Praise for *A*

"Timeless and of the moment . . . A fluent storyteller, Fei entwines this family narrative with harrowing passages about the Rape of Nanjing and the oppression of early Chinese immigrants to America. . . . Squarely and honestly takes on a misunderstood ill—the burden of the so-called model minority."
—*The New York Times Book Review*

"Setting a contemporary novel against the backdrop of the historical changes sweeping across China as the country moves from stark repression to a booming capitalist economy would be a challenge for any novelist, much less a first-timer. Fei, a Chinese American who has lived in Beijing and Shanghai, tackles it with ease and great insight. . . . Rest assured that when the moment arrives to tie up these threads, Deanna Fei has her readers in the palm of her hand. With tenderness and humor, each of the sisters finds love in a way that opens her eyes to the larger world. This is one of those rare novels that delivers on the promise of its opening pages. This summer, no smart woman should leave on vacation without it."
—Chicago Tribune.com

"A quality of longing animates this lovely and subtle first novel. . . . It is exhilarating to read a novel about the nature of female ambition; it is far more exhilarating to find that the novelist doing the exploration is as ambitious as they come. Fei's canvas—a family of feisty women taking a trip together to China—is simple only on its surface. Deeply, *A Thread of Sky* is a novel about belonging, perfection, cultural pressure, how to leave, and what it means to be left behind. Fei's prose is always careful and at times gorgeous, and her handling of magnificent, mind-boggling contemporary China is deft and sympathetic."
—Lauren Groff, author of *Monsters of Templeton*

"Deanna Fei brilliantly captures the richness, confusion, and contradictions of both China and Asian American identity today in her intimate yet epic novel. Told in gorgeous prose with humor and probing insight, *A Thread of Sky* illuminates the past even as it grapples with the opportunities and challenges of an uncertain future."
—David Henry Hwang, author of the Tony Award–winning play *M. Butterfly*

"Lin Yulan, a revolutionary and leader of the Chinese feminist movement, reluctantly returns to her homeland after a self-imposed exile for a guided tour of 'the new China' with her two daughters and three granddaughters in an effort for the nearly estranged women to reconnect. Each woman arrives in China with her own agenda, and each discovers that some shameful secrets are simply too heavy to bear alone. This powerful, intricately woven first novel is a meditation on grief and recovery, strength and vulnerability, and the urgency to leave one's mark on the world. A very promising debut."

—*IndieBound*

"Painterly . . . Fei's writing is precise and exquisite. . . . The characters are beautifully drawn, every sentence is well crafted and the pace is measured. . . . Most will find this well-shaped story satisfying and its prose a pleasure to savor."

—*Mostly Fiction*

"*A Thread of Sky* is a first novel that delivers on all that it promises: it's a family story that explores the connections between generations of women and between the U.S. and China."

—*The Oregonian*

"As stunning and elegant as its cover . . . Fei's portrait of the family, both as women and Chinese Americans, is powerful and important, and wonderfully written by one of the most promising voices in contemporary American fiction."

—*Largehearted Boy*

"Fei stakes a claim in Amy Tan territory with this satisfying tale."

—*Booklist*

"Ambitious . . . Fei's novel does not broker to presenting China as an exotic, unchanging landscape, one that can be claimed by the credit card. Rather, it is a complex and shifting space. . . . The novel resolutely moves outside of sentimentalism and resides in a domestic drama that unfolds unceasingly and with admirable restraint. In this regard, *A Thread of Sky* manages to offer a visually stunning tableau of China's evolution in the twenty-first century without shifting into the superficiality of a travelogue, letting the reader's sense of an already complex geography change as her characters do too."

—*Feminist Review*

"With its mother-daughter conflicts, a feminist message, and an exploration of Chinese roots, this novel will appeal to fans of Amy Tan as well as readers who generally enjoy . . . Julia Alvarez, Gish Jen, and Gus Lee."

—*Library Journal*

"*A Thread of Sky* is a lyrical journey through the heart of contemporary China, and the family of women who make the pilgrimage across these pages are as complicated, broad-ranging, and fascinating as the country itself. Deanna Fei is one to watch."

—Ann Patchett, author of *Run* and *Bel Canto*

"*A Thread of Sky* is a remarkable debut by a gifted young novelist. Deanna Fei is an accomplished writer with keen insight into cross-cultural Chinese American rootlessness and the ties that bind women of several generations. A wonderful book!" —Anita Shreve, author of *A Change in Altitude*

"*A Thread of Sky* is a dazzling, heart-pulling debut. With gorgeous lyricism and rare power, Deanna Fei maps an intricate constellation of loss and love that illuminates the lives of three generations of women. The novel is a startling achievement, braided with history and hope and deep empathy, and it introduces readers to one of the most gifted and captivating storytellers of her generation."

—Bret Anthony Johnston, author of *Corpus Christi: Stories*

"Deanna Fei writes gracefully and with powerful insight and feeling about love and loss, homelands and promised lands, and the various roles of women in family and society. The reader follows her passionately searching characters to China with a brimming heart, and with admiration for a first novelist so full of promise."

—Sigrid Nunez, author of *The Last of Her Kind*

"This had me at the first page. Fei's debut novel is both intensely enjoyable and, I think, *important*. This novel charts the cost of that famous Asian silence between generations, as a family takes in the price of it across several generations. But it is also an intimate portrait of that famous 'new China,' as much of a surprise to Chinese Americans as it is to the rest of us. Truly a book for our times." —Alexander Chee, author of *Edinburgh*

ABOUT THE AUTHOR

Deanna Fei was born in Flushing, New York, and has lived in Beijing and Shanghai, China. A graduate of Amherst College and the Iowa Writers' Workshop, she has received a Fulbright Grant, a New York Foundation for the Arts Fellowship, and a Chinese cultural scholarship, among other awards. She currently lives in Brooklyn, New York.

A Thread of Sky

Deanna Fei

PENGUIN BOOKS

PENGUIN BOOKS
Published by the Penguin Group
Penguin Group (USA) Inc., 375 Hudson Street, New York, New York 10014, U.S.A. •
Penguin Group (Canada), 90 Eglinton Avenue East, Suite 700, Toronto, Ontario,
Canada M4P 2Y3 (a division of Pearson Penguin Canada Inc.) • Penguin Books Ltd,
80 Strand, London WC2R 0RL, England • Penguin Ireland, 25 St. Stephen's Green, Dublin 2, Ireland
(a division of Penguin Books Ltd) • Penguin Books Australia Ltd, 250 Camberwell Road, Camberwell,
Victoria 3124, Australia (a division of Pearson Australia Group Pty Ltd) • Penguin Books India Pvt Ltd,
11 Community Centre, Panchsheel Park, New Delhi – 110 017, India • Penguin Group (NZ),
67 Apollo Drive, Rosedale, North Shore 0632 • New Zealand (a division of Pearson New Zealand Ltd) •
Penguin Books (South Africa) (Pty) Ltd, 24 Sturdee Avenue, Rosebank, Johannesburg 2196, South Africa

Penguin Books Ltd, Registered Offices: 80 Strand, London WC2R 0RL, England

First published in the United States of America by The Penguin Press,
a member of Penguin Group (USA) Inc. 2010
Published in Penguin Books 2011

1 3 5 7 9 10 8 6 4 2

Publisher's Note
This is a work of fiction. Names, characters, places, and incidents either are the product of the author's imagination or are used fictitiously, and any resemblance to actual persons, living or dead, business establishments, events, or locales is entirely coincidental.

THE LIBRARY OF CONGRESS HAS CATALOGED THE HARDCOVER EDITION AS FOLLOWS:

Fei, Deanna.
A thread of sky : a novel / Deanna Fei.
p. cm.
ISBN 978-1-59420-249-0 (hc.)
ISBN 978-0-14-311862-6 (pbk.)
1. Chinese American women—Fiction. 2. Chinese Americans—China—Fiction.
3. Mothers and daughters—Fiction. 4. Chinese American families—Fiction.
5. Domestic fiction. I. Title.
PS3606.E3645T47 2010
813'.6—dc22 2009037246

Printed in the United States of America
DESIGNED BY NICOLE LAROCHE

For my parents,
Mimi Wen-Pi and Donald Li-Tao Fei,
who gave me everything

• *Contents* •

Prologue • 1

Part One

THE ASTRONOMERS

13

Part Two

THE CONSTELLATIONS

99

Part Three

THE STARS

305

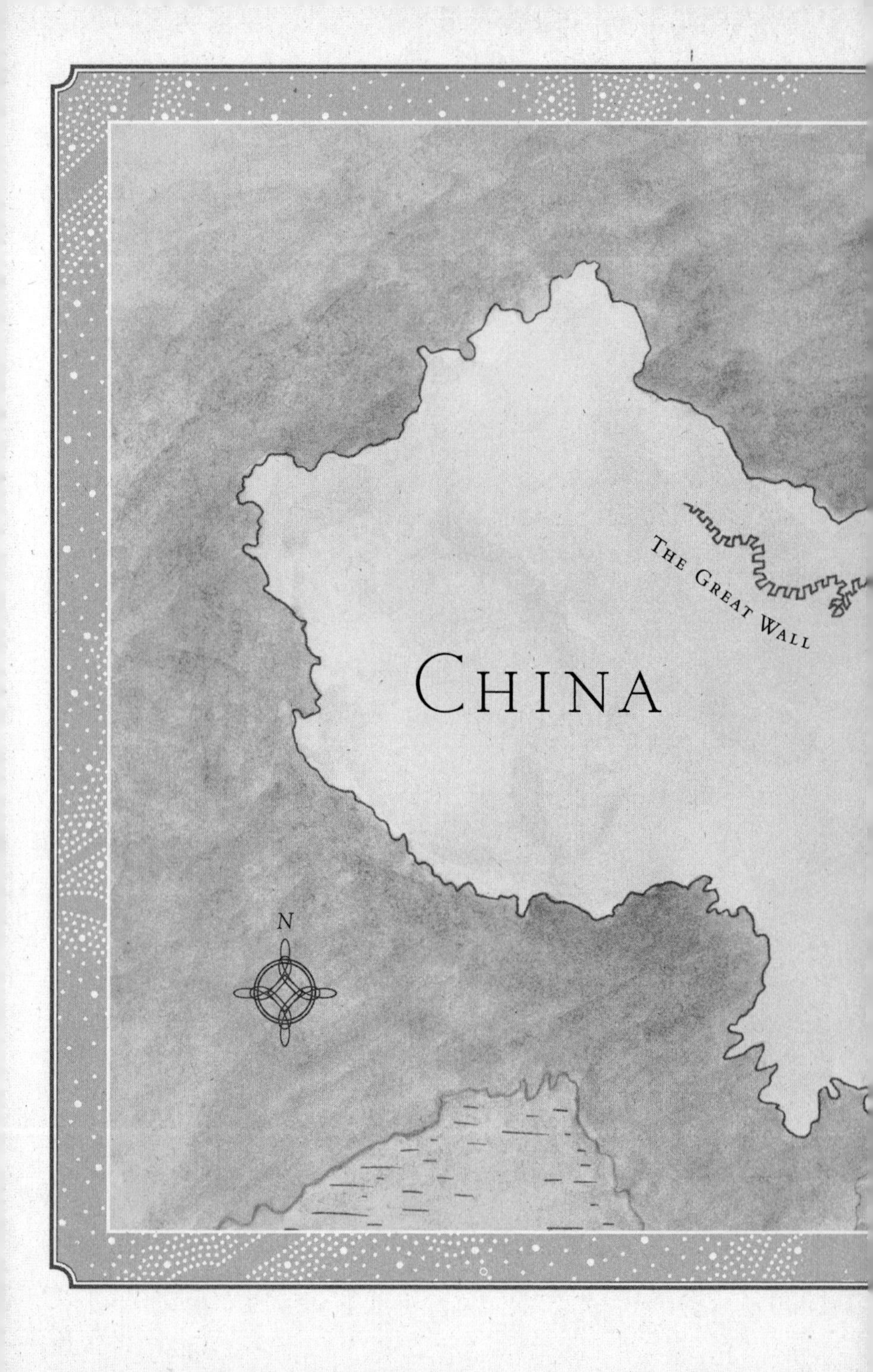
The Great Wall
China
N

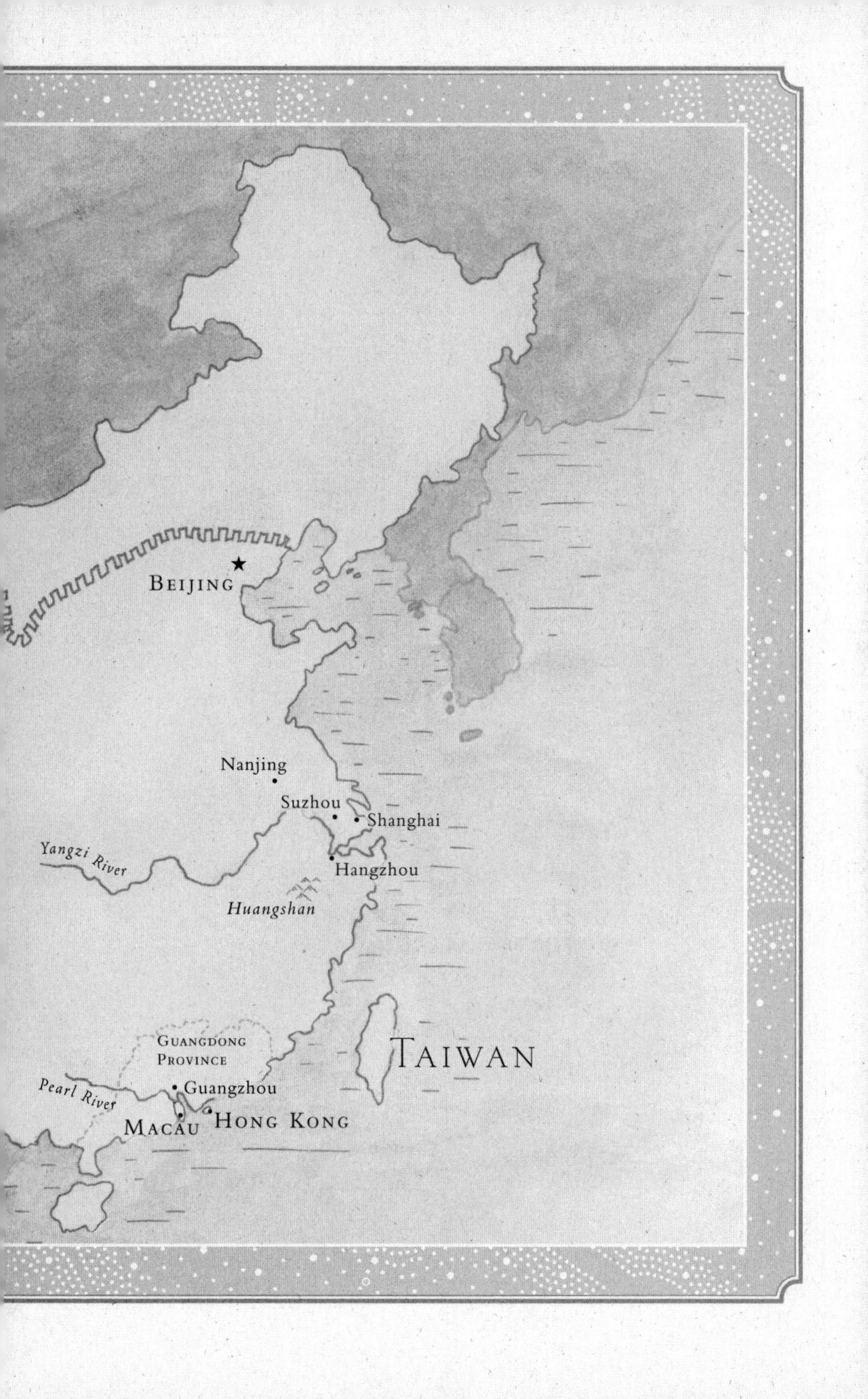
Beijing
Nanjing
Suzhou
Shanghai
Yangzi River
Hangzhou
Huangshan
Guangdong
Province
Taiwan
Pearl River
Guangzhou
Macau
Hong Kong

A Thread of Sky

• *Prologue* •

Irene entered the new millennium alone, watching TV, waiting for the ball to drop—an end, at last, to the buildup. Top ten, twenty, hundred lists, countdowns to the countdown. Experts jabbering about bridging and booming, degeneration and disaster, while ordinary citizens hoarded bottled water and canned food. Since noon, record-breaking crowds in Times Square, just a borough away, celebrating themselves celebrating in Times Square. Now the countdown—quick cuts to cities around the world watching this one—and the glittering ball slowly dropped. So much exertion, yet the timing was never just right. She closed her eyes, the chanted numbers clashing, a countdown to nothing, a vortex of darkness. She opened her eyes. The ball landed: a burst of confetti, whooping, embraces.

Lately Irene had the sensation of falling. Stepping out of the tub, or down a flight of stairs—she didn't slip; it was more the fear of falling, in the moment you know you will and you feel, like a revelation, how thin air is and how clunky your body, unfit to float or fly—but no drop, not yet. She peered into her microscope the other day and saw a black tunnel.

She had to brace herself, breathe deep, and look up. There was nowhere to fall. The floor was beneath her feet.

Once, she'd set out as a genetic researcher to cure Alzheimer's, the disease that seemed more terrifying than any other: your short-term memory, the closer past, the home you'd made, the children you'd raised, all lost in brain plaques and fibrillary tangles—passages blocked, strands caught in knots. What was left? What you couldn't change, couldn't help; the demons of your childhood, the maze of your provenance; gaping voids, lonely death. She hadn't succeeded, of course, and now it was widely reported that falling was the leading danger for old people. Her father had fallen recently, against bathroom tile, alone in Taiwan—a mild concussion, a fractured hip, the beginning of the end. Her mother hadn't fallen yet, but she was eighty this year, alone in California.

Chances were, once you were old, before you fell victim to disease, you simply fell, and never recovered. Irene wasn't quite old, but maybe this was how it started. You got scared to fall, and you fell. You stopped resisting gravity—as her skin did years ago, her shape. Wasn't that life's trajectory? You took off, hung, fell.

She tried to click away from the festivities, but the remote control was unresponsive—Y2K? A dying battery, more likely. She picked up a copy of *Nature*: the numerical memory span of chimps, the lack of P2X1 receptors in impotent mice, the seismic anisotropy of the earth's inner core—and, it being the last issue of the millennium, a countdown of breakthroughs, era by era.

She tried to neaten the pictures crowding every shelf and table, the pictures of her three daughters she couldn't stop taking once she became a mother, just like she used to record every detail in her microscope viewfinder in tables and graphs. There wasn't enough surface area, especially not since one shelf had been cleared for an urn of ashes. All around her, the stillness stretched.

She'd asked Nora to come over, Sophie to stay in, Kay to fly back for the holidays. She'd already prepared herself to be spurned. What were holidays anyway? Ordinary days brightly packaged and stuffed with meaning. Besides, the real new millennium wouldn't arrive for another year.

But the hype had gotten under her skin. This occasion looked historic, sounded momentous. The triple zeroes. The last of this, the first of that. The power of symbolism over science. And now she couldn't shake the sense that this night was presaging the rest of her life.

Five months had passed since Bill had told her about the job in Maine, and she'd said, "At least wait till Sophie's in college," and he'd touched her elbow, said he needed a break. You couldn't take a break from a thirty-year marriage; you could only break it apart. To each daughter, she announced, "Your dad is leaving us." That's how it felt. She'd been his wife; then she became their mother. Saving their hostile glances for her, they gathered to send him off. He dawdled until dusk, fiddling with final chores, making feeble stabs at being their jolly dad, waiting for what? She said, "Okay. Bye," and finally he left. Shutting the door, she said, "Good riddance." It was only the kind of joke she'd made a thousand times before, the way women do, like sighing, "Men," with a head shake. Her daughters said nothing, maybe rolled their eyes, and dispersed. About four hours later, Bill dozed off, drove off I-495 into a tree, and cracked his skull against the windshield.

Irene had gotten the news that night and sat up with it, held it tight, until a reasonable hour in the morning. She knew she'd fallen apart afterward because her eldest daughter had found it necessary to take charge. Nora claimed the body, made calls, wrote checks, and arranged the service. On the phone, Irene's sister, Susan, expressed wan regrets, her brother, Lou, said, "Sorry, sis," and her mother commanded her to be strong. They didn't come; she didn't care. All she knew was that she needed her daughters, that her daughters needed her, that the four of them needed to be together. But after the funeral, her daughters fled—Nora to her high-powered job, her brownstone, and her boyfriend; Kay clear to China; Sophie to her locked room and college applications.

Well, they were twenty-eight, twenty-five, seventeen. Really, they'd resumed being themselves, high-aiming and hard-driving—but higher and harder than she'd intended, farther and farther from her, with a heightened fierceness that she recognized, that made her heart sink.

Anyone glancing around the room would marvel at her daughters' accomplishments. High school valedictorians—two, by summer likely three. Acceptance letters from Harvard, Yale, now Stanford. Awards for outstanding work as a minority female in finance; a Chinese American activist; a student artist. Even beauty—Nora's the most obvious, in her fine nose and long eyes, buttery skin and glossy hair; Kay tall and tan and strong, with a surprising delicacy to her brow and chin; Sophie petite and rounded, a little pouty, with dreamy, downturned eyes imparting a touch of the tragic. Irene had been cute at best, and she couldn't help feeling that this beauty, too, was not a simple inheritance, but something she'd nurtured in them.

Her daughters always took for granted that they were seen, cherished, loved; that, to at least one person in the world, they were everything. She'd taken every picture. She knew each moment and each story. She knew how Nora gracefully angled herself, elbows and hips, even her feet, and often forgot to smile. How Kay's trademark grin, wide and cheesy, kept her from ever appearing as if she'd tried to look pretty. How Sophie hadn't yet learned to time herself and always seemed to get caught fixing her hair, glancing at her sisters.

Even in the latest pictures, Irene could still see the Nora who picked scabs ferociously—not like other children, fidgety and curious, but as if to gouge out the wound itself; the Kay who head-butted a school bully and invited his victim over to play, even though she didn't like the kid either; the Sophie who traipsed around the house showing off sunny watercolors.

And now Irene could look around the room and watch her daughters grow, their bodies lengthening and hardening, their faces lifting and sharpening, all three poising to take flight. She'd tried so hard to capture each occasion that she'd fooled herself about the passing. She'd watched so closely, she'd overlooked the trajectory.

Irene decided to simply wish her daughters a happy New Year. She talked to Sophie's voice mail; perhaps Sophie couldn't hear her phone at her classmate's party. She reached Nora's answering machine; probably a romantic night for Nora and her boyfriend. Finally she dialed the long-distance carrier, the ID and PIN, the international code, the country code, the city code, the local number—thirty-five digits in all, and Kay almost never answered.

"Wei?"

"Kay! I didn't think I'd catch you." Irene sounded fervid. She asked, "Are you drinking champagne? Did you watch the countdown?"

"Mom, it's twelve hours later. And Chinese people observe the Lunar New Year."

Lately, everything out of Kay's mouth was a reproach. *Why didn't you teach us Chinese? How come we never visited Taiwan? Where's my* laojia*?*

Irene would fumble: *Your teachers said . . . I never thought . . . Your* laojia? *Your hometown, New York. I guess they do mean ancestral home. In Taiwan? We moved a lot. Macau? A few months, maybe a year. Me, I was born in Canton. Yes, I mean Guangzhou. Till I was four. No, your grandparents came from villages. Somewhere around there. Well, who really has a* laojia *anymore?*

Irene would try to change the subject to headlines she'd seen: a record-breaking skyscraper, a reengineered river, a Starbucks at the Great Wall—or was it the Forbidden City? Somehow everything she reported was either obvious or irrelevant. Recently she'd warned Kay that in the spring, Beijing would be hit with a barrage of sand from the Gobi Desert, carried over deforested land by strong winds. Kay said, "Mom, I can handle the weather."

Now Kay said, "Can I have Grandpa's number?"

Who? Irene nearly asked. She managed, "Why?"

"I want to meet him. He's my grandfather. Your father."

"He's not up for a visit. He had a fall, he's very weak."

"Why didn't you tell me?"

"You don't know him."

"Isn't that all the more reason? How can you be so detached?"

Inwardly, Irene protested. She'd never cut off her father. She simply hadn't resisted the distance.

Kay's voice was hard. "Does he even know about Dad?"

"I don't know." Irene's vision blurred.

Kay said, "See what I mean?"

The day of Bill's funeral was the last time Irene had her three daughters beside her. Sophie quivering all over, soft cheeks glistening. Tissues disintegrating in Kay's hands, white bits dotting her upper lip. Nora businesslike and gracious, a little jerky in motion. The service was flawless, elegant, and brisk; textbook American, but shorn of religion. Afterward, as if she were facilitating a conference, Nora asked where they should keep the ashes. Sophie suggested scattering them. Kay quavered that she could bring them to China. Desperation plain on their faces, they turned to Irene.

The only logical answer was the one she gave: "We'll keep the urn here, at home." In silence, her daughters surveyed the house, raked pictures of themselves off the highest shelf in the living room, placed the urn in the center, and fled.

Scattering Bill's ashes in China, a place he'd known less than she? He, too, had been born there, then orphaned as a baby, ferried to Taiwan by a spinster aunt who died when he was a teenager, but not before arranging for him to attend college in America—the same campus where Irene landed for graduate school a few years later. He'd never seemed haunted by his past, by his provenance—one reason she'd loved him. In the months before Kay's departure, as he was planning his own, he'd become mildly interested—but in an American way, unencumbered. Scattering his ashes in China made no sense.

Yet now Irene was haunted. Should she and her daughters have worn white instead of black? Should they have burned incense, knelt and kowtowed? Should they have cremated him to bone, not ash? She'd spent her childhood moving—from the mainland to a peninsula to an island, from house to house, school to school, town to town—until, grown, she flew by herself to America. She should have known there'd be gaps, gaps that held such things as a facility with funerals, gaps big enough for a life to fall through.

As a child, she'd never even learned how to celebrate. Not her own birthday, or Susan's; Ma cooked longevity noodles only for Lou, the son. And every Lunar New Year, Mid-Autumn Moon, dragon boat festival, wherever they were living, theirs was the only dark house. Irene would roam and peek at other families, at their red lanterns and paper cutouts, their cakes and coins and firecrackers. At home, if she dared to ask, Ma would spit something about having no patience for tradition and anyhow their father would rather go whoring.

With her own daughters, Irene had improvised each holiday, establishing their own traditions, while Bill mildly grinned from the periphery, shaking his head at all the fuss. For birthdays, candlelit cakes and painstakingly wrapped presents and, after Nora told her about slumber parties, Irene and her daughters lolling puppylike watching Disney movies. Thanksgivings, they devoured a duck dish she invented. Christmastime, the four of them shopped together for one another. And New Year's, before her daughters insisted that wasn't a family holiday, they'd pinch one another awake, count down in a chorus, and drink ginger ale from plastic flutes. In recent years, Bill had pulled her to a few lab parties where she overdressed and laughed too loud. She never was good at socializing, or friendship.

After Bill died, she'd simply collapsed, like a model skeleton might slide off its rack. But if she'd been heir to some hallowed tradition of mourning—wailing and knocking one's head, hiring a phalanx of monks and nuns—she would have honored it to the utmost, aced every ritual, spared nothing. She would have set an example for her daughters. She might have redeemed herself.

Irene wiped her eyes and picked herself up on brittle limbs. After three births, one death, career starts and stops—here was what stood, a house. It had held each daughter since conception. It had held her since marriage. Moving in, she'd felt her life, too, would begin here.

When Bill proposed, he'd told her to make three wishes. They must have just watched a silly movie; she was ready. First, faithfulness. He tapped himself with an imaginary wand and said, *Done*. Second, a permanent home. *No problem*, he said; no one would invade America. They'd raise their kids, grow fat and gray, all in the same house. Third, her own room—a work space, a study. *Easy*, he said, a family of four in a four-bedroom house, the perfect plan. What she had in mind was a space all to herself, one conflict-free zone. Bill was a good man, but perhaps her father had once been a good man, too. She kept that room even after Ma called from Taiwan and announced she was moving in, until Sophie came along and Ma moved out. But there was a new baby, and Nora and Kay clamoring for their own rooms—and Irene was realizing that she couldn't shut herself out.

She peeked into that room now. Everything was stored, filed, in its proper place—a manifestation of Sophie's perfectionism, Irene had thought, but now it seemed she'd been plotting her escape. She'd insisted on early decision, on a college across the country. Back when Nora left for college, Irene's consolation was Kay and Sophie; when Kay left, it was Sophie. Come fall, Irene would be left alone.

Unless Kay moved back after her year in China. She already had a slot at NYU law, a public interest fellowship—and likely no savings, from her years in nonprofit, to pay rent. If Kay was home, Nora would visit. So would Sophie; after she graduated, she might move back in. This was New York real estate—Queens, but New York. What sense lay in the four of them living at four separate addresses, when here stood a four-bedroom house?

Irene could redecorate their rooms. She could renovate the house. Like anything else, it was showing its age—carpet stains, yellowed and cracked grout, some peeling paint, curtains well out-of-date. She could create a separate apartment for her grown daughters. She could make it fun—install a whirlpool or build a deck.

She climbed the stairs, breathing colder and staler air with each step. Kay's room was still brimming and busy; she'd packed for the year as if for a long weekend, and it was possible to understand that Kay didn't miss anything she left, or that she meant to come back.

Irene continued down the hall and opened Nora's door. The room had a lifeless, fossilized feel. Pictures of Nora's high school friends, dusty econ textbooks—and, standing upright in the far corner, Bill's suitcases. They'd been extricated, along with his corpse, from his car, which was totaled. Nora had collected them from Maine.

Irene shut the door and backtracked to the stairs. Holding her alone, the house was just partitioned space. Rooms, doors, floors, walls—all dividers of emptiness.

Her right foot hovered above the first stair. One misstep, and she would fall. She gripped the banister.

The phone rang. Irene bounded down.

"Happy New Year." A pause. "It's me, Susan."

"Happy New Year," Irene trilled, trying to hide her disappointment.

"How are you celebrating?" her sister asked.

"Just sitting at home."

"Alone?"

"Well, the girls are grown." Irene jabbered: Sophie accepted early at Stanford, Nora still a hotshot on Wall Street, Kay hell-bent on becoming Chinese. She let out a laugh, shrill to her own ears.

"That'll pass. How's work?"

"Oh, you know." All they really knew of each other's work was what it wasn't: earthshaking success.

Susan said, "Why don't you come visit?"

Ever since Susan had married and moved to Hong Kong, she'd seemed to have a new sense, albeit sporadic, of familial duty—but she'd never invited Irene before. Of course, tonight was Irene's first New Year's as a widow.

Irene had never met Susan's husband, Winston, never heard of him before her poet sister, who'd reached middle age drifting from one college town to the next, announced the marriage. *You? You got married?* Irene had exclaimed. And Susan had said, as if it was a lesson learned, *Nobody wants to die alone.*

Their parents would die alone, wrecked by war and by each other. Ma a failed revolutionary, mercilessly judging others by standards they, too, were bound to fail. Ba a lifelong womanizer, eighty-six and still shameless; once a powerful politician in the world's most populous country, in the end a lowly bureaucrat on a vulnerable speck.

Why was Irene on her way to dying alone? When she'd raised three beautiful, brilliant daughters in one stationary, solid home? Because of two words and a slammed door?

Susan was murmuring about her spacious apartment, the bay, the food.

"I have an idea," Irene said, and her own words seemed to string themselves together and hang in the air. "A reunion, not just a visit. And not just Hong Kong. China, the mainland. A tour."

"You and me?" Susan sounded rattled.

"You, me, the girls. This summer." It was impossible. They were all too self-reliant, too far-flung, and Irene couldn't pull them together; she needed more weight. "And Ma."

"Ma? You want to vacation with Ma?"

Briskly, Irene said, "The past is the past. She's turning eighty this year. We have to celebrate somehow."

"We never have before."

"But eighty is a big deal. And really it'll be for all of us. Our own holiday."

"Aren't there enough on the calendar already?"

"Oh, but New Year's, Christmas, Thanksgiving—what do they mean to us?" Irene had been at a loss, this past year, on all three.

"Well, what about Lou? And Winston, and—" Susan stopped.

"Just us girls. It'll be fun." Like something she'd seen on TV. Women laughing over jewel-colored drinks. Women sharing deodorants and secrets, caressed by chiffon and a breeze.

"China isn't known for fun."

"We should see for ourselves," Irene said. "You live right there. Why haven't you gone?"

There was a pause. "Who knows. Maybe because it is right there."

China was the regime that had run their family out more than fifty years ago. China was Red Guards, starving masses, rolling tanks. China was men licentious like her father, women embittered like her mother. But what had Irene really seen? Like anyone else, the headlines: China had reformed, *kaifang,* opened up. Hanging peppy banners over its grimmer features and proclaiming itself open for business. Campaigning for the WTO, the Olympics, international esteem and investment. Even luring her own daughter with a scholarship. These weren't just photo ops. In China, it was always a new era, and apparently this was the new era of new eras.

When Irene emigrated thirty-five years ago, nobody had predicted that in the year 2000, all eyes would be on China. The dragon awakening, the global tremors. The formidable potential superpower. Entrepreneurs and scholars and tourists flocking to the great frontier of—what else?—the new millennium.

Never mind the headlines. America was *Meiguo*, the beautiful country—but China at heart was still *Zhongguo*: the central nation, the origin of everything from paper to pasta, the archetypal birthplace. This Irene had always known, without having to look.

She said, "Don't worry. I'll plan everything. I'll start tomorrow—New Year's Day!"

She hung up the phone and tossed out her copy of *Nature,* tucked away the remote control, straightened a few pictures. The stillness of the house now felt different—a note of anticipation amid all the absence.

Perhaps her only legacy would be that she'd given her daughters what she'd never had: a home. They considered it their birthright, like clean water, fresh air, a stable society, citizenship of a country utterly safe from invasion. Now her daughters were taking off, as of course they should—but grief had skewed their trajectory. They were trying to leave it behind, to outdistance her, when what they all needed, now more than ever, was to be together.

Irene couldn't bring their father back, but if she could gather them all for this tour, together they might recover a missing link. Not the notion that Kay was chasing of their *laojia,* their ancestral home—but a new understanding of an old truth, old as civilization itself. A truth about death and life, about generations, about permanence. Then, and perhaps only then, could she and her daughters come back home. *Jia*—family, house, home. In Chinese, it was all one word.

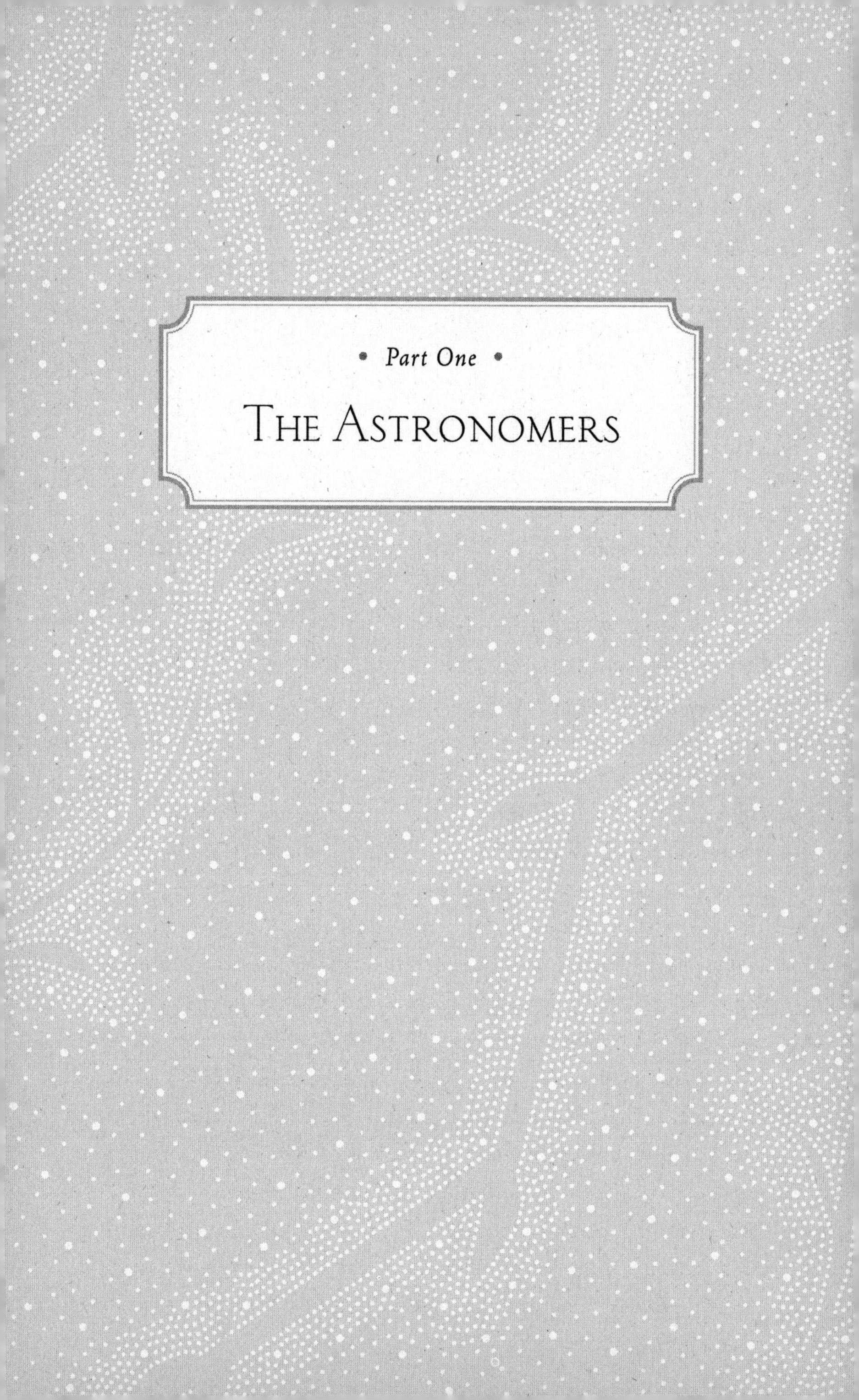

• *Part One* •

The Astronomers

1

Shifting in bed, a sharp stab in her back. Nora grabbed it—a condom wrapper, emptied. Tinsel red—cherry-flavored—the saliva of another woman still glittering on its torn edges.

She thrashed, struggling to get up—she couldn't get up—she woke with a gasp. Jesse lay beside her, innocently snoring. Under her back was the engagement ring. She'd tried it on again last night, after Jesse fell asleep. She must have yanked it off in her sleep.

Gently, she nudged him. "I had another bad dream. You cheated on me again."

He didn't stir.

She stroked his golden hair, the soft pale nape of his neck. "You'd never do that to me, would you?"

He groaned.

She nudged him harder. "You know I could never forgive you. You know that, right?"

He turned to face her. "Nora, you're the one who won't commit."

"That's not true."

"So set a date."

She hadn't even announced their engagement.

His gaze fell on the ring in her hand. "I know you hate that thing. I told you, let's shop for a new one."

She did hate the ring. It was thick gold with a brick of a ruby surrounded by diamonds and sapphires, a family heirloom emblematic of his parents—his corporate-lawyer father who had discreet, not secret, affairs with assistants; his pinched-face mother, careerless, eternally dieting and redecorating their Park Avenue apartment. They even belonged to a country club that excluded Jews, blacks, and Asians—though apparently they'd been willing to bequeath this ring to Nora.

Of course, Jesse was different. He loved her, everything about her—but most of all, her strength, her ambition, even her bitchiness. He was loyal, sweet, accommodating to a fault. When they met, she was already established in finance, while he was moonlighting as a pottery instructor; now, three years later, he was a high school art teacher. He professed pride in cleaning the house, cooking her dinner, being the good man behind a great woman.

Countless times, he'd said, *Give me your hand,* and slid a rubber band, or a circle of twisted tinfoil—even, once, a clay ring he'd molded and glazed—onto her finger. She'd laughed and pushed him away, knowing the option was hers for the taking.

Then her dad died, and Jesse was driving her to the morgue in Maine, helping her compare caskets at the funeral parlor, comforting her every time she cried, holding her upright. She was, through all of it, the big sister—unflinching, capable, first. Only with Jesse did she allow herself to be weak. They were driving home the night of the funeral when she said, "Take my hand. Here's my hand. Take it." He needed a minute to understand. Then he grabbed her hand and kissed the fourth finger. She felt the kiss linger, tingling, as if her finger were already marked. The next day, he came home with the heirloom ring.

A small misjudgment, she told herself. But these dreams had plagued her since then. Suspicious phone calls, a smell on his fingers. A girl in their bed—once or twice, his new student teacher, a honey-haired, milky-skinned twenty-one-year-old who'd divulged a crush. Other times, just a faceless, agreeable girl. Sometimes everyone else had known—her mother, her sisters, every guy on the trading floor. Jesse would be apologetic, but helpless. She'd coldly order him out of the house, or smash his belongings, or kick him in the balls—but she could never hurt him as much as he'd hurt her, with such a simple act, such a common misstep. Even in the worst of those nightmares, he loved her—but somehow he still ended up a bad guy, she his unwitting victim.

They were just dreams. But what if that ring meant he wasn't different after all? From his dad. From the guys on the trading floor—even the nice ones indulged in the occasional stripper or hooker. Maybe, in the end, from her dad. Nora didn't know of another woman, but her father had seemed cheerful, and guilty, in leaving, and that always seemed the easy outlet for men. In a way, she hadn't blamed him. She'd long vowed to be different from her mother, who'd given herself over to her children, and vented her frustration on a long-suffering husband.

But what if her own career didn't pan out? Weren't marriage and motherhood still traps for ambitious women? What if she couldn't help resenting her own husband? Maybe Jesse's goodness, like her dad's, was too good to last. Maybe she, like her mom, would someday grind all that goodness to the bone. And then, if he cheerfully left, maybe she'd find herself saying, "Good riddance"—even if she didn't mean it, even if her kids would hate her for saying it, even if she'd spend the rest of her life regretting it. Her own parents had worn matching plain bands, symbolizing not romance but endurance, until the end. What if they'd set out to be different, too? What if everyone did?

Back when Jesse first moved into the house Nora had just bought, her mother had wailed, "Why? Why not just date? Why make a home with him? What if it goes bad? What if he breaks your heart?" Nora had scoffed: "Then I'll kick him out." She knew how to spot a bad trade and dump it. You cut your losses or you bled to death. But now she didn't know how she could ever cut Jesse out of her life.

And if she married him, wouldn't she be doubly exposed? If they had kids, double that, at least? And how would she know if the relationship had gone bad until it was too late? How could she be certain of not getting hurt? If you don't know who the sucker is, it's you: That was Wall Street wisdom, and she couldn't completely discount it.

The phone rang. Nora was glad for the interruption, until she heard the voice.

"Guess what." Her mother sounded a little breathless. "We're going to China!"

"What?"

"I'm booking us on a tour. Two weeks, this summer. All on me."

"Who's us?" Nora said. Jesse stroked her hand, and she realized she'd tensed all over.

"You, me, Sophie, Kay. Plus your aunt and your grandmother."

Flatly, Nora said, "Why?"

"Well, maybe Kay's right—we're too disconnected."

"From what?"

"You know. Our roots."

Nora had never heard her mother use that word, except in relation to plants. "I can't go. I can't just take off from work."

"You need a vacation. I'll do all the planning. You just have to pack."

Nora recalled her father's suitcases, stashed in a corner of her old bedroom. She'd thought of unpacking them, but he'd wanted an escape from that house.

"I don't know," she said, in a tone that meant no.

"It's a family reunion. Before Sophie leaves for college. When's the last time you saw each other?"

Nora felt a pang of guilt. "I'll call her."

After a pause, her mother said, "You know, Grandma's turning eighty. She might not have much time left."

Grandma: Nora remembered a stout, stolid, self-contained presence—a kind of antidote to her mother.

"Just think about it," her mother said. "Please."

Jesse's stroking was irritating. Nora shook off his hand. He sighed and started to get out of bed. She sat up and grabbed him.

To her mother, she said, "Okay, okay"—meaning she'd think about it.

"Great," her mother chirped.

Nora hung up. Disjointedly, she told Jesse the news.

"This summer?" he said. "You once said we'd plan our wedding for this summer."

"Can we focus on this?" She sounded shrill. "I'm sorry. I'm freaked out. Just the thought of traveling with my mother—"

"So tell her no."

"It's not that easy." Dumb tears came to her eyes. She turned and blinked them away.

Jesse missed it. His face brightened. "What if I went, too?"

Vehemently, she shook her head. "You have to understand. My family—" But since her father's death, she didn't know what that meant herself. She hadn't been back to the house since the funeral. She often screened her mother's calls, and Sophie had become a sullen teenager, and Kay was off in China. Nora had met her aunt once; her grandmother had hardly existed since moving to California. Her aunt and grandmother hadn't even attended the funeral. How could the six of them suddenly be called a family?

"Well, they'll be my family, too, right? Someday."

There was a new, unmistakable bitterness in Jesse's voice. It chilled her.

She reached for his hand, pulled him back into bed, wrapped his arms around her as they lay together on their sides. His embrace was slack at first, but she held it tight, and soon they were nestled close, his heart beating against her back, his warmth seeping into her skin. She still marveled at how their bodies aligned when he held her like this, concave to convex, every curve and joint, even their breaths. As long as she stayed still and soft, and didn't speak, or think too much, the alignment could last.

•

"*Wei?*"

Nora was flummoxed. "Kay?"

"*Wei?*"

"Kay?"

Now she heard static. "Kay? Kay!" With a sigh, she hung up and started over.

This time, Kay said, "Hello?"

"Can you hear me?"

"I could hear you before, but you couldn't hear me."

"I could hear you. I thought you couldn't hear me," Nora said. "But then why did you keep saying *wei*?"

"That's how people here answer the phone."

"But you knew it was me."

"No, I heard you at the end. There was a lag."

The conversation was already tedious. Tersely, Nora summed up her mother's call.

"She knows almost nothing about China. Why wouldn't she ask me?" Kay said. "And a tour? A package tour? You can't get more inauthentic than that."

This wasn't quite the commiseration Nora had sought.

Kay seemed to sense her disappointment. "I've been meaning to call you."

"Me too." And Nora tried to make the announcement she'd practiced: *I'm engaged!*

"I met our grandfather. Mom's dad, in Taiwan. Aren't you curious?"

"Not especially."

Kay sighed. "You're just like Mom."

"Fuck you," Nora said, startling herself. It had been a long-standing joke between them, a charge to level when one was being difficult or anxious or bitchy. But it wasn't funny anymore. Had Kay become so immersed in her life in China that she'd forgotten?

"Sorry," Kay said quickly. "I just meant—did you know Grandma was a revolutionary?"

"A what?"

"A revolutionary—a *gemingjia*—in Guangdong Province, in the forties. A leader in the women's rights movement and the Nationalist movement, during the Japanese occupation."

Nora recalled Grandma stirring and sweating over the stove, squatting to scrub the floor. The undergarments Nora and Kay sneaked into their playtime—saggy thick-strapped bras, panties they could pull up to their shoulders.

"Are you sure?"

"Of course I'm sure. Grandpa's still so proud of her that he carries a picture of her in his wallet. And he said he sees that fire in me, too." Generously, Kay said, "He would've said the same if he'd met you."

Nora supposed she'd known her grandmother had left behind a husband in Taiwan when she moved in with them. But she'd never thought of her as a woman of stature, of intrigue. She tried to picture her grandfather. She had no mental image of him at all.

"Why did they split?"

"I didn't ask."

"It must've been unheard-of back then."

"Well, she was a revolutionary. She had bigger concerns, obviously."

The implication was that concerns about love and marriage should be beneath them, too. Kay's treatment of guys had hardly changed through the years—casual and dismissive. At most there'd been flings, nothing Kay couldn't shrug off.

As if throwing her a bone, Kay added, "They haven't talked in twenty years."

"And you didn't ask what happened?"

"There were lots of questions I didn't get to ask. Anyway, learning about Grandma inspired me. I'm starting an outreach campaign to help local women escape prostitution."

Nora was starting to feel tired, old, and intensely irritated. "How's that going?"

Now Kay sounded defensive. "Too early to tell. How's your job?"

Nora felt compelled to say that she was thinking about joining a microfinance venture, funding poor female entrepreneurs, or even starting her own group. This was true, but she'd been thinking about it for years. Every time she resolved to quit, her bosses would dangle the chance to make history as the first female head of the desk, or the first Asian director—or some newbie would mistake her for an assistant.

"That's a great plan. And now you know we're descendants of a revolutionary!" Then Kay started yammering about her class on Chinese women's history, the street food she devoured for every meal, and her new Beijing friends—for some reason, all male.

Lamely, Nora joked, "Next you'll be marrying a Chinese man."

"What's your image of Chinese men?"

"I'm sure it's one you've worked to debunk."

"Geeky, puny, sexless."

"If you're asking for a stereotype, more or less."

"But if I described them as lecherous, patriarchal, violent—doesn't that ring true, too? The image is the Other, a false construction that expresses Western ideals of Western men, not any truth about Asians."

"Kay, don't run a workshop with me."

After a pause, Kay said, "Anyway, they're just friends."

When Nora said she had to run, Kay sounded equally relieved to get off the phone.

• • •

"My grandmother was a revolutionary." She said it ironically. There was no other way.

"A *what*?" Jesse said.

"That's what I said."

"I didn't know those still existed."

"I guess they did then, in China, according to Kay."

"I'm not sure I knew you had a grandmother, before all this," he said.

"I'm not sure I did, either."

"No family reunions? Holiday visits?"

Nora shook her head, then remembered one visit, the weekend of her high school graduation. She'd hardly exchanged a word with her grandmother. It hadn't made sense that this person who used to care for her, and then disappeared, was there at all. Somehow it was decreed that they pile into the car to stay overnight with her aunt—an aunt she'd never met, in a crummy little house in some Podunk town, everything strange and tense. She found she couldn't describe the strangeness and the tension, let alone explain it.

"Since then, nothing? And you say my family's cold."

"We're not cold," Nora said defensively. "We're just—different. In immigrant families, absence becomes normal, I guess."

"Maybe it is time for a reunion."

"But why in China?"

"Well, you are from there."

She knew what Jesse meant; still, she lashed out. "Are you from Holland, or the Netherlands, or whatever? I don't have any connection to China. It'd make more sense to do a historical tour of Queens."

"Don't get so worked up. I'm sorry I put it that way."

"God, you sounded like your parents."

Their idea of getting to know her had been asking her where she was from, originally; where her parents were from; whether they practiced Buddhism or Taoism. To be more inclusive, they'd pushed her to pick a Chinese restaurant and order for the table. It surprised and amused them that she couldn't read the menu.

Jesse, on the other hand, had thought being sensitive meant overlooking the fact that she wasn't white. "She's American. Like us," he'd hiss at his parents. She thought this was relatively sensitive, too, until she found herself saying, "I'm not. I'm not like you at all." And then found him so clueless that she'd actually tried to use one of those "You know you're Asian" forwards as a teaching tool.

> You know you're Asian if . . .
>
> . . . a trip to McDonald's means stocking up on condiments and napkins.
>
> . . . you ask your parents for help with one math question and two hours later, they're still lecturing.
>
> . . . another Asian shows up and people say, "Is that your mother/sister/father/brother?"
>
> . . . leaving rice in your bowl is a sin.

Jesse had scrutinized all twenty traits on the list—bowl haircuts, plastic on lampshades, fish heads sucked clean. "But you don't do that."

"Of course not. That's not the point."

Being Asian—or Asian American, or Chinese, or Chinese American?—meant something, even if she wasn't fresh off the boat or an activist like Kay. It meant saving, it meant overcompensating. Having to be smarter, tougher, more practical. The fear of good things running out. It meant never being completely at ease. It meant constant guilt toward your parents. It meant feeling vaguely ashamed, even if you didn't know why, even if your family was by no means poor or unaccomplished or spectacularly dysfunctional.

"It's like, everything goes unsaid," she'd finally said.

"Oh, that I get," Jesse had said. "I'm a Wasp."

So that wasn't it, either. Nora supposed her Asian identity was inseparable from being female, and first-generation, and the eldest.

She'd taught Kay to curse at the neighborhood boys who pulled slanted eyes at them and called them Chinks—yes, even in New York, even in this day and age. By the time she was twelve, with Kay skipping alongside, she'd learned to hold her head high against a daily barrage of men professing lust for their Asianness, which meant, she soon figured out, sexy, docile, and inarticulate—men on the subway and the street, in the drugstore and the library, young and old, cocky and shy, sweet-talking and foul-mouthed, men of every race but their own. (No wonder she'd ended up with a man who genuinely believed himself color-blind. And, of course, there was some truth to Kay's lecturing. When Nora dated Asian men, the interactions had seemed strangely familial, and she'd felt compelled to restrain herself from steamrolling them. Unbeknownst to him, Jesse could make her feel inferior simply by mentioning the proper time of day for a cappuccino, or correcting her table setting—and that had actually helped make for a certain equilibrium.)

She'd never mentioned any of this to her parents. She'd always felt responsible for protecting their dignity, her PhD parents who seemed unaware that others sneered at their slightly flawed English, their total lack of hip references. When necessary, she'd guided them. She'd studied other kids' lunches and remedied her father's grocery shopping. She'd studied other kids' birthday parties and told her mother what to buy, or better, bake—though she'd let her think slumber parties meant the four of them swaddled up in the living room.

And yes, she credited her mother with supervising homework, fawning over report cards, making her and her sisters believe they were preordained for success, so that they'd become practically neighborhood celebrities, collecting top scores and prizes all the way through their specialized city schools and into their elite colleges—all of which, of course, only made them typical Asian overachievers.

But Nora had always known, in a way her parents couldn't, how as Asian females in America they were doubly burdened, and she'd forged further, seeking a path that felt groundbreaking—which was, in itself, part of the point. She'd defy any put-downs or pigeonholing, would make a difference by being different—which was only possible in America, wasn't it? Hence her parents' sacrifices, hence the immigration.

She had become a top trader not because she was a money-hungry shark or a pathological gambler, but because she'd willed herself to. Because anything less would have meant utter failure. Her first day on the trading floor, she'd stalked in with head held high, in a sleek new suit and fierce boots, and a guy at her desk said, "Hey, you look like a girl I jacked off to this morning. Hotorientalbabes.com—you one of them?" She'd spent the last four years proving herself, and she couldn't help feeling that it was partly because she'd succeeded that Kay felt secure enough to be something of a subversive, and Sophie would feel free to do whatever she wanted.

Jesse had come to understand this outline, but he would never fully understand that inner drive—that fire, that whatever. Maybe Nora didn't either, because she still failed to see how it could have originated in China, in her grandmother, a grandmother she'd seen once in seventeen years. Besides, that was partly why she'd fallen for Jesse, why they'd seemed to align—he was doubly privileged, with no need to prove anything, except that he was a good guy.

For Jesse's birthday, they went out to dinner with his parents. Nora wore the ring. Between taking important calls, his father asked how Jesse planned to support a family on a teacher's salary. Between tightening her face at every ring of her husband's phone, his mother beneficently offered the use of her new decorator, "a lovely, petite Japanese girl," to bring an Asian theme to their wedding. To fill the pauses, Nora and Jesse drank too much. Back home, they staggered into bed without washing up.

Out of the darkness, he mumbled, "What's wrong with me? Why won't you marry me? My parents are assholes, I guess, but I'm not like them."

"Nothing's wrong with you." She tried to enfold him in her arms, the way he did to her.

"Then what's wrong with you?"

She recoiled. "What do you mean?"

"Nothing's ever enough," he mumbled. "I'll never prove myself to you. I'll never be good enough."

"That's not true."

"Then why won't you marry me?"

"I—I will."

"You won't. You won't let yourself need me. You do need me. But you can't admit it to yourself, let alone to the world."

"Let's not do this now. Please."

"Say it," he said. "I love you. I need you. I want to marry you. Now you say it. You've never said it."

"I love you. I do. But—" She choked. "What if someday you cheat on me? What if someday you leave me?"

"What would it take to convince you? How much certainty would be enough?"

"I don't know." She started to cry.

"Don't cry," he slurred. "I'm sorry."

He fell asleep stroking her hand. In the morning, he claimed not to remember anything.

Every involved conversation was becoming an argument. They argued about the purpose of marriage. They argued about the existence of unconditional love. Once he said, "Okay. You've convinced me. Marriage will doom us. Let's not," and she locked herself in the bathroom and cried silently on the toilet.

She remembered when she could test his embrace, and test it and test it, and feel how he held her tighter, how he loved her at her worst.

She remembered lashing out, in their first year together, after a contraceptive mishap. She'd forgotten her refill of the pill, so they reverted to condoms. The sex felt dry and dull. They kept changing positions. She gave up and waited for him to finish. Afterward, they discovered the condom had slipped off.

Helpless, she raged: Didn't he feel it? No—well, at the very end, he thought maybe— And he didn't think to stop? He was too busy enjoying himself? What the hell would she do if— She couldn't finish the sentence. The prospect of pregnancy had always terrified her. An alien hatching inside her, diverting her nutrients, deforming her body. No way to expel it except by letting her own flesh rip. And then this permanent burden, the rest of her life compromising between her dreams and its needs.

"I'm sorry. I should've been more careful. But would it be so bad? If you wanted to, you know, I'd marry you." He cupped her belly. "I'd like to knock you up."

She pictured him nailing her to a wall with a cheerful whistle. "Now that you put it that way, yes, let's knock me up. Forget my career. Forget my whole life."

"No, of course not. I could be a stay-at-home dad. I think it'd be fun."

"Fun," she repeated. She pushed his hand off.

He sighed. "Relax. We'll get the morning-after pill."

It was the middle of the night. She'd need an emergency appointment. It would take up her morning. What would she tell her bosses? She hadn't even enjoyed the sex. Soon Jesse nodded off. She shook him awake and ranted about Viagra being more accessible than birth control.

He stroked her hand and said, very earnestly, "If there was a pill I could take instead of you, I'd take it."

"And if you could give birth through your dick, I'm sure you would."

"I would."

"Oh, shut up."

A couple of weeks later, when her period came, she felt silly, and a little guilty. But blaming him had seemed the only way to ensure he was burdened, too. And it had bound them tighter, like a role-playing exercise, acting out betrayal and rage, knowing she could stop any moment and see that they were fine.

She supposed they'd still be fine if she'd just quit finance. Too often these days, she came home feeling dirty, exhausted yet pumped for a fight. But wouldn't quitting mean capitulating? None of the white men were rushing to give up their exorbitant bonuses and help those less fortunate. And if she quit, how would she and Jesse pay the mortgage? How could they plan a wedding, or a honeymoon, or anything after that? He said not to worry, but how could she not? And wasn't it a little disgusting, that he could be so nonchalant about money and achievement?

And she supposed they'd be fine if she'd just marry him. But every time she went to sleep thinking *Yes*, she'd wake flailing from one of those dreams. If she then acted needy, he'd reassure her, but more and more grudgingly, since she was the one who wouldn't commit. If she held it in, or if he sighed and retreated, soon they'd be arguing again. And when she heard herself, and couldn't stand herself, she wondered how much longer he could, which only made her more helpless to stop.

She'd meant to call Sophie for weeks, but she no longer knew how to talk to her baby sister. She resolved to do what her father used to: Every now and then, he'd call and ask what she'd eaten for breakfast, relay a weird news tidbit, report mail for her at the house. They'd chat, chuckle, hang up. It was the only part of her life where the expectations were so simple, and so comfortably met.

Sophie sounded instantly suspicious. Every question met with monosyllabic answers.

"Did you hear about Mom's plan?" Nora asked.

"No."

"She wants to do a tour of China together, this summer." She used a bright, neutral tone.

"She didn't tell me anything." Sophie sounded accusatory, as if Nora were part of the conspiracy.

"Well, would you want to go?"

"Like it matters what I want. I'm the last to know everything."

It occurred to Nora that Sophie had been the last to know about their father's accident. When she got to the house, Kay had just been told, and Sophie was just waking up. Now Nora wanted to ask how Sophie was grieving, how she was coping alone in the house with their mother, whether she was scared to leave for college, whether she needed anything from her big sister.

"What'd you eat today?" Nora finally said.

There was a pause. "What do you care?"

Nora let her off the phone.

None of them knew how to talk to one another anymore. None of them knew how to admit sadness, or confusion, or hurt, or fear, because it felt like failure, like weakness. Maybe they never had known, not since they were children. Her father's death had ripped them open, and then they'd scabbed over, too fast, their wounds still fresh under a thick, warped cover. Maybe, in order to heal, they needed to reconnect—not to their roots, but to one another. And maybe this tour of China could be their chance.

She knew her mother was barreling onward with her plan, pretending Nora had given her the go-ahead. Nora wouldn't fight it. She was tired of fighting.

And maybe she and Jesse just needed a break from each other. Maybe that was all her parents had needed, before it was too late.

2

"But it's the summer before my freshman year." Sophie couldn't keep a whine from her voice.

Mom flung the stir-fry around the pan. "I know."

"I'll have just graduated. I'll have an internship. I'll be registering for classes. I'll be packing up."

Mom flinched, as Sophie had known she would, but said only, "Oh, that internship—how'd the interview go?"

"Fine." She'd applied through a city arts program for public school students. She'd been the only thing in the gallery that wasn't perfectly cool, pale, and streamlined, with not a bit of excess—the icily glamorous owner, the exquisite gallerinas, even the stark paintings flat against the white walls. She could tell she was expected to feel disadvantaged and grateful to even set foot in the place, and she did, in spades.

"Well, if the rest of us can take a vacation, so can you."

"But why am I the last to know?"

"You're not. I haven't reached Kay. I haven't told your grandmother."

"How do you know they'll go?"

Mom flung the stir-fry harder. It sizzled, each chunk of pork oozing fat onto the vegetables. "Of course they'll go."

"How come you told Nora first?"

"Someone had to be first."

"I live here with you."

Mom let the spatula clang down. "Set the table, please."

Two sets of chopsticks and napkins and plates, no one across from anyone, food the only focus. Sophie swallowed hard. Sourly, she said, "I'm just saying, I have a life. I need to plan ahead, too."

"Now you can plan on touring China for two weeks. It'll be the perfect vacation for us. An educational, cultural experience—and a family reunion."

A family reunion without her father.

They sat down. Mom filled Sophie's plate with the stir-fry. Sophie picked at her rice, kernel by kernel.

"So Nora called you?" Mom said. "How did she sound?"

Sophie shrugged.

"I bet she's excited about our trip."

"Did she say that to you?"

Mom went quiet.

Feeling a stab of remorse, Sophie ate a sliver of onion, a piece of green pepper, a little chunk of tender pork. The dish wasn't pretty, but it was tasty. She drizzled the brown sauce onto her rice and took another bite.

She was all Mom had left at home, and Mom was all she had left, and she still needed a parent. No more Daddy to crack his corny jokes or suggest junk-food breaks. He used to interrupt her homework, nights Mom worked late, with clippings and coupons—the best burger in Queens, half-priced fried chicken.

Now her dad filled an urn in the living room. Once, she'd lifted the lid and poked a finger inside. It came out gritty and gray. It reminded her of those packets of colored, flavored sugar that came with a white stick to dip and lick. She'd touched her finger to her tongue. It tasted bitter. It tasted like death—an end so final that fire couldn't do anything more to it. Afterward, she'd eaten a quart of strawberry ice cream and thrown it up, and still that taste stayed.

After dinner, she sat on the floor of her room and laid out some of her artwork in neat rows, in chronological order. Sometimes she needed to see her own progress, even starting from a few watercolors she'd kept from way back, where she could see an interesting angle, a little talent. Some of her work made her feel so hopeful it hurt—especially her latest sketches in charcoal, stark yet dreamlike—while others made her wince. Shame was productive, though; it spurred her to do better.

Her portfolio had helped her get into Stanford; her art teacher had singled her out for an award—but so what? She always got ten out of ten on her assignments, but the point was to prove she understood the theme of, say, German Expressionism, not to produce original art. She'd never studied any Asian artists, let alone Asian American ones. How could she hope to break through? She was too self-conscious, too perfectionist. She worried too much about getting straight A's; with her valedictorian sisters, it would've been humiliating if she didn't. She worried too much about her looks; her sisters were thin and gorgeous.

She'd told Mom Stanford had the best fine arts department, but she hadn't even looked it up. Applying there early decision had been, stupid as it sounded, the most impulsive act of her life. Her sisters had gone to Harvard and Yale—like some Asian joke—so the only way to forge her own path was to go far away.

To her mother and sisters, her drawings were cute, just like the pigtails she used to wear, or the baby fat they loved to pinch. Once, when she was nine or ten, she'd deliberately painted something clumsy and inane—a house, a tree, a butterfly. Like every time before, they oohed and aahed. Daddy was the only one who didn't fake it; he was watching football, and just gave it a glance. Furious, she'd gone to her room and ripped up the painting. Since then, she'd kept her artwork to herself.

Sophie filed everything away and checked a blog she'd recently found, posted by a Stanford junior named "mybigfatsecret." This week's entries ran the gamut: *Up 4, down 2, up 2, down 1 . . . Girls, don't forget to hydrate! . . . Your gag reflex is like your clit, gotta find the right spot) . . . Scales are for fish!*

College meant the freshman fifteen, unlimited meal plans, dorms where whole floors of girls became synced in their eating disorders along with their menstrual cycles. There, Sophie had done her research. The EDs, Mia and Ana—in college chat rooms, no need to spell it out. The pro-Mias trading tips on B/Ping. A pro-Ana creed: *Dear Ana, I offer you my heart, my soul, and my bodily functions. I seek your purity and your feather weight. I pledge to be your faithful servant until death.* Even the Mias and Anas in recovery groups posted, for "thinspiration," close-ups of celebrities' protruding ribs, clavicles, hipbones, and ranted against "the haters" urging them to stop killing themselves.

In the desk chair, Sophie's thighs squished against each other. Her gut swelled over the waistband of her jeans.

She reminded herself of her boyfriend, Brandon, and how much he loved her looks, or so he said. He was the coolest guy in the grade. He had his pick of girls, and he'd picked her. Once in a while, she could look in the mirror and see herself the way he said he did—curvy, sexy, beautiful. But he was black; among his friends, "thick" was a compliment. Of course, the Asian girls didn't mean it as a compliment when they asked her, in the locker room, if she was mixed.

She told herself Mom might hear her in the bathroom. But Mom never had. Ever since the accident, the silence of the house felt so impenetrable, no matter if she blasted music, no matter if she gagged.

Her father had said the job in Maine was temporary, and too good to pass up. But Mom had already told her, "Your dad is leaving us"—as if he was sick of Sophie, too. And maybe he was. She could be as moody as Mom, maybe worse. Sometimes she snapped when he was chatty, rolled her eyes at his jokes. Still, she'd figured he needed a breather, and then he'd come back.

Sophie stood up from the desk. Casually, she strode down the hall, past Mom in the living room. Mom looked up and smiled. Sophie smiled back. She entered the bathroom, locked the door, and turned on the tap. Purging was an orderly procedure. The precise push of her pointer and middle finger. The natural resistance, a bit more push—the surge, irreversible—then abandonment. And, after a cool rinse, a lightened, cleansed self—herself, but better.

At school the next day, her throat burned. She and Brandon decided to cut out. With her early acceptance, she could relax a little, even though secretly, she was still aiming for valedictorian. She tried to seem like she succeeded without trying. Otherwise her straight A's seemed so typical-Asian—uncool, unartistic. As it was, some of the kids theorized, half seriously, that the teachers automatically marked the Asian girls as present, gave them A's without checking their assignments.

The moment they entered his apartment, Brandon wanted to have sex. She did, too, at first.

She craved the way she sometimes forgot herself in sex. The first time she and Brandon ever made out, back in September, was the first time she stopped missing her father—only for a few minutes, but she hadn't known those minutes could exist at all. Soon she and Brandon started having sex, and though she usually kept her shirt on, sometimes she forgot about her looks, too. Sex felt like something all her own, a thrilling new discovery. Rationally, she knew her mother and sisters had had sex, but she couldn't imagine them wallowing in it the way she did. The act itself was powerful, something neither she nor Brandon could completely control, something outside of them both. And sometimes she felt powerful, too—like the most powerful girl on earth.

But sometimes it was all unbearably gross—squishy fat, slippery skin, sweat and spit and slime. Then each thrust seemed to thump her lower.

And she wondered what was wrong with him, that he could enjoy it when she didn't, that he didn't mind her keeping her shirt on, that he had no clue about her throwing up. This was one of those times.

Afterward, her throat felt worse. She wondered if she'd pushed too hard with her fingertips. If the acids had already done permanent damage.

"My throat hurts." It sounded more babyish than she'd intended.

"You want a cough drop?"

"Could you make me tea? With honey and lemon." The way Mom made it.

"I can try."

Nonchalantly, Brandon pulled up his pants on his way to the kitchen. By the time he returned, Sophie had fixed her clothes, brushed her hair, and dabbed a little lip gloss.

The mug of liquid he handed her was lukewarm, tan, and cloudy. It tasted awful.

"The teabag was a little dusty," he said apologetically.

"What'd you put in it?"

"Orange juice and sugar."

"Did you boil the water?"

"No, I got it from the tap."

"You can't do that," she said, aghast.

"Why not?"

"You just can't. Bacteria, I guess." Suddenly she missed Mom—her tea, her soothing voice, her cool soft hands stroking Sophie's head and back when she was sick.

Brandon looked embarrassed. Sophie forced herself to take another sip.

"Want to hear my new demo?" he asked.

She nodded.

They lay against each other on his lumpy couch. The first track, "Family Tree," was about his great-grandparents, born to slaves, his preacher grandfather, his dad in prison, his mom waiting ten years and counting for his release. The second was about welfare cereal and cheese. She'd heard most of the material, she'd even been with him when he scrawled some of the lyrics, and everyone at school had already gone nuts when he performed at the last Cultural Day, but she'd never heard it all packaged like this. He sounded professional, ready for radio, if radio ever played what he called the real stuff. He sounded tough and raw. He didn't sound like anyone who could be her boyfriend.

"It's amazing," she said, and felt embarrassed by her word choice.

Brandon smiled, kissed the top of her head, and continued bopping to the beat, occasionally rapping along to his own voice.

She burrowed into him so that his heartbeat muffled the music. Since they'd been together, she'd learned to appreciate hip-hop—not hip-pop, but the real stuff. Sometimes, she could even lose herself in it. Domestic dramas and political rants set to thumping beats, rage funneled into poetry, lessons in overcoming adversity looped with wicked humor and silky hooks. At first, she'd felt like a poser. Like those suburbanites blasting gangsta rap, or hipsters tattooing Chinese characters they couldn't read—of course, she couldn't either.

She'd tried to joke: "Maybe I should listen to Peking opera."

Brandon hadn't laughed. He'd said, "You're a person of color. In America, there's white people, and there's the rest of us."

In that moment, the world had shifted into perspective, like the first time in art class she learned how to start with a dot in the center and two lines, the relationship between depth and angle and distance.

The music stopped short. There was a glitch in the recording. Brandon began to get up, gently pushing her off.

"I have to go to China this summer," she said. "For a family reunion."

His eyes bulged. "Like *The Joy Luck Club*! My mom and I saw that together. We cried like babies."

Sophie had read the book in seventh-grade English class. She remembered a joyful ending. "Not really."

"Aren't you psyched? My family reunions take place at my grandma's house in South Carolina. What's your grandma like? Was she a concubine, with bound feet? Or is she that tough old Chinatown type who can knock you over with an elbow?"

She laughed. "Neither. I don't know. What's yours like?"

"She's the sweetest lady ever, but she'll whup anyone who cusses. She's old, but she can still whup hard. Man, I love her."

"I don't know my grandmother at all."

"But that's family. That's blood. That never goes away."

She shrugged.

Brandon wanted to know whether she'd get to pat a panda, wear a rice paddy hat, learn kung fu.

"Probably," she said. "And eat beetles and dogs."

His eyes bulged again. "Really?"

She laughed. "You're a moron."

He tackled her, put her in a headlock. She wriggled free. He caught her, then hugged her, so tight it hurt.

"I'll miss you," he said.

Her laughter died. "Me too."

He dropped a kiss on her forehead, then started to get up again.

Was it that easy for him to turn away? She'd felt she and Brandon belonged to each other, in a way a more conventional couple couldn't. She liked that her family had no idea. She didn't even mind the jokes in school about jungle fever crossed with yellow fever. His friends talked about black girls being too demanding, white girls too eager to please, Spanish girls too full of Catholic guilt, but they never talked about Asian girls—partly out of respect, knowing how Brandon felt about her, but also because, in their circle, she was unique.

But what if that meant she would also be easy for him to forget? She didn't expect to stay together after high school—she wasn't naïve—but did he plan to leave her before summer? Was she already becoming part of his past?

She blurted, "Sometimes I purge."

He spun around. "What do you mean?"

"Purge, like binge and purge. Sometimes I make myself throw up."

"What are you saying? You're anorexic?"

It was easier to nod than explain. The world of eating disorders was foreign to him, more foreign than tea, maybe as foreign as China.

"Why on earth would you do that to yourself? You're beautiful, every inch of you." He sat back down and caressed her thigh.

Sophie fought the urge to shudder. Instead, she let a few tears fall.

He kissed them, then dried her face with his palm. "How come I never knew? Does your family know?"

She felt a twinge of contempt. Of course nobody knew. She wasn't stupid. "I've never told anyone but you."

"Come here." He opened his arms and squeezed her tight again. "Promise me you won't do it anymore. Promise me."

She loved how his embrace compressed her, made her feel warm and small. "I promise."

Brandon released her and sat back, shaking his head. "Man, you really threw me. I thought that was some shit only white girls did. Rich ones at that."

Inside, she crumpled. She'd thought her confession would make her seem more profound, not just his Asian high-school girlfriend but a person with real problems, like him. After all, he'd never noticed her until the first day of senior year—her first day of school fatherless. In bio, he'd asked her to be his lab partner, and the first time she came over to work on a lab report, she'd ended up telling him about the accident. He'd held her while she sobbed, until she was so dehydrated her lips stuck together.

From that day on, they'd been boyfriend-girlfriend, and she couldn't help thinking losing her dad had made her a deeper, more deserving person, a girl someone like Brandon could love. Sometimes she felt she was that person. But now he was starting to see her for what she still was, the only thing her mother and sisters knew her to be—a baby, a blob of needs and tears.

3

Lin Yulan was somewhat taken aback. A tour of China with her daughters and granddaughters? Seventeen years had passed since she moved to California. In that time, she'd seen them once. She could not remember the last phone call. They were busy, of course, busy with work, busy with school, busy with being busy. She'd been busy in her time, too.

"If not now, when?" Irene said, as if following an outline; Lin Yulan hadn't objected yet. Soon, the implication was, she'd be infirm, or dead. At her age, some body parts were bound to malfunction. Arthritis in her knuckles, knees, and ankles. A strange numbness in her right arm that came and went, ghostlike. But at her last physical, the doctor had pronounced her in excellent health. All in all, she felt quite alive.

"It's your eightieth birthday," Irene said.

Eight was an important number—*ba,* rhyming with *fa,* meaning good fortune, prosperity. But Lin Yulan had never understood why, in America, birthdays were such cause for celebration. Why everyone deserved congratulations for having lived another year. She recalled those enormous productions Irene used to organize for each daughter: an elaborate cake, single-use candles, gifts wrapped in flimsy paper in new boxes in fancy wrappings tied with shiny ribbons—and a rush to take pictures before the weak flames flickered out, before the skinny candles sank into the cake, before the cake itself melted away, before the paper and boxes and wrappings and ribbons all got ripped and discarded. One would think birthdays should be a bigger deal in China, where survival wasn't so certain. Well, maybe people in China nowadays fussed over birthdays, too.

"And the new millennium," Irene said. "Isn't it strange, how the timing works out?"

Recently Lin Yulan had received a letter from Kay in Beijing. Now, that was strange. Her first letter from a granddaughter—in Chinese. Childish grammar and simplified characters, with photos of Kay in Tiananmen Square, in front of a lotus pond, beside a pagoda. Descriptions of her studies, her sightseeing—and many questions about China.

What did she, Grandma, remember? What was it like to be a *gemingjia*? How had she become one? Why hadn't she told them? How had her time as a revolutionary ended? How had she survived incessant war? How had she left the mainland, started over in Taiwan? What was her view now on cross-strait relations between the People's Republic of China and the Republic of China, on independence versus reunification?

Do you ever wonder, Kay had asked, if you hadn't left? If we all lived here? What life might be like then?

Lin Yulan had written back using the Chinese software her son Lou had installed, on the computer he'd given her. She didn't know what Kay knew of her story, or how; whether some record of her life's work had survived on the mainland—impossible. She praised Kay's Chinese. She wrote that she hoped all three granddaughters were safe and well. The numbness in her arm—she kneaded it.

If implied a choice. And one *if* led to another. If her side hadn't lost, if they hadn't escaped, if her children hadn't emigrated, if she'd stayed in Taiwan. One might as well ask who one would be if one's mother were somebody else. An absurd question. Unanswerable.

Lin Yulan asked, "Why China?"

"Where else?" Irene said.

"Someplace new."

"It will be new to us. It's completely different now. We should see it for ourselves."

"What for?" What could they possibly find?

Irene sighed. "For a reunion. For family. For your granddaughters."

Lin Yulan was silent.

Her daughter's voice turned knifelike. "Ma. You don't care to see them?"

Ten years ago, Lin Yulan had remembered that Nora was graduating high school, entering adulthood. She remembered how her own life had forked, and she flew all the way back to New York, without an invitation, to visit the granddaughters she'd helped raise, to meet the baby who was no longer a baby, to tell the stories she'd never told, to present the wisdom she'd stashed away.

One long weekend. The girls treating her as a stranger, Bill exerting cheer, Irene so on edge that Bill drove them all to stay overnight with Susan, who was pale as bone, creeping around her odd house like an ailing cat. When Lin Yulan tried to talk to her granddaughters, they couldn't seem to hear, and they weren't bad children, so she could only confirm what she already knew, that in their world, the new world, the only world that mattered anymore, she was obsolete.

The next morning, she cooked and packed Lou's food for the week. Then she went to tend her garden, where she would see him as soon as he pulled up.

Tucked away on this dully pleasant, slightly shabby block of west Los Angeles was a narrow patch of good soil, bordered by brick halves, for her to cultivate. The other tenants proudly filled theirs with frilly flowers that died in the mildest chill, and were just as proudly replaced year after year.

When she'd moved into the complex, she'd made mulch of the previous tenant's flowers and planted squash, tomatoes, garlic, scallions—things of use. The other tenants had complained; apparently her plantings were insufficiently pretty. She'd ignored the knocks and notes, pretended not to understand. Eventually the super let her be. He was Polish, no stranger to hardship—and old now, frailer than she, with bigger problems than her plantings. Recently there had been an influx of graduate students from the mainland whose parents minded their children, three generations in one-bedrooms, and let them urinate and defecate out in the open, onto the paved walkways and flower gardens.

Today there were trails of slime among her vegetable beds, ragged holes in her squash leaves. Snails—reveling in the gentle warmth of early springtime sun. She caught one munching through a new leaf on her kumquat tree. She plucked the snail, dropped it on the pavement, crushed it underfoot.

Carefully, she checked each branch, each leaf. The kumquat tree was from Lou—a housewarming gift, he'd called it. She'd scoffed at the petite tree, its leaves artificially glossy, its fruit pebble-hard and sour, for show. But once planted, it thrived. Three seasons of the year, it gave fruit. Each year, the kumquats were plumper and sweeter. She ate them whole, each tart bite encased in thin peel. For Lou, she preserved them by sunning them in the windowsill, then soaking them in sugar water.

She caught two more snails munching away at the tree. She crushed them, then went to the basement and brought out her snail trap, a wood plank elevated on two runners. She'd sponged it off when she stored it for the winter, but the underside was still smeared with the remains of previous years.

She was inspecting her tomatoes when Lou pulled up and honked, even though they saw each other immediately; they had their routines. He was driving a new car with no roof, from the dealership where he worked. Over the years, he'd sold knives, then computers, now cars. That was progress of a sort.

"How's this year's crop looking?"

"The snails are back." She spotted one right by her thumb. She plucked it, crushed it, wiped her hands.

"Poor bastards picked the wrong garden." Lou grinned. "You like the car?"

She climbed into the passenger seat. "A car is a car. You don't own it, anyway."

"Jeez, women are tough to impress these days."

They sped off, the wind ruffling their hair. She never asked what they were eating; each week, she let him surprise her. California wraps and smoothies, Japanese ramen, Vietnamese spring rolls, Thai hot-and-sour soup, Korean barbecue, Turkish chicken and rice, Mexican stuffed peppers, even Ethiopian. If he ever repeated, she'd forgotten. She rarely cared for the food itself. She appreciated how he made adventures out of their outings.

He pulled into a parking lot and jogged around to open her door, offer his arm. She pushed him aside and got out herself—another of their routines.

Mischievously, he whispered, "We're eating with black people today. Don't be scared."

"Nobody scares me," she said, because it was true, and because it would amuse him.

In a cracked red vinyl booth, they ate lukewarm fried chicken and sweet limp waffles, with mushy greens on the side. She watched him handle the bones with all of his fingers, sop syrup with each bite of waffle, swallow his greens without seeming to chew. He was past fifty now, but his hair was still jet-black, his face smooth and tan. He was still her son.

She told him about Irene's call.

"Whoa," he said. "Is she serious? Are you going?"

She shrugged.

"Too busy for a vacation?" he teased. "I can feed myself."

She slapped his wrist. "I'll go. I don't have any other grandchildren."

"There's still time for me. Don't worry."

"You have a wife I haven't met?"

"Ma, when I meet a woman dumb enough to marry me, believe me, I'll introduce you." He grinned. "Hey, Susan does. A husband, I mean. Maybe there's time for her, too. In vitro, you know."

"Don't be stupid," she said.

It vexed her that anyone, let alone her own children, could deny that mating and reproducing were biological imperatives, the very basis of survival and progress; that children were necessary investments, to build on your hard-won gains and see you through old age—something Neanderthals must have understood. Of course, it was fortunate to have choices. Lin Yulan, like all women of her generation, hadn't had many. But a sound choice was when to have children, or how many children—not whether to have them at all.

At least Lou was right: men had time. Susan, on the other hand, would leave the world with nothing but poems. Poems were something; words could spark a war, though Susan didn't write that kind. Still, she had a quiet brilliance, a tensile strength—and no one to inherit any of it. She'd finally married, but what for? At her age, she might have saved herself the trouble, and spent her last few decades in peace, as Lin Yulan was doing now.

"You want to go on this tour?" she asked.

"Like hell," Lou said.

"Those girls lost their father."

Soberly, he nodded. "It's sad. At least they're mostly grown."

"If you want to go, I'll tell Irene."

"Nah. This is a ladies' thing."

"What for?"

Lou released his mellow laugh. "To hang out, I guess."

That was a term he'd taught her. When she first moved to California, when he first suggested these outings, she'd say, "What for?" He'd laugh and say, "To hang out, Ma." She'd picture them swaying like laundry, suspended between uses.

"Seriously, are you worried?" he asked. "About you and Irene?"

She shrugged again.

"All that fighting was a long time ago. She didn't have to invite you on this trip. Just be easy. Don't argue."

"Finish your lunch," she said. "Don't tell me what to do."

He shook his head in mock frustration and poured more syrup, shook more salt, resumed eating.

After lunch, Lou drove her to Costco, then the Chinese market, and back to her apartment. He unloaded the supplies, checked her bills, loaded his car with the containers of food she'd cooked that should last him for the week. And, with a salute and a grin, he drove off—their final routine of the day.

Lin Yulan supposed he was right: It was a long time since she had reminded Irene of her duty to leave a legacy, since Irene had told her to get out, since she had tried, in the space of a day or two, to give her granddaughters a sense of the woman she'd been, of the women they should become.

Now it seemed Irene had finally told Kay, at least, about her revolutionary days. So perhaps Irene was finally admitting her mistake. Perhaps all three granddaughters were finally ready to learn from their grandma.

Or perhaps Lou was right that this tour of China was a vacation, nothing more. Its purpose was simply for them to hang out.

A vacation—she did not know how to pack for one. She only knew how to pack knowing she'd never return. Her suitcase sat in the closet. Tucked inside was an old picture, in a silver case. It stayed home with her. If she ever moved again, it would go with her.

China was a new country now, as Irene said. Nothing remained of what Lin Yulan had known, what she'd left. She could think of this trip as a kind of adventure. Like going to these new restaurants each week.

And she was an American now. She had her certificate of naturalization. Lou had helped her apply so that she could receive benefits. She'd studied, once she arrived in California, from a book he gave her. It was her guide to citizenship, and her primary text for learning English.

When she first opened the book, she thought she'd never pass the test. Under a veneer of conviviality, the passages threatened her.

> The opposite of a citizen is an alien, or stranger. You want to become a citizen!
>
> Read this section in front of a mirror: "I am a person of good moral character. By studying this book, I am making progress."
>
> To sum up, a citizen belongs. But nothing in life comes free. Yes, there is a price, but the price is right!
>
> DO YOU KNOW?
>
> a. Is it easy or difficult to become a citizen? ______________
> b. Do you want to be a citizen or an alien? ______________
>
> Now check your answers. (Turn the book upside-down.)

She was instructed to memorize a poem titled "America Is Her Flag." From this poem, she learned stars stood for states, stripes for colonies, "red for courage, white for truth, blue for honor." In China, red was Communist, blue was Nationalist, and white was death.

So she began to understand how to study—without feeling or remembering. Focusing on pronunciation, not meaning; on names and numbers and dates, not her conception of history. *Nation, colony, alien, citizen, refugee, allegiance, security, democracy, progress*—she only had to do with these terms what the book told her to do. And the book did not fail her. She received her certificate. She became a citizen.

The courtroom ceremony began with "Welcome, new Americans" and ended with "So help me, God!"—the last words of the Oath of Allegiance. When she'd read the oath in the book, she'd found this odd, not in its injection of religion—that was everywhere, here—but its ring of desperation. When she repeated it in the courtroom, though, she found it served its purpose. It made her feel grateful.

The day had peaked; time to check the trap. In the strong afternoon sun, the snails had sought shade on the underside of the board, clinging upside-down, even piling on one another. Lin Yulan flipped the board and stomped on it—the crisp crack of the shells, the soft, moist squelch. Firmly, she set the trap back in place. The remains would attract more snails. They never learned, never gave up seeking this shade. Or perhaps she underestimated these lowly creatures; perhaps they sought their lost kin. In that familiar way, her arm throbbed—her arm itself there, then gone.

4

Susan started to dial her sister's number. She hung up and poured herself a drink.

She'd told her father about Irene's plan. The line had gone quiet—so quiet she'd pictured him keeled over. At last he'd said that he wanted to see Ma. That he would meet them at the end of their tour.

She'd called him for the same reason she'd called Irene on New Year's. Because she should, because Winston felt she should. Because, these days, she could afford to be magnanimous. Because now and again she felt compelled to perform some deed, to make some contact, to distinguish one day from the rest.

Susan downed her drink and picked up the phone.

"What?" Irene cried. "Why did you tell him?"

"I called to check up on him. I was making conversation."

"Call him back and tell him no."

"I don't think I can do that," Susan said. Her sister's temper was daunting, but not as daunting as her father's.

"Well, I can't have this! I'm working so hard to plan this trip. How can you have him just show up? And ruin everything?"

Susan decided to treat these as rhetorical questions.

Irene sputtered, "What does he want? He's dead to her. That's what she said. Twenty years ago, when I took her in."

"Maybe you inspired him," Susan hazarded. "All this reconnecting."

Abruptly, Irene asked, "Did he mention Kay?"

"No. Why?"

"Never mind. This is your responsibility. This has nothing to do with me or the girls. If you don't stop him, it'll be on you. You tell Ma. You try and set up their reunion. You know what they're like. Whatever happens, it's on you."

Susan sucked at the dregs in her tumbler. The only temper as daunting as her father's was, of course, her mother's. She said, "I'll call him back."

"You'd better."

"So how's the plan coming along?" Susan's head was buzzing from the liquor.

Irene's voice brightened. "I think I've found the perfect tour. The must-sees in two weeks. All-inclusive, except for overnights in Hong Kong at the beginning and the end."

"Should I book the university hotel? Winston says it's quite nice."

"Oh, I thought we'd stay with you. You said there's plenty of space."

Plenty of space for Susan and her husband. Not for Ma and Irene and the girls. But in that moment, Susan would have agreed to anything to get off the phone. She'd deal with the consequences later.

She hung up and lay back on the couch. She seldom drank so quickly these days. Her life was steady, predictable; it defined moderation. Soon Winston would be home, cooking a well-sauced meat, a steamed fish, leafy greens, soup, rice. During the day, he left her to her whims—saltines, strawberries and whipped cream, coffee with a dash of brandy, nothing—but he insisted on thorough dinners. When they first met, she literally couldn't stomach them. Now she relied on them. He took pride in this. He was a decade older and never had children either. To him, she was girlish, quirky—the one person he indulged and nurtured.

Tonight he brought home, in addition to fresh groceries, a gift-wrapped box. Before she could open it, he said, anxious to please, "It's a travel purse. For China."

She kissed his cheek and gave his rear end a light pat. He smiled and busied himself with dinner. Over his rinsing, scaling, chopping, she told him about Ba and Irene.

Reasonably, he said, "It's not your fault."

"I know. It doesn't matter."

"You don't think Irene will come around?"

"No." She'd never known her sister to come around on anything.

"This trip must mean a lot to her," he said. "Being widowed."

When Susan had heard about Bill's accident, her first thought had been that if Winston died now, decades early, she'd want to die, too. Not because of passion—she'd known passion, and how it went; how, when the winds shifted just a little, it felt like self-immolation—but because without Winston, her life would lose all structure.

She asked, "Should I tell Ba he can't come?"

"How bad would it be if he did?"

She could only shrug.

Winston wiped his hands and patted hers sympathetically. "I wish I could help. This is a very difficult situation."

She held his hands for a beat, then let him resume cooking.

He didn't fully understand, and he didn't claim to. He accepted the situation, the way he accepted her writing or not writing, her moods, her being. "You're a poet," he'd say, every time she disparaged her worth, confessed to countless wasted days, raised the idea, only half joking, of training to be a real estate agent or an accountant. And he did not mean that she had prominent publications, that she'd won prizes. "You're a poet"—a simple fact.

Everyone else she'd ever met, upon hearing it, thrust their own personalities to the forefront—those who proudly declared themselves too stupid for poetry; those who said they might be poets, too, if only they had the time; those who found the idea fanciful, even funny; those who demanded to know where she'd published and where she'd taught and what she thought of so-and-so.

And one man—a man hardly more than a boy—who'd said, *So you have what they call a writer's eye. Where I come from, writers are like anybody, in the pit, wrestling with the world. Here, you watch it like so.* His hand went up, palm out, and slid down air, as though against a sheet of glass. Then the hand closed and knocked on her chest. *Either that, or you have no soul.*

His name was Ernesto. He came from Chile, which had signified to her approximately what Taiwan had to him: turbulent, marginal, foreign. She'd thought she'd known what he meant. She could, at any time, go cold, go distant; this was necessary. Perhaps other poets had better memories, louder voices, more conviction. In order for her to focus on one image, one moment, everything else had to fall away.

Winston turned on two burners and the exhaust fan. He poured oil, slid it around, tossed garlic and scallions. She went and clasped him from behind, her hands meeting over his solid belly, her cheek resting against the gentle slope of his back. He twisted to glance at her, smiled a bit shyly. She was overcome with gratitude, and with it, a sudden, throbbing hunger.

"I'm starving," she said.

He simply nodded and kept cooking, a little faster but steady, thorough as ever. After a minute, she unclasped her arms. She set the table, sat down, and waited for dinner.

The travel purse hung nicely, soft yet sturdy, from her shoulder. It matched her everyday purse—her first real purse, also a gift from Winston, nine years ago. Beige and brown, supple leather, silk lining—the style, apparently, was classic. The everyday purse was meant to hold nothing but a wallet and a single handful of something, she supposed cosmetics. The travel purse was big enough for four handfuls of something, but she couldn't think what.

For decades, she'd carried synthetic bags bigger than her torso, bottomless totes that, for months, held everything she dropped inside—student papers, bills, takeout menus, books, candy, napkins, keys. They'd stretch and fray and rip, and then somehow replace themselves, with some variance in color or logo. Then she'd met Winston, accepted his proposal, and received her first purse. She'd fussed over that single handful—a notepad and pen, her reading glasses—until she learned that in her new life, she hardly needed to carry anything. Everything stayed where it belonged, at home, the same home for nine years now, and she was usually in it.

She did not want to leave it for a two-week tour of China.

Yes, Bill was gone now. Susan had Winston. So she'd called Irene on New Year's. And Irene had sounded so tremulous, so unlike herself, that Susan had behaved completely unlike herself and invited Irene for a visit. She'd pictured herself as a well-appointed hostess. She had not pictured this glass-walled, cream-carpeted flat, this perfect container of her life, overrun by her sister, three nieces, and her mother. Her home, annexed. That had happened once before—just one night, one night only she seemed to remember—and her life had proceeded to fall apart.

She reminded herself she had nothing to hide anymore. And not much to show. No children, no career, not even poems.

She hadn't written a new one in years. Sometimes she tinkered with an old poem, eked out a new phrase or two. Sometimes she wrote refined essays for literary journals that she might or might not submit. Every now and then, she sensed a glow, like the faintest sign of the moon through high clouds, like the aura of some long-absent thing, but she could not see it, let alone name it. And a blank page was quite beautiful on its own, she'd found. There were already so many words, so many voices in the world. She flinched at contributing to the cacophony.

She'd married a nice man and learned to be nice to him. She had a nice home and kept it neat. She even had nice plants; she'd never managed to keep one alive before. Here, in their oceanfront apartment in the New Territories of Hong Kong, every houseplant flourished, burst against the glass. Still, she avoided anything temperamental, anything that promised to flower and drop off. Winston liked orchids, so she'd bought one fashioned from silk.

She'd once assumed her ambition would swell with age, mortality sharpening her desire to capture the world in verse. Instead, she'd settled.

Back when she'd met Winston, a visiting professor of economics in yet another college town in America, her last, it had suddenly seemed crucial that his family had also fled Guangzhou, that, Oxford education and visiting professorship aside, he'd lived in Hong Kong ever since. A plane hop, a train stop, a ferry ride from the mainland, and the decreed gateway between the mainland and Taiwan. It seemed the one right move for her, the one last move.

And it was. But, in moving, she'd lost her hold—long tenuous—on language. Cantonese was the language of her birth, of her parents, of savage private strife. Mandarin was the language of school, of history, of her first success. English was the language of limitless promise, the language she'd striven to possess, only to be awarded a genteel sort of perpetual scrabble. When she married Winston and moved to Hong Kong, she became just another person, another wife—and as mixed-up linguistically as anyone here. Now Cantonese was the language of home, except when the context called for English, or Mandarin, or a mishmash. And English had been the language of authority, until the handover three years ago, when the British passed this territory back to the Chinese, and Mandarin invaded the government, the schools, taxis, TV news.

And now there was no conduit for her poetry. Or was that an excuse?

Was she always too walled off from the pit of life? Was that what Ernesto had meant?

She was not searching for him. In nine years, there'd been no contact, no mentions, few reminders. She was browsing online for books. There was his name. His novel, his American debut. She ordered it, express. It arrived overnight. She finished reading it before she ate a thing. The prose was gorgeous and a bit stilted. The story was grand in scope and utterly narcissistic.

His face took up the entire back cover, black-and-white and starkly lit. He'd filled out. Of course he had; he was in his thirties now. He looked like a Latin matinee idol, inky shadows along his cheekbones, below his pooling eyes, in the indentation above his upper lip. Also printed on the jacket was an e-mail address: ernesto@ernesto.com. How like him.

At twenty-two, he'd arrived in a college town in America, the same dot where she'd just arrived from another college town in America. He had already published a novel in Chile, or what was left of a novel after censorship. No American publisher would translate it, and he couldn't bear the unremitting compromise of translating it himself. He saw linguistic imperialism as his personal nemesis. He believed his calling was to write the great Chilean novel in English, and thus catapult his country and himself to the forefront of world consciousness, at least to those parts with power and a conscience.

When will our stars rise? he used to ask.

No matter day or night—she kept the shades drawn—she'd point to her bedroom window. *They're rising. Look.*

The truth was, she hadn't seen much on the horizon for either of them. She was a poet, laboring with a dictionary and a thesaurus. English was not her native language, as Americans never tired of pointing out. She suspected she'd already plateaued. Ernesto, like her, had studied English since childhood, studied as if his life depended on it. Unlike her, of course, he was young, male, cocky. In his speech, in his stories, he tossed out melodramatic phrasings, pretty clichés, plain errors. When critiqued, he claimed them intentional, integral. When he arrived in America, she'd already been a citizen for twenty-odd years—for more than his life span. He was her student.

Now his star was rising.

Winston had saved her from damp furnished rentals, from pasty academics, from being the Asian lady in each town—there were usually a few others, of course, yet they were each somehow marked, marked in a way that ruled out comfort in solidarity, or even acknowledgment of mutual existence; besides, she did not fit any American's idea of an Asian lady, eventually not even her own. Winston had saved her and wanted nothing in return except the rest of her life.

But her poetry couldn't thrive in such continuity. Hadn't she known that?

You see life in moments, Ernesto once said. *You have no sense of narrative, of cause and effect. One moment burns bright, and you forget the rest.* He gave an extravagant sigh. *As poets must.*

The novelist's craft, he said, *was* the connections. He'd quote someone: "Only connect . . ." He'd say, *Dot dot dot.*

Yes, she focused on life crystallized. He fussed over the in-between. What did it matter, when the other divides were so glaring?

Think of pearls, a necklace. The plot is the thread that strings the pearls together.

Another quote he'd picked up, perhaps from her own syllabus. She'd lifted large parts from her predecessors.

Without it, he continued, *you have only a handful of pearls, useless.*

What use is a necklace?

A necklace, you wear. You wear, you own, you keep.

I don't wear necklaces.

So they bantered, until despair closed in.

• • •

She was feeling panicky, as she hadn't since the handover. At that time, Winston had reassured her that China would be hands-off with their teeming, high-rolling islands, that political ideology would bow to profit. But she wasn't the only one panicking then. The economy plummeting, the rich fleeing, the frenzied demand for British citizenship—a classic case, Winston had said, of the colonized clinging to the colonizer.

Yes, but China always was too close. These days, people like her niece Kay talked of reclaiming their heritage, when really, Susan thought, China retained its claim on you.

She refrained from drinking to quiet her nerves. Instead, she tried to write a poem. A poem about China.

She'd stored decades of stale news bites, tragedy to break your teeth wrapped in metallic irony. Reeducation for anyone resisting liberation. The commune experiment, millions starving to death in unison. The Cultural Revolution, kids damning parents, students damning teachers, poets and painters hanged. The papier-mâché Statue of Liberty in Tiananmen Square, the singing interrupted by tanks. Then the motherland, rehabilitated, retaking custody of Hong Kong and Macau, both of which had done quite well without its supervision.

Winston had been right, mostly. He'd admit their eventual obsolescence as the gateway to China now that China had opened its own gates, but overall, they were still doing quite well. Just powerful politicians becoming figureheads, Web sites refusing to load, a new deference in the press. Just enough to make you watch yourself. Thousands still rallied every year to commemorate Tiananmen, and they could keep rallying. China would do as it wished.

China, childhood, her father. She couldn't keep hold of an image, let alone a moment. She tried switching the language.

A few afternoons kite-flying with her father. He said she was talented.

Once, a strange woman appeared and waved, and he disappeared. For an hour or two, Susan kept the kite aloft, her arms going numb, her legs cramping up, until he came back and said, *Good girl*. She said she'd rather not go kite-flying again. She knew she was rejecting a gift, possibly his last. He said that was fine. He said he'd take Irene.

The splintering wooden handle of the feather duster. Ba would make her pull up her skirt before he used it to spank her. Once Irene threw a tantrum and he spanked her, Susan—because she was older, nearer, quieter? Still, worst was when he beat Lou. Lou would run and laugh. She and Irene would watch, dumbstruck: Was that the difference between a girl and a boy? Was that his talent? When Ba caught him, he'd tie him to the *longyan* tree and lash him. If Ma happened to be home, she'd save him. A certain look from her and Ba would walk away. Ma never tried to save Susan or Irene—maybe because they didn't try to run. More likely because Lou was the son.

Once Lou pelted Irene with rotten *longyan,* the thin brown shells splitting against her dress, the slimy white fruit streaking her legs. Irene screamed at him to get lost, to go and die, and Ma locked her out of the house until morning. Susan understood that somehow the danger was real; Lou was precious, and he might vanish. Whenever he appeared—grinning, hair gleaming, always chewing or leaning against something—Ma relaxed. Of course, Irene could never forgive this. She was like Ma, self-righteous, each labeling the other a traitor.

Anyway, all that was in Taiwan. What did Susan know of China? She'd been five when her family fled. She tried switching the language again.

Ba on his hands and knees. Ma standing over him, menacing. Susan's first memory, her only memory of China. She'd read that first memories were always false, reconstructed from a picture or a story, imaginings replayed until they rang true. A moment willed into being by a wretched poet.

She was inside, peeking out. She could not hear. Perhaps she was covering her ears.

Ba knelt like a dog, his face dripping tears. Because they had to flee?

Because he feared for their lives? Because he'd been caught with a mistress? But then they'd be fighting. This wasn't a fight. Ma squatted before him and slapped him. Then slapped him again. He didn't flinch, only kept crying, one side of his face on fire.

Maybe the moment did need connecting. Susan gave up, in any case, on the poem.

5

Click-clacking in her ears, Kay jerked awake. Her elbow had slid off the table; her face had nearly hit her notebook. A quartet of all-night mahjong players chortled at her over their tiles. She gave them a sheepish smile, then tried to focus on the characters she'd penciled over and over, the last column devolving into squiggles at the bottom, where she'd nodded off.

One hour until her dictation test, intonations of long strings of syllables that had called up, until mere months ago, nothing but a vague and needling familiarity, and now triggered—unless she hadn't studied adequately—romanizations, tones, definitions, grammatical usages, and precise combinations of strokes in precise order.

Her gaze wandered to the window. Outside looked yellow and hazy, the harsh grays of the city in soft focus, tinted sepia. Kay wondered if the glass was warped, or if exhaustion had blurred her vision.

The night before, her mother had called. "I've been trying to reach you for weeks! Didn't your roommate give you my messages?"

"It's hard for me to call back." Besides, she'd heard the news from Nora, though she hadn't really believed it.

"Isn't this exciting? You're so interested in your roots. Now you'll get to tour China with your whole family. I know you haven't seen all these must-sees."

Of course not. She'd intentionally shunned being just a tourist. Her mother was expectant—not only for assent, Kay realized, but approval. She gave it, and got off the phone.

She hadn't slept. She'd surveyed her dorm room, its grimness now precious. She'd flipped through her textbooks, her notebooks, her dictionaries. She'd pulled out her last batch of outreach leaflets, the meager lines she'd spent weeks drafting and typing: guidelines on safer sex, her own contact details, her willingness to help, and an empowering quote from Chairman Mao himself: *Women hold up half the sky*. For the last month, she'd loitered outside karaoke clubs, hair salons, hotel lobbies, offering these leaflets to women selling their bodies under the guise of business entertainment, hair washes, massages. Two women had called—one wanting only money, and one threatening to harm her in a manner she still lacked the vocabulary to understand.

This morning, she'd crawled out of bed before dawn, pressed those last leaflets into her notebook, and plodded to a karaoke club to catch the hostesses ending their shifts, their makeup caked, their slinky clothes stinking. Most stared and sidestepped her, like every time before. A few immediately pushed the leaflets into their purses as if the paper would come in handy. One girl lingered, thin white fingers clutching Kay's last leaflet, and asked, "What is this?"

It's nothing, Kay wanted to say. *Just take it, and I'll go.* But she explained, speaking too quickly, her tones a little off.

The girl cocked her head. "Where are you from?"

Her Mandarin was worse than Kay's. She was a migrant, a peasant. They could be discussing how she'd turned to prostituting herself in a Beijing karaoke club, how she endured it, how Kay could help. Instead, the urgent question was where Kay came from.

"Never mind." Kay smiled weakly and started to leave.

"Wei!" A man in a baggy suit stood in the doorway of the club, the sweep of his ear-to-ear comb-over black and dramatic against the pink neon glow.

The girl crumpled the leaflet in her fist. The man bore down upon them. Kay froze.

"Boss, I don't know her. She gave me this. I don't know what it is." The girl held out the crumpled leaflet.

"What's this propaganda?" The man snatched it with one hand and seized Kay's arm with the other. "What are you doing here? Who are you?"

Kay tried to shake her arm loose. His grip tightened. She blurted, "I'm a student. At the university. An international student."

"International?" His gaze darted between her face and the leaflet. "Where are you from?"

"America."

"You don't look American."

"*Meiguo huaren.*" The term for Chinese American she'd never heard until she came to China.

"So you're Chinese? Where's your *laojia*?"

She babbled, "My mother was born in Guangzhou. My grandparents came from villages, somewhere around there. They fled to Taiwan. I don't know my father's side of the family. He was an orphan. He grew up in Taiwan, too."

"Taiwan is part of China!" he bellowed.

Hastily, she agreed.

He grabbed her notebook and flipped through it. All three of them watched her first scrawls evolve into respectable characters. He snorted, tossed it back, and tore up the leaflet. The scraps drifted into a greasy puddle.

He turned to the girl. "Get out of here."

She vanished around the corner.

The man jabbed his finger at Kay's nose. "If I see you again, I'll have you jailed. You're not a *laowai*. You understand?"

Clutching her notebook to her chest, Kay nodded and hurried away, ducking into this teahouse where she'd dozed off.

Where are you from? That relentless question, long the bane of her existence, and every other Asian American's; the one question that somehow was, to the questioner, of paramount importance. In America, no matter if you were American-born, spoke only English, knew nothing else, the answer that satisfied people was China, or something equally foreign. In China, the honest answer was America, and still people weren't satisfied. No, she wasn't a *laowai*—a white man, the definitive foreigner. Here, Japanese were Japanese, black people were black people, and people like her were oddities, Chinese enough not to merit favorable treatment, foreign enough to be continually shut out.

All year, she'd studied a language that should have been hers from the start, and learned enough to know how little, still, she knew. All year, she'd tried to trace her heritage in a place where history was being razed, paved over, replaced with steel, glass, and neon—and yet where even a pimp wanted to know her *laojia*.

For as long as she could remember, she'd felt the need to constantly resist, or end up conforming. As a kid, she'd made it her business to be not only the smartest but the toughest girl around. In college, she'd protested egregious instances of present-day Orientalism, such as the "Geishas and Concubines" party, an annual campus tradition. In her job at the Asian American Cultural Awareness Project, she'd monitored media depictions of Asians as inferior, exotic, mystical, monolithic, premodern, submissive, devious, buffoonish—eternally foreign, almost never fully human. Then she'd launched a program to teach Chinese American history to students in Chinatown, emphasizing how their people had helped build America as much as anyone. Finally, after years of arguing for the right of those like her to exist in the here and now, to occupy their rightful place as Americans, she'd resolved to learn her own history, to see how it led back—on her own terms—to China.

Of course, the issue of resisting or conforming wasn't quite the same for her here—in fact, she remembered a sense among Asian American activists that they were protecting something endangered. Now, living among one-billion-plus Chinese, few ideas seemed more absurd—but there always seemed to be an easy way and a hard way to do everything.

There was the "foreigner comfort dormitory hotel," and then there was the dorm she'd chosen, with a wooden plank for a bed, a rusty pipe for a shower, filthy squatting toilets. There were shiny taxis, and then there were grimy, teeming buses and subways. There were fancy expat supermarkets, and then there were street vendors, from whom she'd learned how to bargain well enough to live on her meager scholarship—and from whom she'd also bought a handless alarm clock, a toothbrush that shed bristles on her tongue, bags full of rotten fruit snuck in during the weighing. There were American fast food joints and upscale French restaurants, and then there were the local food stalls—which often gave her diarrhea, but even when she consumed nothing but crackers and water, every now and then her stomach would fall victim. This seemed a crucial message, the place itself refusing to be digested. In a way, she'd come to appreciate physical discomfort as a kind of penance, keeping her aware of her boundaries, keeping her from taking life for granted.

How could she bear for her year in China to end with a package tour?

She drank her cold, oversteeped tea and stepped outside, into a choking fog. Sharp pricks on her face and neck—she thought, at first, it was her own hair whipped by the wind. All the pedaling, scurrying masses wore an array of face masks—hospital green, Burberry plaid. Even the beggars had wrapped their faces in rags. Pushing against the gritty gusts, Kay was seized by fits of coughing. She doubled over. "Just don't come back hacking and spitting," her father had said, grinning.

Up and down the street, people were mobbing buses, scuffling over cabs—she didn't stand a chance. Just ahead was the only other person holding still—a little boy in a teddy bear mask, resisting his grandfather's tugging, face turned upward, eyes full of wonder. Shielding her face with her notebook, Kay looked up, too, and saw that the yellow haze was a colossal swarm of sand between Beijing and a blue sky.

By the time she reached her dorm, she was battered and wheezing, nose and throat clogged, eyes burning. Casting about for a washcloth, she paused. The room was full of something, a presence she couldn't place. The floor, the beds, the desks—all a strange pallor. She checked the window. It was closed. Somehow the sand had penetrated, and veiled every surface. She drew her fingertip across the sill, picking up a tiny golden drift. She touched the drift with her thumb; it disappeared into her skin. The sand was finer than any she'd seen before, fine as powder, fine like mist.

"You doofus," her friend Rick said. "Even I knew about the sandstorm."

"How?" His Chinese was pathetic. They'd started in the same class, but she'd sped ahead.

"My mom saw it on CNN."

Kay recalled a warning from her own mother that she'd dismissed. "But seeing it was so surreal. The yellow haze, the blue sky, the way the sand got in everywhere—"

Rick nodded affably. "It was weird."

They were on a bus, just after sunrise, to Tiantan Park—a must-see said to still live up to its name: Temple of Heaven. She slumped in the seat and let her head fall against Rick's arm. After a minute, he slid his arm out and resettled it over her shoulders. Her cheek against his chest, she stared at her lap. She did not know why she'd initiated this contact.

The first day of class, she'd turned toward the voice intoning the most basic vocabulary with the baldest American accent in the room, and saw that he was Chinese—American-born, of course. He caught her gaze, his slanted eyes twinkling from his tanned face, and said, "Now I know more Chinese than my parents or grandparents."

She and the other ABC students were all first-generation and knew a little of the language, even if they thought they didn't—from parents' covert conversations, from a grandmother, maybe from something innate. Rick was third-generation on both sides, descended from railroad workers. She would've loved to introduce him to her Chinatown students, a perfect illustration of how their people were as American as anyone—yet still got asked where they were from. Rick didn't mind that, though. Maybe because he was from the Bay Area, where Asians weren't such a minority. Maybe because he was good-natured to a fault, like her dad.

Since her arrival in Beijing, she'd found herself craving the company of men—their geniality, their simple enthusiasm, their lack of self-awareness and self-doubt. She divided her free time between Rick, an earnest local grad student named Du Yi, and a worldly Beijing entrepreneur named Mr. Wan. All three had, at various times, expressed desire for more than friendship. She'd kept them close while making clear her interest was anything but sexual. In fact, she'd once enlisted them to help her gain entry into a karaoke club—to conduct a little investigation, and to draw the line, as starkly as possible, between her and those women.

Inside the park gates was a hallowed quiet. Strolling down a dirt path, woods on either side, she thought she saw a strange animal scaling a tree. It was an old man, solemnly rubbing his back against the bark. She and Rick stared, then laughed. The old man turned and they hushed; with a dignified nod, he resumed his routine. Deeper in the woods, a tiny figure with a bun of gray hair was swinging from a branch. Kay and Rick squinted all around them, into the tangled shadows still resisting the sun, and saw legions of old men and women, all communing with trees—rubbing, swinging, slapping the bark, stretching as if their arms might sprout leaves.

Even after they emerged from the woods into a more familiar realm of preserved structures with official signage, the park continued to enchant. The Round Altar, every arc and spiral of white marble tiled in multiples of nine, the divine number. Echo Wall, where she stood so far from Rick that she could hardly make out his features, and whispered, "Knock knock." Rick's reply traveled along the wall and vibrated in her ear so intimately that she didn't finish the joke.

And then they ambled through a gate into a vast courtyard and nearly collided with two wizened men absorbed in a kind of dance, flowing and meticulous. One was painting classical characters from right to left, while the other painted the mirror image of each character underneath, both pausing every few steps to dip coarse brushes into plastic pails. The two lines of calligraphy were divided by a long chink in the pavement, a horizon separating each object from its reflection. She began copying the first line into her notebook. The characters were immensely complicated, composed of traditional radicals whose meanings should have been obvious from their images—and surely were, to the other old-timers idly looking on, but not to her. At last she moved to the next line, and saw it was fading fast. She looked back to the first. It was gone.

The men were painting on the pavement with water. Dawn had given way to another day. After another minute, the men dumped out their pails and trundled off.

"We should head to class," Rick said.

"No, not yet," she cried.

"We've seen it." He pointed to the exit, a few yards ahead.

All the old men and women were taking their leave of the park. Tourists were straggling in. Souvenir stands were popping up.

"Can we come back?" she asked, stricken.

"If you want." Rick gave her a curious glance. "I thought you were templed out."

That was a term they'd coined together, early in the year, when one iconic sight after another got checked off: *Well, we saw it. We can say we saw it. Here's proof: a picture.* The Summer Palace, the Forbidden City. Ancient this, imperial that. A university trip to the Badaling section of the Great Wall—by then, she was braced for mobs of tourists, but not for cable cars and donkey rides and a KFC.

"I was, but now my mom's planning this tour, and—" She looked up to find Rick's face directly in front of hers, and suddenly she found herself shutting her eyes, stretching closer, searching for his mouth. Just as he started to reciprocate, she broke away.

He stared. She headed toward the exit.

He caught up. "And what? You're marking your territory?"

There was a new, slight jeer in his tone. She'd disturbed the equilibrium between them. She knew she wouldn't get it back.

"Shang che zhao zhao, xia che niao niao, shang chuang shui jiao." Mr. Wan grinned. "A little saying about bus tours. Get on the bus and take pictures, get off the bus and take a piss, get into bed and go to sleep."

Laughing, Kay laid down her chopsticks and wrote it in her notebook.

Officially, she and Mr. Wan were language partners, though she only refined his accent, while he taught her sayings that, no matter how colloquial, had an elegant brevity that their translations never matched.

She'd met him at a newsstand, where she was trying to read a headline, stuck at five words; she knew each character, yet she couldn't make sense of them together. *La si wei jia si,* she muttered. "Las Vegas," a voice boomed over her shoulder, "great city." He apologized for startling her and introduced himself: "Mr. Ten Thousand—you get it? *Wan*—literal translation, of course. Okay, sorry, not funny. You're ABC, right? I knew at first glance." In a musing tone, he said, "America," and marveled at how American businessmen expounded on what they liked and didn't like about China. "Hey," he said, "China doesn't mind. China's too busy eating your lunch!"

He often invited her to dinners like these, home-style specialties in plush, secluded restaurants unmentioned in any guidebook. He also invited her to business banquets, bar openings, his luxury condo. Perhaps like China, Mr. Wan never seemed to mind her demurrals; he was older, worldly, wealthy, with no shortage of admirers.

Now he asked her, almost by reflex, if she wanted a nightcap. She found herself saying yes.

Instantly, his eyes sharpened. "How about my place?"

She shrugged. "Why not?"

It was strangely easy to accompany him to his grand high-rise complex, called "Platinum Gold Palace Court." To drink a glass of whiskey and feel it drape her insides like warm silk. To go with him to his black lacquered bed.

Over the next weeks, it felt strangely easy to hook up with him, and Rick, and then Du Yi, too, as if it was something they all, including she, had been waiting for. And yet it also felt like a brave exploration, like she was navigating dangerous terrain—not only because none of them knew she was hooking up with the others.

She always stopped short of sex, but she found herself going further with each of them than she ever had with anyone. The further she went, the more unsatisfied she felt, and she didn't want to stop, but she didn't know what else she wanted.

Her restraint elicited Du Yi's approval; among his friends, all overprotected spawn of the one-child policy, morning-after pills and abortions had become as common a rite of passage as a hangover. It amused Mr. Wan, who said, "I thought American girls were *suibian*"—loose, easy. It deeply frustrated Rick, who thought she simply didn't care enough about him.

None of them knew she'd never had sex with anyone. She couldn't shake the sense that sex would be something done to her, rendering her vulnerable, even helpless, an object.

• • •

She agreed to meet Du Yi for drinks. It seemed fair; she'd spent the previous night at Mr. Wan's, and the next day she and Rick were going on an overnight trip to the Great Wall.

The bar was swankier than she'd expected, half the clientele white men. She sat at the bar. The servers ignored her. She picked up a copy of the English-language weekly, another convenience she usually spurned. A pizza parlor opening, a wine bar opening, all-you-can-eat-and-drink champagne brunches—and a thick section of personal ads. Under "Women Seeking Men," the first ad queried:

> Do you have healthy personality and baby-skin heart? Me, lovely tempting local girl seeking for sincere long relationship with successful blond businessman. Playboys and jerks please stay away!!!

Flipping to "Men Seeking Women," Kay read:

> Handsome European male fluent in English and Chinese would like to meet Japanese and Korean girls. NO SPEAK ENGLISH? OK! I LIKE YOU. WE HAPPY.

She couldn't stop reading. "I wish for Hollywood romance." "Do you need a place to stay, rent-free? I want a Chinese girlfriend to take care of me." "Is true love too much to hope?" "You: Chinese, sweet, sexy, slim, petite, and possibly smart. Me: generous, tall, decent-looking Western man—did I mention generous?" "Lonely and beautiful Beijing girl dreaming of fun, friendship, marriage." "I think Asian women are the hottest!!!"

"Ni hao."

Kay recoiled. A middle-aged white man leaned on the bar beside her, his blue eyes traveling the length of her. In America, a contemptuous glare generally sufficed. But there was such offhandedness to this overture, such self-assurance oozing toward her, and in another second, she understood what he was, perhaps unintentionally, signaling: Not only *I want you,* but *Lucky you.*

She spat, "Go fuck yourself."

The guy jumped. So did everyone around her—all local women, she realized, waiting drinkless at the bar for the opportunity she'd just spat on.

By the time Du Yi arrived, his hair carefully spiked, Kay could hardly break out of her thoughts to greet him. He ordered drinks for them both. She finished hers, barely looking at him. She was studying the local women sitting, waiting, hoping, while the white men held court, taking their time, taking their pick.

These women couldn't understand how what seemed like romance, or at least mutual attraction, was shameless capitalization; or the historical context of Orientalism; or the subtext of those English ads—how, for starters, that "Handsome European male" preferred his Asian women inarticulate, if not voiceless; or how such presumptions coiled around people, until they no longer knew how their very identity had been constricted.

For the first time in months, she felt that fire again—what her grandfather had called "the fire of a revolutionary." In English, the words were grandiose, but in his low, gruff voice, they'd had a simple, strong ring. As she made the tortuous trip back from visiting him—by a fifty-year decree, there was no direct route between Taiwan and the mainland—disparate elements of her life in China had suddenly seemed to connect. Her classes on contemporary Chinese history and Chinese women's history, where she'd learned about a long line of female revolutionaries, from Hua Mulan to Qiu Jin, whose political battles were as embedded in the collective consciousness here as the rescue of Cinderella by Prince Charming in the West. Her professors, older women so unadorned, forthright, and unselfconscious that American women seemed, in comparison, to be posturing more than being; and what they'd taught her about the Communist liberation of women. In stark contrast, the new generation of women Kay herself had seen on the streets of Beijing, who had been pushed back to being most valuable as sexual commodities not by a feudalist tradition of female subjugation but by *kaifang,* China's "opening up" to capitalism and tourism. And so she'd conceived a plan to empower a few of those women, to resume in some form the work of her own grandmother.

When she'd told her professors about her outreach campaign, they'd responded with bemusement, as if she were protesting, say, nose-picking. When she'd persisted, they'd shifted to stony rhetoric: Prostitution was eradicated during liberation. She'd tried to look up local organizations devoted to the cause, and never even found a phone number. She'd organized a campus meeting, attracting two geeky Midwesterners who seemed overly interested in both the souls and the services of Asian prostitutes, and Du Yi, who'd later confessed he'd seen her posting flyers and thought she was pretty. And in the end, her last leaflet had become scraps of litter in a parking lot.

She'd aimed too high, too far; after all, she was only a student, still a newcomer, an outsider by birth. But here in this bar, only someone like her could draw the connections.

Du Yi was desperately making conversation. She was on her second drink, without noticing. He never let her pay—not because he was the man, but because here, anywhere in China, he was the host.

She told him about the tour.

"I would like to introduce myself to your family," he said, so earnestly she almost laughed. He misread the tremble in her face and ventured, "I will try to get a visa to visit you in America, but the authorities are very strict. What will become of us when your scholarship ends?"

"I don't know. Maybe I'll stay." The thought hadn't occurred to her before, but why not? After the tour, she could stay.

Du Yi's face lit up. She tried to explain her fledgling idea for a new mission.

"These women?" he said, incredulous. "They're not victims. They're trash. Unworthy of a revolutionary like you."

From him, the word sounded fatuous; he was just as admiring of the way she eschewed cosmetics.

Kay finished her drink and said she needed to get up early. He asked why. She told him about the Great Wall plan. He wanted to know which section. She told him Simatai, the section said to be the most authentic. He said he could take her to a section only locals knew, so unspoiled it didn't even have a name.

She wanted to walk home alone, but they lived on the same campus. By the time they reached the gate, she'd snapped at him a half-dozen times. A little contrite, she made out with him briefly, on a bench behind her dorm.

She'd planned a route of four buses, but Rick had hired a cab, and she was too tired to argue. She slept through the three-hour ride. When they arrived, her eyes snagged on cable car tracks: another tourist trap, another disappointment. She found herself blinking back tears.

But on this overcast, chilly day, there were no cars in operation, no one manning the booths or stores, not even a backpacker in sight. She and Rick hiked a dusty trail that wound around the mountain, sloping more steeply until, halfway up, they had to crawl. A wheezing—she thought it was Rick, and Rick must have thought it was her, until they both turned to find a middle-aged peasant padding in their wake, pink circles blazing on his gaunt brown cheeks.

The man apologized, explained he grew apples for a hundred *kuai* per month—Du Yi's tab last night—and lowered his head. She and Rick had become hardened, of necessity, to beggars; they shook their heads and hiked on. Every time they stopped to rest, the man crept near, discreetly wheezing. At last they climbed onto the Wall, the man a few steps behind. He apologized again and stared at their feet.

Below the crumbling brick were brown spindly bushes, a steep rocky fall, a desolate dribble of a creek. Without looking at each other, she and Rick reached for their wallets. The man stared at the bills they held out and offered to carry their backpacks, guide them along the Wall, lodge them at his house.

"Please," Kay said, "just leave us alone."

He bowed, took the money, and began padding down, pausing every few steps to turn and bow again.

In near silence, she and Rick walked the Wall, the serpentine stretch gorgeously disintegrating into the gray sky and bleak countryside, until the sun set. Soon it was too dark to do much but stay in place. They zipped their sleeping bags together.

Rick had packed chocolates, wine, a pillow. She'd brought water, bread, and toilet paper. The wind flooded their ears like white water. For the first time all year, she saw a multitude of stars shining bright. She could not think how to fill this time and space, and yet she could not let this night just pass away. Rick's arms were a band of warmth around her, his breath sweet and sour. When she tasted it, she turned and cried.

She cried for her dad. For the peasant and what she'd said. For Rick, who didn't know she was crying, only that he'd been rejected yet again. For herself, because she couldn't stop chasing what she seemed unlikeliest to attain—transcendence, her thoughts stilled, a moment to simply be; and even as she lay here, she ached to climb that section of the Great Wall that didn't even have a name.

Back in Beijing, it was balmy, clear-skied, and snowing. Pieces of white fluff drifted overhead, tumbling through streets and hallways, caught in whirlpools of current. "What are they?" she couldn't stop asking. "What is this?"

Rick, of course, had no idea. She called Mr. Wan, who was in a meeting. She called Du Yi, who said it was *liuxu*, which he struggled to define—some kind of annual late-spring dissemination from willow trees. Her teachers said everyone called it *liuxu*, but everyone knew it was really *yangxu*. They wrote the characters on the blackboard. When Kay looked them up, she couldn't find one complete definition. Catkins, or seed pods, from poplar trees, or only female poplars, or cottonwoods, or willows after all.

In America, she wouldn't know the difference, and it wouldn't matter. Here, it was like wind or rain, a sign of the seasons, just part of the weather—another element of this country that took hold of her, even as it eluded her grasp.

6

A warm breeze wafted through the house, caressing Irene's skin as she sat at the computer, rustling all her books and brochures, printouts and notes, carrying just a hint of humidity. The summer was nearly upon her. All the hype about the new millennium seemed not only quaint, but somehow excised from public memory.

She double-checked the flights she'd selected. Just as she was about to click the button marked "Purchase All," she hesitated.

From winter through spring, she hadn't minded the monotony of work, or nights alone in the house. She'd been immersed in her research. She'd surveyed travel agencies, quizzed sales reps, collected brochures, created spreadsheets. She'd scoured guidebooks, encyclopedias, maps. She'd read reviews of tour companies, hotels, landmarks, China itself. She'd clicked through strangers' travelogues and photo albums. She'd made a list of things to pack. She'd made a list of things to buy. She'd shopped for a new camera.

She was harboring something she didn't want the outside world to touch, something only she could bring to life, something that could change everything. It was like being pregnant again.

Sharing the plan with her daughters, her sister, her mother, she'd winced more than once at this new, precious thing being met with a gust of cruelty, the chill of indifference. But they'd agreed, and since then, she hadn't even minded her daughters' daily rejections—not as much. Sophie was staying out later, locked away deeper, sometimes refusing to emerge for dinner. Nora rarely answered Irene's calls, and when she did, she sounded strained and snappy. Once, Irene caught the tail end of an argument—she heard the word *commitment*—and even though she wanted to protect and comfort, to know if her daughter was being denied anything by her boyfriend, Jesse, she managed not to probe.

Meanwhile, Kay had told her she'd met her grandfather in Taiwan, though she was curiously reticent about it, other than demanding why she hadn't known her own grandmother was a *gemingjia* in pre-Communist China.

"Ask her," Irene said.

Sounding defeated, Kay said, "I tried."

Then there was talk of reaching out to local prostitutes, or something equally baffling. And then Kay said she might stay in China after her scholarship ran out. How long? As long as she felt like it. What about law school? She'd defer, or reapply. What about home?

Kay said, "What about it?"

Irene dropped it. For once, she'd heed Susan: This would pass. It was only further proof that until they reunited for this tour, they were all flailing. The very fact of it would prove the futility, even the absurdity, of doing anything afterward but returning home.

When the time came to put her research into effect, Irene had gotten a bit stuck. There were tours for independent travelers, singles, single women, seniors, families with small, teenage, half Chinese, and adopted Chinese children. There were tours in English, Mandarin, Cantonese, Taiwanese. There were luxury, deluxe, standard, basic, and budget tiers. The American companies wantonly used the adjectives *heavenly* and *exotic*, and the people in the pictures looked too—American. The Chinese companies used too many dubious labels—*super value, ultra standard*—and the people in the pictures looked too Chinese. Where did her family fit in?

She'd tried to focus on the sights. China's Ancient Capitals, the Longest River and the Longest Wall. The Real Middle Kingdom, Silk Road Adventure, Hidden Tibet. The Emperor's Southern Tour, Canal Towns of China, Confucius Tour. She'd found herself dizzy.

She'd decided she was trying to take too big a leap, that perhaps she needed some middle ground, a stepping stone between the two shores, a gateway destination: Hong Kong. In all the travel literature, that was its definition. She found a Hong Kong tour company offering no-nonsense descriptions in decent Chinese and English, pictures of transnational-looking Asians, and one itinerary that held her fast: The Must-Sees.

The Must-Sees: the Forbidden City and the Summer Palace in Beijing, the Great Wall, the sister cities of Suzhou and Hangzhou, the glitz of Shanghai, historic Nanjing and the Yangzi River, the spectacular peaks of Huangshan, and last, Guangzhou—maybe not their *laojia*, but its literal translation, their old home.

She'd booked six passages and paid a nonrefundable deposit.

Two weeks on the mainland, bookended by overnight stays in Hong Kong. Visas arriving by mail any day. Transportation, lodging, meals, sightseeing: all included once the tour convened.

Now the convening. She'd compared a half-dozen airlines. She'd plugged in numerous flight times. She'd even studied the layout of the Hong Kong airport. Once she bought the tickets, it would all be done.

She triple-checked the flights, then held her breath and clicked the button.

Filing away all her research, Irene felt a little bereft. But here was a new beginning, not an end. If she could engineer this reunion, she could do almost anything.

She could renovate the house. She could sell it. At work, she could devise a new and thrilling investigative path. Or she could quit.

She could take a little container of Bill's ashes to China. The tour would fall near the first anniversary of his death. Maybe she and her daughters would see a sight and know it was the right place. They'd still grieve, they'd always grieve, but the worst haunting inside them would be put to rest.

When Irene lay in bed, the moon was visible, just a fingernail. She'd once thought she would be an astronomer. She loved how the moon in all its moods, anywhere she went, hung faithfully over her shoulder. She loved staring at the stars, those tiny winking glimpses into the other side of the sky.

She'd soon realized her fascination wasn't scientific. She was scandalized by mankind's shenanigans in space. Man puncturing the moon with a flagpole. Men claiming comets as their namesakes. The litter left by lunar missions—hardware, plastic bags, golf balls. The first astrogeologist had fantasized about traveling to the moon and whacking it with a hammer. He'd never achieved that, but just last year, a spacecraft carrying a capsule of his ashes had been purposely crashed into the lunar plains.

She'd chosen a field where every discovery was truly momentous, linking express purpose and infinite potential to each protein, and every line of research originated in some human suffering. She'd believed, utterly, that there was a genetic reason for everything. Push aside your upbringing. That was circumstance, that was history. Genes held your fate. You could view them up close and calculate a life. You could learn to control them and transform that life.

She'd grown up on an island where nobody around her saw a future—not there. Their government was the true Republic of China, which meant the civil war wasn't over. Any day, the mainland might attack across that narrow strait, or their government might reclaim the mainland. In school, they stood through interminable flag-raisings, pledged loyalty to the Nationalists, bowed to omnipresent portraits of Chiang Kai-shek, the Generalissimo—but the future lay in America, a country so great it could flood Taiwan with aid, and not show it. Most ambitious kids chose science as their route; it was a global commodity, would make them valuable exports. To secure fellowships, they only had to be the best of the best, plus learn English. She remembered telling Ma she was going to be a scientist, and Ma patted her shoulder—not quite affection, but a little recognition: She might not disappoint after all. For Irene, science wasn't just an ambition; it was her refuge.

Her family moved and moved. She understood they were scrabbling to get a foothold in this newly upturned society—but it also seemed their fate to be eternal escapees. They'd barely unpacked their paltry belongings before her parents fought like demons again, before a toxic smog settled again, rendering her and Susan, at least, invisible. She remembered Ma smashing everything in reach, screaming, *Take them. Take them and give me back my life.* Ba said, *You love that boy more than your life. Remember that.* And *You had no life before me.* Ma flung a plate with such force that a shard struck Irene's knee and stayed there, sticking straight out. Neither parent noticed. Trying not to blubber, Irene staggered to Susan, who plucked out the shard and scolded, *Why were you standing so close?* The two of them had little guidance in how to care for each other.

They moved and moved, as if searching for something they'd lost. But every time they moved, they lost something else. She learned to disdain toys, friends, landmarks. The one constant was her future in America. Every exam pointed her path, like runway lights.

And then she landed, lugged her trunk to her dorm, and found five other students fresh from Taiwan watching their host grill cheese sandwiches on a radiator. That was Bill, still a college senior. Since his own arrival, he'd welcomed each new contingent with this dinner.

He became her guide. More: her America. This beautiful country—of gold hair and gold mountains, blue eyes and blue oceans, Hollywood chases and kisses, songs honeyed as if love were the only subject fit for music—was in shambles, with the Vietnam War, the police crackdowns, the campus sit-ins like stage-set refugee camps, even the willfully tattered fashions. Susan was at another university studying poetry, a long flight away that neither of them could afford, or tried to take. Meanwhile, Bill shone as though his goodness couldn't be contained; it sparkled from his eyes and filled out his shoulders and crinkled the corners of his grin.

He took her to Burger King for, he said, America's best onion rings, to Dunkin' Donuts for America's best coffee. He drove her to a mall and bought them matching checkered bell-bottoms. He thought her brilliant, himself diligent: "You'll always outshine me, and that's A-okay."

Indeed, she was assigned to the highest-profile professor, invited to design her own project. There was a prevailing notion, then, that Alzheimer's was caused by aluminum in drinking water. She'd help disprove this, and assert the supremacy of genetics. In the next few years, she'd pick up publications, prizes, offers. Bill was her age, and soon her lab assistant. They worked side by side in that cool, constant dusk, snuck into supply closets to cuddle, paid little mind to the shaggy Americans chanting, drugging, dancing themselves into a stupor.

She felt like the first woman—or the first Chinese woman—to be lucky in love. For the first time, she took her sights off the future. She was living the future. It was her present.

Until she found herself married, home-owning, pregnant—and absolutely panicked. In America, parenting was a *subject*; she studied. She lay swelling, taking careful notes, suddenly weeping. In Chinese, there were only good or bad kids, no good or bad mothers. But it turned out that everything you did, everything you didn't even know you did, might affect your children as intrinsically as each protein of a chromosome. Every developmental phase, every interval of the daily schedule, was a chance to love them. And she would learn how. She would get it right.

And so she, with a PhD at twenty-six, an envied arsenal of lab techniques, a rare combination of precision and vision, stayed alone in the house with a baby. She breast-fed, diapered, cleaned; Bill joined a biotech team, attended lab picnics, presented at conferences. He was, as he said, not brilliant—he was probably meant, in another life, to be the proprietor of a family restaurant, or a sports commentator, or a chatty pilot—but he was male, and smart enough, and from Taiwan, so the easiest path to citizenship was science. Also, colleagues and mentors enjoyed his company, wanted to work with him, wanted to help him; it astonished her that in science, this made a difference. She watched the baby nap, charted the baby's bowel movements, even weighed the baby every hour. She did not feel the way she was supposed to feel.

Perhaps she was doomed—doomed by her own mother. Perhaps her baby wasn't a lovable creature. And Bill had wanted a son, a direct, true heir. He'd been nice about it. He was an orphan. How could she blame him?

One afternoon, she peeled a bowl of grapes for the baby. She pierced each tiny pucker and lifted off slivers of purple-green skin. Her eyes ached, her fingers cramped. She persisted until there sat, between her and the baby, a bowl piled high with glistening, seedless, skinless grapes. The baby couldn't have cared less.

Irene sliced each grape into perfect halves. Still the baby was unimpressed. Irene deposited a grape half into the little curled fingers, indiscriminately grasping, like sea anemone. The baby lifted a fat arm and smashed the grape. Pulp splattered Irene's face.

She snatched the bowl and ate the grapes herself. Popped them one by one, three at once, a whole handful. The zingy sweet juice burst in her mouth. An errant seed crunched, acrid. The baby watched, mesmerized—approving. Suddenly the baby grabbed the last grape half. Irene slapped its fat little hand.

The baby wailed. Irene ran to her study and shut the door. She turned on a fan, louder and louder, though she mostly heard her own breathing. Finally, she turned it off. Quiet. Deathly quiet.

She remembered that last grape half. Had she skinned and sliced each grape into the perfect object to lodge in a baby's throat? If she could hit a baby, what wasn't she capable of? She was one of those women made demented by motherhood. She'd killed her baby. She'd have to kill herself, too. She crept into the kitchen.

The baby—Nora—wasn't dead. She was busy smearing grape pulp across the tablecloth. Nora saw her and smiled—smiled hugely, wet eyes full of love. Irene cried. She lifted her baby and hugged her hard, crying into her neck. Nora hugged her back, warm, soft, and grapy. This, Irene realized, was as unconditional as love got. She didn't need to prove her worth. The love was hers. It was her. She let it reign.

Each moment as a mother became something to hold, to capture. For the first time, the past was precious, too—this new past, this history of her own making.

Bill was perplexed: What about day care, what about her career? She couldn't explain, and soon she didn't have to, because she was pregnant again. A family of four in a four-bedroom house—wasn't that the plan? Her field was being revolutionized in her absence—recombinant DNA and ligases, the keys to the future. A former mentor was nominated for a Nobel; her former peers were all tenure-track. She had her own project, eclipsing everything else: two daughters. Two daughters to love, so much they soon accepted kisses and hugs automatically, like vitamins. Two daughters whose first steps, first words, first successes on the toilet felt like firsts in human history. Two daughters to protect from ever feeling inadequate for not being sons.

At last she returned to the lab, the oldest postdoc, the only mother. Her days had been divided into intervals the length of her daughters' attention spans, and now she distracted and interrupted herself. She worried about the lunches she'd packed, about a rash or a runny nose, about whether or not they missed her. She mislabeled specimens, contaminated a cell line, made simple miscalculations in her data.

There was no mystery. The longer your hours, the purer your thought, the higher your chances for success. And once she realized she'd lost the basics, she began to lose the rest—her daring, her vision, her purpose.

She'd never be the charismatic scientist who made great copy or electrified conferences. She'd never distinguish herself through elegant articles or inspiring grant proposals; her prose was serviceable. It amazed her that Susan had remade herself as a poet in English—though, if you lived life by and for yourself, what couldn't you achieve?

At the very least, Irene would distinguish herself through her daughters. Not like Ma, who'd treated her and Susan as disciples; as if, being daughters, they were duty-bound to be *lihai*—extraordinary, fierce, unstoppable—while Lou could simply be. Irene would never force her daughters to prove their worth to her. They would always know they were the most special beings on earth. They were, from the start, *nenggan*—talented, ambitious, determined. Bored by soft furry things, scornful of simple answers, eager to stand apart from their peers. Sometimes she feared the genes she'd unknowingly passed on, but as a mother, she'd come to believe in nurture over nature. She'd prepare her daughters for success, and pray they'd be fulfilled—what else was there to do? Raise them to seek happiness? That seemed crueler than raising them to be revolutionaries, an even greater guarantee of eternal restlessness, eternal searching.

"You're not yourself anymore," Bill said once. "You have no passion left for me." She didn't bother denying it.

Like any man, he did things that would infuriate any woman. Pointed out a crusty dish she'd washed. Complained about undercooked rice. Sat watching sports when she arrived home to find one daughter with a disaster of a science project and another developing a fever and nothing for dinner. His standard response to her distress: *Ah well.* Like any good man, he tried to help out—always, she felt, with a flourish: *See how good I am? See how easy this could be?* She hated that her career was falling short of his, when she'd aimed so much higher. She hated when he felt sorry, she hated when he shrugged it off. And he was a good man, a good dad, tolerant, fun, easy—wasn't that plenty?

Then, out of nowhere, Ma called: She was moving to New York, Ba was dead to her, she'd help raise her granddaughters. Of course, this wasn't really out of nowhere. Taiwan had been rocked by the realization of its worst fears: expulsion from the UN in favor of Mao's regime and relegation to renegade province; the abandonment by America, their great protector, who tossed over more money in place of acknowledgment of its existence, as if it were bastard progeny.

To Irene, until then, all this had felt like international, official recognition that Taiwan was never a home. She'd hardly considered the fate of her parents. She and Bill had never visited. There was little money, and nobody asking, and they'd heard of others returning, expecting a red-carpet welcome, only to be suspected of disloyalty, and arrested, imprisoned, even sentenced to death.

Now Ma was leaving Taiwan to move in with her. Why her? But she knew why. Lou was a swinging bachelor in California. Susan was drifting from town to town, as if she were doomed—by the economics of poetry, by the tightfistedness with tenure, by her ineptitude with faculty politics, maybe by her own conviction, even if she didn't know it, that she deserved no better—to reenact their childhood. Irene had her own family, a true home. A refusal rose in her throat, and stuck there.

So she had to become inured to her daughters running not only to Dad but to Grandma when she scolded. Her daughters grimacing at her stir-fries and begging Grandma for sugary treats Irene never had as a child. Her daughters barely noticing when Irene called them *nenggan,* and basking when Grandma called them *lihai*. And while this grandma was a stranger to her—placid, reticent, lenient—Irene knew her mother still had an agenda. Every now and then her daughters would ask her, apparently out of nowhere, why she'd taken Bill's name, or when she would become a famous scientist.

When Irene vented to her husband, Bill said, "Ah well." Or "She's not so bad." Or "How *is* work?"

Then, all at once, work started to become everything she'd hoped. And Ma could preside over the house, because Irene had results. Earthshaking results. For three years, she'd tried to generate a line of transgenic mice exhibiting the amyloid plaques found in the brains of Alzheimer's patients. At that time, Alzheimer's was becoming widely recognized as a real disease, not a function of aging—in fact, the fourth leading cause of death in the developed world. Research funding and global attention were exploding. The biggest obstacle was the lack of an animal model to help elucidate the origin and progression of the disease and how it might be treated. Irene had a strong hunch about those sticky protein deposits, but many researchers suspected they were an effect, not a cause, of the disease. Other hypotheses centered on neurotransmitter deficiency, glutamate receptors, neurofibrillary lesions, neuron death. Without an animal model, they were all fumbling in the dark.

For three years, Irene had injected myriad gene sequences linked to amyloid deposition into fertilized mouse eggs. These specimens had been born and bred, born and bred, with no sign of the condition. Now, all at once, she had a line of mice exhibiting, at six months of age, deposits of the sticky protein in the hippocampus and cerebral cortex—the parts of the brain associated with attention, awareness, and memory.

Viewing the sectioned brain of a sacrificed specimen under her microscope, seeing the smattering of plaques, stained violet, for the first time, Irene felt her heart beating so rapidly, she pressed her hand to her chest, to help contain it. She forced herself to bide her time, recording every possible sign of pathology—scratching at the cage walls, climbing in a circular motion on the inside of the lid, incessant jumping. At seven and eight months, she sacrificed more specimens, and found the plaques multiplying and thickening. At nine months, she launched a set of memory tests.

In a pool with a hidden platform, normal mice paddled until they found the platform and came to rest, soaked and quaking. After that, each time they were set into the pool, they'd swim straight to the platform. Her transgenic mice, by contrast, paddled frantically every time until they chanced upon the platform. Again and again, they paddled for their lives as if each plunge into the pool were their first.

Exultant, Irene brought her results to her director, who pounded out a grant proposal with her project as the linchpin and directed the other postdocs to work on reproducing her model. There was talk of a press release, an immediate and prestigious publication, the need for protection from competing labs, even of patenting her discovery.

At home, Ma patted her shoulder. In the middle of the night, Bill popped a bottle of champagne, and Irene savored his embrace, as she hadn't since they were students.

Perhaps another researcher would have felt pure joy at such phenomenal success, this one-in-a-billion chance of her labors paying off at this magnitude. Irene had the sense that she was, at long last, fulfilling her duty.

Once again, she was driven by the momentum of her work. She stayed in the lab past her daughters' bedtime, rushed back before they woke. She donned her mask and gloves as unthinkingly as underwear. Her eyes became so accustomed to the fluorescent glare of the underground animal facilities that daylight seemed unnatural.

While the other postdocs analyzed the DNA of her transformed mice, hoping to pinpoint the crucial gene sequence, Irene pressed on to a grander ambition. What if, having afflicted her mice with Alzheimer's disease, she subsequently cured them? What if, having destroyed their memory, she now restored it? She read up on an array of new compounds that seemed to impede Alzheimer's by any number of hypothetical mechanisms, and set about procuring them. In the eyes of her colleagues, at that time, she could do no wrong.

Then she discovered she was pregnant again.

When she told Bill, his shoulders sagged. Ma barged into their argument and said, "Of course you should abort. Motherhood is not a cause. I named you after a revolutionary."

Bill had helped her pick *Irene*, and she'd gladly exchanged her father's surname for his—the American custom. Irene Shen, a new woman. No longer the namesake of Qiu Jin, Ma's own icon, who abandoned her children, husband, and home to overthrow feudalism, and was captured, beheaded, and martyred. Irene had vowed not to saddle her own daughters with such history. She'd given them names she loved for no particular reason, names they could make their own. And they'd started their own lineage of sorts: She'd named Nora, she and Nora had named Katherine (though she was immediately Kay); she and Nora and Kay would name the new baby.

The truth was, Irene had intended an abortion—until her husband suggested it, until her mother insisted on it.

She knew it was another daughter. She was, like both times before, violently ill, alternately retching and nearly fainting. Nora and Kay, as if in sympathy, caught chicken pox, then stomach flu. For two weeks, Irene called in sick for all three of them. She told her daughters about the baby. She reclaimed them from her mother.

Now her research had an inexorable deadline. After she gave birth, she'd return to work, of course. This time, she'd look into day care. Maybe rely on formula. Still, in science, anything could happen in her absence.

She decided her best bet was to conduct a quick battery of experiments and hope for results, no matter how preliminary. She set aside a control group, then divided the rest of her transgenic mice into groups of three. Over ten weeks, she gave each group daily injections of a different compound. Then she sacrificed one specimen from each group. The brain plaques of one appeared to be clearing.

The promising compound was related to an extract of *Amanita muscaria*, a poisonous mushroom, and thought to enhance the activity of certain receptors in the brain. She transferred another group, then another, to the same regimen. When she mapped her data points, she saw a constellation.

She pictured her mice briskly swimming to the resting platform. After that first plunge, they'd remember. She would show the world the first line of Alzheimer's-afflicted mice—and then the first line of miraculous recoveries. Before she could set her mice into the pool, they started dying.

First two, then ten, then dozens dropped dead in their cages. An unforeseen manifestation of the pathology, or a side effect of the treatment? In curing her specimens, had she killed them?

The catastrophe had a mundane cause: a virus. Bad luck, or a momentary lapse—and an outbreak. Infectious ectromelia had developed among her treated mice—latent, then possibly activated by experimental stress. The illness spread by blind passage to her control specimens, then to all the rest. No outward symptoms, until they started dying.

Her belly swelling beneath her lab coat, Irene desperately tried to isolate the survivors. Within a week, they too were dropping dead. The remaining few limped on gangrenous paws with pocked noses and crusted skin, and had to be immediately incinerated.

The other postdocs were ready to give up. Some asserted her success had been pure dumb luck in the first place, the kind that would never strike again. Others quietly questioned her data.

Fourteen hours a day, Irene tried to retrace the steps she'd taken to produce her transgenic mice. She'd kept meticulous records, as always—charts of her procedures, graphs of her results, pictures of the brains of every sacrificed specimen, sectioned and stained—but the key could have been the smallest adjustment in technique, the smallest change in sequence, a chromosome still to be mapped, a gene no one had yet identified. If not for her records, she herself might have doubted what she'd achieved.

Her model now existed only in photographs. Of course, a model that couldn't be reproduced might as well have never existed at all.

When she finally disclosed her pregnancy, she was granted a six-week leave. She told herself she might return sooner.

Failure in the lab was forgivable, of course. Daily failure permeated the lab like the sterile sunless air. But reconciling oneself to failure for the sake of a third child—there was no forgiving that.

One night, perhaps a week before her due date, Irene was clearing out her study to make room for the baby and she saw herself in the mirror, distended and squatting in a housedress. Ma caught her with her face in her hands.

"For the last year, you've had that fire inside. Don't let it die."

Irene could not rise to face her mother without an undignified struggle. "I'll be back at work in no time."

"Think how you were with Nora and Kay, when I first arrived."

This was, of course, her own fear. Irene turned away from her mother.

"You should have aborted," Ma said.

When the baby was not a bundle of cells, not a fetus, but Irene's third daughter preparing to push her way into the world.

"You had three children." Irene clasped her womb, as if to shield her baby's ears. "Do you regret it?"

"Regret? I had no choice." And Ma launched into a speech about a woman's duty to make a difference, Irene's chance to leave a legacy, not to mention all the privileges afforded to her in this modern era, in this free country—privileges those who came before her had been denied.

All Irene could think was that Ma had never regretted having Lou. And if the baby Irene carried now were a boy, perhaps Ma would consider this birth worthwhile.

"This was my choice," Irene said. "And this is my house. And you can call Lou and tell him I want you out."

So Ma packed up. Nora and Kay wailed, and blamed Irene. Bill said, "Sorry, Ma," in a tone that made it clear whose side he was on.

Irene suspended her research and birthed her third daughter. Nora and Kay, in their rapture, quickly forgot Grandma. The three of them named Sophie.

The six weeks became six months, then a year. With Sophie at her breast, Nora and Kay rushing to school and back, endless cycles of hungry mouths, dirty diapers, outgrown clothes, haircuts and checkups, birthdays and holidays, Irene couldn't quite remember why her lab work had been so crucial. Mouse eggs, trick pools, mushroom extracts, sliced brains, stained plaques. It began to seem a phantasmagorical realm, even a sadistic joke. Let others pick up where she had left off. No one else could be the mother of her daughters.

Then Bill began disappearing at night. He'd ease out of bed and drive off. Sometimes he wouldn't change out of his pajamas or grab his wallet, he'd just take his keys and drive off. She found a speeding ticket—ninety miles per hour, 2:15 a.m. She would not ask. She would not rage. There were her daughters, two upstairs and one in the crib. This was her home. There were joint accounts and mortgage payments. This was permanence, or as close as she'd get.

Resentment roiled and sometimes spilled over. But mostly, she contained it. She vented only when she had to, when it felt necessary and just, when she would have otherwise imploded.

The year had become three. At last, with Sophie ensconced in preschool, Irene tried to return to her old lab. The director offered her a teaching assistantship, a position she'd held as a graduate student. She could have devoted herself to teaching—offering up hard-won knowledge to thankless youths chomping to surpass her. She could have strived for professorship—someday, at a third-tier school. But she'd have to move for an opening, and move again. She refused.

She joined a pharmaceutical company—becoming, in the eyes of her former colleagues, not only a has-been but a sellout. Scientists were increasingly abandoning academia for private institutes and for-profits, but they were wooed, they entered as stars; she asked to be used. She was allowed, at first, to direct her own research, once again working to engineer the first animal model for Alzheimer's. No one else had succeeded yet.

The previous year, someone had finally identified the main constituent of brain plaques as a novel peptide, beta amyloid. Soon someone else would discover the amyloid precursor protein gene. Increasingly, her own hypothesis about the causal role of amyloid in Alzheimer's looked to be the right one all along.

But all she achieved now were negative results, negative results. When she mapped her data, she had a multitude of scattered dots, the occasional vague cluster—but no constellations. It was possible she'd lost the ability to see those constellations.

Eventually, she was ordered to pursue another scientist's lead, studying protein-folding in yeast. She was relieved to trade her mice for this fungus—single-celled, oval-shaped, reproducing simply by budding. To quit trying to formulate her own radical proposition, quit devoting herself to proving it. To become a pair of hands, pulling or not pulling her weight, producing or not producing results that would, at best, replicate those of another researcher.

"The girls can fend for themselves for a week," Bill said once. "We could have a second honeymoon. We could take a road trip."

"A road trip?" she said. "A road trip?"

Sure, he said, the two of them on an open highway, wind in their hair, hiking in the woods, sleeping in a tent.

"We're not vagrants," she said. "We're not refugees."

Grievances had accumulated between them until there were more sore spots than not. But no one ever died of splinters.

Just when the house was paid off—this house she'd sacrificed her career, or at least a path or two, to keep—her daughters began to leave.

Nora buying her own house, letting her new boyfriend move in. *Why?* Irene couldn't help asking. Why the hurry to move out, and why make a home with this boy unless she was sure, and if she was sure, why not marry? Jesse was blond, handsome, charming; he seemed, from the little Irene knew, like a good guy—but she knew her daughter, she knew eventually that wouldn't be enough, even if it should be, even if she loathed herself for the fact that it wasn't.

While Irene was trying to explain this, Bill told Nora, "Set aside a room for my retirement," and they laughed.

When Kay became fixated on China, Bill clipped articles, found goofy Web sites, even turned on a Chinese news channel for Kay, who couldn't understand a word, but watched raptly, as if the language were a secret code. Gamely, he tried to answer Kay's questions, and when he couldn't, he was easily excused, of course. For Irene, it was a dark tangle she had no desire to touch, though she knew she was being found wanting.

"Do you remember leaving China?"

"No."

"You have no memory of it? Wartime? Packing up? Fleeing the place?"

Irene recalled a dark flurry, wailing sirens, sudden voids. She shook her head.

"What was Taiwan like then?"

Irene shrugged. Kay persisted. It occurred to Irene that Americans these days hungered to write tell-all memoirs, chart family trees, even trace their DNA—not to illuminate the future, but to revel in the past. Everyone wanted to find and display their link to some shameful history, some buried tragedy, thinking somehow it made them special, when really, what could be more ordinary? She supposed in this young, rich country, people felt too light and free. They wanted weight; wanted to feel themselves tethered more solidly.

So she said, "It was miserable. We were poor."

"But you were the mainlanders, the elites."

Irene remembered shacks where they all slept in one room, she and Susan on one cot, Ma and Ba and Lou on the other. Brown water from a spigot in the street. A stove shared by six families. Lizards and spiders crawling freely through windows. The windows were just four-sided holes. She couldn't remember any pictures of herself. She realized she didn't know what she looked like as a child.

"Maybe compared to illiterate peasants. Maybe compared to the native Taiwanese. They were barefoot. They didn't have tables or chairs." In the face of Kay's skepticism, she said again, "It was miserable."

Bill said, "It wasn't so bad."

"I was talking about my own childhood," Irene snapped.

Reprovingly, Kay said, "Dad was an orphan."

Then Kay won her scholarship, just a year of language study, but Irene knew her daughter wouldn't stop there, and she couldn't help saying, "You could learn Chinese here." Kay rolled her eyes.

Bill gave her a high-five and said, "Just don't come back hacking and spitting." And they laughed.

And to Sophie, even before she finalized her Stanford application, even as he plotted his own escape, Bill said, "Get there early and grab the best bunk."

An old friend of his was heading the biology department at a small university in Maine, and offered—or had Bill requested?—a visiting lectureship.

"At least wait till Sophie's in college," Irene said.

She always knew that if they split, she'd be blamed. She saw how her daughters cringed when she sniped at him, rolled their eyes when she appeared to seethe over nothing. She hadn't actually envisioned herself alone in the house, permanently. She supposed she hadn't believed he would really leave. The last nighttime drive had been years before. She'd assumed he, too, had settled into the resignation of middle age.

He said he needed a break. A break—not divorce—the *yet* hanging, unsaid, between them. He needed a break and he decided to drive off on his own road trip, as if he were still an individual, one man. Well, he was.

What called to him from Maine? Open roads, rolling hills, burbling brooks? A patient mistress? Or simply her own absence?

She would not ask. And she didn't ask, or scream, or smash anything. At a volume that wouldn't wake Sophie in the next room, she denounced. He'd been itching to leave since their third daughter was born. He thought she didn't know, but she knew about his high-speed drives, his nighttime hankerings.

"I would just drive," he said. "Alone. No destination."

She told him not to insult her intelligence.

He said, "Why didn't you ask me back then? Why didn't you ask where I was going? Why didn't you ask me to stay?"

She told him it had been too late then, and it was certainly too late now.

But it hadn't been too late then. It was now.

Irene closed her eyes. Darkness—but not the falling kind. The kind you needed in order to see, against it, a glimmer. However tenuous, the glimmer was there, so clear in her sights that she could almost feel it in her hand.

Her mother and her sister, herself and her daughters—they had all set out, in a way, to be astronomers. Focused on chasing the unattainable, on charting the unknowable, and forgetting what made them who they were, what gave meaning to their lives in the end—the connections between them. It was time they all remembered.

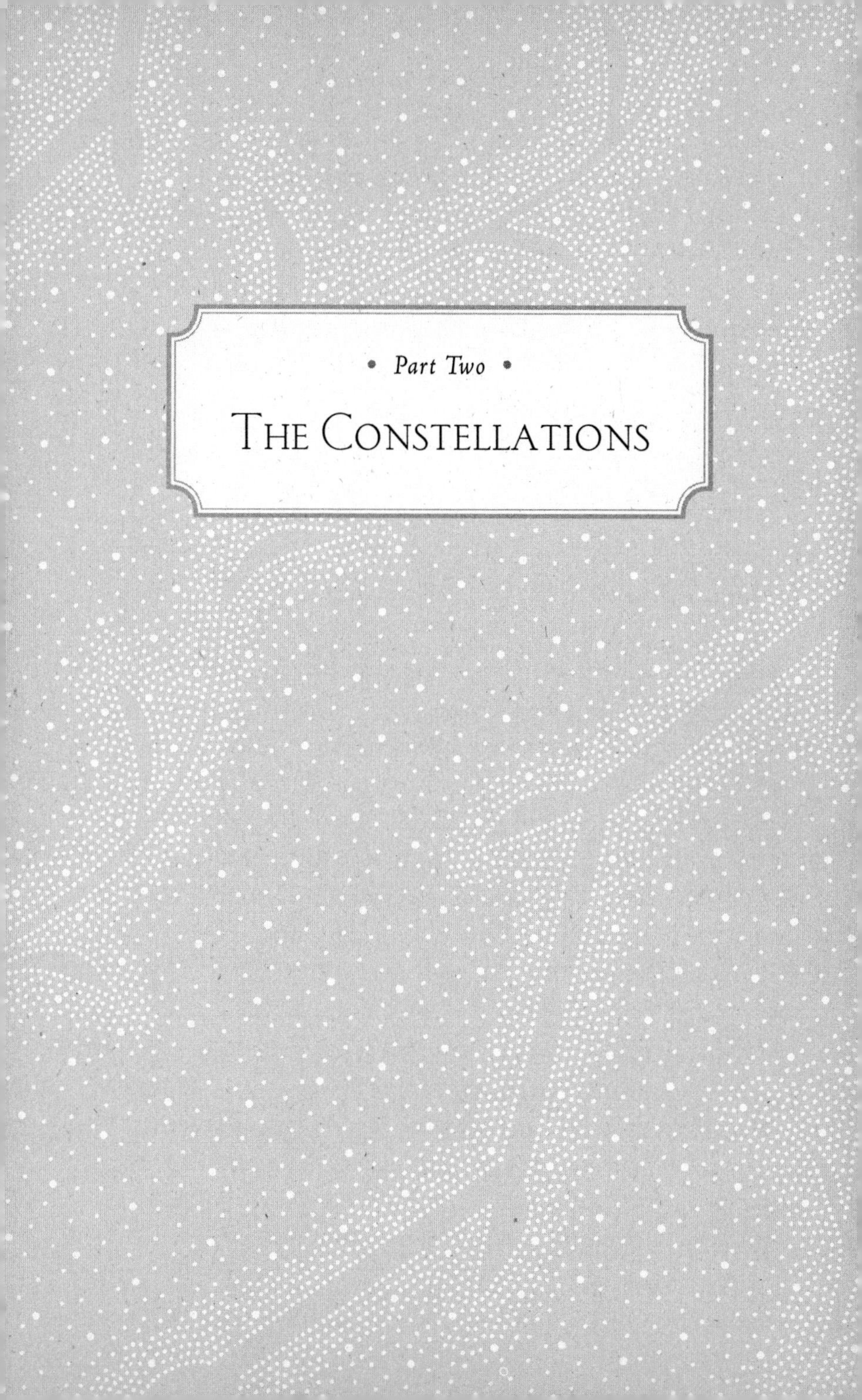

• *Part Two* •

The Constellations

7

Cool summer separates, stretch cotton, silk jersey. Jeans, a sundress, a pair of sweats. Casual sandals, dressy sandals, flip-flops. Five everyday bras, one strapless, one sports. Twenty pairs of underwear. Tampons—she'd be due mid-tour. For the flights, a cardigan and cozy socks. A bikini, though Nora didn't foresee a hot tub or a beach. All of it felt absurd, as if she were packing for a romantic getaway.

From her nightstand drawer, she took out the ring. Six weeks ago, she'd thrown it out with the rest of Jesse's belongings, as she was throwing him out of the house. He'd cheated on her with that honey-haired, milky-skinned, twenty-one-year-old student teacher.

He'd been distant, staying late after school. One night, he went to a staff party, while she dozed off on the couch. When she woke, he was asleep in bed. Strange that he'd tiptoe past her and leave her to sleep on the couch. She studied him. His hair was damp from a shower. He still smelled of liquor. She thought she remembered a start, a quick click, when she'd passed him at the computer the other night. All his e-mails were on the computer—her computer.

You're a sweet girl. Your mouth is actually sweet. I shouldn't even be writing this.

Certainty at last, a breakthrough, like a fist hurtling through glass.

By the time he woke from the noise, she'd made a heap in the foyer. His shoes, his jackets, a stack of baseball caps—the outermost layer of his stuff.

"Nora? What the hell?"

She faced him. "How could you." It wasn't a question.

He hopscotched from bewilderment to indignation to confession. A kiss the other night. The first, nothing else had ever happened, he swore.

And then?

Once, he rasped. Once, it happened once.

He meant sex. She realized she'd been praying he would say, *Then nothing. One kiss, that was it.*

"Tonight?"

He hung his head. "Last night."

Last night. *Last* night. She remembered brushing their teeth together last night. Ten-year treasury bonds were up 4/32 at close. He'd said he'd be late again, so she ate a slice of pizza on the way home. He fucked that girl.

She said, "Why not tonight?"

"Tonight I told her, never again." He slumped to the floor, his face in his hands. "It's been awful. It felt so wrong. I wanted to tell you."

She left him there and picked up where she'd left off, stalking between each room and the foyer. He followed her, apologizing, pleading, proclaiming his love, begging for forgiveness. She worked fast. She'd had a whole house, fully furnished, complete sets of everything, before she met him. She supposed she'd done some accounting all along.

She tossed his clay sculptures, which were surprisingly durable. His clothes, his papers, his books. His CDs, his old tapes. His toiletries. His laundry. His cell phone. His cell phone charger. Soon she was down to his cereal, his vitamins. And then pictures of him, of them—the glass didn't shatter, only sank on top of the heap. She made the mistake of pausing, and he managed to grab her, engulf her in his arms, and she softened and collapsed.

He carried her to bed. He'd betrayed her, yet this was their bed. Those were his arms, his loving arms, his hands, warm and strong. How could he? Now it was a question. When exactly, where exactly, how? What words? What thoughts? What feeling? The questions were infinite and terrifying. How could he?

"I don't know." He was crying. "I'm not like my dad. I'm not that kind of guy."

Was she this kind of woman? She'd never thought her dreams would be quite so accurate—suspicious messages and smells, an agreeable girl, a common misstep. Wasn't she prepared? She gathered herself and stood up.

"Get out. Get out of my house."

He blathered about their three years together, and the rest of their lives, and how could it all end like this?

"Like this," she said. "Just like this."

"I'm sorry. I messed up. Let me make it up to you. Please, let's make a fresh start."

"It's too late. I said get out."

"Nora, I wanted to marry you. I begged you to set a date."

The ring—of course. She plucked it from her nightstand and tossed it onto the heap.

His voice was hoarse. "What do you want me to do with it?"

"Put it in the trash. Or give it back to your parents. Or give it to that girl. And while you're at it—"

The pill—she'd only gone on it because he whined so much about condoms. Before him, she'd insisted on condoms with every guy, every time, but Jesse hated the constriction, the barrier between them. Her first weeks on the pill, just after he moved in, she was so nervous she had trouble swallowing. For a few months, she even ingested every fourth-week placebo, just in case. Giving in to him felt like a betrayal of herself, but so did falling in love. She'd loved the new flow of their lovemaking, the bare tremors, how they stayed melded, sometimes drifting to sleep together.

Had he worn a condom to fuck that girl? She gathered the rest of her pills and tossed them in the trash. She grabbed his key chain and twisted off the keys to the house—her house.

By dawn, he was gone.

In the aftermath, she tried to throw herself into work, but the more she let the rhythm of the trading floor pound through her, the deader she felt. Halfheartedly, she tried to quit, but while the flattery and the promises had lost their allure, the taunts—"You going soft? Can't cut it anymore? Hearing your biological clock?"—made her pause, and by the time her bosses unleashed their scare tactics—"Got a clever little business plan? Don't come crying back to us. Nonprofit? Who are you kidding?"—she was out of comebacks. She would quit, but not just yet.

For the first time since her first year in trading, she barhopped with the guys after work, matching them shot for shot. One night, she found herself on line for the single bathroom with Kurt—the one who, four years before, had greeted her on her first day on the floor with the line about Hotorientalbabes.com, who now had a pregnant blond wife and a one-year-old at home. Suddenly they were kissing. She couldn't remember how to kiss anyone except Jesse, but she had to try. They fell into the bathroom together. Kurt groped her ass, her breasts, and leered, "Not bad." She fled—out the bathroom, past the other guys, into a cab.

Since then, she and Kurt had returned to their well-honed ripostes, but she didn't need to know what he'd told the guys—that she was desperate, that she was easy, that her body was only "not bad"—to know that she'd slipped a few notches from her precarious perch.

Still, if dumping a cheating boyfriend was a test, she'd aced it. In one night, she'd thrown Jesse out. Spot a bad trade, you dump it. Cut your losses or bleed to death. But it didn't feel like the bleeding had stopped yet.

Every time Jesse called, and she attacked him until he broke down, and she felt momentarily strong, or victorious, or simply worn out, and hung up. Every day he didn't call, which was every day now. Every dinner alone, every night in the house. Mail addressed to him, telemarketers asking for him. His chores—the trash, the dishes, the garden debris—piling up. Every time she looked at the shelves he'd been so proud of building, the chair that had molded to his shape, the blanks on the walls where their pictures used to hang. The house itself—her house—betraying her.

And the ring. She'd found it in a dark corner of the foyer, when she vacuumed for the first time since he'd left. All she could think to do was toss it in her nightstand drawer again.

Now she picked up the phone and calibrated the coldness in her voice. "I still have your ring."

"Do you want to keep it?"

"No. I'm flying out in the morning. You want to pick it up?"

"I'll come over right now."

And just like that, he was coming over. Coming back. She packed her toiletries. She zipped her suitcase. She told herself this would be the last test.

When the bell rang, her heart jumped. She was opening the door by the time she realized she'd left the ring by the bed. Jesse stepped inside as if he still lived here, then stopped short. He wore frayed khakis she'd bought for him. His hair was a little shaggier than she liked. There was a patch of razor bumps on his cheek.

"You look tired," he murmured.

"Just busy packing."

"So you're really going."

She nodded. "Let me get the ring."

He reached out, and stopped before he touched her. "That's not the real reason you called me over—is it?"

"Yes."

"It's not the real reason I came," he said. "I'm sorry. I had to say it one more time. Before you fly off, even if you never want to see me again—please understand, I never meant to hurt you."

"So you cheated by accident?"

He sighed. He shoved his hands deep into his pockets.

"You knew that was my worst fear. The thing I could never forgive."

"Nora, you win. You're right." His voice was low and drained. "I still love you, but I can't fight anymore. I just hope someday you can forgive me."

She was trembling. "Never."

He sighed again, a complete exhalation, the sound of finality, and turned to leave. "Have a safe trip."

She slammed the door. *Good riddance.* She covered her face. Through the kitchen window, she saw her father's shoulders flinch and hunker. Her mother's sneer. The next jolt killed him.

She ran onto the stoop. Down the sidewalk, Jesse turned. His profile was angular, a little sinister, and ravishing in the glow of the streetlamps. The humid night air wrapped around her, and her insides sickened and thawed.

"Wait!" The exclamation sent her gasping.

He caught her. Entangled, they staggered up the stoop and back inside. They stood in the foyer again, breathing hard, and it seemed one of the safer things to do was to kiss. They kissed. She broke away. She lurched deeper inside the house. He followed. Once in the bedroom, she felt a sob rise up her throat. She swallowed and sank to her knees. His fingers worked her hair, her scalp, as if he were working clay.

She was his student teacher, newly nubile. She was a hot Oriental babe. She was his victim, almost his wife.

She reeled backward, her arm grazing her suitcase. On the floor, he clasped her from behind. She strained to feel their bodies align, but they clashed and scraped. Knuckles and knees, elbows and nails, a cold rivet and the rough jaws of a zipper. He pushed against her, inside her—the rawness of skin against skin—and finally she felt nothing but an eddying ache. Her arm flailed—a handle. She clutched it. She'd let go of everything but this grip and this motion. She clutched her suitcase handle as she cried out and came.

Carpet burn on her shoulder, hipbone, ankle. She saw a dead moth under the bed, an old barcode on her suitcase. Her hand released the handle and limply curled beside her face. He was pumping fast, his breathing coarse and labored. She was unprotected.

"Wait," she croaked, just as he groaned and plunged deep.

Panting against the nape of her neck, he started to caress her breasts. Guilt radiated from his hot breath, his sweaty touch. She shoved him out and away.

"Nora—"

"What." It came out a near sob.

"I'm sorry. I'm so sorry."

She got up and focused on fixing her clothes. After a minute, so did he.

The phone rang. It was her mother. Was she packed? Was she bringing a hat? What about sunscreen? What might they both be forgetting?

"Yes," Nora said robotically. "No. Yes. I don't know."

"Is your alarm set? You want to stay over tonight? So we can head to the airport together?"

She said, "I'll come over."

"You will?" her mother exclaimed.

Nora hung up and pulled her suitcase upright. "I have to go."

"Who was that?" Jesse asked.

She didn't answer. She avoided his gaze, twisted away from his outstretched arms, turned her back as he left, saying it again: "Have a safe trip." She heard the door shut.

And there sat the ring on her nightstand, glinting meanly. She grabbed it and pushed it in her pocket. She felt, at her core, a kind of gathering and hardening. Like a muscle she'd been flexing all her life, so that when the time came, it wouldn't fail her.

But tonight, it had failed her.

The house was even more cluttered than Nora remembered, littered now with suitcases, carry-ons, printouts, takeout containers, even a baby spoon she'd used to feed Sophie. Perched above it all was the urn holding her father's ashes. Gray granite with white streaks, cool and heavy and simply shaped. It had seemed to atone, as much as any receptacle could, for the indignity of his departure, of his corpse. It looked slightly off-center now. She reached up to adjust it. Her hands came off clean, as if it had just been dusted.

"You're here!" Her mother flew out from her bedroom and pulled Nora into a tight hug. "You look pale."

"I'm fine."

"You're working too hard. This vacation will be just what you need."

Sophie skulked out of her room. Nora hesitated, then hugged her. For the briefest moment, Sophie felt small and soft again.

Her mother beamed. "Two daughters back home, and soon I'll have the third. Oh, look what Sophie got at graduation." From a shelf full of awards, she lifted a new one—Sophie's valedictorian plaque.

"Congratulations. I'm sorry I missed it. Work was hectic." Nora had known she couldn't bear an entire morning seated beside her mother in the audience.

"It was stupid," Sophie said. "They named four valedictorians. We all had the same GPA."

Sophie disappeared back into her bedroom. Nora sat on the edge of the couch. Her mother bustled around, proffering snacks and drinks, fussing over Nora's luggage. Her mother asked about her work, her house, then Jesse.

Nora set her jaw. "We broke up."

Her mother gaped. She'd hardly known Jesse; Nora had preferred it that way. She'd never shaken the sense that forging romantic relationships, intimate outside connections, somehow meant dispossessing her mother.

She said, "It's fine. I'm fine."

"What happened?"

"It's complicated."

"Was there another woman?"

"What makes you think that?" Nora snapped.

"I just thought—weren't you planning a future with him? Isn't that why you wanted to live together?"

"Actually, he wanted marriage and kids. I didn't."

"Why not?"

Nora was silent.

Hurriedly, her mother said, "So you're in that house all alone? No wonder you wanted to stay over. You can stay over anytime, you know. I haven't touched your room. If you want, we could fix it up. You could even move back."

Nora recoiled. "Thanks, but I'm fine."

Her mother smiled bravely. "Well, it's perfect timing, isn't it? For a holiday with family."

Nora noticed her mother still wore her wedding ring. Those bands had always seemed so fixed on her parents' fingers, she hadn't remembered her father's until the funeral director gave it to her, after the cremation. Nora couldn't help thinking her mother ought to take off the ring, to stash it away. Her father had died leaving her mother. If he were alive and well in Maine, her mother wouldn't be, to the world, a strong widow—only another wronged wife.

Avoiding her mother's gaze, Nora stood up and said she was going to bed.

In her old room, she set down her suitcase beside her father's luggage.

She left the door ajar and opened a window, hoping for a breeze. The ring was a hard, solid lump in her pocket. A faint smell rose from her clothes, the clothes Jesse had pushed and tugged. She balled them up and stuffed them deep into a corner of her suitcase. From her dresser, she dug up a prim nightgown, never worn, that her father had bought at a going-out-of-business sale. He'd snapped up everything under five dollars, and she and her sisters hadn't wanted any of it. Against her skin now, the nightgown was comforting, loose cotton, cool and sexless.

Long ago, this had been her grandmother's room, bare of memento or adornment. Her grandmother used to sit in a recliner reading Chinese periodicals, her eyes traveling up and down the columns of characters, turning the pages from left to right. Sometimes Nora would lie on her stomach and do homework by Grandma's slippered feet. Occasionally, they'd look up and joke: "You're reading backward." "No, you are." They shared a kind of coziness that dissipated whenever her mother showed up. Nora would watch her mother lash out at Grandma, would overhear furious arguments she couldn't understand. And when Grandma announced she was moving to California, where Uncle Lou lived, Nora had stomped to her mother and said, "It's you. You drove her away."

From downstairs, she could hear her mother still bustling around. She shut the door and lay in bed, unable to sleep, barely able to breathe.

"Look what I got." Her mother presented a box of cookies and a bag of popcorn, beaming. They were at LAX, waiting for her grandmother.

Nora accepted a cookie. It cracked apart when she took a bite. "It's stale," she said, and dropped the pieces back in the box.

Her mother gave a determined smile. "Remember when you used to dictate what to serve for your birthday? Ice cream cakes, instant cake mix—whatever it was, you were so dead set."

Nora said, "Shouldn't Grandma be here by now?"

Her mother's smile faded. "Lou's probably late."

Across the passageway, Sophie trudged out of the restroom, skirt riding up her thighs, hair hanging over her face, flip-flops barely lifting off the floor. Her body was curvier than Nora's, but her face still looked unformed. She seemed to teeter between a babyish pliancy and a defiant sexuality. As she passed a sports bar, two men leaned over the counter, looking her up and down, while crisp travelers whisked by her, their carry-ons veering too close to her bare ankles. She was nearly eighteen, just a little younger than Jesse's student teacher.

"Just in time," her mother said, presenting the food and beaming again.

"I'm not hungry," Sophie said.

"Oh, come on. Nora said the cookies are stale, but the popcorn's still warm."

"I said I'm not hungry."

"But you didn't eat anything on the plane."

"Because I'm not hungry."

"But—"

Exasperated, Nora said, "Give me the popcorn."

Now the only sound among them was the crunch of popcorn in her teeth.

The reconnecting Nora once had in mind seemed less likely by the minute. On the flight over, they'd all adopted Sophie's tactic—a sour, wary silence. Nora wondered if her mother thought the tension might magically lift once they set foot in their homeland.

There'd been a time when Nora kept hearing—from schoolmates, from strangers—how she ought to fly to China and find herself. These days, any references to her roots were ironic—except her mother's. When she mentioned this trip at work, people only wanted to spout their own expertise. China was the next superpower. China was a bubble. The billion-plus potential consumers, how to grab a piece. Where to buy the best counterfeits. Of course, China was simply a place tourists wanted to see. The mist, the mountains. The immensity, the history. But the image Nora had gleaned from Kay was of an unsanitary country only a martyr would enter.

A strangely familiar scent wafted to her. Hand cream and vitamins, Tiger Balm and milk tea. A tap on her head—she started, the bag of popcorn falling to the floor.

Beneath a white cloud of hair and the wide curve of her forehead, her grandmother's eyes glittered, keen and deep set. She looked much like the Grandma Nora remembered—solid and robust. *She doesn't have much time left,* her mother had said. But her grandmother didn't exude frailty, much less impending death.

"You haven't aged at all," Nora said.

"You're still the same. Always *fa dai.*"

Nora was surprised she remembered that phrase—daydreaming, staring into space. Her grandmother used to scold her for it. *Wei!* she'd exclaim, or clap in front of Nora's face, just missing her nose.

While her grandmother exchanged distant greetings with her mother and Sophie, Nora had the strange sense that she was regaining a long-lost confidante.

"Was Lou late?" her mother asked.

"I told him to stop so I could buy presents. A grandma should bring presents, right?" Her grandmother reached into her purse and brought out two necklaces—big loops of colorful plastic beads, both undeniably ugly.

Nora and Sophie chorused their thanks.

Frowning, her mother picked up the popcorn and cookies, dumped them in the trash, and started for the gates.

"Wait," her grandmother said.

Nora turned back.

Her grandmother handed her a small round tin. She sniffed at it—dusty fruit and cool metal. Grandma used to produce a tin whenever Nora showed her a perfect test score, or stomped upstairs after arguing with her mother. Inside, enveloped in wax paper, were candies hard as marbles, coated with a mysterious powder that wasn't sugar—it was like waiting itself, before the tart, sweet flavor came through. She looked up with a smile, but her grandmother was already briskly walking ahead.

She wondered if the grandma she remembered would console her now in a way her mother couldn't—or if her heartbreak would seem trivial, unworthy of a former revolutionary's notice.

At takeoff, Nora watched the landscape of palm trees and concrete tilt, miniaturize, and slide into the ocean. Once the plane started cruising through an unbroken pale blue, she reclined her seat and closed her eyes. She often napped more easily in motion. She'd wondered if her father had been lulled to the moment of death, or if he'd jolted conscious, tried to wrest back control of the car, before careening off the freeway.

She kept her eyes shut tight, twisted against her seat, finally fell into a cramped sleep.

She woke extremely unrefreshed. The recycled air carried a whiff of rotten peanuts. The flight attendants were making their laboriously chipper way down the aisles with meal carts. "Chicken or noodles? Chicken or noodles?" In some time zone, it was dinnertime.

Her grandmother chose noodles. Nora chose chicken. She ate a roll with frozen chips of butter, speared some overtenderized meat, and spooned out the spongy bottom of her cake, leaving the thick gelatinous top quivering. Soon their trays were collected, tray tables stowed. And that was dinner: an efficient, thorough simulation, pre-prepared and plastic-contained, instead of the trial she'd endured every night since Jesse left.

A movie was playing overhead, a romantic comedy—the kind of movie no one in her family would watch on land. In the row in front, her mother and Sophie had clamped on their headphones and turned their faces to the fuzzy screen. Beside her, Grandma rubbed ointment into her joints.

Politely, Nora asked, "Are you excited to go back to China?"

Her grandmother shrugged—a heavy, considered gesture.

Nora waited. Her grandmother was quiet. Nora turned to her window again. The sky was still cloudless, now cobalt, the horizon shot through with pink. On the overhead screen, a man was about to marry a woman, but since it was early in the movie, it had to be the wrong woman.

The seat belt sign lit up—turbulence ahead. Through the crevice between their seats, Nora craned to make sure her mother's and sister's seat belts were fastened. Her grandmother's eyes were now closed, a blanket covering her seat belt. Gently, Nora reached to check it.

Grandma slapped her hand away with a barklike laugh. "You think I've never flown before?"

Disconcerted, Nora apologized.

The promised turbulence set in. Nora tried to let her body shake with the plane. Beside her, Grandma stared straight ahead, face placid.

What kind of woman will you be? Suddenly Nora remembered Grandma asking this, as she and Kay sat eating something sweet and sticky Grandma had made. *A strong woman or a weak woman? Great or ordinary? The kind who holds us back, or the kind who pushes us forward?* Nora said, *A strong woman,* and for good measure, added, *A great woman.* Kay, her mouth full, bobbed in agreement. Grandma asked, *How?* Nora said, *I'll beat boys at*—she thought of the school math competition, outer space, the White House—*whatever they do.* Kay said, *I'll help people.* Grandma said, *Right. Because this*—the sweep of her arm encompassing the kitchen, their own busy mouths and twiggy bodies, the whole house—*is not enough.*

"Still *fa dai*?"

"Sorry." Her grandmother's keen eyes were trained on her. Nora stammered, "Why did you leave Taiwan?"

"To help raise you and your sister."

"But why did you leave—Grandpa?"

Grandma's face tightened. "It was time."

"Do you ever regret it?"

"No."

Nora swallowed. "I just broke up with my—Jesse, my boyfriend."

"You suffered, with your father's accident. He didn't hold up?"

"He did, but then—he wanted to marry me, and I kept putting him off, and—"

"What? Another woman?"

Nora could not admit it.

Her grandmother said, "In hard times, most men fail. Their true character shows. Be glad you didn't tie your life to his."

Nora nodded.

"So you got rid of him. You were not weak." Her grandmother's eyes were like feelers, probing for cracks.

"I threw him out."

Her grandmother nodded. "Your career is most important, of course. I don't fully understand what you do, but I understand you control money. You have power among men. As a woman, you are considered a trailblazer."

Nora hesitated. Didn't that sum it up? She'd never considered finance until, having been lauded as valedictorian and "ass-kicker" of her high school, she entered Harvard and poked her head into a new stratosphere, one she hadn't perceived before, ruled by golden boys who didn't bother to swagger, whose nonchalant naming of their prep schools seemed like a secret code, who subtly and unmistakably pegged her as lower class. She chose econ as her major, leaped into the recruitment frenzy, emerged with a prime offer—and discovered it was common knowledge that the female new hires, all 10 percent, had also been screened for their looks.

She set to proving herself with ninety-hour workweeks, reaping excellent reviews and big bonuses, but like any junior banker, she was just a paper pusher, a glorified accountant. If she simply put in her hours, followed orders, and didn't make mistakes, she was considered a good worker. Good, of course, wasn't good enough.

She heard trading was the real action, where money and power were hers for the taking, if she dared; where there was no genteel ladder-climbing, only winners and losers; where she could, from the start, call the shots. She finagled a transfer and set to proving herself again.

She learned to woo clients and make them listen. To catch code errors in the bond books and see the big picture of the markets. To be a team player and to be completely selfish. To take abuse when she screwed up and give it right back when she felt she was right. To win, and lose, like a guy—no self-effacing, no apologizing. Even to laugh as one of the guys when they told detailed blow job jokes, created spreadsheets for rating assistants' breasts, presented her with a "Hot Oriental Babe" nameplate—by then ironic, an affirmation that she was one of them, not one of *them.*

She said, "Something like that."

"Good for you, for now. You must be strong. You must keep asking yourself—"

"What kind of woman am I?"

Grandma nodded, looking a little gratified.

Nora had always thought she knew. The kind of woman who'd never let a man betray her? The kind of woman who'd never let him back in? The kind of woman who simply said, *Good riddance*? The kind of woman who—like her mother, like her grandmother—ended up alone?

She blurted, "Is it really that simple? What kind of woman are you?"

Her grandmother's face tightened again.

The turbulence had passed. Nora steeled herself. "I'm sorry. Never mind."

Grandma patted her hand. "*Suan le.*"

Another phrase Nora remembered, an echo of her own: Forget it, drop it, never mind.

8

Sophie rinsed and spat, rinsed and spat. There was still an old sourness, mixed now with the soapy-sweet taste of baking soda. She stared in the mirror. In this cool, gleaming bathroom in the Hong Kong airport, she looked worse than ever. Washing her face had made her nose shinier, her zits redder. Her hair was greasy and clumped near the roots. She dabbed concealer and brushed her hair. There was no help for the excess to her cheeks, her chin, all the flesh obscuring the bone.

At the luggage carousel, Nora, Kay, Mom, and Aunt Susan seemed not to notice the suitcases circling by, while everyone else crowded and craned. Sophie set her shoulders and headed toward them. It was like she'd graduated only to end up in some nightmare summer camp where the clique of skinny, self-assured girls was her family, and she was stuck with them day and night, on the other side of the world.

"There's the valedictorian!" Kay said.

To Aunt Susan, Mom said, "That makes all three."

"Wow," Aunt Susan murmured. "Congratulations."

Sophie said, once again, "It was stupid. They named four valedictorians this year. We all had the same GPA." And while everyone else, including

Brandon, had had a whole posse of relatives to applaud them, she'd only had Mom.

To Kay, Mom said, "Have you lost weight?"

Sophie had already noticed that Kay was thinner than ever, every joint striking. Next to Kay's legs, her own looked like stumps.

Kay shrugged. "I had some digestion issues. I'm better now."

"What do you mean?" Sophie asked.

"Diarrhea."

Mom said, "Didn't I warn you about the street food? What if you have a bacterial infection?"

Kay turned to Sophie again. "That's an awfully sexy skirt for my baby sister." She patted Sophie's butt.

Sophie twisted out of Kay's reach. The last time she'd worn this skirt, Brandon kept saying, *Damn*, as if he couldn't believe his luck. At home that morning—yesterday morning, she supposed, or by Hong Kong time, two nights ago—it looked summery and flirty. She'd thought it would be comfortable for the flights—airy, elastic. But now it looked obscene. She looked obscene—overfed, oversexed. She longed for a pair of sweats.

They'd hauled their suitcases off the carousel and were heading for the exit when Aunt Susan said, "Where's Ma?"

Mom gave a little start. "Sophie, go tell Grandma we're ready."

Why her? Because she was the youngest, the most pliable. She'd forgotten about her grandmother, too. Her grandmother was sitting by the customs forms, behind an abandoned cart.

"Grandma," Sophie tried to call, but it sounded like she was calling a pet. "Grandma, we're leaving."

Unhurriedly, Grandma gathered herself. She stood for a moment, as if taking stock of Sophie, then began walking with her free hand cupped, as if for a child's fingers to slip inside.

Sophie suddenly remembered that Grandma had visited once, when she was maybe seven. Mom had seemed so tense about Grandma's arrival that Sophie decided to curl her hair and wear her fanciest dress to the airport. The night before, she wet her hair, slathered it with gel filched from Nora, and braided it all over, pulling her scalp so tight her eyes slanted. She spent the whole night in a painful and delicious delirium, certain that the more she suffered, the prettier the curls would be.

In the morning, when she pulled off the rubber bands, each braid burst, exuberant and kinky as a clown wig. She was one giant frizzball. Mom spotted her and cried, "What did you do?" Sophie went blubbering to Nora, who tried to tame the hair, wielding a spray bottle and a stiff brush, while Kay and Daddy guffawed. Finally Nora clamped a headband onto Sophie's hair and declared her adorable. All the way to the airport, her hair seemed to expand until it was wider than her flounced skirt and puffed against her sisters' chests. Daddy kept looking at her in the rearview mirror and laughing so hard the car rocked.

To her own surprise, Sophie took her grandmother's hand.

The smell of hot, rich food wafted out as Aunt Susan opened the door. Sophie's stomach twisted. Inside, sunlight was pouring through a glass wall, glinting off stainless steel, even shining off the snowy carpeting, which their suitcases marked like sled tracks. Open, minimalist space—and no privacy.

"Winston?" Aunt Susan called. Her voice was barely audible above a whirring and clatter. A balding, bulky man was beating eggs while operating a blender.

"Winston!" Mom shouted helpfully. Her voice could cut through concrete.

He jumped. "Hello, hello."

He wore a neat comb-over, straw slippers, an apron snug around a substantial belly. He looked much older than Aunt Susan, who was still pretty in a faded way, and thin—not that strained look of older, dieting women, but delicately framed, as if more flesh simply wouldn't fit. Now Aunt Susan slipped beside Uncle Winston, and even as they murmured to each other, she appeared younger and looser, as if, until then, she'd been holding herself tight. Aunt Susan was, Sophie noted, the only married one. She wondered if settling down with an uglier, older man and not having children was the only escape from female insecurity and resentment.

Sophie went to gaze out the spotless balcony doors. Golden sand and vast rippling blue and, toward the misty horizon, a cluster of islands that looked somehow connected deep down, like a giant's fingertips just breaking the surface.

She and Brandon had made it to the end of high school. After this tour, she'd have the rest of the summer to spend her evenings with him and her days at the gallery, and then she was off to Stanford. To the dismay of every teacher, Brandon hadn't applied to college at all. He'd decided to focus full-time on his music, because he believed in hip-hop as an entire way of life, and that was, in their context, heroic—but it also meant that soon his life wouldn't include her. He hadn't said that, but she knew.

When it came to other girls, she'd started testing him—playfully, of course: "Is she hot? Would you do her?"

At first he'd refused to play along. "You're my girl. No one's hotter."

"But if you had to. If someone had a gun."

"Nope."

"Okay, if they paid you."

He'd guffawed. "How much?"

"How much would it take?"

"Well, that depends."

This had become their game. They'd point out innocent passersby, name teachers at school, make up price lists for first base through home plate, laugh until their stomachs hurt. It made her feel stronger somehow, more secure that he belonged to her, but also that she could handle the inevitable—until they crossed some invisible boundary, and then nothing could get rid of her gross feeling but purging.

Uncle Winston spread the dining table with golden popovers, an enormous omelet sliced like a pizza, glasses of fresh papaya juice. The juice was safe, only high in sugar. There was just a touch of cheese in the omelet. Sophie ate deliberately, in slow, careful bites.

Politely, she said, "Uncle Winston, this is delicious."

He gave a shy smile.

To Kay, Mom said, "Bet you haven't eaten like this all year."

"No, but last week, I ate dog."

Everyone stared at Kay.

"Are you joking?" Sophie asked. "I thought dog-eating was a myth."

"It's a specialty. I just wanted to try it." Kay plucked another popover and slathered it with butter. "Mom, you never ate dog? When you were little?"

Mom shook her head.

"But Beijingers say the Cantonese eat anything with legs except furniture."

"Do you see us eating cockroaches?"

Kay looked as if she were about to ask Grandma, who was calmly sipping her juice.

Sophie asked, "How was it?"

"Tough, gamey. My friend Rick found a little fur."

After a pause, Aunt Susan and Uncle Winston suggested an outing—a sampan ride, Victoria Peak, the history museum.

"Something relaxing. The sightseeing starts tomorrow. And tonight, we'll have a slumber party." Mom turned to Sophie and her sisters. "Remember? Staying up in the living room, eating ice cream cake, watching Disney movies?"

Only Kay managed to smile back at Mom. She'd been away all year.

"Shopping is our top tourist attraction." Uncle Winston seemed to have studied, in the last hour, how to steer the conversation. "You could all stroll along Women's Street while I prepare dinner."

Grease in the back of her throat, her stomach pushing against her waistband. Sophie told herself she could shop for shoes, sunglasses, earrings—things that fit anyone.

The Hong Kong subway was like no subway Sophie had ridden. No jolting or screeching, no pushing or cursing, no perverts lurking, not a mark on the shining surfaces, not a crackle in the automated announcements, which were pleasantly intoned in Cantonese, Mandarin, and British English.

An escalator propelled them up so fast she worried they might all pitch onto the pavement, but once the street came into view, she didn't even glance down to step off. Such verticality, the skyscrapers space-age, the alleys steep as ski slopes, and in every direction, more *everything* for sale than she'd ever seen—hypertrendy clothing, futuristic electronics, improbable fruit, riotous flowers. Teeming on all sides, their noise thick as smog, were Chinese people—Chinese people in suits and school uniforms, pedaling bikes and hailing cabs, posing on billboards and sweeping the streets. The scattered white businessmen and tourists were the ones who looked misplaced.

Yet even these crowds paused and parted for her sisters. Nora and her bikini-ready body, sleek hair, sculpted face. Kay taller, flatter-chested, and boy-hipped, as unadorned and nonchalant as an off-duty model. In New York, sometimes Sophie got her share of attention on the street, but just a paltry share—mostly from black and Latino men, and only when she showed some skin. Here, the few glances directed at her held a passing curiosity, not desire, certainly not awe. Meanwhile, the admiration lavished on her sisters seemed utterly beneath their notice.

Women's Street was a pedestrian mall crammed with stretch jeans and metallic dresses, push-up bras and platform sandals, shrill vendors and grabby girls. Nora and Kay paused to laugh at a rhinestoned, tasseled, heavily padded bra. Mom and Aunt Susan idly fingered some silk scarves. They were dallying at being the kind of women this street was designed for. To Sophie, it was a microcosm of a new universe where she was flailing. Their way was nobler, but weren't they missing something? Those moments when a number on a scale or the fit of a skirt sent you skyrocketing or nosediving—they were torturous, frivolous; they detracted from the important goals; but didn't they make you feel alive?

"This would look nice on you, Sophie," Nora called, holding up a lace-trimmed top. Kay agreed and found a simple pair of black pants. For a moment, she thought they were humoring her, pretending she was still their adorable dress-up doll, no such thing as body type. But they were selecting clothes for themselves, too, and Mom was bustling over to help, and Sophie realized they were all uncertain of their roles now, of how to behave like a family again.

She accepted the outfit and allowed herself to be ushered to the fitting rooms—sheets hung with clothespins. No walls, no mirrors. The clothes seemed to fit. She lifted the sheet. Her sisters emerged, too—Nora's dress clinging only where it should, Kay's jeans slung just so. They converged at a full-length mirror.

She looked like the runt of the litter. The clothes bunched at her chest and crotch, where her fat strained the fabric.

Mom frowned. "Hmm. Do you have the right size?"

"It doesn't matter. I don't want anything."

She hadn't let Mom take her shopping in years. Now Mom held her in place in front of the mirror, adjusting her neckline and waistband. Everyone looked her over. A group of local girls paused to look, too. Everyone here was skinny, some even skinnier than Kay. Her sisters fit in. So did Mom and Aunt Susan. She stuck out more than the white people, nearly as much as Brandon would. In America, her body type was average—

medically, statistically average. Who wanted to be average? Not Nora or Kay or Mom, and certainly not Sophie.

Nora said, "Sophie, that looks pretty. It's just—do you want me to find—"

"I said I don't want anything."

She scrambled into the changing area and left the shirt and pants in a heap. The saleslady squawked; Mom called after her. She glanced behind and saw Nora picking up the clothes. She might as well have announced a body-image problem.

Where to turn in this maze? Years ago, on family trips to the mall, she and Daddy would sneak off to the food court and cruise for free samples—tiny cups of creamy soup, halved jalapeño poppers, sticky chunks of fudge.

She finally found a sunglasses stall and desperately busied herself trying on frame after frame. Vendors buzzed around her, now offering pills—bust-enhancing, skin-whitening, diet.

She squirmed away from them and, through a pair of purple cat-eyes, caught sight of Grandma. She'd forgotten about her again. Grandma sat in front of a fruit stand, on what appeared to be a milk crate. Sophie took off the frames and pushed past the vendors until, one by one, they found other prey.

"Why aren't you shopping?" Grandma asked.

"Why aren't *you* shopping?"

"Me? There's nothing for me here."

"There's nothing for me either."

"You want to sit with your old grandma?" Grandma pulled out another milk crate from beneath the display table, ignoring a man barking from just inside the shop.

Sophie sat. The heat settled on her skin, heavy and moist. She felt an urge to rest her head on Grandma's shoulder, and after a moment, she did. Grandma's shoulder was ample and soft. Sophie let her eyes close.

"*Wei*," Grandma said. "You're the youngest. You shouldn't be so tired."

"I know," Sophie said. "But I am."

A rumble—she looked up. The sky was laden with low, heavy clouds. Even as she watched, the rumble gathered, then spread, a warning that the sky couldn't hold its weight much longer.

9

At the Beijing airport, Kay's visa was amended from student to tourist, and then her passport, along with everyone else's, was handed to the tour guide, who stuffed the stack in his fanny pack and led them straight to a tour bus. A whole row of plush seats for each passenger, the air-conditioning so high she was covered in goosebumps by the time they pulled up to Yiheyuan, the Summer Palace—the first sight she'd seen nearly a year ago, when she'd arrived in China on her own.

She'd never felt so alone as when she entered the arrivals terminal tugging her suitcase and fumbling with strange currency, her passport, and her "introduction"—a sheaf of sternly stamped papers with her picture attached, her face peaked and hopeful, a staple through her forehead. She scanned the waiting families and company reps and tour guides, even though she knew nobody was there to greet her. Hawkers swooped, offering her rides for three, four, six hundred *kuai*. Then a hand closed around the handle of her suitcase and a man beckoned her to follow, promising a fair price over his shoulder. He looked familiar, like a distant cousin or a friend of her dad's. "Two hundred," she called out, her tone more pleading than commanding, and hastened after her suitcase.

When they arrived at the university, she felt so grateful she wanted to hug him. Eagerly, she hefted her suitcase from one decrepit office to the next, only to discover there'd be no welcome, no orientation, only a pockmarked young clerk who asked what she'd paid for her ride and promptly sniggered. He sniggered again when she declined his offer to upgrade her to the "foreigner comfort dormitory hotel." She forced a winning smile and asked him to direct her very first day in China. "*Yi-heyuan*," he said, and slapped down a map.

She left thanking him profusely, repeating the three syllables, adding the map to her trove of papers that she couldn't read, that seemed to hold her fate. *Yiheyuan*—an ancient temple, a bustling market, a secret garden? She found her dorm room, which looked just like the decrepit offices, only smaller; met her roommate, Tomoko, who could only bow in response to her own idiotic gestures and grins; and changed her clothes, grabbed her camera, and shoved her suitcase under her wooden plank of a bed, venturing out again before she lost her nerve.

On the street, she'd never felt so lost. People with grim faces and dark baggy clothing stared hard and pushed past. Bike riders elbowed her with their handlebars and lurched on. Buses seemed to take pleasure in threatening to crush her. Each time she stepped off the curb, she doubted she'd make it to the other side alive. And just as she was managing a stride, she was besieged by beggars—squalling brown-skinned boys, hardly more than toddlers, then a young man scuttling on the ground on his hands and buttocks, his legs crossed behind his head. Shaking a bowl of coins in his teeth, he seemed sent to warn her that no matter how disoriented she felt, she had no idea how twisted life here could get.

Her throat filling with dust, she passed a KFC, a McDonald's, a Starbucks, but she forced herself to keep walking until she found an authentic-looking teahouse. Ready to savor her first pot of tea in China, she got served a bag of Lipton. When she tried to pay, she found her handbag agape, an empty space where she'd tucked her cash.

She stammered and stammered before the manager let her go, eyes narrowed. She stumbled back to campus, scanning the pavement. The pockmarked clerk calmly told her about the little migrant boys trained to pickpocket. "But I didn't feel anything," she said, wanting to add, *I'm from New York*. The clerk sniggered again. "Of course you didn't." She turned away and he called, in a tone close enough to kindness, "Just take a cab."

She hailed a cab and, instantly, it stopped. She pronounced the three syllables and it zoomed there. *Yiheyuan*—the Summer Palace—of course. Bronze phoenixes and cauldrons, incense burning before gold Buddhas, a rippling lake skimmed by dragon boats and punctured by red pagodas. She toured it, snapping picture after picture. It was all incredibly—picturesque. She couldn't shake the sense that a crew had finished painting and packed up just before her arrival, either to compensate for her sufferings or as part of a conspiracy whose sinister depths she had yet to fathom.

Nearly every picture came out blurry or off-kilter, like documentary evidence of her weakness. She trashed all but one, self-timed, of herself by a lotus pond. The scene looked archetypal, as if lotus ponds could be found around any corner in China, and somehow her grin looked effortless.

Now their bus joined a fleet of tour buses in the parking lot, and their group began disembarking to join a fleet of tour groups. First Tommy the tour guide, slender and orange-haired, bouncy on space-age sneakers. Next a honeymooning couple, George and Joyce, who looked like siblings, both Toronto-born Cantonese, sporty and cheerful. Mr. and Mrs. Wong, Hong Kongese retirees, both about five feet tall and under a hundred pounds, their movements birdlike, their hair the same improbable black. Then Mr. Chu, a beady-eyed Hong Kongese corporate computer something or other, and his son Byron, who looked about Kay's own age, half-white, lean, and handsome, with copper skin and hair. Finally, her mother, her aunt, her grandmother, her sisters, and herself, with a sigh.

In her two days' absence, the summer heat had reached full blast, baking the city listless, its native life given way completely to a tourist circus, no mystifying element in the air, only hot dust and faint rot. In a way, it reminded her of the atmosphere in the house after her father's death.

Mom nudged her and pointed to Tommy bypassing the giant snake of a ticket line—the tapering lifeless tail, the alert body, the vicious fat head attacking the booth. "All-inclusive, see? Can you imagine if we'd come on our own?"

Kay nodded. She was trying to be a good sport.

Mom clamped on a visor. "Did you girls bring hats?"

Nora ignored her. Sophie was fixing her hair in the dark window of a parked cab. Kay shook her head no.

Mom clucked. "Didn't I warn you about the ozone layer here?" She waved at a vendor wheeling a cart from one tour group to the next. He had no hats, only parasols, flowered and lace-trimmed. Mom asked for three.

Quickly, the vendor sized up her mother, tossed the parasols in a bag, and said, "Very cheap, only one hundred!"

"Mom, don't," Kay said.

"I don't mind the money."

"I'm not carrying that," Sophie said.

"Why not?" Mom asked.

"It's a parasol."

"No one will laugh at you," Mom said. "People here take sun protection seriously."

Kay supposed that was true. Lisa and Summer, the two local women who'd responded to her own ad in that English-language weekly, often expressed dismay over how carelessly she tanned.

Her mother was already digging out a hundred-*kuai* bill.

"Wait." At least Kay could bargain the price to something less ridiculous. She gave the vendor her starting price. His glee faded. They careened from warfare to flirtation to comradeship, until they were just a few *kuai* apart. Tommy had returned with their tickets. Everyone was watching and waiting. The vendor held firm, which meant it was time for the final tactic. Kay started to walk away.

"Oh, let's just let him have it." Mom thrust the hundred-*kuai* bill into the vendor's hand.

He pocketed it, grinned at Kay, and padded toward the next tour group.

Mom patted her arm. "It's nothing."

"He's not a charity case. There's a ritual involved. Everyone bargains here."

Tommy cleared his throat. "Are we ready?" He spoke in accented English, his cloying tone somehow both servile and disdainful.

He gave a commanding wave, and the group started off. Mom tried to pass out the parasols. Nora and Sophie waved her off. Kay took the whole bag and started forward.

"Wait." Mom brought out her camera.

Her sisters were stone-faced. Kay grinned until her face hurt.

Mom lowered her camera and turned, but not before Kay saw her face sag.

Her sisters walked on either side of Kay, dragging their feet in silence. Kay found herself afraid of conversation. They hadn't been together since the funeral.

She tried pointing out the ornately painted pagoda eaves, the hundreds of lions carved on the balustrades of the footbridge, but her sisters didn't bother to feign interest. She tried catching up with the group to hear Tommy's narration, but he was speaking Cantonese, the dialect her mother and aunt and grandmother were born into, which to Kay, aside from the odd word, was still indecipherable. Soon she was simply pausing where Tommy paused, looking where he pointed.

Lunch was at a "seven-star foreign visitor restaurant" decked out with

Christmas lights, pink tablecloths, and bowing waitresses. The food was goopy, deceptively tasty, and quickly gross. Around every table sat other sweaty, duped tour groups.

Next on the itinerary: Tiantan Park. Since that morning with Rick, Kay hadn't had the chance to revisit it.

This afternoon, the sweltering woods were abandoned. All along Echo Wall, tourists jostled and shrieked. In the courtyard, vendors circled like seagulls, tour groups were being head-counted, and a few elderly locals had been reduced to fanning themselves on benches. The only thing for her group to do was click away with their cameras, which they did, Mom the most relentlessly, and then Tommy led them to buy souvenirs—postcards, stuffed pandas, T-shirts, mugs, all emblazoned as if Tiantan were a brand.

Her grandmother sat by the gift shop entrance, looking profoundly solitary, and profoundly unmoved.

A little timidly, Kay sat beside her. "It must be strange for you, this tour."

"It's not bad."

"But being back in China, after so many years."

After a moment, her grandmother nodded.

"Do you remember fleeing?"

Grandma nodded again.

"What was that like?"

"It was—" Grandma shrugged. "It was war."

Kay had waited most of the year to reach that era in her history class, but the unit had focused exclusively on the triumph of Chairman Mao and his loyal masses. When she tried to ask about the other side, she was only told, once again, that they were a corrupt elite who got soundly and justly defeated.

She'd asked her parents about that fateful journey from the mainland, but her father remembered nothing, while her mother seemed to feel affronted by her questions. After meeting her grandfather, Kay had written a letter to her grandmother. Her grandmother's reply was quick, typed, and devoid of answers.

All the links to her own history seemed to have vanished during that flight, as if they'd dropped into the strait. Kay had studied, in sociology, the difficulty among immigrants of revisiting the past, but she couldn't resign herself to such loss.

"Grandma, hearing about your revolutionary work really inspired me."

Her grandmother gave a little start. There was a flicker in her eyes.

Carefully, Kay said, "You were a prominent leader for women's rights, and against the Japanese occupation."

Her grandmother nodded.

Kay waited. Her grandmother was silent. Flustered, Kay tried to explain her latest campaign—the personals she'd read, the ad she'd placed herself, her two respondents whom, despite her best efforts, she couldn't say she'd helped. At last she stammered, "I know this kind of work is always hard, but how do you know when to give up? How do you know when to move on?"

"As long as you can keep fighting, you don't give up."

"Well, when you left China, when you gave up your revolutionary work—"

The flicker turned flinty. "I had no choice."

"Kay, do you like this? Should I buy you one?" It was her mother, waving a silly souvenir.

Now the rest of the group spilled out of the gift shop, and Tommy herded them all toward the bus. By the time Kay turned back, her grandmother's face was placid again.

Kay supposed she still hadn't studied enough, hadn't found the right questions. She feared she never would.

A few months ago, she'd received a Lunar New Year card from her grandfather, containing just twelve words—her name, a well-wishing message, and his name. The characters looked textbook-perfect, until she looked close: each stroke was composed of tiny oscillations. Someday soon, those oscillations would become even shakier, more erratic, and then cease completely. She couldn't bear for that card to be their last exchange, and yet, though she carried the card in her backpack, she hadn't managed to reply.

Olympic-size pool, sauna, and gym beneath the lobby, French and fusion restaurants on the roof. A glass elevator trimmed with gold lights glided up and down, reflecting off the glass walls, the glass doors, all the shiny surfaces becoming mirrors against the deepening night.

Brightly, Mom said, "After such a long, hot day, isn't it nice to be in a fancy hotel?"

"But look around—we could be anywhere." Kay had exhausted her good sportsmanship.

"Tomorrow we're going to the Great Wall. So it'll be pretty obvious where we are."

"Which section?"

Mom shrugged. "The must-see section."

"No. It's a tourist circus." Everyone looked a little startled at her intensity. "My friend Du Yi told me about a section so unspoiled it doesn't even have a name. Let me take us there."

After a pause, Mom said indulgently, "Okay. You be tour guide for the day."

No one objected. They wanted only to duck into the comfort of their rooms. While they paired up, washed up, and went to bed, Kay walked through the glitzy lobby and outside, wandering away from all the hulking multinational hotels that had devoured the district until she found herself on a familiar-looking street.

An orange-hooded pay phone, a wonton stall, a convenience store. A rickety fruit stand whose proprietor lounged in nothing but pajama pants, with offerings from peaches and bananas to guavas, mangosteens, rambutans, others she could name only in Chinese. An "adult health" shop with contraceptives and sex toys openly displayed. A hair salon where pink neon and bare legs indicated the full range of services.

She'd launched her second campaign as humbly as possible, placing a simple ad in the English-language weekly under "Cultural Exchange": "Seeking Chinese women seeking Western men. I'm an ABC who'd like to hear your story."

Lisa, her first respondent, was tall, porcelain-skinned, and pretty. She'd hoped Kay was a Chinese American man who might be her savior. Sweetly, she said, "For my story, you can pay me. If you can spend your days like this, you can afford it." She settled for meeting at Häagen-Dazs, ordering sundaes that cost Kay a week's worth of her own dinners. Lisa's current boyfriend, a sixty-something Brit, was stingy, she said, and between his monthly visits, she barely scraped by. Besides, she'd caught him advertising in the same weekly for threesomes under the heading, "You, me . . . and you."

The only daughter of small landlords who'd been "sent down" to toil in the countryside during the Cultural Revolution, Lisa had studied English in college and still did intermittent secretarial work, which she loathed. Her freshman year, a Taiwanese businessman had taken her as his mistress and paid her tuition; her parents asked no questions. He was her first, and her first love, but senior year, he dumped her for a freshman. Thinking *laowai* would be more romantic, "more Hollywood," she started accepting dates from Western men she met at bars, at Starbucks, at McDonald's. Again and again, she got "swindled" by lowly salesmen, students, and drifters claiming to be successful entrepreneurs, professors, and journalists, while the few men with real money broke her heart—but at least, Lisa said, she'd always extracted fancy vacations and gifts, even from "the losers."

Kay asked how that differed from cash transactions, and Lisa threw down her spoon so angrily Kay thought she might slap her. Kay hastened to apologize, blaming her poor Chinese, until Lisa glanced at her melting sundae. She tossed her hair and picked up her spoon. Kay let her eat in silence until she seemed mollified.

At their next meeting, Kay tried to explain exoticization and fetishization, asking Lisa what she thought lurked behind the Western fascination with Asian women. Lisa said, "Obviously, we have nicer skin and figures. We know how to manage our men. And we age better." Anyway, she reminded Kay, she'd already decided to set her sights on a Chinese American. When Kay tried to explain her concerns further, Lisa said, "If I wait longer to have a baby, my figure will never recover. Do you have a brother?" When Kay found herself speechless, Lisa offered to introduce her to friends who'd known truly evil "white devils"—for, she said, a modest commission.

Summer, Kay's second and last respondent, had sleek hair down to her hips and very large, low-hanging breasts. She declared, "We Sichuan women are spicy like our food." Dryly, Kay said, "And hot like summer?" Of course, the pun didn't translate. The elder of two daughters of pig farmers (who, as members of an ethnic minority, were exempted from the one-child policy), Summer had left home at sixteen and worked in a doll factory, a hot pot restaurant, and now a shoe store, where she slept at night on a display table, in order to save for her sister's tuition. Why did she date *laowai*? "To fuck! Bigger penises. Isn't it true?" She pressed until Kay admitted a lack of expertise, which Summer found hilarious.

Summer cursed her exes with gusto—"That fat turtle, fuck him, fuck his mother"—while insisting she had great fun. Without prompting, she said she'd only charged once. The guy was American and ugly, made fun of her underwear, and wanted to shave her pubic hair. She let him screw her, then demanded money, and when he refused, she smashed a picture of his girlfriend holding a cake and threatened to call a gangster cousin. Later, she admitted she'd begun charging when a *laowai* was particularly unattractive or unpleasant, or when marriage seemed absolutely unattainable.

Summer hoped Kay would write a racy exposé about modern Chinese urbanites in which she'd figure as the sexpot star. "Just get it banned, and it'll be an international bestseller, and we'll both be famous." When Kay explained her motivations, Summer listened intently, then asked, "Why don't you marry a rich *laowai*? You're so lucky, you grew up with them. Marry one and you can follow your dreams." Her own dream was to design shoes. She showed Kay a pair with hand-painted musical notes and lightning bolts.

After a few of these sessions, Kay found herself completely muddled. Lisa and Summer weren't hapless victims. In fact, she wasn't sure who was prey. Maybe Du Yi was more right than not. Maybe the transactions were, however warped, equal.

And would Lisa be better off as a full-time secretary, Summer as a factory worker or a pig farmer? Weren't they simply pursuing their best economic opportunities in this new China? And wouldn't marriage to a Westerner—any Westerner, even a "loser"—set them and their families for life?

In America, Kay and her sisters and every other Asian woman—and every person of color, maybe every woman—were forced to be representative. Why should Chinese women in China be burdened in that way?

Perhaps she should have focused instead on the plight of those twisted cripples, or the pickpocket boys, or the Great Wall apple farmer. Her heart ached for almost everyone in this country, even as she knew that was wrong, too.

She'd refrained from setting up more sessions, but then Lisa and Summer insisted. They wanted to keep talking. They wanted to know what the other looked like and whom she liked better. Lisa brought her wild vegetables and peanut brittle from her hometown. Summer offered to paint her sneakers. They asked concerned, detailed questions about her diarrhea, and independently fingered the same culprit: the bottled water she bought from migrant peasants on the street. They couldn't believe her stupidity. Those peasants, they said, salvaged bottles from the garbage, filled them with tap water, and resealed the caps. Their suspicions were validated. Once Kay stopped buying those bottles, she hadn't had a flare-up.

So Lisa and Summer had helped her in one small but definite way. It was time to stop deluding herself that she could do that much for them.

Every day, Du Yi asked if she was staying. Mr. Wan had promised to find her lucrative stints tutoring other local businessmen in English. Rick had offers to work as a business consultant, a bar manager, an editor at that English-language weekly. He said he'd stay if she would, as if it were a dare. In her last days before this tour, all she'd really managed to do was cram for her finals and convince Rick to join her in sampling dog meat. Their relationship, in particular, was getting more fraught the more she professed nonchalance that it was ending, even as she refrained from saying good-bye, from confirming that she was really leaving.

She'd told herself that when the time came to leave, she'd be ready. Now her scholarship was over. She had a certificate to show for all her studying. She had two days to vacate her dorm, and the thought of moving back into her old room, of living in that house alone with Mom, made her shudder.

If she left, how would she ever come back? Rationally, she knew it was simply a long flight—the same flight her family had just hopped. But she couldn't shake the fear that, at any time, an absence could become permanent.

She bought fruit and water for tomorrow's excursion, then went to the pay phone and dialed Du Yi for directions.

"Wait," he said, as she was about to hang up. "Let me accompany you."

"No, thank you."

"When will I meet your family? When will I see you again?"

"I don't know."

"Will you stay?"

She'd been drawn to his earnestness, but now he just seemed lacking in dignity.

"I don't know." She hung up.

Immediately, she felt a little remorse. She thought of calling Rick or Mr. Wan, but they felt so far away. Even this ordinary street where she now stood felt like a replica, as if she'd already left the real city and would never find her way back.

In the morning, Kay paced the stretch of corridor her family occupied, trying to tamp down her anxiety. "Let's go! Sneakers, please. And parasols—just kidding!" She decided she'd better wait downstairs.

In the hotel lobby, a man with sinewy shoulders and high cheekbones sat smoking on a loveseat. He turned: Byron. The corners of his eyes were a vulnerable pink against the copper of him.

"Jet lag?" He exhaled smoke.

"Just heading to the Great Wall."

"Aren't we all?" He shook out another cigarette and lit it with the one still burning between his lips.

"We're going to a section only locals know."

"Then how do you know it?"

"I've learned my way around here." She sounded defensive.

He looked amused. "So you're leading the female bonding today?"

"Are you and your dad here for male bonding?"

He shrugged. "I guess he's finally decided to give it a try."

A little thrown, she tried to think of a helpful reply. Just then, her mom, sisters, aunt, and grandmother stepped out of the elevator.

"Have fun," Byron said, with a smirk.

She ignored him.

Outside, liberated from the tour, her family began to stretch and turn, absorbing the place through all their senses. The city cooperated this morning, imbuing its ordinary happenings with an extra glow—people biking in business attire with tufty-haired kids perched behind, old men playing chess with scraps on the pavement, old women sweeping store-fronts with hand-bound brooms, the savory smell of *baozi* wafting from stacked bamboo steamers. Kay bought a half-dozen and, after some hesitation, everyone took one. Biting into her own, she held her breath. Sometimes the outside was mushy, the inside a hard lump. But these *baozi* were luscious, the dough hot and pillowy, the savory pork filling bathed in its own juices.

The bus station was just far enough to require a healthy exertion. The bus line was just long enough to make them feel lucky to squeeze into seats, which looked like they'd been rescued from a junkyard. Their stop was a brown and dusty town, stalled like so many others somewhere between a pastoral village and a strip mall. She found the lot Du Yi had described, where minivans were for hire, and bargained just until everyone felt self-satisfied. The ride was just bumpy enough to feel adventurous. The air-conditioning was broken, but gentle breezes swirled around them, and lush greenery occasionally brushed into the open windows as they wound higher and higher. At last the driver pulled over.

Kay jumped out. There it was, more spectacular than she'd imagined—a tarnished tiara atop a rocky green peak, the watchtowers like points where gems were once set, all shrouded in a haze of dust like magical smoke.

No souvenir stands, no touts. No cable car. No paved steps. Barely a path—a jagged fissure in the brush sharply angled toward the sky, like a bolt of lightning from the earth.

"Wow," Mom said.

"We're supposed to climb this?" Sophie asked.

"*Wa*," said her grandmother, her eighty-year-old grandmother.

"Oh no." Kay clapped her hand to her mouth.

Her grandmother couldn't climb this section of the Great Wall. Kay herself would struggle. Cheeks blazing, she checked the time. By now, the tour group would be well on their comfortable way to Badaling, to ride the cable car and take pictures and buy souvenirs, to check the Great Wall off their list. Certainly that was preferable to standing here like this.

"What should we do?" she finally squeaked.

Mom said, "How about the four of us try to climb? Aunt Susan will wait with Grandma."

Grandma nodded. "The Great Wall is not new to me."

Kay mumbled, "We should've stayed with the tour. I'm sorry." In her mind, Byron's smirk bobbed to the surface.

"Don't be so hard on yourself. We all make mistakes."

Mom's tone was so eager that Kay winced. Before another silence could take over, she said, "Okay. If you're game. Let's go."

The trail was barely wide enough for one, the incline just gradual enough to get a foothold. Kay tested each spot, instructing her mother and sisters to step where she stepped. A slip could be fatal. Soon the dirt path became even steeper and sandier, and the weight of the water and fruit in her backpack kept pulling her back. She tried to crawl, but everywhere she placed a hand or foot, clumps of earth loosened and fell, exposing skeletal rock.

Behind her, Mom and Nora and Sophie were breathing hard, scratched by shrubbery, slipping in their sandals.

"Let's turn back," Kay huffed. "It's too dangerous."

They looked at her in surprise.

"We can make it." Mom wiped her mottled face with a sleeve.

"This is good exercise," Sophie said.

"We're almost there," Nora said. "Look."

Kay craned. The climb was surprisingly short, cutting right up the mountainside. She steadied herself. She lifted one hand, one foot, the other hand, the other foot, and then crumbly gray brick sat at eye level.

After some heaving and tugging, the four of them stood on this unnamed remnant of the Great Wall, broken off on either end. While

Kay focused on catching her breath, Mom and Nora and Sophie scrambled from vista to vista, exclaimed at a waterfall, peered out the sentry windows.

"What is this, really?" Sophie asked. "All I know is that you can see it from outer space."

Mom smiled. "Actually, that's a myth. But ask Kay—she's our tour guide today."

Kay found herself stammering. "The Great Wall was built to guard against Mongolian invasion. But it didn't work—I mean, there was Genghis Khan. Well, it worked for a while." She hadn't studied the Great Wall. It had seemed too entrenched in the Western imagination to be worth studying, like foot-binding or kung fu. She'd only tried to see it, properly, and that was hard enough.

"When was it built?" Sophie asked.

"A thousand—no, two thousand years ago." The difference of a millennium. "Mom?"

"Some sections were added later, while others were destroyed and rebuilt. But yes, construction started two thousand years ago." Mom fished out her camera. "Smile!"

After Kay and her sisters had posed for a dozen shots, they all sat down to rest, letting their legs dangle over the mountainside. Kay handed out the water and fruit, keeping a badly bruised peach for herself.

Mom said, "You know, sometimes at home, I get this strange feeling, like I'm going to fall."

"You mean those dreams where you're falling and falling, and suddenly you wake up?" Sophie asked. "I've heard they're common among high achievers. Falling represents fear of failure, loss of control."

"No, it happens when I'm awake. And it's not the actual fall, but the moment before. I had a similar feeling when I was pregnant, all three times. A fainting feeling—my blood and nutrients diverted to you girls. So maybe this is like a phantom pregnancy, now that you're all grown."

After a long pause, Nora said, "Maybe you should see a doctor."

"Maybe. Maybe I have some imbalance, literally." Mom forced a small laugh. "Anyway, all I wanted to say was, now that I'm here with you girls, up high, now that I actually could fall—well, I feel just fine. Better than fine." Mom smiled directly at Kay. "And I'll feel even better once I have you back home."

Kay sucked at her bruised peach, still fat with sweet juice.

Even as she began to lead the way down from this nameless section of the Great Wall that had beckoned her for months, that she hadn't even enjoyed climbing, the thought that she might never see it again made her vision blur, and she nearly lost her footing.

10

Susan released a long sigh, and felt like she'd held it for years. She and Ma were sitting in shade at the foot of the mountain, on a large rock that made a passable bench, though its newly upended appearance didn't make for much peace of mind. This was a rest stop for tumbling rocks, not for two old women—one middle-aged, one plain old. And this being China, there was no cement siding, no orange netting, not even a warning sign. There was a section of Great Wall for Irene and the girls to climb, and for Susan and Ma, there was shade.

Mosquitoes attacked her, then buzzed and danced, amused by her swatting. If Ma was getting stung, she didn't show it.

Susan was itchy and hot and hungry and thirsty. When they made it back to the hotel—if they made it back in time—they'd get Peking duck, "special treat," Tommy had said. All she wanted was dinner at home with Winston. Or at least a hotel room with her own husband, instead of Ma.

The first overnight stay had taken place, and her life had not fallen apart. That night, to express sympathy for her predicament, not to air any grievance of his own, Winston had noted that Ma and Irene and the girls hadn't asked him one question about himself. This hadn't even registered on Susan. Now her life with him felt more solid than ever, those walls waiting to contain her once again.

"So you've been to the Great Wall before?" she asked.

Ma made a scornful noise. "I never had leisure to sightsee back then."

Susan swatted at a mosquito buzzing by her ear. Ma reached into her handbag and passed her a fan. Susan wondered if Ma carried anything else handy—repellent, food, water. Her new travel purse sat on her lap, ladylike and useless.

She flicked at the metal clasp of the fan. It snapped open, catching the web between her thumb and forefinger. She silenced a gasp, sucked quietly at the smarting skin. Ma said nothing.

"Kay should've given this more thought," Susan said.

"She's a spirited child."

"She's not a child anymore."

"I'm her grandma. When you have children, you can tell me who's a child."

Susan sighed again. To her and Irene, at least, Ma was never anything like this indulgent "Grandma." As a mother, Ma had done her duty. She hadn't become a dead branch on the family tree, hadn't squandered her biology. And of course that made sense, more sense than how Susan had spent her fertile years, incapable of raising a plant, let alone a child.

Susan fanned herself. The exertion cooled her face, but made the rest of her even hotter.

A few weeks ago, she'd finally called Ba again, thinking that at the very least, she needed to be able to say she had—and that maybe he'd forgotten, changed his mind, been advised by his doctor not to fly. Instead, he'd demanded their itinerary. An hour later, he'd called back to dictate his own.

Then he'd asked if Ma knew about his plan.

"I don't think so. I don't know. Maybe she heard from Irene," Susan lied.

"You know her daughter came all the way from Beijing to see me?"

He meant Kay. He'd probably forgotten her name. "Did you enjoy the visit?"

He grunted. "That girl has more fire than you or Irene ever did."

Playing one female against another—in old age, that longtime habit of his had probably become an involuntary tic. Brightly, Susan had said they'd all see him soon.

In eleven days, Ba would board a plane to Hong Kong. In twelve days, so would they. Susan hadn't told Ma or Irene.

She'd tried to imagine best-case scenarios. If Ma simply agreed to see Ba. If they carried on a brief, civil conversation. If they laughed, a bittersweet laugh that buried the past. If they promised to stay in touch, exchange medical updates, grumble about their children. If they decided to spend their remaining days as husband and wife again. All preposterous, the first not much less than the last.

Susan fanned herself harder. Her stomach rumbling, the mosquitoes buzzing, even Ma's breathing, all rising to an unbearable drone. She snapped the fan shut.

"You seem in good health," she said.

"I am," Ma said.

"Ba isn't so lucky."

The droning seemed to pause. Inside, Susan started to cower.

"So?" Ma snapped.

"I just thought you should know."

"It means nothing to me."

Ma meant, of course, not only his health, but Ba himself. Susan let the droning swell between them again.

How was she to stop Ba? Or tell Ma? Or tell Irene to deal with it? She'd only tried to do her duty as a sister and a daughter. She'd called Irene, then Ba, and made conversation. How was she to have foreseen any of these consequences?

At last, four shiny black heads appeared in the brush, faces pink, sweaty, and self-congratulatory. Ma abruptly stood, the rock teetered, and a sharp patter hit Susan's back—an avalanche of pebbles and dirt. Such a rush to greet the mountaineers? Yet Susan shook out her shirt and followed to hear their tale of courage and triumph.

•

"Nice ring." Nora's tone was odd, breezy yet searching.

Susan looked down at her left hand. Her diamond ring was catching the afternoon rays, shooting tiny rainbows throughout the back of the minivan.

When Winston had first presented it to her, she'd stared until he said, anxiously, "It's platinum." She still wasn't sure why that mattered. She still didn't know how many carats, or what cut. It was her first jewel, her first piece of jewelry. She knew Winston loved seeing it lodged on her finger, and she knew it impressed other people. To her, the stone seemed as prosaic and flavorless as refrigerated red roses, but inherent beauty wasn't the point. A diamond was a standard. It allowed others to assess your worth to the man who'd promised to keep you for life.

Susan noticed her niece's face was no longer a girl's—no lines or spots, but a tiredness around her mouth and eyes, a new gravity. Everyone else had dozed off. She fumbled for conversation.

"I heard you're quite a star on Wall Street."

"I've had a good run. It's time to move on." That same odd tone.

"To what?"

"Something more meaningful, I guess. Not that trading was just about money to me, absurd as that sounds."

"Being a trailblazer."

Nora's brow lifted in surprise, then furrowed, as if she were trying to work out a difficult riddle. After a moment, she said, "Didn't you teach? Poetry, right?"

Susan was taken aback. She never expected strangers to have heard of her, or people who knew her to have read her work. But for her niece to ask, *Didn't you teach poetry?* Like, *Were you somebody, once?*

She nodded. Nora waited. Susan feigned a yawn. Decorously, Nora turned to the window, and Susan closed her eyes.

Irene had raised such obviously outstanding daughters—sharp, ambitious, good-looking to boot. She'd bequeathed them Ma's self-righteousness, perhaps not realizing they'd be finished with American exceptionalism, historical ignorance, and entitlement. They were in the vanguard; others were laggards. They set out to better the world, and held themselves above it. They rebelled against a luxury tour and led their eighty-year-old grandmother to a crumbling mountain, and considered that some kind of progress. And they could not conceive of her, their aunt Susan, having gone out into the world with as much hope, foolish or not, as their own generation now.

When the tour group reconvened for dinner, the others seemed less than rapturous over their official Great Wall expedition, and just as overheated and undernourished. Irene gushed over Kay's tour-guiding. To her credit, Kay gave only a sheepish grin. Everyone ate each allotted portion of Peking duck as it came, meat, skin, scallions, sauce, all preassembled.

Afterward, Tommy herded them to an art gallery filled with ornate silk screens. An old woman sat on display, too, flicking a needle through a door-sized screen, fashioning a pair of fat white cats fluff by fluff—the pricking of tourist consciences, live. Irene announced she'd buy a silk screen and summoned her daughters to help her select one, sending Tommy and the gallery manager into a tizzy. Susan made her way to a bench and found herself seated beside Ma—sidelined and waiting once again.

Why were the two of them here at all? Six women, three generations, two sets of sisters—for the mathematics, for the symbolism? Her own unthinking invitation to Irene had been a handy excuse. Irene's grand plan revolved around her and her precious daughters. Susan and Ma were included as gestures; at most, buffers for that core group, the center of the universe.

So why was any of it Susan's responsibility? It probably wasn't her phone call that had inspired Ba, either. It was Irene's own plan, if not Kay's visit.

Susan waited until Irene chose a silk screen, until they were released to their hotel rooms, until Ma stepped into the shower. Next door, Irene stood at the mirrored bureau with a pair of tweezers, yanking at tiny, obstinate roots.

Susan took a deep breath. "Ba will be waiting for us in Hong Kong at the end of our tour."

Irene's hand stopped in midair. "What?"

Susan repeated it.

"Didn't you call him back?"

"Yes. He wouldn't listen."

"How could he arrange this by himself? How does he know we'll meet him? How could he just show up if you said no?"

Susan shrugged. "You want to leave him stranded at the airport?"

Irene slammed down her tweezers and wailed, "What'll we do?"

Susan was relieved at the plural pronoun. "We have to tell Ma."

"You know she won't see him. You know this will ruin the whole tour."

"We don't know that for sure."

"But this is our holiday! This is our chance to reconnect!" Irene seemed deaf to the irony of shouting such sentiments.

"Maybe that's all Ba wants, too—a chance to reconnect."

"Then let him plan the next reunion," Irene snapped.

Susan noticed the sound of the shower—one of the girls. For the first time, she started to form a plan of her own. "I think Kay put the idea in his head, actually."

Irene pressed her lips tight.

"And I think the girls should tell Ma."

"You must be joking."

"She's their grandma. She won't get mad at them. She might even listen." Susan thought she could see the dueling forces in Irene—maternal instinct versus self-preservation.

Irene hissed, "They have enough to cope with. They lost their father."

"They might find some consolation in seeing their grandfather." Susan was impressed at her own boldness. "Maybe that's what Kay was after."

"He was never a father to us, let alone a grandfather to them." Irene's hands had curled into fists at her sides, a gesture Susan remembered from childhood, a gesture of frustration and near-defeat.

Easily, Susan said, "Doesn't he deserve a chance to redeem himself?"

Irene set her palms flat on the bureau. "What exactly did he say? When he came up with this scheme. When you told him my plan."

Susan was a little thrown. "That he wants to see us. That it might be the last time. Something like that."

"Did he actually mention his granddaughters? Did he ask about me or you?"

"Some things can be left unsaid."

"Are you his mouthpiece? His mind reader?"

"He's eighty-six. You expect him to keep up on your lab work, or Sophie's grades, or—"

"No, I don't," Irene said crisply.

Susan stared at her sister, at her sister's defiant face in the mirror, her sharp eyes and jutting chin—and at her own profile, wan and skinny, confined to the edge of the frame.

"He wants to see Ma," she said finally. "That's all I know."

Irene nodded. "And if you want to do his dirty work, go ahead. Leave me and my daughters out of it."

"Dirty work? Imagine your time was near. Wouldn't you want one last chance to see your—the one you—" Susan couldn't finish the sentence.

The bathroom door opened. Sophie emerged, toweling her hair.

Susan murmured, "I was just leaving."

Sophie gave a faint smile. "Good night."

Susan turned to her sister. "Good night."

Irene, face stiff, didn't answer.

In the corridor, Susan leaned against the carpeted wall to catch her breath, and remembered one Mid-Autumn Festival, many years ago. She and Irene gnawing on duck wings they'd bought on the street while the other families feasted, then sitting on their dark stoop watching the neighborhood girls gather for their yearly game of catching the moon's reflection in water-filled cups. Ever the newcomers, they weren't included.

Suddenly Irene grabbed her hand. *Let's chase the moon. It's always following us. Let's chase it down.* At first Irene had to drag her, around the house, through inky alleys, down red-lantern-lined streets. Then, as Susan saw how low the moon hung that night, orange and full like it might drip, she saw a possibility. They ran, spinning and darting, panting and plotting: *Right. No, left. No, this way!* She was still caught up in the chase when Irene stopped, stamped, and scolded, *You're too slow.* It was probably their only attempt to celebrate a holiday together.

Susan decided to call Winston. He would sympathize, though he might also remind her that Irene was widowed.

As children, Susan had vowed never to marry at all, while Irene had vowed never to marry a man like Ba. Bill had seemed the opposite—hearty, handsome, wholesome, like he'd been fed on American milk and beef, good humor and crisp air—while Ba was slight, mean-eyed, twitchy-mouthed. He looked as if whoever made him had been stingy, and he behaved as if he needed to recompense himself for the rest of his life with women, with power, with power over women.

In the elevator, she joined a pair of businessmen who, once they hit the lobby, trundled into the hotel bar. It radiated cheap jazz and an amber glow, with backlit lettering over the doorway: *Passions.* She veered away, bought a calling card from the front desk, encased herself in the mottled glass of a phone booth, and found herself dialing Taiwan.

The phone rang and rang. At last: "*Wei?*"

"Ba. How are you?"

"What?" he barked.

"It's me." Her voice cracked. She cleared her throat. "Ba, it's me. How are you?"

"I was asleep."

"Sorry. I wanted to tell you—we're in Beijing. We arrived yesterday."

He grunted.

She was a girl again, craving his notice, trying to be worthy of his time. "Today we saw the Great Wall. Tomorrow—"

"Is everything set?"

"Yes—" She wavered. "Yes. Winston will meet you at the airport while we finish our tour. Then we'll all come see you."

She wondered if he'd say he wanted to see only Ma. But he grunted again, more agreeably. They hung up.

He always thought she didn't know how he tried to manipulate her. She knew, probably better than he, but somehow that merely enabled his manipulation. Only one other man had ever done that to her.

She needed a drink. What would Ma say if she raided the minibar? She was fifty-six, for heaven's sake. There was Passions—she ducked in. Her elevator companions sat with two tensely smiling, tarted up girls. She slid into a booth and ordered a martini. It came tinted brown and tasted ghastly. She drank it in large sips, holding her breath.

More than a decade ago, in a September week of drizzle and mist, she'd met Ernesto in a wet parking lot. She was leaving a faculty dinner where the department chair had assigned her to give a talk on the state of Chinese poetry. She was going home to the little yellow house she'd rented, thinking why not, a whole old house instead of another generic one-bedroom, why not an address she might remember a year later. But it was too much space. Scared to wander, she kept to the bedroom and left the other doors closed. The cracked parquet floor, destroyed during a summer keg party, stabbed the soles of her feet and snared her hems and socks. At night, ladybugs swarmed through the torn window screens and whizzed overhead while she tried to sleep.

She was thinking of how she should have retorted ("You speak English. You have a wife. Why don't you give a talk on the state of British marriage?"), and wondering if she'd take him or any other man at dinner to her bed over the semester, when she saw a glistening creature, features fine and pointed as a swallow's, lit by a bulb strung over a heaping dumpster. He was watching a man pull away in a station wagon. He didn't step back when it ground through a puddle and splattered his pants, which were white and belted too tightly. He raised his middle finger and issued a stream of curses she couldn't quite distinguish. They sounded as if his tongue had savored, then twisted each syllable. They sounded bewitching. Through her rain-streaked windshield, he caught her gaze and smiled—though later, it seemed more a sneer. She rolled down her window.

When his accent rang into her car, she thought perhaps he worked in the back of the restaurant. The town wasn't diverse; they never were. When he opened the door and the light blinked on, she thought he might be an exchange student. She didn't ask. He didn't, either.

His eyes were liquid and large and darker than her hair. His upper lip stuck softly out, a pink morsel of unconscious flesh. His skin was pale, but all the men she'd known were pale. Pasty academics in each town, each semester, pasty and droopy-shouldered and much too clever, with some keening frailty that was the only thing resembling fervor. They were cold, and left her colder—a wan victory, but easily repeated. His skin was pale and tender like the undersides of her own arms, like her inner thighs, but all over. Every part of him a secret, uncovered for her. Pale and glowing like the moon.

In her bed, ladybugs whizzing overhead, they both closed their eyes. (He kept his shut tight as a newborn's. She peeked.)

A few days later, he walked into her classroom. Creative Writing 1, fall

1989. That night, he knocked on her door, glistening in drizzle and mist. The next night, and the next, she let him in.

She kept the shades drawn. They lolled in bed, unwashed and unclothed. He killed ladybugs, smearing black on the walls, flicking maroon to the floor. They made meals of spiked coffee and saltines, canned oysters and vodka. They both grew even paler and gaunter. Night bled into day into night, until she needed to write, and made him leave. He took pains to wound her before he left. She didn't know where he lived. She had no way of reaching him, outside of the classroom, until he knocked on her door again.

The little yellow house was their world. Outside stretched wide, flat, and bright, and more forbidding than ever.

Their affair felt like a culmination of how she'd lived for twenty-odd years. No continuity, no sense of future. Everything could fall away, and did, except this single pearl, this beautiful thing. That thing was him, until it was a poem—no in-between. Her poems flourished that year, cool and spare, with sudden, luminous blooms.

In class, he fretted about his novel, taunted the sunny-haired students writing in earnest detail about fishing trips with Dad, glowered when she critiqued his critiques. *You are not qualified to teach fiction*, he once erupted. The sunny heads spun in unison. *I'm more qualified than you,* she said, and lifted the next double-sided, double-spaced story.

The first semester ended—seven weeks of poetry, seven weeks of fiction. He asked if he should refrain from signing up for the second. She shrugged. *What I am asking, Professor,* he said, *is would you be seen with me then?* She shrugged again. She wasn't affecting coldness. She didn't know what would happen next. She was never good at planning.

When she walked into the classroom, he was waiting. He stood over her desk and whispered, *I won't have you seducing another student.* Blood surged and made her dizzy.

She began to appease him, him and her own hunger. They drove to greasy spoons where they'd each have gotten stares alone, too, sucking up milkshakes, eating chicken-fried whatever. They drank at a dive in the next town where she'd hand back her martini glass when she wanted another; Dave the bartender had just the one, uncracked from an old gift set. They started to gain weight and color.

Still, in the house they kept to the bedroom. Ernesto asked about the dim closed rooms, about using a desk, a dresser, a bed for when she needed to be alone. But to her the unused spaces had become necessary, buffers between passion and poetry, inside and out, together and apart.

In certain lights, he made her swoon. But when his patchy stubble bristled, when that upper lip curled, the times she caught sight of his delicate frame slinking out of the men's room—she'd tell herself, *Soon, this flame will die soon.*

You need me. Until you don't. And I never learn my lesson, Professor. He snarled the last word. She looked away until his face was wistful and pretty again. *Each moment I take as the truth,* he said, like a plea. So she did not say: *Each moment is the truth. To try to string them together—that is* fiction.

Along with the pearls, they had another bit of banter—funny, until it was bitter: He was her hotheaded Latin lover, she was his inscrutable Asian. Once, at Dave's, a woman hissed, *Lookit the chink and the spic.* Like the title of a children's fable: The Chink and the Spic. The woman was perfectly matched with her mate—both doughy and heavy-set, with faded frizzy hair, pale tired eyes, plaid flannel shirts.

I am going to throw a pretzel at her, Ernesto announced, and he did. It bounced off one boulderlike breast. The woman smashed a bottle. Her mate picked up a stool. Dave came to their defense but, he warned, they were on their own next time they looked for trouble. They retreated to the little yellow house again.

She was no town personage—not a college dean or a church deacon, not even a noteworthy collector of steins or lamps. She was just an Asian lady, the Asian poet lady to some. She hid less from the possibility of professional censure than from the acknowledgment, in the form of public scrutiny, of their perfect futility.

If not for their perfect futility, she never would have kept letting him in.

Ernesto became more difficult to appease. He declared he loved her, and demanded she say it, too, and say it again, say it louder, tell him how much, tell him for how long. He asked about next year, and sulked when she explained her contract, her lack of control. He wanted her to know every detail of his asylum application, his visa problems, but she couldn't help him. He presented her with plants she didn't want, and blamed her when they withered. He bought a tank and a pair of tropical fish that ate each other's brilliant tails until one died. The other died one day later. He bought another pair, and another.

He panted and cried out in his sleep. He howled when she told him to go. He announced there were others, and bloodied his fists against the door when she refused to raise an outcry.

We are star-crossed lovers, you and I, he used to say. Always *you and I,* as if she might think he meant himself and another. He loved the sound; he thought it meant their union was blessed. Even after she explained, he kept saying it, another joke until it was no longer.

Us? she'd scoff. *I'm twice your age. You're a boy. A beautiful, petulant boy.*

You try to hold yourself like so. He stood back, flattened and rigid. *But nobody wants to die alone. Obviously.*

She held herself like so, sure and cool as a sheet of ice, while he coursed through the spaces beneath, between, inside her; while she began to believe in their subsistence, in living a life of tonights; while the end of the year closed in and the start of the next loomed, impossible and inevitable; until the little yellow house proved a battered farce of a world, like an internment camp, like a bomb shelter; until the moment it collapsed.

• • •

After three drinks—the second and third, whiskey straight—Susan still wasn't sleepy. She was cold in the air-conditioning, itchy and restless. On her way through the glittering lobby to the elevators, she stepped into a warm air current, an electric hum—the business lounge. Unmanned cubicles, cushioned chairs, dozing computers.

Almost silently, key by key, she typed *ernesto@ernesto.com*.

She typed, *I see your star is rising.* She added, *Congratulations.* She modified this: *Congratulations from your old professor.*

She backspaced to *rising.* She started a new line: *Meanwhile, I've settled.*

That second semester was nearly over when Irene called to announce Nora's graduation, Ma's visit, the whole family driving to her house. *Like a slumber party,* Irene chirped. Susan could have said no. Mouth dry, she asked where they'd sleep. Irene said, *Don't you live in a house?* Not Irene's idea of a house. Damp closed rooms, rented chintzy furniture, stained mattresses she'd never touched. She could have said no.

She swept Ernesto's effects—paltry, damning—into one of her totes, and put it by the door. His upper lip trembled: *Can't I have one drawer?* She refused. She raised the shades. She spread new sheets. She scrubbed and sprayed. The house reeked. Dead and dying plants, the last pair of fish, passion and weakness—they'd sense it, she was sure, they'd probe the junctions in her foundation she'd been trained to seal and reinforce, they'd find every patch of dry rot. He sat in the middle of her bed like an Indian figurine and demanded not to be swept out. *If you have a soul,* he said, *prove it now.*

She decided these lines about her soul were gibberish, him falling victim to assimilation—assimilation of a sham native culture, just as she'd found herself saying, more than once, *In China, we have a proverb . . .* Dot dot dot.

We are star-crossed lovers, you and I. She laughed a crazy laugh.

Ernesto kicked a plant. The pot broke and spilled across the cracked parquet floor. She never mopped it all up. She didn't try very hard. At least the family stayed out of her bedroom. All summer, gravel and soil, ceramic and root embedded themselves in her soles.

Just like that. Poof. He gestured as if flicking magic dust. *To you, I—us—this—never existed.*

It existed. Later, it wouldn't. This was not a contradiction. It wasn't even strange, if you saw time as rotational, not linear. When you see the moon, you say, *There's the moon.* The moon shows a different face every time you look, each one true. You don't say this, but you know.

For the last time, they went to bed. Then she offered dinner in town, at a well-lit establishment. In the parking lot, they paused before the grimy window of a pickup. "Clean me," someone had traced. Underneath that, the work of another hand: "Bite me."

At dinner, the stares felt compassionate, as if she and Ernesto emanated such heartbreak, others couldn't help but overlook the particulars. She ordered a dirty martini, wanting the bitterness. It tasted only of brine.

She said she didn't know if she could, but she'd try to stay, if he would. She said maybe they'd find a way to stay together, somewhere else, if not here.

He told her his application for asylum had been denied, his family struggling to pay more tuition, his student visa soon expiring.

You're a citizen. If you married me, we could stay together anywhere, here.

She spilled her drink. It seared her skin. A wife—not her, not his.

He said he didn't mind if they never had a child.

She laughed another crazy laugh.

His upper lip curled. He went to use the men's room. She didn't see him slip out the back door.

She found him in the parking lot, in the passenger seat of that pickup. Through the grimy window, through the scrawled words, she saw his head in the lap of a man with a square-jawed straining face, a bristly salt-and-pepper beard.

• • •

Susan discarded the message and headed for the elevators. A girl was inside the phone booth she'd vacated, her voice sharp and broken, the sound of a fierce creature wounded. A bang, then a louder bang—the door swinging open: Nora. Susan jabbed the up button. One elevator began a leisurely descent. Mustering surprise, Susan turned.

Nora looked alarmed, then resentful. She was Irene's daughter, all right. She muttered, "It's nothing. I'm fine. I was talking to my—Jesse, my ex."

Without thinking, Susan asked, "Was he unfaithful?"

"What's with you and Mom and Grandma? Why do you all assume that?"

Susan apologized. Nora's eyes were still narrowed. "Because of your grandfather, I guess."

"So he cheated on Grandma? That's why she left him? And moved in with us?"

"I think by then, it was more about starting a new life."

"By then she was old," Nora mused.

Four years older than Susan was now.

"Until then, they were happy?" Nora asked.

Susan let out a short laugh.

"I mean—things were different back then, but—" Nora's brow furrowed again. "Did she catch him cheating?"

"I don't think he tried hard to hide it."

"He cheated more than once?"

"All along, as far as I recall." Susan added, "She wasn't very pleasant, either."

"She was a revolutionary, right? So how could she stay for as long as she did? And why did she finally leave?"

Susan shrugged. As Winston sometimes clucked affectionately, she had no head for history. Nor for cause and effect—there, Ernesto was right.

The elevator doors opened. Susan felt too tired to step in. She sank onto a loveseat. Nora looked at her curiously, then sat beside her. They watched the doors close.

In a rush, Susan said, "Your grandfather wants to see your grandmother again. She doesn't know this yet, but he'll be waiting for her in Hong Kong."

"Let me get this straight," Nora said. "He cheated on her throughout their marriage, she hasn't spoken to him in twenty years, and now he wants to pop back into her life?"

Susan nodded.

"How romantic."

Susan heard an off note in Nora's sarcasm, a hint of buried feeling. "Maybe it is," she said. "Whatever they did to each other, however long they've been apart, they've never forgotten each other. Now she's eighty. He's eighty-six. And this will be their last chance."

"At what?"

"That's up to them."

Slowly, Nora said, "Kay told me he still carries her picture in his wallet."

"I didn't know that. I guess I'm not surprised."

"How will you tell her?" Nora asked.

"Actually, that's where you come in. If I tell her, she'll think I've been conspiring with him against her. Your mother doesn't want to deal with it, because she's afraid it'll ruin this trip. I have a feeling that if your grandmother hears it from you, she just might listen."

"Me? You want me to tell her?"

"Well, you and your sisters. I suspect you're her favorite." For all Susan knew, this could be true.

Nora seemed to accept it. "You think she'll agree to see him?"

"I think they're both too old to live with such bitterness."

"What if she can't forgive him?"

"At least you'll have given them this chance."

Nora was quiet.

The elevator doors opened again. Susan stood and entered. Nora followed. With a small wave of tenderness, Susan patted Nora's hand. It seemed an auntly gesture.

"Discuss it with your sisters. Come up with a plan. If anyone can make this happen, it's you."

Soberly, Nora nodded.

The strange thing was, Ba's plan now had a different ring—a valiant deed rather than an opportunistic scheme, an offering rather than a demand, dramatic rather than preposterous—and, yes, romantic.

It was sixty years since Ma had married Ba, twenty years since she'd left him. A love gone bad, a sea of bitterness: such an everyday thing. As ordinary as the tide, and perhaps as relentless. But tides turned, too.

11

Irene ladled congee into Kay's bowl, then her own. Nora was sitting beside Ma, out of her reach. Sophie had refused to get up for breakfast. So had Susan—not that Irene wanted to see her this morning.

"Today's our last day in Beijing," she said brightly. "Kay, you're all packed, right?"

Kay slurped her congee.

Irene remembered when her daughters used to gag when she tried to feed them congee. Goop, they called it.

George, the honeymooner from Toronto, asked Kay, "So you've been studying Mandarin here?"

Kay nodded. "And contemporary Chinese history and Chinese women's history."

Irene noted a round of impressed glances from around the table: an ABC who embraced her Chineseness, who didn't scorn the traditions, who felt such a pull to her mother country.

Ma said, "And tell about your work."

Now eyebrows rose as Kay started to ramble about prostitutes and personal ads.

Irene patted her arm. "So *nenggan*." She meant to evoke all the times she'd praised report cards and honor certificates with that phrase, one of the few in Chinese her daughters could never forget, but Kay stiffened.

"So *lihai*," Ma pronounced.

Kay ducked her head, looking pleased in spite of herself.

"Save the hookers." A murmur, sardonic, from Mr. Chu's son Byron.

Mr. Chu said, "The world's oldest profession, in one of the world's oldest civilizations. You thought you could eradicate it?"

Irene bridled.

Kay said, "I just thought I could help."

Pleasantly, George's wife, Joyce, said, "After such excitement, you must find this tour a little dull."

"Um—not really," Kay said.

Everyone laughed—partly out of relief at the change of subject.

"With five thousand years of history, China is an endless study."

Kay sounded a bit robotic, Irene noticed, but this elicited a round of approving nods.

George asked, "Were you always a China scholar?"

"No. I used to work for the Asian American Cultural Awareness Project in New York."

"Save the Asians," Byron murmured.

Kay kept her gaze even, only her cheeks burning a little brighter.

Mr. Chu asked, "And what's your plan now?"

"Probably law—public interest."

"Public interest? Is that another way to say your parents will pay your rent?" Mr. Chu chuckled, and now his son looked abashed.

Irene turned and said, "We'll fly home and figure it out together. You know, I—" She wanted to say, *I quit!* Like a victory. It seemed so many things could count as a victory for an American woman now—splurging on four-hundred-dollar heels, bed-hopping like a man, declaring *I quit!* There was Ma's stony face. "I might quit."

Kay exclaimed, "No! Really?"

"I could use a fresh start."

"Me too," Nora said.

Kay spun. "No! Really?"

Irene and her daughters stared, then laughed. Their laughter tumbled across the table, her daughters' laughter ringing of their childhood selves, tinklings only she—the one person who'd known them their entire lives—could hear, and the others shifted like intruders and began to leave.

"If I'd known, I would've planned a longer holiday for us," Irene said. "Maybe a resort after this."

Nora's face shut down. "I haven't quit yet. My bosses always beg me to stay." To Ma, she explained her plans in microfinance.

"That seems a cause worthy of you," Ma said. "When a woman has that fire inside, she must be vigilant to not let it die."

Solemnly, Nora and Kay nodded.

"Too late for me. I sacrificed my career for you girls long ago." Irene smiled hard.

Her daughters glanced at each other and began wiping their mouths, setting down spoons.

Irene followed them out and grabbed Kay's arm. "Are you packed or not?"

"I have one suitcase. So either way—" Kay stopped.

"We fly out first thing tomorrow." Irene fought to calm her voice. "I'm sure you've seen today's sights—the Forbidden City and Tiananmen Square. You go to your dorm and pack up. We'll pick you up tonight."

The arm slipped away. Her daughters disappeared. Irene stood alone in a hotel corridor.

That glimmer—had it gone? If she still had it in her sights, still felt it close at hand, maybe she could cope a little better with Kay's reluctance to leave or Ba hijacking her plan. So far, every one of her offerings had met with indifference, if not flat rejection. Even Nora's breakup had only widened their distance.

There was nothing to do but try to hold tighter.

• • •

Zi Jin Cheng: jin cheng, forbidden city; *zi,* violet, the color of the North Star, where the emperor of heaven was said to reign. Ever since it had opened to the public, just months after her family had fled, it was simply *Gu Gong,* Old Palace, as if it were like anything else the Communists had nearly razed and then reopened with a ticket booth. But it was like nothing else.

If Irene painted, she would have tried in vain to re-create these colors—true royal blue, the yellowest gold, and imperial red, stately and dark, not Communist red, primary, common.

The world's largest palace complex, the seat of imperial power for over five hundred years, with each placard noting at least three dates—construction, destruction, reconstruction—the Forbidden City had not escaped the Party touch: bare lightbulbs, broken English, discolored display cases. But what had survived dynastic coups and peasant revolutions could withstand any makeover.

Fragments of Tommy's narration and facts from the placards fused with knowledge Irene had always possessed. Eight hundred buildings symmetrically arrayed. A hall for every purpose—for banquets, for official exams, for meditation, for reading, for the empress to be served by eunuchs, for the emperor to practice abstinence before sacrificial rites. Nine thousand chambers designed to hold priceless treasure. She remembered school trips to the Taipei museum, viewing the trove secreted from here by the Nationalists and said to be rightfully theirs, along with the whole nation. Now she saw how it belonged here, in this compound that was indeed a city in itself, bound by an impassable wall and a riverlike moat: Only China could contain it all.

She saw, too, the sacrifice of ordinary lives permeating this magnificence. The orb hanging over the royal throne, designed to crush anyone who dared sit without sovereign power. The well where Cixi, the concubine turned empress, ordered any possible enemies drowned. The 250-ton marble sculpture, hauled from great distances by hundreds of thousands of men, mules, and horses; they waited for winter and slid the stone here by digging wells, drawing up water, pouring it ahead of them, and waiting for their path to freeze.

Everywhere, the marriage of form and function, of science and art. The majestic wall, shaped to be impossible to scale, the brick made of sticky rice and white lime, the cement of sticky rice and egg white. The grounds laid in crosswise layers that not only prevented assassins from tunneling into the inner court but resonated at a certain note with each footfall. The dragon heads on the eaves that spouted rain from their mouths, draining the roofs. Bronze urns that weighed four tons and held four tons of water each. In the face of such mortal genius, who needed to believe in an all-powerful Creator?

At the gift shop, Irene bought a coffee-table book and a set of glossy prints. She wished she could buy a little bronze in all its tarnish, one fragrant shard of sandalwood. Didn't she have a right? Part of her reached all the way here, some part that had been sitting lonely in America. Even though she didn't identify with the masses, even though the masses didn't seem to identify with her for a second—she didn't know whether it was her clothes, her carriage, the Mandarin she'd learned in Taiwan and, for over thirty years, used mostly in private with Bill, so that it had become not only outdated but coded—her Chineseness was intrinsic, innate. She couldn't help but feel it.

To Kay, the salient feature of China was suffering. Her efforts on behalf of this nation's downtrodden were noble, charitable, and misguided. She was only a visitor. A visitor to America would seek out the Empire State Building, the Statue of Liberty, the Grand Canyon, the Golden Gate Bridge. The essence of a country was in its highlights, not its lowest common denominator.

Irene trailed the tour group to lunch, then to a jade emporium the size of a truck stop. Jade in every shade of green, and purple and brown and white; jade bracelets and pendants, brooches and combs, statues and vases. How could so much jade be real? She uttered that idle remark to a salesman, mostly to hear her own voice, and as though to complete her mystification, he yanked a hair from his head. He whipped out a lighter, wrapped the hair around a bracelet, and held it to the flame.

"See?" he said.

She did not.

He explained that only the cooling property of real jade could keep the hair from burning.

"Oh," she said, and couldn't think what to say next.

Nora and Susan were leaning over a jewelry case with four shopgirls at the ready. Irene moved toward them. Whatever they liked, she'd buy it for them.

Their talk was hushed. They weren't looking at the jade at all.

"Has he tried to contact her before?"

"Not that I know of."

"Do you think she secretly wants to see him, too?"

"It's possible."

"What does he want to say to her, after all these years?" Nora caught sight of Irene.

Susan paled.

"How dare you." Irene's words were slow and thick, her tongue weighted.

"It just came up," Susan mumbled.

"Grandma has to decide for herself," Nora said. "You can't stand in their way."

"She decided twenty years ago."

And Irene had taken her in. Not Susan, whose phone number had changed once or twice a year back then. Not Lou, who'd invited Ma to America. "I'm a bachelor, sis," he'd said on the phone. "I've got a one-bedroom. Anyway, she wants to help raise your girls."

"People change their minds," Nora said.

"Not her."

"You don't know that."

Irene knew Ma's bitterness was bottomless. She knew Ba's inability to consider the feelings of another. She knew Susan's talent for complete detachment.

"You don't know them. You just want to take a stand against me." Her voice broke.

The shopgirls twittered and dispersed. Nora bit her lip and looked away. Cold stone and glass, fluorescent lights tingeing everyone's skin yellow-green. That falling sensation—Irene swayed, and caught herself on the display case.

A little wobbly, she walked past all the jade, past the bench where Ma and Sophie sat by the entrance—they glanced at her curiously, without sympathy—and outside. The sun was merciless. Tommy and the driver were lounging across the front seats of the bus. She knocked. They stared as though she had no business boarding, as though she hadn't paid for six passages.

The driver finally pulled the lever. She climbed the knee-high steps, clutching the railing, and sat toward the rear. She tried to feel the solidity of the seat, to stare straight ahead at the rows of headrests.

Last year, when Susan had called to report Ba's fall, Irene's whole body had seized up. Her father sprawled on his bathroom floor, cold tile against his skin, unable to reach the phone, no one to hear his cries. Family scattered far away, not knowing how long before you were found, before you were missed, before anyone thought to wonder.

She'd cried, "At his age, falls are fatal. It's the end. It's just a matter of time."

"Wasn't it already?" Susan said, before assuring her that she'd spoken to Ba's doctors, arranged for a few safety modifications to his apartment, sent a check to the woman who'd found him—a woman who called herself his goddaughter. They both knew what that meant.

No one deserved to die alone, no one—but the truth was, if any man was suited to it, if any man had treated others as if he was already fated to it, that was Ba. And if any woman could face such a fate without fear, that was Ma. Irene had lived a life in opposition to theirs, and for herself, she couldn't imagine a more terrifying end.

Certainly, Alzheimer's was tragic. These days, one new case every minute—her generation now the most likely victims. The loss of memory much less linear than once believed, but a relentless progression toward degeneration and death. Such parallel processes in the neurological and physiological systems that sometimes she couldn't help marveling at how much more neatly connected—even beautifully connected—was the disease than anyone's results.

In the cortex, the breakdown of vast numbers of nerve cells. A marked decrease in acetylcholine, a neurotransmitter of messages. A marked increase in beta amyloid, the peptide forming those brain plaques. The disabling of whole networks of cells. In the hippocampus, increasing vacuoles—mysterious voids within certain cells. Eventually, so much wasting away that empty spaces, literally, could be seen in the head.

Meanwhile, episodes of confusion, disbelief, rage. Loved ones transposed—a wife for a daughter, a daughter for a stranger. Moments of clarity, soon forgotten. Being doomed to unknowing repetition, reduced to infantile emotions and needs, becoming an impostor in your own life. The loss of simple words. The loss of rationality, the brain grappling for explanations for the inexplicable. Accusing others of theft—how else could so much have been lost? Always wandering—in many victims, incessant walking to the point of exhaustion. Forgetting your own diagnosis, your own forgetfulness, your own tragedy. Eventually, forgetting how to chew, how to defecate. Total dependency, perhaps a vegetative state, until death.

There was little humanity in this, and no dignity at all. But the suffering was unknowing. Nothing could hurt, because nothing was connected to remembrance or hope—not even loneliness. If you fell victim to Alzheimer's, you'd be the one departing. You wouldn't be the one abandoned, the one left alone.

Why shouldn't she quit? Her latest assignment at the pharmaceutical company was simply testing one drug candidate after another, testing perhaps a thousand in all, with little regard for gaining a better understanding of the underlying mechanisms. A few treatments had gone from her lab to early trials—one of them an advanced version of that promising compound she'd injected into her line of transgenic mice years ago. So far, all had failed.

In the last two decades, elsewhere in Alzheimer's research, there had been frenetic progress. The amyloid cascade hypothesis—that accumulation of beta amyloid initiates a series of events ultimately leading to neuronal dysfunction, neurodegeneration, dementia, and death—was now widely accepted. Just five years ago, the first bona fide, reproducible mouse model had finally been reported. Now dozens of promising treatments were in the pipeline. Yet no one had yet discovered the actual cause of those protein deposits. For the vast majority of cases, no one had found a definite genetic link. All the small discoveries might soon coalesce into a major breakthrough—even a revolutionary one—but perhaps not in her lifetime, and certainly not bearing her name.

Once, she'd loved holding the instruments of science, funnels and beakers, Petri dishes and pipettes, test tubes and syringes—all containers of life. Now they weren't much different from a spatula or a vacuum cleaner—all tools and gadgets. Once, she couldn't get enough of gazing into microscopes. The wonder of it: Give her this fixed field of view, one tiny round window, and she could see infinitely. These days, she peered down and saw a black tunnel.

If she quit, few would object; few would notice. But then what? Like those poor mice in the pool, she only knew to keep going, or go under.

Back to where they'd started that morning, but across the street, and from this vantage, Irene saw that the entire zone was designed to make a person feel as easily squashed as an ant. The street wider than a highway. The interminable, impenetrable façade of the Forbidden City. The crowds on Tiananmen Gate straining for a view around shotgun-wielding guards, stiff as toy soldiers, above the portrait of Mao, the famous wart on his chin the size of her own face. The square itself, concrete and more concrete—save two long strips of perfect grass, off-limits—spiked with poles so tall she had to lean back to see the flags. Eleven years ago, she'd cried as she watched the demonstrators being mowed down. But no one should have been surprised. Tiananmen Square was paved for tanks to roll between the monuments and museums.

Their group joined the line to enter the mausoleum where Mao's body was embalmed in wax. Apparently, Tommy had no authority to bypass it. This line was serious, single-file, and slowly moving, moving; guards shouted at anyone who stood still long enough to allow a gap. Irene focused on taking even steps, in time with the feet in front of hers.

Inside the tomb, the stepping became mincing, then inching. The distance between feet disappeared, bodies collided. Laid out in a crystal coffin was something that looked like Mao, also like a wax model of Mao. Irene craned and stared like everyone else, swiveled to prolong the viewing, turned back again for one last glimpse as they got pushed out.

The others in her tour group looked politely solemn, a bit thoughtful, a touch ironic, mostly blank. They were all exiles or the children of exiles, prospering well enough under capitalism and democracy to pause during a luxury tour to view the Chairman's preserved corpse. Meanwhile, the others in line were nearly all members of Chinese tour groups, and wide-eyed—with fear, excitement, awe? Irene had no idea.

"That's pretty weird," Sophie said.

Nora asked, "Is that the custom here?"

Suddenly worried that they were thinking of their father's funeral, Irene fumbled for something she could say with authority.

Loudly, Ma said, "Some say Mao's body rotted long ago, and they had to keep it secret. So in there is just wax. No dead body."

Heads all along the line spun, scandalized eyes seeking the source of that voice.

"Ma," Irene hissed. "Hush. Not here."

Ma waved her off. "When you die, your body needs to rest. To do that to someone's body, even his—" She shook her head. "I would never want it."

"Don't worry. No one wants to embalm your body." Susan sneaked a rare grin.

Nora and Sophie stared, then laughed.

Irene turned before she could see Ma's expression.

Outside, a crowd had gathered around the main flagpole to watch soldiers lowering the flag to the tune of the national anthem, in time with the setting sun. Irene slid her gaze up the pole, past the flag, and saw a bird on fire—a phoenix—a kite. More: a soaring rocket ship, a dancing butterfly, a leaping lion. Their strings blended into the fading sky.

"Look," she said, lifting her arm to point, but her daughters, her sister, her mother were already looking upward. She wasn't sure what they saw, but she let her arm drop.

At first sight, Kay's dorm was merely drab, a block of concrete in a plot of dirt. In the lobby, young people—a few Africans, more whites, many Asians—sprawled on mangy chairs, emitting streams of cigarette smoke and language—all sorts of language, including multiple strains of peculiar Chinese. The hallway was dingy, its entire length lit by one bare bulb. The air was hot and dank, then suddenly putrid.

"Ugh!" Nora and Sophie held their noses.

"That's the bathroom," Kay said.

Irene ducked in for a survey. Two stalls of splintering wood, rusty pipes for showerheads, murky puddles all over the floor. Stained, chipped sinks with no hot water taps. Four squatting toilets, three of them clogged. Lidless trash cans overflowing with used toilet paper, used sanitary napkins, visible human waste.

In Kay's room, the light flickered and flickered before dousing everything in an unsavory glare. The room was dirty, the kind of dirtiness that never washed away, that was in the construction itself. Nothing was joined right—the ceiling to the walls to the floor. It wasn't solid, wasn't whole, didn't protect its inhabitants from the elements.

"This is my side. That's Tomoko's."

Tomoko's half had flowered cloths, checkered sheets, framed pictures of a rotund couple who must have been her parents. Kay's half was flagrant in its wretchedness. The floor, bare rough cement. The wall, jaundiced and cracked. Her bed, a wooden plank.

Two small brown cockroaches crept, unhurried, underneath. A fat fly buzzed and banged itself against the one grimy window. Irene went to shoo it out. The window had no screen. The panes were glued to the frame with brown crud that smeared her hand.

She couldn't help saying, "You wanted to stay on here?"

"The local students live eight to a room," Kay said. "They consider this luxurious."

"All the international students stay here?" Nora asked.

"The scholarship ones. There's a hotel dorm if you pay extra."

"I would have paid extra for you," Irene said.

"I didn't want to."

Sophie said, "Well, lots of people live worse than this. Even in America."

"They don't have a choice," Nora said.

Irene gave her a grateful look. Nora didn't notice.

"For once, I'm not in the mood to debate," Kay said. "Let's get out of here."

Irene nodded. She'd sooner lick the floor than delay that.

A thin girl with a cherubic face appeared in the doorway, looking petrified at the sight of them. Blushing and bowing, she squeaked, "*Duibuqi,* pardon me."

Behind her stood a tanned, muscular young man wearing a baseball cap. Seeing Irene, he quickly took it off and smoothed his hair.

Kay was locking her suitcase, back to the door. "Hi, Tomoko. We're just—Rick."

"Uh, hi." The young man seemed caught between introducing himself to Irene and answering Kay's stare.

Tomoko ducked her head and tiptoed past. "*Duibuqi*, pardon me." She kept her head down as she retrieved a book from her desk.

"Bye, Tomoko," Kay said briskly. "Good luck with your thesis."

Tomoko bowed a few more times, then scurried away.

Rick smiled at Irene. "The two roommates couldn't be more opposite, huh?"

Politely, Irene smiled back. She didn't know if this boy was part of the pull for Kay to stay, but if he was fond of her, he could follow her to New York.

Kay motioned to him. "I'll walk you out."

Their voices from the hallway were as clear as if they'd stayed in the room.

"I've been looking for you everywhere. I've been trailing goddamn Tomoko. I took that consulting job. I'm staying."

"Oh. Well, we leave tomorrow."

"So that's it?"

"I don't know."

"You weren't going to say good-bye?"

No response from Kay.

"How can you act so indifferent?"

"I have to go. We'll talk later."

Kay returned expressionless. No one asked about the hapless Rick. Instead, Sophie bowed and squeaked, "*Duibuqi*, pardon me." Irene's three daughters laughed.

"That's not nice," Irene said.

"I know, but she drives me nuts," Kay said. "At first I thought it was the language barrier, but it turns out she's the worst stereotype of Asian females—meek and voiceless."

Nora and Sophie nodded.

"She's Japanese," Irene said. "If she was raised that way—"

"The other Japanese girls aren't like her."

"Well, if that's her nature—"

"Mom, imagine if that was our nature. Wouldn't you have raised us to speak up?"

Yes, because they were her daughters, not because they were Asian females.

Irene didn't want to debate, either. She just hadn't expected all three daughters to be so contemptuous. American at birth, they believed they had a common cause with that poor girl, and saw her as a traitor.

She was tempted to blame Ma, but perhaps she shouldn't have raised them to feel quite so special. It became a barrier between them and others. It became a burden. Who could live up to their standards? Certainly not her. Probably not themselves.

Night had fallen, allowing the shabbiness of the campus grounds to recede into gentle shadow. Irene thought to tell her daughters about the ashes she'd packed, but the moment felt so tenuous, just bearing their togetherness.

How would she start? *Girls, guess what I brought?* And how to explain? How she'd searched the house for a suitable container, and finally filched a glass vial from the lab. How she'd opened the urn, and realized a funnel would have been handy, too. How she'd found a baby spoon all three daughters had used, and scooped five tiny heaps. How she'd wrapped the vial in a scarf Bill had bought her years ago, and tucked it in the innermost pocket of her suitcase.

How she harbored a notion that she and her daughters would recognize a proper resting place, scatter this portion of Bill's ashes, and feel the haunting become remembering. And then they'd go home as a family again.

On either side of the path, a mysterious rustling and murmuring. Irene squinted: human silhouettes melding. On every bench, a couple. Embracing, kissing, more. She thought she saw one pair splayed on the dirt.

Kay noticed her staring. "That's the Chinese students. When the sun goes down, they make out everywhere."

"When I was in school, if you were spotted walking with a boy, you'd get reported."

And those regulations had enforced what she already knew: a bad love corrupted your life. The authorities were protecting not only your chastity, but your heart, your time, your energies. Romance was no game. When you were ready, you channeled it into your own home, your own family—if you were lucky, into permanence. Otherwise, you'd probably suffer for nothing.

"This must be the American influence. Everything—*suibian*." When was the last time Irene had needed to fill in a blank with Chinese? Now she remembered the translation. *Suibian*: going with the flow, easy, anything goes.

Kay said, "Societies evolve constantly, while the homeland, for immigrants, is a fixed memory."

"But you only see—what you see."

"I'm no expert. I just want—I wish I could—" Kay shook her head as if shaking off water or dust. "I just don't feel ready to leave."

Irene wanted to somehow comfort her daughter, to explain that she couldn't always control her fate, though she could convince herself the course of her life was chosen. But she only hailed a taxi and made sure Kay's suitcase was securely loaded into the trunk.

12

In bed, Nora cupped her breasts. They felt inflamed, a little tingly. Through her thin silk nightgown, the hotel sheets were coarse. In the dark, she rummaged through her suitcase for something cozy, and came upon the balled-up jeans with a lump in the pocket. She hit the light and grabbed one of Kay's T-shirts.

Kay stirred. "Jet lag?"

After a minute, Nora told her the news about their grandfather. She'd wanted to sort it out for herself first, but she didn't know what to sort.

Kay bolted upright. "It's like he read my mind. How could that have been good-bye?"

"What?"

"When I saw him in Taiwan."

Carefully, Nora said, "According to Aunt Susan, he wants to see Grandma. It'll be their first chance to see each other in twenty years, and it might be their last. And they have a lot of unfinished business. He was unfaithful, and she's never forgiven him."

"Still, he must want to reconnect with all of us."

Kay didn't understand that hurt, how it blotted out everything else, and

Nora couldn't spell it out for her. She'd told Kay the same reason for her own breakup that she'd told her mother—her aversion to marriage and children.

Kay dug into her backpack. "Look at the card he sent me."

Nora opened the card, red with gold embossing. "I can't read this."

"Just look at how fragile and beautiful those characters are. Think how long they took him to write."

To Nora, they just looked wobbly. "You carry this around?"

"I keep meaning to write back, but I don't know what to say."

"Well, you hardly know him."

"He's our grandfather. I'm the only one who seems to care." Kay grabbed the card and slid it into her backpack again.

Nora decided to change the subject. "How do you feel about leaving Beijing?"

Kay shrugged.

"Seems you and that guy Rick became more than friends."

Kay nodded, a little sheepishly. "It wasn't serious."

"He seemed serious about you."

Kay blurted, "I hooked up with my other guy friends, too."

Nora stared. "Rick didn't mind?"

"He didn't know."

"So you were cheating?"

"Like I said, we weren't serious."

Could Kay really be so impervious? Suddenly Rick's chiseled, genial face seemed tragic.

Nora asked, "Do you remember Grandma lecturing us, when we were little, about the kind of women we should be?"

"I wish I did. What did she say?"

In the face of Kay's eagerness, Nora found herself mumbling, "Strong or weak, great or ordinary—that kind of thing. That's all I remember."

"I wish I remembered," Kay said again. "So when should we tell her about Grandpa?"

Nora said she needed a few days to form a plan. After all, only she truly understood the question her grandmother would confront: If she agreed to see him, if she finally forgave him, what kind of woman would she be then?

Nora turned out the light. In an instant, Kay was snoring.

Two nights ago, Nora hadn't been able to stop herself from stepping into a phone booth in the hotel lobby and dialing Jesse's cell phone.

"Where are you?" he'd asked.

"Where are you?" It was quiet where he was—inside somewhere, someone's apartment. That last night, she'd let him think she had someone calling her over, someone who wasn't her mother. "Never mind. It's not my concern anymore."

"I'm not with her, and I won't be, if that's what you're asking."

"So she really was just a fling."

"Less than that."

"So you threw away our future for less than a fling."

"Nora," he said. "You called me."

Sourness spread on her tongue. "That last night—I shouldn't have called. You shouldn't have come."

"I was glad you called. I wanted to come. I wanted to ask for forgiveness."

"What does that mean? One last fuck?"

"No. It means for you to see that I'm sorry, I'm really truly sorry, and I wish I could make it up to you, but maybe there's no way. For you to see that I never meant to hurt you, even though that is what I did. And maybe—for you to see where I was coming from. The truth is, I never imagined cheating until you treated me as if I was already doing it."

"So you decided you might as well do it."

"That's not what I'm saying. I was just so tired of trying to prove myself to you."

"And that sweet girl happened to be waiting."

"She is a sweet girl—but that's all. You're the one I wanted to marry. To love unconditionally. You made it clear you weren't ready."

And how could she ever be? You could love your family unconditionally—your parents, your sisters, even a grandmother you hardly knew. Not the man who held your heart in his fallible hands.

She burst out, "What kind of guy cheats because his fiancée isn't ready to set the date? And then asks for forgiveness with one last fuck? And you didn't—we didn't—you knew I'm off the pill."

There was a pause. "You are? How would I know?"

"I threw them out in front of you."

"There was a lot thrown out that night. I guess I didn't think about it."

What was her excuse?

"Are you worried?" he asked.

"I'm fine. It's not your concern anymore."

"Nora, if anything happens, we'll deal with it."

Without warning, a sob escaped. She slammed down the phone. She didn't know what he felt. All she hit was plastic against metal, setting off shockwaves from her hand to her own chest.

Another flight, another airport. Another bus to another hotel. She and Grandma sharing a room this time—her aunt's suggestion—and back on the bus again. Tommy passed the microphone to their new local guide, a young man who yapped incessantly in Cantonese, though even Nora could tell his accent was off.

Her mother translated snippets. "The saying goes, 'The sky has heaven, the earth has Suzhou and Hangzhou.' They're sister cities, two of the world's most beautiful."

The streets outside looked like every other Chinese street Nora had seen so far, hectic and gritty and gray.

The local guide glanced at Nora and said what sounded like a punch line. Her mother cast an apprehensive glance at her and translated. "Suzhou is famed for its handsome men, Hangzhou for its pretty women."

"What's the joke?"

"Oh, he said you could shop for a husband here." Now her mother's glance was sympathetic.

Nora turned back to the window. In New York, twenty-eight was a prime age to be single—single and fabulous, as they said. It hadn't occurred to her that she might be taken for an old maid tagging along on a family vacation.

The Humble Administrator's Garden: Nora read enough of the placard by the gates to gather it was built by a corrupt government official who, retired and remorseful, devoted the rest of his life to this garden. She entered the garden and was enfolded in green. Weeping willows hanging their heads, the longest of their feathery tresses skimming the ponds, dusting the ground. Pools of opaque emerald water, with stone sculptures that seemed to float in the center, and lily pads so large and velvety they looked like fairy-tale creations, home to tiny pixies and talking toads.

Overhead, Nora suddenly heard birds. Under her feet, the paths were paved in patterns, every pebble arranged by color and size. Slipping away from the group, she followed one diamond-checkered path and found the pebbles forming leaves, flowers, a pair of cranes.

Her wandering led to more wandering. Paths branched off to crown hills, drop into water, loop pavilions, reconnect by bridge. She climbed stone steps that were steep and roughly carved, as if designed to make a girl reach for a guy's hand, and sat in a shady nook where sunlight flickered in the leafy shadows like candlelight, on a bench made of an irregular slab balanced on two wedges of stone—Jesse would have admired it.

Below her, in every direction, were local couples strolling arm in arm, canoeing the canals that latticed the garden, taking pictures of each other, asking other couples to take pictures of them together. Most looked younger than her, but gave off a thoroughly settled air. They seemed to feel no need to prove themselves above such conventions—such romance.

Making her way down the steps, Nora spotted a sign: the Pavilion for Listening to Pain. She followed the arrow, circling twice until she found it, a small empty chamber, the walls austere and gray, the air cool and still. Inside, the sounds of birds chirping, leaves rustling, water gurgling were subtly amplified and fine-tuned.

Listening to pain. A space to step inside and attend to it, before stepping out again into a world full of life. She wondered if that was the original purpose of a temple, a church, a mosque.

Religion was never discussed in her family. Worship of a holy father, an afterlife in heaven or hell—such ideas simply had no place in their house. Only in this life, on this earth, in their time and place and society, could they strive to transcend limitations. That was always her reason for being, wherever it came from, and in a way, her father's death had seemed like the ultimate test.

That morning, when she'd arrived at the house, her mother was a small, silent, rigid heap on the couch. By the time her sisters started sobbing, Nora had taken charge.

First, the body. She proceeded toward it in inexorable stages—the nicely paved interstate, the nearly empty parking lot of the morgue, the doors revolving her into cold sanitized air, the stark echoing corridor, the cot sliding out like a drawer to present the body bag, white and just translucent enough to reveal the outlines of a body. The zipper unzipping, steady and ruthless—in that antiseptic chamber, the sound of those tiny metal teeth unclenching was like something ripping. A palm-sized bald patch toward the back of her father's head, she'd never seen it so clearly, shiny and clean and intact—the surrounding hair still more black than white, matted flat—his face a jagged mess, like he'd been smashed to pieces, then hastily stuck back in place.

The closed casket was, it turned out, the only obvious decision. She had no precedent. If any relatives had died in her lifetime, she didn't know of them. Her mother was no help—frozen into a mute, defensive crouch, as if by speaking again, she'd risk admitting guilt. And Nora felt the guilt. She felt it, even though she was utterly blameless.

When her mother announced, "Your dad is leaving us," she'd kept her composure. When her father called and said, "I guess your mother already got to you," she'd matched his determinedly lighthearted tone, chatting about Maine, enthusing about the opportunity. The day he left, she'd driven to the house as if it were a holiday, and when he seemed regretful, almost as though he didn't want to leave, she'd given him a reassuring hug, and told him she'd take care of everyone. She'd held her tongue when her mother said, "Good riddance." At home, when Jesse said, "Whoa. That's harsh," she'd finally snapped, "What's she supposed to do? Beg him not to leave?" Jesse just held her. It had been a hard day, and she was allowed some kind of emotion.

Planning the funeral, she'd wished for an organized religion for the first time in her life. There were many guides, but nothing that fit her family. She found one that outlined Chinese traditions—for funerals, weddings, birthdays, "and other customs"—but it was written by a white woman. She found another that circumvented God, but insisted on humanism. She found herself left with green funerals, do-it-yourself funerals, and one called "I Died Laughing," which purported to bring a sense of humor into the proceedings. In the end, she'd called the funeral home Jesse's family had used for generations.

She'd given clear, bare instructions—simple and elegant; no embalming, no viewing, no Bible reading—not quite realizing what a brief service this would make. The director suggested including a photo slideshow, but it wasn't until she was sifting through all the albums and boxes at the house that she realized how few showed her father, in focus and centered. Her mother always took the pictures, the lens trained on her three daughters. Nora compiled what she could, including her parents' wedding photo, though that felt like a lie. The director eased her through the rest: burial or cremation, urn, flowers, even the eulogy.

Where to keep the urn—that was the only place, in the end, she'd gotten stuck. Her mother finally roused herself to answer, "Here, in the house." Nora helped her sisters place the urn on a shelf, and then she left. She'd done everything she could. It would never feel like enough.

She gathered herself and rubbed a slight chill from her arms. She had no idea how long she'd stood in this chamber. Stepping out, she spotted another sign by the door: the Pavilion for Listening to Rain. She went to reread the first sign. It looked etched by hand, a hand that had missed one tiny line.

Just as she rejoined her group, a van pulled up beside them, and out stepped a bride, a groom, another bride, another groom—four Chinese couples in all, the brides in poufy white dresses and pasty makeup, the grooms with lacquered hair and tuxedos pinned to fit. Last came a frenetic photographer, who directed the first couple through a variety of poses under a willow tree: the groom on one knee with the bride gazing tenderly down, the bride sitting amid the white gauze of her skirt and the groom standing robustly behind, the two stiffly kissing, each curving an arm overhead to form a heart. Then the photographer waved for the next couple to take their place. Hastening out of the way, the first bride tripped on her hoop skirt, revealing scuffed black sandals buckled over nylon socks.

The rest of Nora's tour group was staring, too, their expressions quizzical, bemused. Nora didn't need to scan the faces of her own family to know that they wore a cast of contempt.

Love and marriage had always seemed not only beneath her, but somehow dangerous. She'd never been able to imagine her engagement being, in her family, a joyous occasion to celebrate. At best, it might've felt like an unavoidable rite of passage, like getting her period.

To Mom, Kay said, "*This* you can blame on the American influence."

Sophie said, "Sure makes me want to shop for a husband here." She glanced at Nora, and Nora realized her baby sister meant to offer a little commiseration.

Tommy was urging everyone to head back to the bus. Nora fell into step with Sophie, behind her mother and Mr. Chu.

"Three daughters, eh?" Mr. Chu said. "Now people say daughters are better than sons—they stay closer to home."

As if having three daughters clearly called for consolation.

"I wish that were true." Her mother gave a rueful laugh.

"The oldest is not married yet?" Apparently he was indifferent to their proximity.

"She's very independent. A big success on Wall Street."

"Ah. Now if the middle one were more business-oriented, she could've been a valuable corporate liaison in Beijing."

"Well, as she said, her focus is social justice."

"Your third is much younger than the others."

"Yes."

"She doesn't look like the others, either. She's more—well, here they say prosperous." Mr. Chu chuckled.

Sophie's face stiffened. Nora stopped to adjust her sandal, letting her mother and Mr. Chu get farther ahead.

She said, "He didn't mean—"

"I know what he meant."

"He's an idiot." Nora wanted to tell Sophie how beautiful she was, but that seemed demeaning, too. For a few minutes, they walked in silence. At last she said, "I have some news. Our grandfather—Mom's dad, in Taiwan—"

"He wants to see Grandma," Sophie said. "I heard Mom and Aunt Susan arguing."

"Oh." Nora was a little thrown. "Well, it's up to the three of us to make it happen. How do you think we should tell her?"

Sophie shrugged. "Just tell her."

"But we can't just say, 'Grandma, remember the husband you haven't seen in twenty years, the one who cheated on you throughout your marriage? Well, surprise!' "

"If you don't care what I think, don't ask."

Nora sighed.

They'd reached the bus, where Tommy and the local guide flanked the doors, waving them aboard. The next stop was a silk factory, where Tommy presented their group to the factory guide with the air of a cat bearing freshly caught prey.

"Since when is this a must-see?" Kay said. "What's next, a mall?"

Yet Nora found herself mesmerized. In one room, workers extracted brown bugs from cocoons of white fluff and dropped the bugs into one pail, the fluff into another. In the next room, each ball of fluff was stretched thin and flat. In the third room, workers stood and pulled each corner of the fluff until it became a misty veil covering a rectangular table. They added another veil, and another, until there was a snowy pile, and then they wrapped the pile in cloth and sewed it up. Nora wasn't sure what it was, but she wanted one.

Her mother's eyes reflected her own desire. "Silk quilts. A local specialty."

In an instant, Tommy, the local guide, and the factory guide surrounded them, touting the powers of silk quilts: soft as clouds, light as air, warm in winter yet comfortable in spring.

"These prices are ridiculous," Kay said. "Someone's getting a fat cut."

"It is a matter of quality," Tommy said coldly, and the factory guide launched into an ardent discourse on silkworm species and disinfectant, thread count and weight.

Nora and her mother were sold. Desire was contagious: Grandma agreed that a silk quilt would suit California weather, which perked up Sophie, and then Joyce and Mrs. Wong began stroking the quilts, too. The industry banked, of course, on the fear of missing out, that chronic fear gnawing at travelers—but Nora didn't want to miss out on this. Eagerly, she stood in line with the others to hand over credit cards and receive their quilts in vacuum-sealed carrying cases.

Then Tommy led them to an auditorium and said, "A fashion show for you," as if to reward them for their compliance. Set to a step-aerobics beat, the fashion show consisted of a dozen silk *qipao*, identical except in skirt and sleeve length, modeled by long pale girls who awkwardly minced, batted eyelids, attempted coy smiles.

Nora found herself intensely discomfited by this seemingly concerted effort to conform to stereotypical depictions of Asian women, and how the models reminded her of herself, in a basic, bodily way—not only their hair and eyes, but the shape of their upper arms, their knees, even their calves. Unnamed traits that she shared with her sisters and her mother, even her aunt and her grandmother, that she rarely saw honestly depicted.

There was a strange heaviness in her middle. She went to find the bathroom. In the corridor, she nearly collided with Sophie. An odor—foul, faint, sour. She felt a ripple of nausea before she realized the odor itself was of vomit.

"Did you throw up?"

Sophie jumped. "What do you mean?"

"I smell vomit. Are you sick?"

"No. I don't smell anything."

Nora sniffed again. The smell was on Sophie. Sophie sidestepped her and ducked into the gift shop.

Maybe the smell wasn't vomit. Maybe it wasn't on Sophie. Maybe she had thrown up, but didn't want to admit it.

Mr. Chu's comment, Sophie's face stiffening. Sophie's fit at the Hong Kong market. Sophie in the bathroom, at every stop. Nora's baby sister, bulimic?

In the bathroom, Nora had to hold her breath and stare at a fixed spot on the wall.

Sophie pushing a finger down her throat, acid burning her insides, mouth over this toilet—a squatting toilet, actually a gutter—for the sake of losing weight?

In the gift shop, Nora found her hunkered in a corner. Seeing Nora, she looked panicked.

As casually as she could, Nora asked, "Are you sure you're okay?"

"Yes."

"Are you enjoying the sightseeing?"

"Not really."

"We could bail on the rest of the day. Maybe hang out at the hotel?"

Sophie nodded as if she suspected a trap but couldn't resist the bait.

Nora found her mother and pled a stomachache for them both: Probably the same dish at lunch—yes, that fish—no, no doctor—yes, of course they could manage, they'd simply . . . And Nora realized she didn't know where they were, the name or address of the hotel, how to get a cab. She'd moved hundreds of millions in bonds and didn't have a cent of local currency. Like an infant, she blinked.

Her mother went to Tommy, who conferred with the local guide, who turned to the factory guide, who convened his staff. By now, everyone had overheard. Mrs. Wong proffered a vial of pills from her purse. Mr. Chu pointed out the bathroom down the corridor. A worker offered toilet paper.

"What kind of stomachache?" Grandma asked. "Gas, constipation, diarrhea?"

"I ate that fish, and if I'm not running for the bathroom—" Kay noticed Byron standing by, smirking, and she blushed.

At last a taxi was called, Nora accepted a wad of cash from her mother, and she and Sophie flopped into the backseat.

It was her duty to try to help Sophie, but there was no way to raise the subject without forcing a confession of failure, of weakness. She supposed she could offer a confession of her own in exchange: for Sophie's eating disorder, the real reason she'd kicked Jesse out? Would that be an equal trade? Would she have to throw in the fact that she'd let him back in?

She couldn't help wondering what her grandmother would think of such a modern, self-inflicted, feminine condition as bulimia. But being a teenager was riddled with insecurity, and so was being single again. In the last weeks, Nora had bought new heels, a sexier suit, her first jar of eye cream. She wasn't shopping for a husband. She was terrified that she'd driven Jesse out the way her mother had driven out her father. That she'd exhausted the love of the one man who loved her as much as her mother did, loved her more than any other man ever would, now that her father was gone.

The cab ride elapsed in silence. At the hotel, she and Sophie ducked into their separate rooms.

Nora pulled the balled-up jeans from her suitcase and reached into the pocket. If she'd worn the ring instead of stashing it in a drawer, if she'd simply set a wedding date, if she hadn't been haunted by those dreams, wouldn't she and Jesse still have a future?

They'd met her second year in trading, when she signed up for an evening pottery class; she wanted a counterpoint. Jesse was the instructor. He was lanky, dirty blond, undeniably handsome—but his hands were what kept her attention. His long, muscular fingers, with knobby knuckles a tinge darker than the rest of his skin; his palms, wide and deeply creased; his nails, stubby and rosy under a crust of clay. The whole class, all twelve women, tried to get near him, but he wasn't interested in them or their handiwork. At the start of each session, he'd demonstrate wedging, pinching, coiling, then leave them to fashion pretty vessels, while he set to making things that were strange and useless and stunning. Over her slimy mound of clay, Nora watched him.

Clay was magical in his hands, like leather, or jagged metal, or blown glass. His sculptures seemed on the verge of action—about to spring or melt or fly apart. She began staying for the open studio hour, smoothing cracks and bumps, checking for symmetry from every angle. He'd look at his latest piece, just look, as if waiting for it to move or talk. Sometimes he'd slice it up, mush the chunks together, and make something new by the end of the hour. Across the oven-warm studio, they began to exchange bits of talk like scraps of clay, randomly broken, intimately shaped, at turns promising, at turns hopeless.

After the last session, as she was trying to perfect her last vase, he laid a freshly washed hand on hers and said, "Let it be. Let's get a beer."

Before him, she'd quickly discarded every boyfriend—one who admitted a preference for Asian girls and remarked, not with pleasure, how "feisty" she was; one who said that, as a future doctor, he needed a wife who'd make their house his haven; one who always considered his sexual needs paramount; others with subtler flaws that were no less fatal.

After just a few months, she asked Jesse to move in.

She'd spotted her house when she visited an old friend in Brooklyn one weekend: a brownstone three stories high and sixteen feet wide, newly renovated, described by the broker as "cozy and charming." Her friend said, "That means tiny and weird." But for her, it *was* cozy and charming. The other bankers were buying up generic glass boxes in Midtown for millions. She bought a whole house: two bedrooms, a living room and parlor, kitchen and dining room, even a little garden. All clean, open space, completely uncluttered. Prewar moldings, restored parquet floors, pressed-tin ceilings—and an ultramodern kitchen, stainless steel appliances, sparkling bathrooms. It seemed, in almost every way, the opposite of her parents' house, that contemporary, characterless brick box crammed with mementos of her and her sisters—pictures, awards, outgrown shoes, plain junk. Not least, she admired her new neighborhood—how *neighborhoody* it was, whereas her parents' house might as well have sat in the suburbs, with lawns and stoops and sidewalks for show.

But once she moved in, she found she couldn't quite join the neighborhood, not by herself. She tried to take strolls but found herself walking too fast. She brought the Sunday paper to coffee shops but couldn't blend into the contemplative ranks. And the locksmith, the cable guy, the alarm system guy, the boiler guy, the mailman, all seemed to think it unseemly that she had this house to herself. At work she was used to being, as they said, the babe among big swinging dicks—but in a context that garnered kudos, not contempt. If she had to prove anything here, it was that she wasn't an overprivileged bitch.

Then Jesse moved in with a few boxes, and at once, her house became their home. He befriended the servicemen, raked and hammered, lifted and swept, kept her in bed through the weekends, held her hand as they strolled and kissed. He infected her with a languor that finally enabled her to feel the neighborhood's embrace.

And she gave him direction—anyway, she tried. She encouraged him to devote himself to his sculpture, at least for a while, but he scoffed at an MFA, of pursuing it as a career. He derided his father's offers to put him through law school. After some talk of teaching disadvantaged kids, he applied for a job at his own alma mater. The truth was, she gave a legitimacy to his lack of ambition. His vocation was to be supportive of her. They'd be different.

She slid on the ring. There was some comfort in its chunky weight, its solid old shine, even its fustiness.

Could she ever get back to that moment when she said, *Take my hand*? When tying her life to his seemed the safest thing to do—the only safe thing in the world? If she took him back, couldn't they make a fresh start? But what kind of woman would she be then? For as long as she could remember, she'd lived her life as an unending test—her grades, her major, her career, her dates, her father's death. And Jesse's betrayal had seemed to wreck everything she'd built, to blot out her very identity.

She pulled off the ring, pushed it back in her jeans pocket, and stuffed the jeans into her suitcase again. Beside it sat her grandmother's suitcase, a frayed hem peeping through the zipper. For all her revolutionary work, for all her talk of fire and vigilance, Grandma had endured her husband's unrepentant womanizing for decades. So what kind of woman was she?

Nora lifted the lid of her grandmother's suitcase. Wrinkle-free synthetics. Lotions and pills. Taupe trouser socks. Those thick-strapped bras, those baggy panties.

She probed deeper—for what? Even if she found a lifelong diary, she wouldn't be able to read it.

At the bottom, a cold metal thing. She pulled it out—a small tarnished silver case. She opened the clasp.

An old picture, black-and-white, scalloped edges. A little boy with plump cheeks and a large head, lightly fuzzed. He wore shorts and a long-sleeved shirt buttoned all the way up, the collar indenting his soft neck. His fingers fumbled at the buttons, and he seemed to be glancing at his own little legs, his brow crinkled, as if worrying whether they'd hold.

It had to be her grandfather. Nora had never seen a picture of him before, yet somehow she recognized this boy, and knew he was family. Strange that her grandmother would choose to remember him as this little boy, not much more than a toddler, defenseless and harmless. But Nora herself carried an engagement ring she'd loathed, that had never felt like her own—and now seemed to evoke something more enduring than Jesse's betrayal or her fury.

Her grandmother and her grandfather were nearing the end of their lives, both alone, both haunted. Her grandmother had transported this picture of him from China to America and back—unaware that he, with her picture in his pocket, would soon embark on his own long-awaited journey, to see her again. They still missed each other, still loved each other—what else could explain this pull across so much time and distance? And if she agreed to see him, if she finally forgave him—after all these years, but not too late, not yet—perhaps that could be an act of strength, not weakness.

Nora closed the frame and tucked it back inside her grandmother's suitcase.

13

She was not bulimic. She knew how that sounded. People—girls especially—couldn't deny anything anymore. *I'm fine. Nothing's wrong. I'm not bulimic.* The truth sounded just like a lie.

Sometimes she ate until it hurt, to fill the pit inside, to smother that gnawing—but who didn't? And sometimes she threw it all up. But the official definition was twice a week for three months. She only did it when she felt like it. A binge/purge here, a binge/purge there. Or a week straight and then not for a month. She was still getting her period, she wasn't losing her hair—she was hardly even losing weight.

She wasn't like those girls on talk shows, or the half-dozen at school who'd shriveled to seventy pounds, whose cave-eyes glowed when people called them sick or emaciated, and she didn't want to be—though she admired their willpower, and their kind of glamour, the same kind as a suicidal painter's. She just wanted to be thinner.

The way people analyzed it, clucked about it, shook their heads, wrung their hands, you'd think an eating disorder was an outrageous travesty, a catastrophic disease. In fact it was rational. Maybe not reasonable, but rational. Society mandates skinny. And consumption, and self-improvement. So here's a way, in theory, to have it all. Eat your cake and fit in your jeans, too. Don't lose control, and it's called watching your weight. How was that a disease? Alcoholism, depression, ADD—okay. Even seventy-pound anorexia. Not whatever she had. She didn't *have* it. She did it. When she felt like it.

So far, on this tour, she'd purged every day. There wasn't much to binge on, but purging was almost easy. The hotel bathrooms were more soundproof than the bathroom at home. The squatters were slippery, with puddles and smears everywhere, but she managed. At the silk factory today, there'd been no toilets at all, only a gutter, but there was a sink with no stopper, just a hole, the open mouth of the pipe. No splash-back, and with her stomach nearly empty, the stink actually came in handy.

Privacy was the only real challenge—in her family, on this tour, in this country. Her lot in life, as the baby of the family, was always being subject to everyone's scrutiny—her weight, her height, her hair, her teeth, every part of her body. But compared to Chinese people, her family believed fervently in privacy. For Chinese people, it seemed not to exist as a concept. They just stared, stopped in their tracks and stared, and if you gave them a dirty look, they still stared, not in the least embarrassed. They picked their noses in public, hung their ratty underwear in the street. Those couples on Kay's campus—not even the ickiest couples at school made out clumped in one spot. And the bathroom stall doors extended only from chest to knee, as if they'd calculated the bare minimum that made you higher than an animal: not enough to have dignity, just to be human.

Not even the lack of privacy had thwarted her, until today. Nora had delivered her from the group, but now she'd watch her even more closely, sniff her when she emerged from a bathroom, jump at any chance to pity and judge her. Sophie could never tell her, or any of them, not even if someday she wanted help. They'd speculate and strategize, like they were doing to Grandma.

She wished they'd all leave her alone. She wished she were back in the city with Brandon; she wondered if he was already starting to forget her. She wished Mr. Chu would keel over.

She tried to keep herself occupied with the TV. Dynasty dramas, the men thundering around in silk robes and long ponytails, the women simpering in floury makeup. Deadly earnest news. Variety show singers belting out what sounded like one national anthem after another, amid lots of steam and rainbow lights and dramatically gesticulating dancers. Dubbed action flicks with unrecognizable stars, as if any gun-firing, car-chasing white guy was good enough. The commercials looked like American parodies of commercials, and she caught one striving for English: "Crony Underwear: Your most intimate friend."

On the music channel, cheesy white boy bands were crooning their hearts out to China. Even worse, much of the local pop was masquerading as hip-hop. Do-rags, gang signs, breakdance poses, *word* and *yo* inserted here and there. Even one girl with Afro puffs who called herself Cocoa.

Sophie turned off the TV, feeling vaguely ashamed. It was understandable that Asian Americans didn't own much cultural space yet, but why didn't Chinese people in China? Then again, why shouldn't they co-opt hip-hop if they wanted, when all over America, the co-opting itself had become a joke? Even her dad had gotten it. Once, he'd said, "Sophie, you're so unfat, hanging out with your dad on a Friday night." Mid-bite, she'd said, "Huh?" He'd grinned. "You know. Un-*p-h-a-t*." She'd laughed so hard she'd choked.

Sophie picked up the phone—the dial tone was a strange pitch—and followed the instructions for calling America. It was late there, but Brandon liked to stay up working on his music. After all, he was done with school for good.

"Hey you! You still remember me, you jet-setter?"

His voice made her feel warm all over. "I'd rather be there with you," she said.

"Come on now. You're on vacation in China! How many people get to do that? Tell me what you've seen so far."

"Some pretty gardens and parks. Tiananmen Square and the Forbidden City. The Great Wall—that was cool."

"Man, I'd trade places with you in a heartbeat."

Trade places, instead of being here, or there, with her? "Is something wrong?"

"My dad just got denied parole again."

"Oh no." She hadn't known he was up for parole. Brandon hadn't told her.

"Anyway, go on. I want to hear more about your trip."

She hesitated. "Brandon, I'm so sorry—"

"It's all right. I've said all there is to say about it. Tell me more about China."

"I don't know. It's a package tour. We get rushed from place to place."

"And? What else?"

"There's some family drama. My grandfather's meeting us at the end of our tour. He wants to see my grandmother, for the first time in twenty years. But no one knows how to tell her."

"Hmm. Well, if she wants to see him, she will, and if she doesn't, she won't. Right?"

"I guess." Obviously, everything she said seemed trivial compared to his troubles. She blurted, "I've been throwing up."

"I hope you don't mean what I think you mean."

She was silent, trembling.

"I thought you stopped. You promised me."

"I know."

"I don't get it. You have everything going for you. A solid family, Stanford, your art—"

"Don't worry about it. It's not your problem anymore."

There was a pause. "Now what do you mean by that?"

He was already getting sick of her. So let that be the reason. It wasn't her, it wasn't even a part of her. It was something she did, when she felt like it.

"Nothing. Forget I said anything. I have to go." She hung up.

She was feeling dehydrated and faint. She knelt before the minibar.

Potato chips, chocolate bars, coconut milk, instant noodles. She reached for a bottle of water, took a long gulp, and put it back.

She closed the cabinet, trembling harder. There was only one way to feel in control again.

One by one, from the undersides of her fingers, she pinched back the excess. The skin whitened, revealing the fine shapes underneath. There was safety, and truth, in seeing the bones.

She reopened the cabinet and finished the water. She drank a can of diet soda. She tore in.

Her first time had been a few days after the funeral. Any guidance counselor could analyze that.

She was home alone. She was hungry. On the pantry floor, she found bags full of groceries, a receipt curled on top—her dad's name and credit card, the date a day before he died. Amid his preparations to leave, he must've forgotten to put away these last purchases for the house.

She started with a few slices of raisin bread. She felt like she'd never be filled. She ate the whole loaf, half plain, half toasted and buttered. Then a box of pecan cookies. Once she'd eaten an obscene amount, why stop? A hunk of cheddar cheese. A stale pound cake. Cream of mushroom soup. She made it all vanish.

She didn't feel the pain until she burped. She staggered to the bathroom, holding her stomach. Then it came up, by itself, in a rush. What was left inside after that, she forced out. And then, the weirdest part—she felt great. She *was* great. She could loose this monster, ripping packages with its teeth, cramming food between dripping jaws—and then tame it. She could careen into a total wreck—and then reverse out of it. She could turn back time.

• • •

In the bathroom mirror, her cheeks looked swollen, her eyes bloodshot. The first two knuckles of her right hand were raw pink, the two knuckles that her teeth scraped. They'd never betrayed her before.

Sophie gathered the wrappers and containers and stuffed them in a pocket of her suitcase. Then she curled up in bed and picked up the phone again. She had to call Brandon back. She still wanted the rest of the summer with him. His sweet full-lipped kisses, the way he closed his eyes when she rubbed his freshly shaven scalp, how easily he moved through the hallways of their school and his housing project. But if a stupid argument could hurt this much now, she wasn't sure how she could handle breaking up later on.

She redialed the international code, and then her fingers dialed a number she hadn't dialed for nearly a year. She nearly dropped the phone when it rang.

The automated greeting: "Hello, you have reached"—and now her father's voice, enunciating his own name: "Bill Shen."

"Daddy! Are you there?" The voice mail beeped. She slammed the receiver down.

Could he be alive? Was there a conspiracy? A horrible mistake? His funeral—closed casket. The urn of anonymous ashes. Violently, she shook her head. Her father was gone. They—Nora, Mom—must have forgotten to deactivate his cell phone.

At the funeral, she'd stared at the shiny wooden lid of the casket and pictured him as a skeleton. His dimpled cheeks, his thick arms, all his warm sturdy flesh—gone. That hadn't happened, of course. His body was there, smashed up, maybe starting to rot. She understood why Nora had decided on closed casket. And she understood Nora had taken charge when no one else could. But she wished she'd seen the corpse. She was a visual person. It would've been more cathartic.

Scattering the ashes might have helped. She'd imagined climbing a peak or sailing onto the ocean and flinging them to the wind, watching them catch the light, spread, vanish. But, again, she was overruled. Anyway, hiking and boating had no significance to her family. She'd probably gotten the idea from a movie.

Sometimes she tortured herself with what-ifs. What if she'd told him to drive off earlier, brewed him coffee, called his cell phone just as he got sleepy. A few times, she'd tried to test whether he'd heard what Mom said before he drove off. She'd turned on the TV, then stood in the driveway. All she could hear was a distant garbling, but she didn't know if the volume was right. She'd tried rushing out of the house while Mom was midsentence, which gave her a little bonus satisfaction, but Mom fell silent before she could shut the door, and the satisfaction quickly soured. Anyway, even if he'd meant to leave forever, to escape the house for good, he hadn't crashed on purpose.

She pulled the sheet over her head and cried until she was, finally, emptied out. At last she stretched, wispy and lithe in her dark detergent-scented tent, and dozed off.

A new perspective: standing on Tiger Hill, surveying this city, Suzhou. The old gray stacked-tile roofs and new gray construction sites. The hill itself, gray brick on gray steps on gray rock, with a nearly black pool. Even the tree trunks were gray, and the sky filled with billowing clouds.

She stepped under a pavilion, into a frame—the eaves and pillars and carvings directing her to a tableau of sky, tree, earth, water, perfectly composed. Whoever designed it knew just how to limit your field of vision so that you were stilled by the view, and when anything moved into that frame—a bird, another tourist, your own sleeve—the intrusion startled, and became part of a new, fleeting composition. It reminded her of something she'd tried to capture in her own art.

In the last year, charcoal had become her medium. She'd discovered she could capture images and moods in gradations of white to black, in light and shadow, more honestly than she'd ever done with anything but pencil, and then only with painstaking sketching and erasing. She'd never liked paint; it made her revert to childish colors and shapes. Charcoal was so stark and understated, it made her bold. She could produce infinite effects with a few strokes, a few smudges, a variance in pressure.

For her final project, she'd done a series of charcoal drawings, three different views of a house at dusk: the first, as one of a row of houses on a hushed, slanted street; the second, front and squared, a stark version of a childish crayon drawing; the third, through a window, panes of glass separating two figures hunched over a silent dinner. She'd gotten an A-plus, though she knew herself that she hadn't quite achieved her vision.

Now she felt an ache, a lovely ache, in recognizing her own glimmering of an idea utterly realized centuries ago—so utterly it must have been a cliché.

The scattered placards promised intrigue—the Sword Testing Rock, the Pavilion for Fetching the Moon—but the explanations were only in Chinese. She went to join the others, staring into the dark pool, and caught a snippet from another group's tour guide: "So the sword is said to still be in there. No one knows for sure." She stared, too. A flare in the murk, then another—goldfish, sluggish and bulbous, eerily aglow.

Crossing a footbridge, she spotted another English sign, fortuitously profound, like a child's haiku:

Guides Attention:
Don't say any word on bridge
In order to avoid jam

The jam-causing sight just across was a leaning pagoda, dignified in its decrepitude—the culmination of all this gray, crooked, cracked beauty. People were lining up to pose in front of the pagoda, giggling as they imitated its posture. "It's leaning today, it may topple tomorrow," another tour guide said. If she were the pagoda, she might topple onto these gawking tourists.

Past the pagoda was a garish temple that their local guide indicated was the official highlight of Tiger Hill. Unimpressed, Sophie watched bony, shabby workers padding up and down a long stone staircase, hauling pots of flowers hung from poles balanced across their bare shoulders. At the bottom, more workers squatted to arrange the flowers—red, yellow, purple—all over the gray rock and brick. The workers were short and brown; she wondered whether that was part of the cause or the result of their backbreaking labor, which was for nothing, worse than nothing. She supposed this was another kind of Chinese aesthetic, bunching lots of colorful things together, the more colors the better, the more things the better. They might as well tape balloons and streamers to the leaning pagoda.

"Feel better from yesterday?"

Sophie jumped. It was her grandmother. "Much better, thanks."

"Maybe your stomach is too American for food here."

Sophie nodded. "What's the guide saying?"

"Some old story." Grandma listened and translated bit by bit. "Tang Mu had eight wives, but was still unhappy, so he prayed to Guanyin." She pointed inside the temple at a fluid sculpture of an almost-smiling woman. "He knelt on each step and *koutou*." She knocked her forehead and pointed to the stairs. "Altogether, fifty-three times, praying to find his true match. Then, dizzy, he sees this beautiful woman, also praying—for a husband, I guess—and loses his balance. She laughs, without showing teeth. She leaves without raising dust. She walks down steps with no sound." Grandma gave a dismissive wave.

"Then what? She became his ninth wife?"

Tommy was already calling for the group to head down the hill.

Grandma gave a slight, wry smile. "Perhaps."

At a leisurely pace, they descended the hill together. Sophie stole intermittent glances at her grandmother's stolid face. Her grandmother didn't need anyone's strategizing, any more than she herself did.

And Brandon was right. There was no crime here, no serious trauma, no sweeping injustice. His problems were so much more real and raw; cinematic, soaked in color, like zooming in on a galloping horse's haunches. This stuff with her grandparents was like a dried bouquet—brittle, dusty, and faded.

Sophie started to say, *Grandma, Grandpa wants to see you, and if you want to see him, great, if you don't*—But she faltered. "Grandma—I could visit you, from Stanford."

"That would be nice. But don't worry about me. I have my little garden. I have Lou."

Sophie wondered how Uncle Lou and a garden could fill up a week, let alone a life. No plans, no goals? At eighty, she supposed, passing time was the goal.

Grandma added, "I know you'll be busy. I was busy at your age, too."

"You went to college? I mean—did girls go to college back then?"

"Some did. I was meant to. But then the Japanese invaded—the country, the city, my village. They killed many people. They set my family's house on fire. I escaped, again and again."

Sophie stared. Grandma's face was utterly calm. An invasion—people said her neighborhood had undergone the Asian Invasion. She tried to picture brutal foreign troops swarming the streets, but her brain could only conjure aliens and zombies. She tried to picture the house in Queens on fire. She and Mom fleeing. Unable to reach her sisters. Flames licking the urn. Her art portfolio, her Stanford acceptance letter, her transcripts and to-do lists—all ashes.

"So what did you do?" she asked.

"Instead of a university student, I became a revolutionary. I published a journal—I wrote, edited, distributed. I led protests. I made speeches. *Kang Ri, jiu guo*—Resist Japan, save our nation. That was the urgent call, but impossible without *nan nü ping deng*—equality for men and women."

Sophie wondered how to explain this to Brandon. *My grandma wasn't a concubine type or a Chinatown type. She was a revolutionary.*

"Did you succeed?"

"Well, eventually the Japanese surrendered."

"Oh, after Pearl Harbor? After America bombed Hiroshima?"

"Yes, but we Nationalists had fought for eight long years by then."

"The Nationalists—the elites?" She'd heard that somewhere.

"The Nationalists founded the nation. They were the ruling party. In my province, anyone in politics would be Nationalist. It meant what the word means. A united nation, men and women, rich and poor."

"But you were a revolutionary—against your own party?"

"I was a revolutionary for the principles of our republic, which had never been realized. *Minzu*—nationalism, sovereignty, the right to self-determination, to freedom from foreign domination. *Minquan*—democracy, power for the people, civil rights for the entire citizenry. *Minsheng*—people's livelihood, the right to the basic needs of food, clothing, shelter, transport."

"Why would anyone oppose those principles?"

"The republic was founded eight years before my birth. Never in my lifetime was it not under siege. Before the Japanese invasion, the Nationalists fought the warlords and the Communists. After the invasion, there was a brief truce, a united front, between the two parties. The Nationalists fought the Japanese, while the Communists mobilized the peasantry. So the Nationalists grew weak while the Communists grew strong. As soon as the world war ended, civil war erupted. The Communists won, and people like me had to flee."

If civil war divided America now, what would the two sides be? Would Sophie end up on the same side as her mother, as her sisters? The same side as Brandon?

She asked, "Do Nora and Kay know all this?"

"Some. But I don't know how much they understand." Grandma patted her shoulder and pointed to a bench. "Time for me to rest."

They'd reached the base of Tiger Hill, a clutter of souvenir stands that looked like a small-scale Chinatown: gaudy purses and fans, cushion covers and table runners, tea sets and chopsticks, dangling good-luck doodads. Sophie paused by a food stall where locals were sucking up noodles, popping whole dumplings. Food was a basic need. People ate when they were hungry, and then they stopped. It should be that easy.

A hand on her arm—Kay, grinning. "Come. Don't tell Mom." She tugged Sophie into an alley lined with food carts.

"I'm not hungry."

"Try this."

Kay kept a firm hold on her as they watched an old man spoon batter onto a grill. He spread it in a perfect circle, thin as paint, then cracked an egg on top. When it was mottled yellow and white, he brushed on sauce, sprinkled chopped scallions and cilantro, laid a kind of fried wafer on top, and folded it all up. Kay held it, sizzling and oozing, to Sophie's lips.

Sophie shook her head, too vehemently. Before Kay could react, she took a bite. She couldn't taste it for the roiling inside. She couldn't remember how to judge food by pleasure, not safety.

"Yummy, huh?" Kay said. "Eat it. I want one for myself."

And the thing was in Sophie's hands, weighty and hot as a bomb. The only way to make it disappear was to eat it.

Munching away, Kay led her to another cart. Plump pyramids of stuffed sticky rice, wrapped in leaves and tied with string. One for her, one for Kay. Sophie tried to eat like Kay, like a person unfettered, for hunger and for fun. She forced herself to taste the rice, dark and fragrant with soy sauce, the sweet mealy morsels of chestnut, the chunks of pork squishing and melting on her tongue. She could do it. She could do it when she tried.

"Girls? Where are you?" It was Mom.

"Uh-oh." Kay's eyes twinkled. "Stuff it. Quick!"

Panicked, Sophie swallowed until she held nothing but oily leaves and string. She flung them on a heap of litter on the ground and swiped the back of her hand across her mouth, her chin.

Kay laughed. "You look so scared."

Mom was holding up a dress, severely cut silk with no stretch, a tiny collar and sleeves, a long slit. "Want a *qipao*?"

Kay grimaced. "In college, the white girls wore those as party costumes."

"Well, *qipao* were designed for Chinese women's figures."

Sophie tried to stay calm. Her worries were trivial, products of peace and prosperity. All day, she'd focused on important issues—the aesthetics of Chinese gardens, the local laborers, her grandmother the revolutionary, civil war. But everyone, everything conspired against her.

Tommy was starting to herd the group to the bus. The lard was coating her throat, the carbs expanding in her stomach. By the time she reached a bathroom, all the fat would be in her bloodstream, impossible to expel.

14

On the bus from Suzhou to Shanghai, Lin Yulan tried to rest, but through the cushioned seat, she could feel each bump of the road in her bones.

Ever since the interminable flight to Hong Kong, her tendons had knotted and cramped, the soreness extending even to her fingertips and gums. Every day meant hours of walking, the bus jolting, more walking, more jolting. Every meal hard to digest, a chore to chew. Every night, a strange bed, a strange bathroom.

This vacation, as Lou had called it, was the first time she'd left America since she had emigrated. The first time she'd set foot in China since she had fled. The first time she'd traveled with her daughters and granddaughters. Each first the last. At eighty, one could be certain.

And it was her chance to soak in her granddaughters' careless vitality, to see her daughters with silver in their hair, to feel how life branched and branched.

Traversing the new China, all three granddaughters had become inquisitive about her past. But all of Nora's and Kay's questions were, to her, unanswerable. Only with Sophie did she have, in scattered moments, the feeling of hanging out that she had with Lou.

Yet she still could not refute the hard truth she'd voiced more than seventeen years ago. In fact, it was clearer than ever now. Irene had let her fire die, and with every breath, she exuded regret. Of course, Lin Yulan's fire was long extinguished, too, but she'd had no choice.

Twenty years ago in Taiwan, she'd turned sixty and was pushed out of her hard-won position as a local magistrate. She attended a mandatory party for her mandatory retirement, where her superiors spoke platitudes and raised glasses, more to her husband than to her. Her attention strayed around the banquet hall to the brass phoenix-and-dragon with blinking lights for eyes, to the carrot swans and turnip roses adorning the plates, reissued with each course. An ordinary retirement party, for an ordinary old woman.

Bolted inside a bathroom stall, she overheard two poised young women from her department gossiping: How could she abide that lecherous husband? Who couldn't keep his hands off the interns and new hires? Especially when—they'd heard somewhere—she'd been a prominent feminist in her day. Well, that was then. She was old. No point in leaving now, was there? All at once, Lin Yulan understood that her life was over if she did not leave.

With a vigor she had not felt in years, she marched out of the bathroom, startling the young women, and left the party to call her children—all three citizens of America already. Lou on the West Coast, Irene on the East, Susan somewhere in between. Lou breezy, Susan vague, and Irene struggling, with two daughters of her own.

So Lin Yulan packed up and flew to New York to make one more attempt at leaving a legacy. She would raise her granddaughters to be the kind of woman she once was, the kind of woman she'd raised her own daughters to be. And, in so doing, she'd free Irene from the duties of motherhood to make a revolutionary discovery. Like the invention of the birth control pill, by a China-Taiwan-America transplant like themselves.

Or the fact that male biology was to blame when no sons were born—so many wives abandoned for no reason, including Lin Yulan's own mother, who'd urged her father to find another wife, and was then left to die alone in her ancestral village.

Lin Yulan became Grandma, cooking and cleaning, doling out comforting pats and tinned sweets, learning to satisfy her granddaughters' trifling, burning wants. On occasion, she prepared speeches in her head, but they sounded mythic or mundane. They made no sense out of context. And she didn't have the vocabulary in English, while little Nora and Kay couldn't grasp the complexity in Chinese. Besides, on American TV, grandparents were laughable creatures, toothless and deluded. She'd kept quiet, thinking there would be plenty of time.

Irene seemed to have acquired a peculiar notion in America: that motherhood, something females in every society, females of every species, had carried out for all of history, was a grand achievement, worthy as a career, a noble *choice*. Still, during Lin Yulan's tenure as Grandma, her daughter gradually refocused, that flame inside her rekindled, and soon there was success, a big step toward curing some malady of the brain, a memory sickness. Irene's eyes gleamed bright with hope that she would indeed make her mark on the world through science. But then she got pregnant again. An accident—she said so. Then why let it stand in her way?

Even from her willful daughter, the tantrum that followed was confounding. So much shouting about choices. It was her choice, didn't she have the choice, wasn't that the point of the movement, now women have the choice. She seemed to mean not having to make any choices. Not this or that, but this and that, this then that. She was a fool.

Lin Yulan tried to remind her of what she had to already know. If she wanted to talk about choices, motherhood was not a choice; it was the given. The choice for a woman was to push and strain forward, or to be part of the backward pull. Life must be lived for the long view, to set an example for generations, rather than to seek temporary ease. And those positioned to make a difference had a duty to do so, to assert their power outside the home, to make public contributions, the kind that might go down in history, if history were ever fairly written. In her own era, the War of Resistance had opened the gates, and she'd stormed through. She'd understood that only by merging the causes of nationalism and feminism could either be won.

Equality was to be gained not by pointing out grievous injustices, not by courting well-deserved pity. Hers was not a society that could afford to be moved in such ways. Equality had to be earned. Women had to prove their worthiness of full citizenship by fully shouldering the responsibilities of citizenship. And if, as an individual female, you had to work harder than your male counterpart, personally sacrifice more, for less recognition, that was to be expected. That was how you knew you might leave a legacy.

And Irene was so fortunate, married to a good, honest man, living in this new, free country, not needing to wait until it was brought to its knees before it recognized half its citizenry. Not to mention all these methods of control, all these *choices*—if not to unfetter herself, then what for?

Irene's sputtering was as self-righteous as it was senseless: How dare you suggest my daughters are worthless? How is that progress? You can keep your long view. You have no right to judge. I'll do whatever I want. I never wanted to be like you.

Lin Yulan had never imagined that in one generation, the concept of women's rights could become so absurd. No one had the right to do whatever they wanted. No one should. Progress didn't mean having it all. Everything in life was a trade-off. Nothing was spared from this, not children, not anything.

Lin Yulan harbored no illusions. She had no patience for those who did. So, after helping to raise two granddaughters for three years, she packed up and moved to California, where Lou lived.

He never had a fire, only two considerable talents. One was charm, the other a capacity for contentment—at least outwardly, at least to her. He'd once dreamed of being a movie star, unaware how little value his face would hold in America, but his adjustment was quick. If there were deep disappointments there, unlike with her daughters, she could not see them. It was always enough for her to watch him eat, to hear him laugh—to hang out with him, her son.

Night had fallen thick by the time the bus hauled them to their hotel. Once again, when room keys were handed out, there was some strategizing, which she was never privy to, and she and Nora were paired together again.

She was washing up for bed when there seemed to be a kind of uprising: the girls gathering in the corridor, wanting a taste of Shanghai's notorious nightlife. Lin Yulan inquired about their safety. They found this amusing.

She remembered the third necklace for Kay, still in her purse, and made them wait while she retrieved it.

On the drive to LAX, it had occurred to her that a grandma should bring presents, and she made Lou pull off the highway and find a gift shop. Lou said the girls would prefer cash, but what did he know of granddaughters? When she spotted those necklaces, she thought they were just the thing. Shiny, colorful, fanciful—but plastic, very durable; the kind of bauble she'd never had herself, never granted her daughters.

The necklaces had elicited feeble thanks from the girls and a grimace from Irene. A bit flustered, Lin Yulan had found candy in her purse and pushed it into Nora's hand.

Now Kay's excessive enthusiasm confirmed something was wrong with the necklaces—the colors, the size, she didn't know. Of course, since birth her granddaughters had been glutted with shiny, colorful, fanciful things—barrettes, birthday cakes, wrapping paper and ribbons, so many photos they seemed to be growing up inside a memorial to themselves.

Lin Yulan bade them good night and tried to settle her body into yet another strange bed.

15

The way to "do" Shanghai, Kay had heard, was to live it up. Shopping and feasting, drinking and debauchery—here, that was sightseeing. She'd thought an expedition to the city's famous bar strip might provide some much-needed levity for her and her sisters, but she hadn't pictured this. Bar after bar, bar above bar, bar under bar, bars as far as they could see—and, from curb to curb, a sea of revelers, a wild clamor over blaring electronic pop, and the smells of sweat, booze, perfume, piss, smoke.

A floppy girl was being dragged into a cab by her date, her stilettos scraping the pavement. A guy was puking between his shoes while his friends smoked over him, faces purple with severe Asian flush. A mob of international schoolkids, maybe thirteen years old, hooted as one of them clambered over the hood of a taxi, the driver cursing and honking. On the sidewalks, Uighur men furiously spiced and flipped mutton skewers, little kids brandished dark skinny roses at every man with a date, beggars dipped blackened hands into the passing waves. Fashionable urbanites calmly navigated the chaos, while potbellied white men with local girls in tow swaggered as if the sea would part for them. It did.

At last Kay and her sisters squeezed into a relatively tame bar, dropped into a booth, and collectively exhaled.

"Look at that." Laughing, Sophie pointed to the drink list, titled "Cocktails and Pussytails."

Kay wondered whether it was accidental or intentional, the work of an earnest local or a prankster expat, and then wished she could stop wondering.

"I want a Long Island iced tea," Sophie said.

"That's a strong drink," Nora said.

"So?" Sophie snapped.

Kay waved for the waitress, who flounced over in a way that signaled she'd rather serve *laowai*. When Kay tried to order in Chinese, the waitress only gave a contemptuous stare. "Long Island," Kay finally said, and the waitress flounced off. She returned sloshing three mud-colored drinks, which she banged down.

"I don't really want that," Nora said.

"Oh, come on." Sophie looked slightly contrite.

Kay said, "Here's to a vacation from this vacation." The glass was sticky, the liquid fizzy, acrid, and overpoweringly sweet. She gulped it down, hoping to quell a strange flutter inside.

In Suzhou, after her sisters had pleaded stomachaches and escaped to the hotel, she'd lingered by herself along the ancient canals, trying to touch it all—the rough marbled walls of the houses, the steps crumbling right into the water. She was dipping a finger into the silvery littered surface when she saw Byron's face rippling beside her own. They both paused, staring at each other's reflection.

Finally he said, "They've tagged Suzhou the Venice of the East."

She ventured, "As if it were a knockoff."

He explained that this canal system was much more sophisticated; that, back when Suzhou was a major city and Shanghai a sleepy fishing town, the canals served as the main infrastructure for trade, transportation, and sewage. But most of them had been filled and paved over, he said, giving a dismissive wave toward the canal they stood over: "It's dead water. Purely cosmetic."

"Isn't it historic?" she asked.

Historical preservation, he said, was a Western notion. At that point, they had to walk on, but they'd spent the rest of the afternoon walking together.

He told her he was back in Asia only for the summer; he was getting his master's in architecture at MIT. He asked how she'd become interested in the cause of Chinese prostitutes. She eyed him warily, trying to detect a smirk.

"Sorry about the sarcasm at breakfast the other day. My dad brings out the worst in me," he said. "I'd really like to know."

In a rush, she told him about the night she'd gathered Rick, Du Yi, and Mr. Wan to take her inside a karaoke club, where a dozen "hostesses" sat waiting in a row. Mr. Wan selected three of them in an utterly practiced manner, then explained, "Client entertainment. Unavoidable." In a dark, smoky room furnished with musty couches and a video of Asian women frolicking in a garden, Du Yi busied himself inputting ballads, Rick stared at the hostesses as if they were another species, and the hostesses stared suspiciously at Kay until Mr. Wan told them she was from overseas. Soon they were naming the poor provinces they came from, coyly comparing Mr. Wan's handsomeness to Du Yi's and Rick's, and suggesting "games"—a breast contest, a butt contest, something involving the insertion of a lit piece of paper and a well-timed fart.

"*Why?*" Kay had blurted.

Mr. Wan had looked at her as if she were a cute, slow child. "Why do you think?"

After Du Yi sang a few songs, they asked for the check. "Waste of our time," one hostess muttered. On the way out, Mr. Wan recounted his first time at a karaoke club, when his business mentor tossed bills all over the cruddy carpet and instructed the girls to strip, cover themselves in honey, roll around, and keep the bills that stuck. "And they did it?" Kay couldn't help asking. Mr. Wan said, "They enjoyed it."

The next day, she'd set to launching her outreach.

Byron simply raised his eyebrows. She waited for a wisecrack.

"I can see how that experience would light a spark," he finally said. "I want to hear how you got started with that Asian American organization, but I assume the answer's complicated, and we're getting herded off to dinner."

All through dinner, she berated herself for rattling off such detail and rehearsed a simple explanation. When Byron motioned for her to join him in a dim corner of the hotel lobby, she said, "The short answer is, Asian Americans have always been treated as foreigners, and I wanted to change that."

"I want the long answer," he said.

So she found herself telling him what sounded like the story of her life—at least one version. Growing up facing down racial taunts that, upon puberty, mutated into racial come-ons. In college, her roommate asking where she was from, originally, then rhapsodizing about Thai food; a floormate wanting to consult her on feng shui; a society throwing a "Geishas and Concubines" party, and when she expressed consternation over the girls' getups—satin bursting at the seams, eyes drawn slanted, hair pinned with chopsticks—being told it was an annual tradition, and "ironic." Withdrawing, becoming the quiet Asian girl in seminars, spending weekend nights in the library, until she learned, in sociology, how to interpret such incidents in the context of Orientalism—the dominant discourse of an exoticized, essentialized "East" in the superior, modern "West."

She researched the psychological effects of racism, finding studies that showed the more subtle it was, the more damaging; and racism these days was nothing if not subtle, mostly unintentional, and ubiquitous. She surveyed the other Asian students and found a pattern of being caught between impossible choices—either obligingly answering the same questions about birthplace and food and quaint customs, or being invisible, or being the hostile person of color in the room; seeking social comfort in Asian cliques and risking the charge of being a typical Asian, or accepting honorary white status and risking the charge of self-loathing; a general sense of not belonging, even as they felt they had no right to complain. After all, they weren't being denied jobs or mortgages, only space to exist as they were.

She joined the Asian Students Club, and reformed it—showing Asian American movies, or at least contemporary Asian movies, not kung fu flicks; focusing meetings on sociopolitical issues, not dim sum; petitioning against future "Geishas and Concubines" parties—none of which made her, or the club, very popular, but she was learning that she couldn't mind being thought tedious.

Then she joined the Asian American Cultural Awareness Project to spotlight how popular culture both encapsulated and perpetuated biased treatment of Asian Americans, drawing connections between the media depictions and the societal patterns. The images of Asian women as sexual objects, and the countless men who actually tried to use "*Konichiwa*" or "Where are you from?" as pickup lines. The images of Asian men as inscrutable villains, and the congressional persecution of Asian Americans who dared make political donations. The newspaper headline "American Beats Kwan for Olympic Gold"—as in Michelle Kwan, the three-time American figure-skating champion—and surveys showing Americans willing to vote for a president of any demographic over Asian. The occasional supporting roles that allowed Asians to speak native English, as long as the main characters were white, and the self-congratulatory willingness of whites to accept Asians into their midst—as their girlfriends, their coworkers, even their adopted kids—as long as the status quo, their sociopolitical dominance, remained intact.

She wrote letters, organized boycotts, circulated petitions. Every time she felt sure of progress—a public apology, a groundbreaking show, an Asian American rightly rising to prominence—something she'd thought could never happen again would happen again; for instance, her own senator doing a "ching chong" impression on the radio. Constant vigilance was necessary, and exhausting. She lived in a painful state of heightened awareness, like walking outdoors with dilated pupils. She could rarely watch TV or read a paper without feeling angry, or paranoid, or defeated. She was even tempted, at times, to say, *So what?* Maybe there just weren't enough Asians in America. Maybe they just hadn't been around long enough. Maybe they just needed to wait.

Her director wanted to start a mentorship program in Chinatown; Kay had the idea of teaching Chinese American history. First, she had to study it herself. And she learned how the same cycle she confronted was a small-scale version of a century and a half of Chinese American history, each visible advance met with a backward shove.

At this, Byron looked dubious, so she gave him a crash course: They were "the indispensable enemy," a people to be imported or expelled, exploited or excluded, whenever convenient for the ruling class, starting with the first migrants—coolies bought to solve a shortage of African slaves; gold prospectors turned laundrymen and cooks; railroad workers who fulfilled America's manifest destiny, paid the price in twenty thousand pounds of bones shipped back to China, and were barred from every official ceremony.

Many of these first Chinese Americans learned English, changed silk caps and cotton shoes for cowboy hats and boots, adopted Western names and intermarried, all while establishing Chinatowns, organizing labor strikes, opening their own schools, keeping their own census. Meanwhile, they fell victim to widespread lynching and arson; were defined by the courts as either Indian or black, depending on what kept them more powerless; and were given the distinction of being the only ethnic group ever banned from all public schools and targeted with a specific exclusion act. Until World War II—when Japanese aggression made China an ally, Chinese Americans enlisted in the armed forces at twice the rate of the general population, and Chinese people in general suddenly seemed deserving of humane treatment—that act remained in place.

To this day, each generation relived the same struggle, granted opportunities for economic advancement, but not cultural or political power. The wave of her own parents, when the prevailing stereotype shifted from dirty heathen to model minority. Then a wave of scientists and engineers specifically recruited to strengthen the American military during the Cold War, only to be suspected of spying. And the latest arrivals, hungry to leave a China where a bowl of rice was no longer guaranteed, and finding all paths to citizenship blocked just when American businesses needed a new labor force to exploit.

After she'd absorbed this history, she stood before two dozen fifth-graders with the mission to empower them with it, these kids who, unlike her, couldn't defend themselves with native English or American-born status. When she tried to start a discussion of racism, nobody spoke. Some were sitting up solemnly, as if they might get tested. Some were whipping out video games every time she turned her back. When she asked if they often confronted the question "Where are you from?" she got a few nods, a little more attention, so she reminded them that all Americans, except Native Americans, were immigrants; that they could reply, *America, New York, Chinatown*, and consider the question answered.

Then a boy piped up, in a heavy accent, "But I come from China." The other kids snickered, but he seemed not to notice. His hair was bowl-cut, his glasses thick and plastic. He might as well have stamped "Fresh off the Boat" on his forehead. "Where you come from?" he asked.

Queens, Kay said, with a wink.

The boy launched into urgent Chinese—first Mandarin, which she at least recognized, and then what she guessed was Fujianese. She could only shake her head. Soon the whole class broke into Chinese and laughter, and though she realized they were ridiculing her at least as much as the boy, she wasn't sure what was funny—perhaps that she, unlike them, expected to be treated like any other American.

Over the next months, she refined her curriculum, combining historical success stories with present-day outrages, tailoring discussions to their varying language levels, but the boy never spoke up again. And the more she taught, the more ignorant she felt—so she applied for a scholarship to China.

She stopped talking.

When she got the award letter, her dad gave her a high-five. She asked if he'd visit her in Beijing. He said that was a great idea. But he was leaving for Maine first. She figured that by the time he visited, she could show him around, converse with him in Chinese. Maybe something would jog his memory. Maybe, together, they'd even track down long-lost relatives, trace his half of her lineage. Just as she was preparing to fly off, he died.

Between her and Byron was an expectant silence. Finally he stood. She stood, too.

Sheepishly, she said, "I didn't get to ask how you got interested in architecture."

He put his hand on the small of her back. She felt that strange flutter inside.

"Come out with me tomorrow night," he said. "There's a place I want you to see in Shanghai."

"Ni hao."

Two middle-aged white men stood over their booth, one tall and leering down, the other short and slightly abashed. Kay grimaced, eliciting a giggle from Sophie. At the giggle, the leer broadened, and the tall man began to squeeze next to Sophie, his thick hairy arm hovering over her bare shoulders.

Kay burst, "Get away from her."

The men stared, then released hearty laughs. "Where are you from?"

"New York," Nora said tightly.

"Well now, don't get worked up. Here we are in Shanghai, all far from home. So, the Big Apple, huh? All three of you? Now hold on, are you related?" The tall man grinned. "Three sisters?"

"Fuck off," Kay hissed.

He recoiled and held up his palms. "Okay, sweetheart. Just making friends."

The two lumbered away. Stranded in the middle of the bar, they stood clutching their beers.

"Let's play a game." Sophie wore a defiant little grin. "How much would it cost for you to hook up with either of those guys?"

"You're joking," Kay said.

"Duh. The whole game is a joke."

"Just because we can joke about it doesn't mean we should."

Sophie rolled her eyes. "Nora, name your price."

Nora gave an uncertain laugh. "Um—a hundred million."

Sophie grinned. "I'd say a billion."

"Oh. I guess that makes me cheap."

"Okay, now him." Sophie pointed to a blond thirty-something.

"He's not that bad. If I were hard up—maybe half a million."

"Man, you *are* cheap!"

Kay sat back as they laughed. The waitress returned to offer another round. Rather than speak, Kay nodded. Three more mud-colored drinks were sloshed over and banged down. She quickly emptied hers. Now Sophie was pointing to one of the few local men in the bar, maybe the proprietor. He looked a little like Mr. Wan.

Nora wrinkled her nose. "Twenty million?"

Before she could stop herself, Kay said, "Why so much?"

Sophie looked highly amused. "What's your price?"

"I'm not playing this game. I would never put a price on it."

Sophie snickered. "You'd have sex with him for free?"

"Sex? You said hooking up. I've never—" Kay broke off and sucked the dregs in her glass, but she'd already said too much.

Nora looked incredulous. "You've never what?"

A little defiantly, Kay said, "I've never had sex."

Sophie's jaw dropped. "You're a virgin?"

It was clear, from her tone, that Sophie wasn't. Kay and Nora looked at each other, and tacitly agreed not to ask.

"What about Rick, and the other guys?" Nora asked.

"I told you, it wasn't serious." She'd even clung to that term, *hooking up*—a temporary fastening, completely detachable.

"No kidding." Nora still sounded disbelieving.

Kay shrugged and gulped her drink. Now she saw Nora and Sophie glance at each other and agree to drop the matter.

They sat in silence, Sophie sipping her drink, Nora fidgeting with hers. Kay wished she hadn't interrupted their game, not least because she couldn't recall when they'd last laughed so blithely.

"Did you both know Grandma was a revolutionary?" Sophie finally asked.

"Just since I met Grandpa," Kay said.

"I found out when Kay told me." Nora looked a bit apologetic.

"Of course I'm the last to know," Sophie said. "To think that when I first met her, I had an Afro."

Kay couldn't help laughing. "I forgot about that visit. I don't remember talking to her. I don't remember being curious about her at all."

"That was my high school graduation," Nora said. "We visited Aunt Susan. I just remember not wanting to give up my weekend."

"Didn't we stay in a funny yellow house?" Kay asked.

Nora nodded. "In some Podunk town."

"There were dead plants everywhere, and two fish that kept eating each other's tails."

"I remember that," Sophie exclaimed.

They were all warming with nostalgia for an event simply because it was a little piece of their shared history. Kay reached further back. "I got up to pee late at night. There was a guy at the door, talking to Aunt Susan."

"What kind of guy? A boyfriend?" Nora asked.

"Couldn't be. He was this skinny kid with a Spanish accent. He didn't look much older than me at the time."

"How old was Aunt Susan then?" Sophie asked.

"Late forties, I guess. He must've been her student."

"In the middle of the night?"

"What were they doing?" Nora asked.

"Just talking." Her aunt's profile ghostly in the doorway. The kid, the guy, had a pale pretty face, fast-moving full lips, an urgent lilting voice.

"What student goes to a teacher's house in the middle of the night?" Sophie said.

"What's your theory? Aunt Susan was having an affair with a Latino guy half her age?" It sounded less ludicrous than she'd expected.

"How come you never mentioned this before?" Nora asked.

Kay shrugged. "I was half asleep. I just forgot." She really had. She couldn't make any sense of it, so the memory had tucked itself away, completely undisturbed, until tonight.

"Let's try asking her." Sophie looked titillated.

"It's her business. But I don't know. Our family's full of secrets. Maybe it is time to get them out." Nora set down her drink, her expression keen, then clouded, then keen again.

There was another silence. Sophie looked ill at ease.

Kay tried to grin. "I've shared enough tonight."

"Jesse and I were engaged."

Kay stared at her sister. "I thought the reason you broke up—"

"It was complicated. I couldn't get myself to set a date. I never even told anyone we were engaged."

"Why did you say yes in the first place?"

Nora hesitated. "It was the night of Dad's funeral, and I—" She trailed off.

Sophie stared into her drained glass. Kay bit her lip. Were they supposed to discuss their father? How he'd died? What their mother said just as they watched him leave for the last time?

At last the waitress flounced over again. They declined another round. She slapped their check on the table. They paid. Immediately, the waitress cleared their glasses, wiped the table, and waited for them to leave. Kay and her sisters got up from the booth. On their way out, she spotted the two white men who'd approached them, now merrily seated with two local women, butchering Chinese phrases to giggling applause.

She tapped Byron's door, counted to three, and scuttled away.

"Hey." A loud whisper. He jogged down the corridor. He must have been listening for her, waiting fully dressed.

His eyes were on her chest. Her hand flew up to cover herself, just as he said, "Nice necklace."

Kay blushed furiously. "It's from my grandmother." The necklace wasn't her style, but it was the first gift from her grandmother she could remember and, she felt, symbolic—of what, she didn't know.

He touched the small of her back again. "Let's go."

"Where?"

"You'll see."

He seemed to be steering her with his fingertips. Trying to quell that flutter inside, she said, "I can walk without your help."

With a smirk, he gestured toward the elevator buttons. "I'll let you push."

She jabbed the down arrow.

They zoomed through deserted dark streets in a cab, their knees nearly touching, a little heat radiating through the thin olive linen of his pants. Where was he taking her? What if he reached for her now, here on this discolored cloth-covered backseat? Somehow this felt more dangerous than any of her time with Rick or Du Yi or Mr. Wan.

The cab screeched to a stop, just short of an old beggar crossing the street. Kay lurched forward, grabbing Byron's leg, while he raised a protective arm in front of her, bumping her breasts.

"Sorry."

"Sorry."

She turned her hot face to the window. After another dark, quiet stretch, she saw an eerie expanse, white beams radiating upward like searchlights from a massive construction pit. Blocks of old courtyard houses smashed, chunks of roof and wall buried in debris. A few halves of houses were still standing, defiant and doomed. On a balcony against one lone wall, a few pieces of laundry hung from a bamboo pole, abandoned and helpless.

"Look," she said, because she wanted him to see, and because the silence was too freighted.

He leaned over to peer out her window, then leaned back, carefully avoiding contact.

"And you're against preservation?" she asked.

"That's not exactly my stance. If the new buildings preserve the essential functions of those old houses, then yes, I'm against preserving the structures themselves."

She would've debated anything to sweep past that moment of her hand on his leg, his arm on her chest—but she now found herself aching for these houses. "You know they're building luxury condos or corporate offices or a department store." She couldn't see his expression. If she turned, their faces would be too close. "Why not preserve the structures themselves? Why not preserve the Suzhou canals?"

A little reluctantly, as if he didn't want to prove her wrong but had no choice, he said, "What function are the canals serving? What concept do they embody? Nothing now but nostalgia. Looking pretty for tourists."

"They are pretty. They're beautiful. And what's wrong with nostalgia?"

"They're stagnant, literally. Nostalgia prevents renewal."

He was more knowledgeable than she, but he was missing something. "You said historical preservation is a Western notion. But Suzhou is packed with Chinese tourists. And if those structures weren't preserved, for Westerners, locals, foreigners, us—then they'd be gone."

He didn't say anything. He didn't seem to feel the import of that word.

"How else would people remember?" she asked. "How else would we learn our own history?"

She finally turned. His copper eyebrows were slightly crinkled. His bottom lip was dry.

"History in this country takes care of itself. It doesn't need to prove its existence. It just is. The Chinese have always experienced demolition, on a massive scale, with each war, each revolution. And they didn't use stone like the Romans. The buildings weren't meant to stand forever. Cities are cities to them, not museums, not graveyards. They've always rebuilt. And when they rebuild, say, a temple, they call it the same temple, and it *is* the same temple, even if every scrap of the original is gone."

"But there's never been development like this before."

"Here's how preservation works. They mark off one aspect of a city as historically significant—a few canals, a section of Great Wall, one *hutong*. They display that as an artifact. They restore it to death. And then their conscience is clear to bulldoze whole neighborhoods."

"So you do care about those old houses."

"No, I care about what's built in their place."

She blurted, "I don't know if I'm ready to leave. I feel like I'll never see any of it again."

"Leave China? I didn't know you were thinking of staying. What would you do if you stayed?"

She could only shrug.

"China's not going anywhere." His words were flippant, but there was some empathy in his tone.

Their cab pulled up along the banks of a dull, sludgy waterway. When she opened the door, she was blasted by a foul wet smell. The buildings hulking overhead looked like giant rotting cardboard boxes. The ground was a mess of cracked pavement and dirt, rock and broken glass, a few malformed trees seeming to grow out of sewage.

"Welcome to Suzhou Creek," Byron said. "We're going to an architecture studio in a converted warehouse. A friend of a friend lent me a key."

They picked their way over the pitted terrain, their arms occasionally brushing. Idiotically, she started to chatter. "I don't know much about architecture. It seems so macho. Building higher and higher. Mine's bigger than yours."

He laughed—had she heard his laugh before? It was husky and hearty; it died quickly. "Architecture is about space as much as buildings. Having said that, it's definitely a male-dominated profession." He stopped. "Here we are."

A black gleaming, huge and seamless. It was just a door, one pane of glass, but it looked like a portal to another universe. He opened it. She stepped into complete darkness and held still, even holding her breath. He hit a switch and light spilled down. The walls were collages of brick and plaster, whitewash and paint, with entries that looked like workers had hacked them out. Before her, the ceiling stopped short. One wall simply went up, past the height of any ladder she'd seen, past where there should have been ceiling and floor, another ceiling and floor, maybe another.

"It isn't finished yet," he said.

They climbed a staircase that seemed to be molded from one massive pour of concrete. The light reached only halfway up. She thought she could make out open spaces and solid walls in the gradations of shadow ahead, but she couldn't be sure which was which. Just when she couldn't take another step, he reached for another switch and more light washed down. The cavernous spaces kept unfolding, up and ahead and around each corner. In one, empty birdcages hung from wooden rafters over a matrix of glass-partitioned workstations, on which sat blueprints, graphs, sketches. In the next, glossy photos of old windows and doors dangled from mobiles, slowly twisting, over mismatched living room furniture. She couldn't tell what was design and what was accident, what was redone and what was preserved and what just wasn't finished yet. It seemed to transcend all her definitions.

Partitioning one room was a screen of a strange material, luminous and crinkled, like pearls pounded into paper. She went to touch it. He grabbed her arm. She'd nearly stepped on a miniature complex of buildings and grounds—*space*, he would say.

"Oops. What's behind that? Some secret project?"

"I think it's the bathroom."

She laughed, tripped on a floorboard, and banged into a wooden beam. A creak from high above—then a dry downpour. Startled, she looked up into a shower of dust. She covered her face, too late. Her eyes seared. A whimper escaped.

He held her face in both hands and blew—a quick strong breath on each eye, then a long soft breath across both. "Blink."

Her eyelids felt like sandpaper against her eyeballs. "It hurts."

"I know. Blink."

She blinked. At last tears seeped out. As they leaked down her cheeks, the searing slowly subsided. She turned out of his grasp to wipe her face, but her hands were sooty.

"Come here." He took her by the hand and led her behind the screen. They stood beside the toilet while he tore off a wad of paper. He carefully swabbed her eyes, then let her take over. In the mirror, they looked like characters in a school play—she a coal-stained street urchin, he a silver-dusted prince.

"Can you handle one more level?" he asked.

"Of course," she said, mustering some dignity.

She followed him around another corner, up another set of stairs, and onto the roof. The air was hot and muggy but alive, electric. They stood under a billowing creamy canvas draped over bamboo poles propped at haphazard angles, wired together at various joints. Just overhead, white orchids in plastic pots seemed to be suspended in midair. They were strung from the poles by clear thread. It—all of it—was dreamlike, breathtaking. What did any of it mean? She had no idea. She just wanted to keep looking.

They sat on the edge of the roof. The air hugged her dangling legs. Past her own feet she could see the creek, black and glinting from this height, and scraps of industrial waste carelessly—almost grandly—flung about. A bridge spanned the water, the occasional car streaking orange light toward rows of skyscrapers bedecked in neon.

Gradually, her eyes closed. Whirring and clatter, almost like her mother's kitchen sounds wafting up to her old bedroom. Sounds of construction, no doubt. She imagined sneaking into a site and conking out like the laborers she'd seen in Beijing, sprawled corpselike amid lumber, drywall, the remains of their lunches.

"Whoa." Hands clamped on her shoulders. "Careful. Stand up."

She let herself be pulled backward and upright.

Byron looked truly scared. "You were falling asleep. Let's head back."

There were no cabs in sight. They trudged and trudged. Her feet seemed to be coming loose from her legs, her legs from her body. Soon they passed another construction site, an office tower, a monstrous middle finger sticking up at the rest of the city.

"That is just wrong," she said. "Isn't it?"

"I suppose it is."

"How can you stand it? So many buildings like this, and new ones going up every day, when they could be—like that." She tilted her head back.

"A building takes a lot of planning, a lot of manpower. I'm still a student. But I'm checking out a few more projects tomorrow. Right now this city, opportunitywise, is every architect's dream."

So he, too, wanted to make his mark on the world, maybe this part of the world—yet he could also let some things be. Maybe because he was a man, or because he was half white, or because architecture—a building, a construction site, a model, a blueprint—was easier to see than social progress. Or maybe simply because he was who he was.

A burst of light—fireworks? No, yet another construction site. A trio of workers perched high, shirtless, unhelmeted, unharnessed. Sparks flew from their drills and cascaded past the open sidewalks, onto parked cars, into the littered street. Some died on the way down; others burned out as they skipped across the pavement.

16

Susan drifted past pearl necklaces, pearl rings, pearl brooches—dainty, tacky, bridal. A miniature horse made of pink pearls—appalling. Until someone bought something, they were all trapped in this "pearl emporium" on the outskirts of Shanghai. That seemed to be the tour company's strategy. That, and the manufacturing of moments for people like Irene.

Every time they were ushered off the bus and through a gate and told what to see and buy, Irene rushed to raise her camera and pull out her wallet. One simulated moment after another, each flat or garish or dull. A true moment had nearly taken shape when they'd stood on the Bund yesterday—the tidal waves of migrant workers at leisure, the dark oily river, the space-age skyline built on marshland, its highlight a TV tower that was not only cocked like a rocket but flanked by a pair of globes, across from the stately row of neoclassical buildings preserved since the time of "No Dogs or Chinese People" signs and Shanghai's designation as the Whore of the Orient (what was the Whore of the West?)—the radiance gathering, until Irene's flash popped.

Susan paused. Dimly glowing in a glass case before her was a single black pearl. A black washed in blue and green and violet. Lunar blue and peacock green and star violet. It gave off light, but kept some for itself, secreting it inside.

A saleswoman appeared at her side. "Beautiful, isn't it?"

Susan nodded.

The saleswoman unlocked the case. "You have a keen eye. This pearl is not like the rest. It's ancient and natural. It came from the sea, from an oyster. It's a perfect sphere—the rarest kind."

She handed Susan the pearl. The size of her knuckle, the pearl wasn't set, strung, pierced, or glued. Just one pearl, unwearable, useless. Susan cradled it in her palm.

"Pearls are oyster shit, right?" she heard one of the girls—Kay?—say. "Isn't that weird?"

It was. The waste product of such a humble creature reflecting its sky, the underside of its shell, that gasoline-puddle iridescence. Eventually an oyster spat out its pearl, she remembered—but perhaps it was, nonetheless, its only treasure.

"The rest of our pearls are cultured. Don't misunderstand—cultured does not mean fake. A skilled farmer opens the shell of a freshwater mussel and inserts live tissue from another. From there, the process is the same. The mollusk coats the foreign matter with nacre, the same material it uses to build its shell." The saleswoman paused from her textbook diction. "I'm sure you know all pearls symbolize lunar qualities—hidden brilliance, secret life—but I have never seen a more perfect example than this pearl. That must be why it's been left untouched."

"How much?" Susan asked quietly. All at once, everyone else jostled near.

"You want that?"

"What for?"

"Are you sure it's real?" That was Kay.

Irene sighed. "Kay, we're not at a street market."

"This is China," Kay said. "They sell fake water."

Gazing straight at Susan, the saleswoman said, "It's easy to tell a fake. If you rub this pearl against your teeth, you can feel the natural surface. You can feel it is not factory-smooth. If I scraped it for you with a knife, you would see powder, not a plastic bead inside. But I think, with this pearl, you can trust your eye."

Irene took the pearl and held it to the light. "It's pretty, but what can you do with it?"

Susan took the pearl back. She could hold it. She could keep it.

"How much is it?" she asked again.

The saleswoman stated the price. Susan jumped a little. She'd never bought such an expensive thing, a thing to simply hold and keep.

"The price would be double in Hong Kong," the saleswoman said. "In America, at least triple. But that's irrelevant. You will never find a pearl like this again."

Everyone was turning away, taking Susan's stillness for loss of interest—everyone but the saleswoman and Irene.

"You really want it?" Irene asked, taken aback.

"What the hell," Susan said. "I'm fifty-six."

"You can afford it?"

"It'll be Winston's anniversary present for me. Birthday and Christmas, too."

She and Irene and the saleswoman laughed. Another perk of marriage—always useful in conversation, for camaraderie among women, for a bit of deflection. Susan reached for her wallet. Her new purchase would fit nicely inside her travel purse.

"Well, eventually the girls can inherit it." Irene laughed again.

Susan nestled the pearl into its velvet box, its man-made home, and vowed to have it buried with her.

Later, the girls were in her room—her and Sophie's room. The pairs had been switched—had they planned that, too? Three lithe bodies surrounding her middle-aged body, six shrewd eyes trained on her tense face.

"That night?" she said. "What about it?"

They said they'd been reminiscing. That yellow house, the dead plants, the cannibal fish. Kay hearing voices in the middle of the night and seeing a man at the door. A man—a boy?—with a Spanish accent. In the middle of the night. At her door. Her student? She nodded, then shook her head. Why had he come to her house in the middle of the night?

Her little yellow house overrun. Six invaders who'd never doubted their right to all the space they could occupy. Snoring and sighing from every room she'd kept closed. Ernesto in her doorway, his eyes like black ice. Seeing her face through the grimy window of the pickup truck in the parking lot wasn't enough for him, apparently.

You know, I actually prefer men. They feel more than you do. In one encounter, they feel more. But no matter how American, they can't marry me. I thought you would. Why do you think I kept coming back to you? You fading old poet, you Asian with no soul. You're not even a real professor. I never loved you.

And then he started to sob in her doorway. Her Latin lover, a sobbing boy.

I think you knew about them. You never let yourself love me. I think you knew.

She thought she knew. She thought she couldn't be devastated, not completely.

Let me in this time, for real. Let's go back to bed. Tonight never happened. Please, let's pretend.

He was always unafraid of melodrama, cliché, error. She closed the door, still holding herself like so—intact, upright. But there was a creaking and moaning, as if her insides were collapsing—her guts, her bones—or, perhaps, her soul.

She had not thought of a niece's footsteps on the cracked parquet floor.

Now, like an act of charity, Kay suggested he'd been disgruntled over a paper, a grade. There was sympathy in Nora's gaze, maybe remorse. Sophie was wide-eyed, as if she'd stumbled upon a generally dignified creature in heat and couldn't avert her gaze.

Susan managed to say that she didn't know, couldn't remember. Then she cleared her throat and asked today's date. She pointed out that the tour was more than half over. That time was running out. That in less than a week, their grandfather would be flying to Hong Kong.

Instantly they were abashed. Hushed and anxious, they said they hadn't come up with a plan.

She reassured them, in an auntly way. She'd help deliver the news. She'd bring them to Ma tonight—right now, in fact.

So the four of them marched into the corridor. Susan knocked. Ma opened the door, looking a little gratified at their visit.

"Ma, the girls have something to tell you," Susan said.

And she stood back, already braced. She'd learned long ago to cover her ears without lifting her hands.

And then she was typing again into a dusky electronic hum: ernesto @ernesto.com. *So your star is rising,* she wrote. *Meanwhile, I've settled.* She hit return. *Where are you?* She hit return again. *You once said I had a writer's eye, or no soul. Do you remember what you meant? I once thought I knew.* She read what she'd written, then deleted back to *you?* Electricity crackled, air vents hissed. *Bite me,* she typed, and clicked send.

What had she done? She considered yanking the plug, smashing the screen. She covered her face. She was losing herself here on the mainland. She needed to be home with her husband.

She'd met Winston in September, too, one year after the first time she saw Ernesto in a parking lot, one summer after the last time she saw Ernesto in a parking lot. She'd barely finished that second semester. She'd drunk alone at night. She'd shattered Dave's one martini glass. She'd intermittently sustained herself on instant noodles and calcium chews. She'd sat through workshops silent, called one student a twit, misplaced an entire bin of final portfolios, while Ernesto watched, lip curled. She'd been lucky to get her next job, where Winston turned up as a visiting professor, eager to cook Cantonese dinners and claim her with a diamond.

The computer beeped. Susan startled. A new message, from ernesto @ernesto.com. A string of numbers and one word: *Please.* A secret code? Ten digits. A phone number, with no hyphens or spaces. In her purse, she found a tissue and a pen. At the end of each stroke, the fibers tore.

Walled in a phone booth, dialing, she realized the area code was familiar. His voice was deeper, slower. He was ten years older, too. She wasn't twice his age anymore.

"Your e-mail," he said. "Now that was a poem."

"So where are you?"

"Madison, Wisconsin."

Another town she'd inhabited for one semester. He hadn't asked, but she said, "I'm in China. On a tour."

"A book tour?"

"Sightseeing."

"Yes, of course. My mind—it's brutal, this. Have you seen the reviews? No, because there are almost none. And it feels like rape. I was raped as a boy, did I ever tell you?"

He'd been drinking. He had told her, in a story and in his sleep. She wished she'd been drinking, too.

"I bought a black pearl today. It made me think of you."

"A black pearl. A single pearl, not a handful? Now that is even more useless. So I am the pearl? But I always argued for the thread. What is the metaphor?"

"I don't know. Passion. Poems. Something I've been missing."

"So come," he said.

"What?"

"You already have a suitcase, yes? Your passport, American. You just go to the airport and purchase a ticket. Now planes fly from China anywhere in the world, isn't that right?"

"I can't come."

"You contacted me. And not just to say congrats. Let me guess. You have a husband now. A nice man, a nice house. Maybe even a nice ring—diamond, of course."

"Yes."

"You know, I married, too. Now I'm a citizen like you. I'm not your student anymore. In fact, you can call me Professor."

She was silent.

"Or not," he said. "Just come. My wife and I lead separate lives, just as you and I once did."

"What about my husband?"

"Do you love him?"

Did she love him? Did she love him? When they married, it hardly mattered. Winston was everything she hadn't known she needed until she met him. He was nourishment, he was moderation. He was steadiness, he was structure, he was home.

"Obviously not," Ernesto said. "So he is not my concern."

She asked, "What will you give up?"

"Me, I will give up nothing. You understand?"

"No. I never did."

"I will not sweep you out like you swept me."

"I didn't know what else to do."

In a mature, reassuring tone she'd never heard before, he said, "I know. It's okay. It was long ago. And, after all, it's like I always said—we are star-crossed lovers, you and I."

A sound broke free from her throat, part laugh, part sob.

"So come," he said. "And take off the ring. Diamonds don't suit you."

Hands shaking, she pulled. "It won't come off."

"Pull harder. Then throw it. Throw it far away."

She pulled until the ring popped off her knuckle and flew through her fingers to the floor.

"Good enough," he said. "I heard it fall. Now hang up and head to the airport."

From a corner of the phone booth, the diamond glittered. On her finger was a ghost of a ring, a band of pale skin, slightly withered. It started to glow even as she hung up.

17

Washing up, Irene thought she heard a commotion. She swabbed her face dry and stepped into the corridor. The door to Ma's room was ajar.

"I'm your grandma," Ma shouted.

Sophie's eyes bulged.

"Of course you are," Nora said.

"Yes, and he's our grandfather," Kay said.

"Is he? Because you have his blood? Blood means nothing!"

Susan stood rigidly against a wall. Irene glared at her, but it didn't carry. Susan had already dissociated from the fray, and Irene herself was retreating into the backdrop. Her daughters, meanwhile, were like safari-goers stumbling upon an unknown beast.

Kay said, "I met him in Taiwan. He told me about your revolutionary work. He—"

"You don't know him. You don't know what kind of man he is." Ma's chest heaved. Her shouts were scratchy, embattled. It cost her now, this rage. "What has he ever done for you? Why should you side with him over me?"

Tremulously, Sophie said, "We're not siding with him. We're just telling you."

"You don't have to decide anything now," Nora said. "Just think about it."

"I don't need to think about it. I decided twenty years ago."

Kay said, "If you saw how weak he is now, how his hands shake—"

"Good. Let him die."

Irene's daughters were stunned into silence.

Briskly, Irene said, "Okay, Ma. We get it. *Suan le*."

She motioned to her daughters, and they started to follow. They had an inkling now, of the kind of mother who'd raised her. Of what she'd overcome in teaching herself to be another kind of mother. Once the door shut behind them, she'd enfold them in her arms. She'd keep the past at bay, where it belonged.

But Nora hesitated and sat back down—this was her room. Kay and Sophie ducked past. Irene didn't catch their glances, but she felt them, tiny bullets. *Let him die.* The echo suddenly so loud, she might as well have said it again: *Good riddance.*

She could've reached out for the thousandth time. Instead, she said, "Didn't I tell you?" No one responded.

Hangzhou, said to be heaven on earth, was getting drenched with rain by its supposed counterpart. West Lake, the inspiration for classical poems and paintings, the setting for romantic myths and presidential retreats, was a giant gray pocked puddle.

Irene's sneakers were waterlogged, her socks cold sponges, her pants soaked to the knee. A silly old song looped through her head. *It's my party and I'll cry if I want to—cry if I want to—cry if I want to*—of course, she couldn't. She could only keep slogging through.

At least the weather had subdued Ma. Not even she could rage while holding an umbrella upright in this downpour, avoiding the spikes and drips of other umbrellas, trying not to slip on the muddy, rocky terrain.

Feilai Peak, Lingyin Temple—if not this afternoon, then never. Why was Feilai Peak so named? And why was it carved with so many Buddhas? the local guide intoned, as if someone had asked. Then he promptly recited a legend involving an Indian monk, the peak flying over, the destruction of villages, and locals hobbling the peak with chisels. Indeed, nothing about this mountain, landscaped and staircased, suggested any aerial power. And why was Lingyin Temple special? the local guide continued in this irritating rhetorical style, and ushered them toward the Buddha inside—the largest Buddha of its kind in China, the largest sitting Buddha on earth, or something.

The group moved as one blob under a hodgepodge shell of umbrellas toward a cave whose placard promised the famous sight of "a thread of sky." Irene peered into the entrance—a swarm of jostling bodies and mucky shoes—and said she'd wait outside. Her daughters raised their eyebrows, the local guide and Tommy pursed their lips, Mr. Chu reminded her the admission was prepaid, George and Joyce said it would be a shame to miss out, Mr. and Mrs. Wong privately twittered; even Susan's expression, even Ma's, deemed her behavior unseemly. Irene ignored them and went to sit under a nearby pavilion, on a damp bench.

All around her, Chinese tourists eagerly hopped and skipped, pulling disposable slickers over their suits and dresses, tying plastic bags over their freshly permed hair and polished shoes, grinning and flashing peace signs. For them, traveling their own country was an unprecedented luxury, along with so much else in the new China, and they would not be thwarted by rain. Well, she wasn't one of them. For her, in this age of hype, of globalization, of time being the only commodity that ran scarce, that promised to run out, she supposed the only true guarantee any tour could offer was disillusionment.

A bolt of lightning, the sky cracking open, a searing, blinding flare. It mended itself almost instantly, even before the thunder crashed hard, triggering a collective cower, scattered screams.

Irene scurried into the cave. *A thread of sky*—she mouthed it to herself. Light radiating through a pinhole in the cave ceiling. She pictured an undulating line, alive and fine against the dark. The kind of thing you couldn't help but reach for, knowing there was nothing to grasp.

She scanned the ceiling, the walls, the corners. She couldn't see it. Every time she spotted a glow, it turned out to be the flash of a camera. Her own group was on the opposite side, separated from her by several other tour groups.

Straining forward, she found herself trapped behind two tall strangers.

"Do you see it?"

"Where?"

"There."

"I don't see it."

"Right there."

"That? Is that it?"

"I can't see what you're seeing."

She craned higher, focused harder, and finally saw a faint glimmer, up high and constant. She nearly tapped the first stranger to ask, *Is that it?* Could it be? All this, for that? She would've humbled herself to ask Tommy or the local guide, but they'd exited. Was she looking from the wrong angle? Standing too far, too close? Maybe the weather was wrong—the sky too gray, the cave too damp. Maybe the light was getting blotted out by all the tourists and their picture-taking. Keeping her own camera zipped in her purse, Irene gazed at the glimmer until it seemed imprinted. The moment she stepped outside, she could no longer see it, except when she closed her eyes.

Next was a boat ride—lake water sloshing up, rainwater spattering down. Abruptly, Ma pointed out what they floated toward, a statue standing over a tomb. A slender woman with a resolute face, long eyes looking into the distance, left hand on her hip, right hand on the hilt of a sword, its blade blending into the carved pleats of her skirt.

Kay read the inscription by Sun Yat-sen, the father of modern China himself. "Qiu Jin! But the sculpture's wrong—she never wore skirts."

Ma nodded and began to speechify. Qiu Jin the *gemingjia*, who left her husband and children to join the movement to overthrow the Qing rulers, seeing that gender equality was impossible under feudalism. Who crusaded for women's independence and education, against foot-binding and slave-marriages. Who founded a women's journal and directed a coed military school and composed a resistance song that schoolgirls used to sing. Who, through it all, wrote poems that would, Ma said, "make you try to fly." Whose final battle plan was leaked to government troops and who, at thirty-two, was beheaded by starlight.

Irene's daughters listened solemnly, while the other group members cast curious glances. Of course, most families did not consider revolution a career goal.

Ma wasn't finished yet. She, their grandma, had been compared to Qiu Jin. "And I named your mother after her—you didn't know?"

Her daughters stared at her. "We never knew," Kay said.

"I'm no revolutionary." Irene meant it wryly, but it came out pathetic.

"You could have been, in science." Ma turned back to Irene's daughters. "Instead, she focused on the three of you."

Irene's daughters nodded, unsuspecting that Ma did not mean this as a compliment.

At last, dinnertime. Tonight Irene felt thankful for a dry chair and a hot meal. Hangzhou specialties, the best meal of the tour so far. Beggar's chicken, wrapped in lotus leaves soaked in Shaoxing wine, baked in mud, and broken open at the table. Celery shoots stir-fried with the sweet white petals of lotus bulbs. River shrimp tossed with tea leaves. Stewed fatty pork, each hunk steeped in dark fragrant sauce and served in a clay cup with a soft bun to sop it up.

She ate, she made sure her daughters ate, and she waited for the day, if not the rain, to end.

The rain didn't end, but it waned, and as they sat in a tea factory the next morning, the patter sounded more soothing with each sip of Longjing tea. The tea factory guide, a pretty woman with a dulcet voice, gently directed their senses to the tea, in all its incarnations.

Its nutty aroma, its delicate crispness when chewed dry. The perfect confluence of climate and timing held in these burlap sacks, and the labor, of course, the handpicking of the most tender shoots during the one-month annual harvest, the drying and roasting performed with ten distinct and precise hand movements—see the old woman on the porch now, a bare withered hand swirling tea leaves in a fired pan. In their glasses (not cups), brewed with hot (not boiling) water, each leaf sinking to the bottom and, once unfurled, actually two baby leaves stemming from a heart. Its taste—a pungent absence of taste, of the grassiness or bitterness of other teas, lauded by a famous poet as the supreme taste—tapering to a slight lingering sweetness.

The desire it ignited among emperors of old and magnates of today, the prices its finest samples commanded by the pinch. Its powers against colds, flu, bad breath, bone and tooth decay, stress, high blood pressure, heart disease, cancer, aging, death itself, all of which Western science was now scrambling to test, extract, and bottle, when "we"—an inclusive nod, and everyone in the room hastened to return knowing nods—had always taken this for granted: Drink tea. This tea, if you were lucky.

Irene bought tea, more than anyone else, and signed without checking the total. She wasn't, as Kay thought, a dupe. Here was one more guarantee: the delight she gave Tommy and the local guides and the factory guides and the salesclerks when she pulled out her wallet, and the pieces of this country she took into her possession. Soon she'd have to buy another suitcase to carry them home.

And out of that suitcase, maybe she could begin to fashion a new life. A new pastime, at least. Studying Chinese antiques, silk embroidery, classical poetry—why not? Maybe her career would have played out completely differently if, instead of Alzheimer's, she'd researched green tea. Or ginseng, or acupuncture, or whether eating fish really made you smarter.

Outside, the clouds were swiftly opening, the sun finally gracing the stage, and at the suggestion of their suddenly leisurely guides, the group set off on a stroll around West Lake, its surface now a vast sheet of silk, shrouded by a deep stillness none of them could puncture. The mood wasn't just Irene's wistful state of mind, the Longjing tea in her system; it stretched well beyond her narrow borders. The sky melting into the mountains, faint enough to be mirages, melting into the water, all pearly gradations of pink and blue, swirled with the haze of a sweet languid dream. The scenery wasn't spectacular, but it lulled you, drew you into its shimmering folds, filled you with a slow heavy pleasure that was, at bottom, indistinguishable from an ache.

It became clear that this setting was meant for lovers. They knew it, all the Chinese couples now nuzzling on benches, holding hands on the paths designed for two, adorning the lake as fittingly as the silvery fish at its banks, the flitting birds, the swaying willow trees. Soon George and Joyce, and even Mr. and Mrs. Wong, stepped out as pairs, as model stable compounds, while the rest of them continued to drift and straggle, single reactive atoms that, grouped, remained formless.

The local guide pointed out Broken Bridge, where the legend of Bai She began; a tradition lived on of girls waiting there to meet prospective grooms. Across the lake were the remains of Thunder Pagoda, where Bai She was said to have been crushed. Plans were under way for a reconstruction that would encase the ruins at its center.

Kay had caught a bit of his Cantonese. "Oh, I studied the story of Bai She."

Ma nodded. "Everyone should."

Eager to please, Kay said, "In every Chinese folktale I've read, the women are such strong, complex characters. And of course, there's no Disney rule that a happy ending means a wedding."

"Did you approve of *Mulan*?" Byron was lingering close to Kay, smiling slightly.

Kay seemed caught between responding to him and seeking Ma's approval. "The movie? I watched it at AACAP. Nothing offensive, really. But they added a love story, when 'being a Mulan' actually means rejecting the conventions of romance and marriage. And they made the moral 'Be true to yourself,' when the original message was about the duty to fight to better society."

Perhaps sensing a safe topic, Nora asked, "What's the moral of Bai She?"

Kay paused. "Actually, I'm not sure. The story's so complicated."

Ma prodded her. "Tell it."

A little nervously, Kay began, "Bai She—literally, white snake—was an immortal who lived in the heavens. One day, she and her best friend, Qing She—green snake—decide to explore the human world, and transform themselves into a beautiful woman and her maid. They land here at West Lake, spot a handsome young man, and follow him to Broken Bridge. When they get caught in the rain, he offers his umbrella. He's a mere mortal man, a poor scholar named Xu Xian, and even though Bai She can't reveal her origins, they fall in love and get married."

"So far, it could be a Disney movie," Nora said.

"That's just the beginning. They set up a medicine shop together—she sees the patients, he dispenses the herbs, they treat the poor for free—and soon she gets pregnant. But then an evil abbot tells Xu Xian his wife is a demon who will devour him, and instructs him to feed her a special wine that wards off spirits."

"He's the bad guy?" Sophie asked. "A monk?"

Kay and Ma nodded.

"But she is a demon—a snake—or whatever."

"Well, in one version the abbot is just enforcing heavenly law against marriage between humans and immortals. But in most versions, he's vindictive because their practice has prevented him from fleecing the poor. Anyway, one night Xu Xian gives in and pressures Bai She to drink the wine. She takes a sip and rushes to bed, begging him not to look. He pulls the curtain to find, in place of his beloved wife, a big white snake, and he dies of shock right then and there."

"Being a mere mortal man." Byron again.

After a beat, Nora asked, "The end?"

Looking a bit flustered, Kay said, "Eventually Bai She wakes as a woman again, sees her husband's corpse, and flies off to find a magical herb to revive him. Since the herb isn't meant for humans, she's forced to battle the celestial guards until the head immortal becomes so moved by her determination that he lets her go. The herb brings Xu Xian back to life, but then—in one version, she convinces him nothing happened. In another, he can't forget the sight of the white snake. In any case, somehow he gets lured to the abbot's temple and imprisoned there. Bai She tries to rescue him, but being pregnant, her powers are weakened. She finally retreats, gives birth to a son, and then—in one version—"

Nora and Sophie groaned.

"Old stories are like that," Ma said.

"I'll wrap it up," Kay said. "In the end, the abbot traps Bai She under Thunder Pagoda. Some say she's trapped there to this day."

"And so she is a symbol," Ma proclaimed. "For Chinese women. For the women's rights movement. We all feel the weight, the oppression. And we remember the evil of men—their cruelty and weakness, when a woman's power scares them."

"For heaven's sake," Irene said. "She's not a woman. She's a snake goddess. And it's just a story. A love story—that's why girls still wait on the bridge."

In a conciliatory tone, Nora said, "It's an interesting take on a love story—the easy part is getting married."

But Ma was already facing down Irene. "If you don't know the significance of Bai She, you don't know anything."

Ma was right: However the legend had originated, in their time, in the movie, the TV serial, the opera, Bai She had become a feminist heroine. But Irene was right, too. She said again, "It's just a story. A love story."

Anxiously, Kay said, "Some versions have a happy ending. Qing She defeats the abbot. Or the son grows up and the two of them free Bai She together."

"What about the mere mortal man?" Byron asked, innocently enough.

Kay seemed flummoxed. "What about him?"

"Well, he dropped out of the story."

Kay looked to her grandmother.

"He was disloyal. He's dead. He's nothing," Ma said.

"Enough," Irene said. "If you don't want to see Ba, don't. We don't need to hear any more about it."

"You? You're the ones who raised him from the dead," Ma shouted. Her chest was heaving again. "How long has he been scheming? Why did you bring me all the way here?"

There were many ways to answer that. Irene said she didn't know.

Even amid the ensuing stir, Ma spitting something about a worthless daughter, Nora and Kay and Sophie trying to intervene, Susan retreating to invisibility again, the guides gathering the group—not because of their quarrel, but because, as always, it was time to move on—the mood remained somehow unbroken. Eventually Irene resumed strolling. Nora and Kay, looking childlike and unnerved, stayed with her. Sophie stuck by Ma, the way she'd stuck by Bill—unaware, of course, that if either of them had prevailed, she wouldn't exist.

After a few minutes, Nora said, "Grandma needs to let it all out. Then maybe she'll get over it."

Irene recoiled at the absurdity of these American mantras—*Get over it. Let it all out*—just as she saw that to her daughters, they seemed irrefutable. She supposed here, too, her Chineseness was dominant: the innate observance of containment, the knowledge that the weight of the past endured, that there are burdens people must carry.

As if sensing the direction of Irene's thoughts, Nora added, "Maybe she'll never get over it completely. But enough to just hear him out, before it's too late."

Resolutely, Kay said, "She has to see him again. We all have to."

At first, Irene had thought her daughters' interest in this matter sprang from the compulsion to defy her. Then she'd seen how it struck a particular chord in each of them. To Sophie, it seemed profound, the stuff of art. For Kay, it was a strenuous dig into what had been painstakingly buried. For Nora, it was a bet on an abstract fate—with someone else's money, but her own pride, on the line.

Now she understood: Her father had become a stand-in for their father. And no matter how well she knew that Ma wouldn't see him, that she'd meant it when she said, *Let him die*—no matter how much she wanted to protect her daughters from that cold certainty, there was nothing she could do.

Lightly, she said, "That Byron seems interested in you, Kay."

Kay shrugged.

Nora murmured, "Could he go where no man has gone?"

Kay blushed.

"What?" Irene asked.

Quickly, Nora said, "Kay rejects her suitors, that's all."

Obviously the joke wasn't meant for Irene's ears. But here was a chance, at last, for mother-daughter confidences. "Well, that's fine. When it comes to choosing your mate, you girls have a world of options. Your grandmother wasn't so lucky, and look what it's done to her." She reached for a phrase or two that seemed of their generation. "All I'm saying is, don't settle for anything less than the one."

"But that idea is absurd," Kay said. "*He's the one. We're soul mates. It was fate!* As if out of the billions of people in the world, this one was designed just for you—and lo and behold, he's not an old Tibetan goatherd."

"You've never been in love. That feeling when everything seems to align—" Nora stopped.

Irene asked, "Did you think Jesse was your soul mate?"

"Who said I believe in soul mates?" Nora snapped.

"I'm just asking. No one talked about soul mates when I was growing up. I'm not sure what it means. When I met your father—" She trailed off.

Bill and his goodness, his twinkle, his promises, compared to Ba and his meanness, his arrogance, his mistresses. Ma had made her choice mid-war. Irene had made hers as a clueless immigrant, hungry for a home. She and Bill had picked each other out of a pool of seven. They seemed to have so much in common—everything seemed to align—when maybe it was just thrown into sharp relief.

Or maybe they had been soul mates, until they became parents. Maybe they could have remained soul mates, if he'd taken a little more proprietary interest in her daughters—their daughters—or if she'd taken a little less. Or if—recently she'd caught a few talk shows—he'd said something like *I hear you,* instead of *Ah well.*

Then what? He'd be alive now? In their empty nest, they'd rediscover each other? Or he still would have left her and their three daughters for Maine?

In Chinese, the word was *yuanfen*—fate, fortune, luck, or none of those really. Something between opportunity and destiny; a concept her daughters probably couldn't grasp. You'd say you and another person have *yu-*

anfen if the threads of your lives converge, whether they intersect at a crucial point or become intertwined.

Bill had meant to leave her—did that mean they didn't have *yuanfen*? He'd died in the act—was that *yuanfen*? Maybe after a few months in Maine, he would have come back. Or maybe not. Maybe her *yuanfen* was still ahead, some twirl of the thread she hadn't reached yet. But what was *yuanfen* then, but consolation for your lot? Maybe she no longer grasped the concept, either.

Kay broke the silence. "We're brainwashed to believe love should lead to marriage, which was instituted for economic and social control, but now also means lifelong companionship, sexual passion, intellectual stimulation, compatibility in child rearing, division of housework, money management—everything. Nobody feels completely fulfilled, since that's impossible, so hello consumerism—*Buy this and they'll love you!* No wonder our culture doesn't produce a Mulan, or a Qiu Jin, or even someone like Grandma." Kay was passionate in what she was saying, but she was also desperately trying to steer them out of dangerous territory.

"So you could fall in love and not want all the rest?" Irene asked. "Marriage, children, a home, a sense of permanence? When you're ready?"

"I don't think I'll ever be ready," Kay declared.

Nora shrugged, her face expressionless.

"I guess you girls are too modern for me." What was love, then, if unmoored from the foundations of society? So disembodied and lofty, it must be terrifying to seek, let alone find. Was that progress?

Kay said, "Actually, there are matriarchal, matrilineal tribes in southern China where, traditionally, the women take temporary lovers. They raise children communally. And they govern their villages and perform physical labor."

"That sounds exhausting." A little facetiously, Irene added, "Are you sure these tribes weren't invented by men?"

"The men have paternal duties and contribute financially. But there's no pretense that the male-female bond—love, sex, whatever—is a stable foundation. There's no societal fallout to a breakup."

"Then what's the foundation?" Irene asked.

"The bonds between women, between women and children, I guess."

What if they'd all started with the premise that romantic love expired, that fidelity was futile, that the lasting connections would be among the six of them—among Irene and her daughters, at least? Wasn't that what she'd hoped they'd see when she first conceived of this tour?

As casually as she could, she said, "Why not?"

"Why not?" Nora repeated. "We don't get along with each other any better than we do with men."

Nora and Kay laughed, and then Irene did, too, with an effort.

That night, Irene was sitting alone in her hotel room when Tommy informed her that she owed for minibar charges and an international call from the last hotel. He read out the number. She asked him to repeat it. She told him to bill her at the end, and to repeat the number one more time.

She sat on the edge of the bed and picked up the phone. Reflexively, the pattern of her fingertips, the melody of the numbers, prompted her mind to clipped requests—milk and eggs, the dry cleaning. Then his voice, his name, a beep, and silence.

Bill's cell phone was in his briefcase, which she'd tucked in a closet. Its charge must have run out long ago, but not the service. It was one thing Nora had overlooked.

Tales of grief always seemed to begin with the ordinariness of the moment. *I got the call at work. We were sitting down to dinner. I thought he was asleep.* But there was nothing ordinary about the day Bill died. After thirty years, he'd just driven off.

Before he did, he set up the bills to be paid automatically, just as he packed his toothbrush and razor and cholesterol pills, made sure no boxers or socks were loose in the laundry. Everything he wasn't taking that was clearly his, not theirs, he filed and boxed and stored. He tried to tell her particulars of the boiler, the recycling, the satellite dish, and ended up leaving a folder of notes—his role in the house, so compact. At the time, all of this seemed a parting shot: Even in leaving her, he was a good man.

The night before he left, neither of them slept. She hadn't banished him from the room. Sleeping in the same bed hadn't meant much for a long while. They lay silent, their awareness of each other's awareness like another presence in the room. Just as night began to let up, he said, "You never asked me to stay." Her back was to him, yet she shut her eyes tight. She thought she had. *At least wait till Sophie's in college,* she'd said.

In her first years in America, the word that confused her most was *leave*. To leave was to go, but if something was left, it stayed. Once she'd picked a silly fight and Bill shook his head and walked away, and she chased him and cried, "Please leave!" He stared, laughed, and kissed her. It was one of their earliest fights, when even the pain of love was a delicious novelty, like the first bite of an ice cream cake shooting through the thin enamel of her front teeth.

He was a good man. This was the essence of Nora's eulogy, and the refrain, utterly heartfelt, from everyone else. It seemed the best and most crucial thing to say, not only about him, but about any man. It was what Irene had known about her husband from the start, and what he'd want said about himself. It was true. And he was gone. And he'd excised himself so considerately that whether he was gone for a year or forever, the view for her was much the same. The view—but not the feeling.

She missed Bill. She missed him. His bulky shoulders, his stupid jokes, the way he always bought too many groceries, the way he lumbered to the bathroom half asleep. Even the shaven stubble he left in drifts around the sink no matter how many times she told him to wipe up—

white flecking the black in recent years, and sharp as splinters. It wasn't emptiness inside, but a force she'd kept down for nearly a year, now surging, as if she were trapped alone on a plane with a punctured cabin, pressure leaking, and she could plunge into thin air, or sit and burst out of her skin.

She whispered, "Please stay," and laid the phone back in its cradle.

18

Such nerve he had.

The life she'd lost, the life he'd stolen. The rumors, the truth worse than the rumors. The thunderous fights, the decades of tight-lipped endurance. The day she left: He stepped out, she packed up. A one-way ticket, her one suitcase. Everything she left behind—he could rot in it. The tongue-tied character she became in English, the apron-clad grandma she became for the girls. The peaceful life she finally made for herself in old age, in California.

In her own home, Lin Yulan was strong, self-sufficient, active, autonomous. On this tour, she had to just keep up. And she could have, if not for her failing body. Aching joints, blistering feet, diarrhea—such were the afflictions finally dragging her down.

Meanwhile, her daughters and granddaughters complained, heaved loud sighs, cursed at mosquitoes—one bane she'd outlasted. Mosquitoes, like men, prefer younger, softer flesh—eating tofu, as the saying goes.

The numbness in her arm was spreading. Soon it might be like a phantom limb, a part of herself she carried around, though it no longer knew it belonged to her.

Her body had always had a will of its own. The way, long ago, it answered to his touch. Eagerly conceived from his seed. Susan, Irene, her son: like one, two, three. Another she aborted. Another who died unborn. And there would have been more, had she not refused his touch completely. Of course this was the lot of women of her era, of every era preceding her daughters'—but it also seemed that her body was bent on betraying her.

Now, for the first time, her mind was betraying her, too. Waking in so many different beds, she kept forgetting why she could not do as she wished; why she could not tend her garden, eat her weekly lunch with Lou, be left in peace. She could not keep straight the day, the date, even the year. She could not always remember why she was being rushed from strange city to strange city, ordered off cold vehicles and through forbidding gates, forced to pack and unpack and pack again. She had to keep reminding herself: This was a vacation. In a few more days, she would be allowed to return home.

And now Irene said she didn't know why she'd brought her on this tour. Was it on account of him? It seemed *he* had told Kay about her revolutionary days. Had he inspired the curiosity of all three granddaughters? Had he directed her daughters to wait for her to weaken, then set this scheme in motion? Had he orchestrated this tour from the start?

Yet they stared at her now, like she was a crazy old woman, crazed over old wrongs. She'd never had patience with tradition, she wasn't given to nostalgia, she did not look back. They were forcing her to. They were pushing her into the past.

A giant arm rising from the grave, disembodied, sculpted from stone. A hand groping for rocky earth, a tattered elbow pushing up against the branches of an evergreen tree. A wide barren stretch of jagged gray. A path of survivors' footprints, indented in concrete. A broken wall, with grotesque figures of staggering victims carved in relief. Music from hidden speakers, breathy and high-pitched, more fitting for a haunted house than a massacre memorial.

Gaudy strings of stacked paper cranes adorned the passage to the burial site. Their tour group entered the mass grave, separated from skeletons on either side by glass. Bones and earth in graduated layers, like terraced rice fields, an efficient design, actually picturesque. Yellow sandy earth, patches of young moss, and bones—perfectly domed skulls in profile, a whole rib cage, many shards. Loose limb bones, one end neatly knobbed, the other end shattered. Bones are slender to the point of elegance, as if meant to be admired as well as used. A wonder they don't break more easily than they do.

Explanations were posted for the grisliest remains, explanations that further bewildered. A woman's jaws nearly unhinged, open wider than in the worst scream, because she'd died with something much too big jammed into her mouth. A sixteen-year-old with a foot-long iron nail drilled into her pelvis. Such invention, such effort, to maximize shame and pain.

The crowds jostled forward, pushing her against the glass. She withdrew. Above all their heads, ripe sunlight seeped through the evergreen branches onto the pavement covering the grave outside.

The Nanjing massacre, only the most sensational of its kind. This memorial, built on one of many *wan ren keng*—ten-thousand-corpse pits that marked the invaders' progress. If you mapped them so you could see the web that stretched across provinces, sucked the life out of cities, suffocated whole villages, and then looked close, you might find the threads of her own life in those years.

Xiao luan ju cheng, da luan ju xiang. In times of small chaos, reside in the city; in times of big chaos, reside in the countryside. The village of her youth, like every village, had been besieged by bandits who attacked with ropes, rods, and guns in the middle of the night, faces painted and bodies naked. She was fifteen when they struck next door and left the watchmen hanged, the servants and grandparents bound, the father and sons beaten, the mother and daughter raped, the house ransacked. Her family packed up.

In the city, she climbed up the high school ranks, served as class president, won the principal's notice with her essays on social justice, was told she'd be one of the chosen few to attend college. Every day after school, she prowled the university campus, dazzled by the fiery student speeches, the women's basketball team, the giant sapphire of a new swimming pool.

Then the Japanese invaded. The city terrorized, the university shuttered, the pool seized as a shit pit for their horses.

Back in the village, she honed her arguments: the continuing subjugation of women, the atrocious waste of their capabilities, how a backward, divided nation had no hope for strength and sovereignty.

The man who would be her husband, one of a visiting delegation of local officials, saw her work posted on the school wall and sent it to the leading women's journal—this when women's journals were devoted to revolution, not housekeeping and fashion. At eighteen, she became a major new voice in the movement, attracting notice throughout her province, garnering comparisons to a legend.

She mistook him for a benefactor, and soon her savior.

The countryside was safer, not safe. Japanese troops periodically stormed through to hold competitions for most women raped, most men killed, most brutal methods. Each time the crier spotted troops approaching, she and her family tramped over the hills to hide out in neighboring villages. The last time they tramped back, theirs was one of the houses on fire.

Uncles and aunts and cousins fell victim. Her father was taking his second wife and new son to Singapore. Her mother, health failing, was determined to die in her ancestral home.

The man who would be her husband offered not only protection, but the chance to stay and fight, a vision of their lives joined and given to their nation.

When he brought her to his village, his mother—his father's first wife, who, as befitted her status, took him from the third wife—puffed incessantly at her water pipe while she surveyed Lin Yulan, then sent her to wait in the courtyard. Lin Yulan heard every word of the appraisal: not pretty, stubborn forehead, thick turnip legs. He told his mother she could rot in her feudalist mentality if she couldn't see that his betrothed was headed for greatness.

Lin Yulan didn't see, back then, how a person could be so righteous in his politics and so depraved in his personal conduct. Men like him claimed to fight for women's rights, flaunted a wife like her as a badge of modernity, rode the cause to prominence, then made fools of the cause and the wife. She'd actually believed adultery was a feudalist condition. At least under feudalism, first wives were given due status. She paraded as an example to Chinese women everywhere while he made whores of her followers. *Gua yang tou, mai gou rou*: hanging a lamb's head to sell dog meat.

Ahead of the tour group, she walked aboveground again, then into another hall, cool and dim. The carnage catalogued: a Japanese soldier's diary, a rusty bayonet, a newspaper clipping of Tokyo celebrating the latest death tolls. Appeals submitted by ordinary citizens and Western missionaries to the government—but there was no government then. There was no China. Only a puppet regime controlled by foreign imperialists, the Nationalists trying to unify from the south, the Communists trying to mobilize from the north, warlords all across. No common language, no common interest, until the Japanese gave them one: resistance.

At each juncture, she was one of the lucky ones, the survivors. In Guangzhou, his salary was paid in rice, rice mixed with sand before weighing. Every time the Japanese attacked, they fled on foot. During air raids, they rafted downriver. Just before the city fell, they escaped with her firstborn in a picker's basket. At every chance, she made feverish circuits, writing speeches by gaslight, delivering them to desperate crowds, organizing thousand-strong protests, coordinating takeovers of municipal buildings, insisting she be arrested along with her male peers, distributing her journal even after a collaborator was assassinated by a Japanese agent, even as her second child arrived, her third.

You cannot memorialize every loss.

Black-and-white photographs enlarged to dizzying pointillism. Up close, the faces, especially, made no sense. Young men digging their own mass graves. A makeshift marching band of starving children. Women in neat formations, escorted to be raped and killed. Women the ages of her daughters, the ages of her granddaughters. A wrinkled old woman, perhaps older than she, post-rape, slumped on the ground and staring into the camera, black tape belatedly covering her privates. A scrawny eight-year-old girl, post-rape. Rape and rape and rape. Other women, unphotographed, had their *bi* used as openings into which soldiers rammed a whole arm, a beer bottle, a bamboo pole, a bayonet, and killed them from inside. Those left alive—how many conceived, how many carried to term? These days people still warned against marrying Nanjing natives, for fear of Japanese blood.

Once she returned to her journal offices to find a naked corpse on the doorstep with a dog maw-deep. A woman, of course, right breast hacked off, left breast hanging by shreds and too rotted for even the dog, who kept to the face and neck. Lin Yulan had to demonstrate her resolve against such threats. She got hold of her daughters and marched them to the corpse, collecting supporters on the way over. She chased away the dog and, gripping her daughters by their collars, one tottering at each knee, delivered an impromptu speech about generations of women, legacies of defiance. The dog crept back so many times that, midway, she called for a burlap sack and heaved the corpse inside, headfirst. Then, putrid hands held aloft, she finished her speech.

The rest of the group entered the hall. Her eyes strayed to the English text her granddaughters read. 中国畏复: "Bring China to her knees in terror." So this language of the New World, always "he" and "his," shifted to the feminine in this context.

She turned a corner and gasped. Staggering out of the shadows, something two-headed, half alive. Sunken eyes staring into hers for help. She had the presence of mind to cover her mouth, muffle a cry.

Mannequins—a woman carrying a dead little boy in her arms. A mother with ghastly eyes, glazed with agony, carrying her dead son, bloody limbs dangling.

Bitter liquid burned up her throat. She swallowed it.

"Looks like ketchup," a girl whispered to her boyfriend.

Sharply, Lin Yulan turned. The young couple blushed and murmured an apology. Lin Yulan turned back to the figures. The blood did look cheap. Dribbled paint, tomato red. A cruel joke. A cruel display. Cruel and fitting.

She found a bench just outside, where cold air leaked onto her each time visitors exited.

A memorial like this was necessary, even though the Party hadn't seen fit to build it until a half-century after the fact. These dead deserved national mourning; much of the world had no idea; those responsible had yet to apologize. And yet it made little difference. Those who remembered would always remember. Those who didn't would never understand.

Memorial or no, when a nation had the motive and the means to subjugate another, it would try. The Japanese were deluded imbeciles, boasting they'd conquer this vast patchwork of territories in three months, believing the restoration of riches and power to the divine ruler of their puny islands was worth rivers of Chinese blood. They needed to ravage everyone in their path, because in the midst of their holy war, they could not deny that their victims were all too human.

When America dropped bombs on Japan, it was a cinematic attack on a two-dimensional population, a calculated wipeout of millions. When the Japanese raped and slaughtered the Chinese, it was an intimate act. They fortified themselves by acknowledging the humanity of their victims, and desecrating it.

Their methods were the most monstrous, but their aims were not unique. The line of imperialists who came to carve up the empire was long and illustrious. The British, opium in one hand, firearms in the other. The Russians, the French, the Germans, the Dutch. The Manchu ruling family—foreign conquerors, too.

Not to forget the *neigui,* the demons within. The bandits, among whose ranks, everyone knew, was at least one friendly neighbor. The peasants who served as guides for Japanese troops. The officials who saw more promising careers as turncoats. The Nationalist leaders who hoarded riches while their soldiers, barefoot and hungry, looted from those even more powerless, thus helping to hand the support of the masses to Mao—or who themselves joined the Communists, who, never having been the ruling party, were able to call their victory a revolution, even as they banished true citizens like her, claimed credit for everything they'd achieved, then revealed themselves to be as rapacious for power and profit as the rest.

The greed of men, age-old and ineradicable. Men who believed borders existed to be trespassed, women to be used.

Her side had actually won. Their united efforts drove out the Japanese, they celebrated in the streets, her husband got a splashy promotion, she got a trophy position and a certificate. The rumors became deafening and she made plans to leave him, even with three small children. Then civil war erupted, and once again, she had to flee with him, with only what they could carry.

At the end of the day, they stood over the Yangzi River, waiting for the sunset. Nanjing was one of the three Chinese cities called furnaces, and even at this hour, the heat was so oppressive it seemed impossible, a momentary blast, but it didn't pass; she could see the air buckling under its weight. This bridge had been built to commemorate the Communist capture of the city, back when it was the capital, and the country she'd risked everything for was still her country. Lone fishermen slowly poled junk boats over the wide brown-gold river, looking unaware the last century had come and gone.

Her granddaughters were leaning against statues of Communist soldiers, lifting their luxuriant hair, rolling iced sodas over their supple necks.

"Three hundred thousand. How come I never knew?" Sophie said.

"Three hundred thousand in just one city," Kay said. "Ten to thirty million nationwide. Well, the way history is taught in America, how would you know?"

"That memorial." Nora shook her head. "Maybe it's wrong to critique the aesthetics, but—"

"No, it isn't," Sophie said.

Then Irene hushed them, with a glance in Lin Yulan's direction.

As if her feelings needed such safeguarding. As if their idle talk could rattle her, after a day spent plodding through the vestiges of a war that had wiped out all but one course for her life to take. As if the problem wasn't their treachery, but that she could be distressed by any mention of the past.

The sun was sinking now, but the low clouds, the heavy smog, the thick murky water, seemed to slow its descent, soaking its yellowest light into their depths.

Three hundred thousand, ten million, thirty million. The Nationalists never finished investigating the true death tolls before the Communist takeover. For decades, the Communists maintained silence, out of reluctance to acknowledge the Nationalist resistance, and out of shame. Then they learned to trumpet their victimization as part of the new nationalism, drowning out opposition to the new "Communism"—the pursuit of capital amid censorship and corruption.

The numbers staggered only if you didn't know what life was like then, even before the Japanese. How many men died at war; how many women died in labor. How babies starved with nothing to drink but their mothers' spit. How willingly poor parents would sell a child into servitude, give a boy free to a good family. How easily a sonless woman could claim another woman's as her own. How three children saved wasn't bad.

People forget. Life is common. Life is cheap.

19

Another tomb, another memorial. The streets of Nanjing looked enticing from the bus—airy, clean, lined with exuberant palm trees—but the bus kept driving through them to the next memorial. On the massive steps of this one, Nora pushed herself to climb faster until she was panting, thighs and calves taut, the others far below.

She was glad for the physical exertion; for the heat, unrelenting and external. She'd come to depend on the sightseeing for distraction, even moments of wonder, but always, too quickly, her attention turned inward again. Even at the massacre memorial the day before, her horror had soon subsided: *Well, wasn't the Holocaust worse? That text panel actually says, "Alas!" What day is today?*

It was the day her period was officially late.

She'd worn her sports bra for three days now; still her breasts were sore. The heaviness in her middle had become a steady presence. The flesh there was warmer than the rest of her, and tender, as if it could hardly contain some reaction inside.

At the temple in Suzhou, she'd found herself bowing her head, praying to a god she'd never heard of before. She'd told herself that if she convinced her grandmother to see her grandfather, she wouldn't be pregnant. If she finished her rice, if it rained again. If she wasn't pregnant, she'd devote the rest of her life to nonprofit. She'd be nicer to her mother. She'd forgive Jesse. She'd take him back. And if she was pregnant? Wouldn't she be more tied to him than ever? Even if she got rid of it? What then?

Before her was a dim chamber where someone important lay, but she didn't know who; she couldn't read the signs, and she wouldn't feel anything anyway. All around her, the crowds were swirling and fizzing with excitement, as if they might spill back down the steps. Their jabber steadily surged until someone hissed for quiet, and then, just as a hush spread, the jabbering rose again.

The rest of her group was nearing the top of the steps—except her grandmother, who lagged well behind. Tentatively, Nora descended to her side. Her grandmother was huffing, sweat collecting on her forehead, her determined tread faltering. Nora held out her arm, but her grandmother ignored it.

When they reached the top, Nora offered, "That was a hard climb."

"For Sun Yat-sen, we should all climb. He was a good man. A great man." Grandma pointed to the characters inscribed in gold over the tomb entrance, under grand eaves of lapis blue. "The Three Principles of the People—he gave his life for these. Nationalism, democracy, livelihood."

Nora tried to feel the import, but it seemed impossible to properly appreciate such privileges if you'd always had them.

Misreading her blankness, Kay explained, "This was built before the civil war, after the founding of the republic. Democracy as opposed to monarchy and feudalism, not Communism."

As if on cue, several touts barged into their midst, brandishing key chains, postcards, disposable cameras. Everyone laughed a little—everyone except Grandma. Loudly, she proclaimed, "This memorial was built by the Nationalists. That blue is the Nationalist color. The Communists had nothing to do with it."

If Nora's grandmother hadn't ended up on the losing side, she might be publicly remembered today as a revolutionary, and Nora might be one of the proud masses earnestly paying tribute to a forefather whose legacy she could trace right to her own grandmother. Instead, after all the fighting was over, her grandmother had found herself betrayed by her nation and her husband.

The night they'd told Grandma, after her mother and sisters and aunt left the room, Nora found herself and her grandmother seated opposite each other, on the edges of separate beds. Her grandmother's chest was still heaving, as if the eruption wasn't over.

Nervously, Nora had asked, "Grandma, what did he do to you? Did you catch him cheating? You can tell me."

In a strangled voice, Grandma had said, "One day, I followed him."

"Where? What did you find?" A shadowy underworld of red silk and opium smoke, a shameless seductress, wild tangled limbs. Or a genteel session under the sheets with an ordinary woman, just younger and sweeter.

Grandma had flinched, as if remembering where she was, clamped her mouth shut, and shut herself in the bathroom.

Descending the steps of the memorial, Nora found herself a little dizzy. She took it slow, holding the handrail. Behind her, Grandma's breathing was labored. Nora let go of the handrail and offered her arm again. This time, Grandma accepted it, with a grim set to her lips. Together, they aligned their feet on each step before taking the next. The others were already close to the ground.

As lightly as she could, Nora said, "Why didn't you ever tell us that you were a revolutionary?"

"You wouldn't have understood."

"Maybe not when I was a kid. But all the years since you left—"

From the thronged square, someone was waving—her mother, camera raised. Nora held herself and her grandmother in place and tried to smile.

"Why did you move to California?" Nora was a little surprised by her own question.

They took several steps before Grandma said, "Your mother and I fought."

"About what?"

Grandma was silent, eyes trained on the granite steps.

"The night Dad died—he was moving out," Nora said haltingly. "And Mom said something she'll probably regret for the rest of her life. She'll never have the chance to see him again. Death is final."

Stone-faced, Grandma said, "Yes. It is."

"Now you have the chance to see Grandpa—maybe for the last time. And if you would just see him, at least you won't have to live with that kind of regret."

They stepped and stepped. They were most of the way down.

"Grandma, I understand how it feels to be betrayed. Jesse cheated on me, too."

Grandma snorted. "You'll never understand."

Nora was shaking. "Whatever he did to you—twenty years later, he still loves you. Don't you want to see him before it's too late? Don't you miss him at all? Don't you still love him?"

"Pi!" Grandma spat.

Nora remembered that word, too. It meant ass. It meant bullshit.

In her agitation, she stumbled, her arm still linked with Grandma's. She caught herself on the handrail but sent Grandma lurching. Her grandmother hit the granite, legs splayed, blouse bunched, revealing a pale section of loose veined flesh and the frayed elastic of her panties. Nora tried to look away, even as she rushed to help.

"Are you okay? I'm so sorry—"

"*Suan le*," Grandma hissed. She waved Nora off and struggled up by herself.

Nora had taken to riding in the first row of the bus, alone with a wide hurtling view. The others couldn't bear to watch the local style of driving—

the swerving from lane to lane, the frenzied honking at peasants pedaling bicycles loaded like pickup trucks, the passing contests that, until the last second, seemed bound to end in a head-on collision.

For the first time, they were speeding past real countryside: stooped farmers in rolled-up slacks and pewter-skinned water buffalo wading through waterlogged fields of soft green shoots, each paddy bordered by pinched ridges of soil in an interlocking pattern seemingly dictated by the earth.

Nora closed her eyes and dreamed of a ghost—a little boy. An old black-and-white picture—no, a sonogram. Her baby. His head was grossly large, his body shrunken and gnarled. Only she could revive him, by letting him suckle her breasts. But they were dry, hardened like potatoes. Jesse kneaded them—no use. She ran to find a candy to put in the baby's mouth. Jesse wept. The baby was dying.

She jolted awake.

Kay had sat beside her, looking concerned. "What happened with Grandma at the memorial?"

A little groggy, Nora said, "I raised the subject of Grandpa again."

"She still seems upset. Maybe we should let her be. The rest of us will see him."

"No. We can't give up on them." Nora tried to temper her voice. "We haven't even told her about the picture in his wallet. And—don't tell anyone, but I found a picture of Grandpa in her suitcase. I know she wants to see him, too. She just can't admit it yet."

"Really? How did you find it? What did it look like? When was it taken?"

Nora felt the need to protect the boy in the picture from Kay's scrutiny. "Let's just give it one last try."

Kay looked dubious, but she nodded.

The sky was blue-black now, hanging heavy and close to its fragmented reflection in the rice fields. Oncoming cars flashed blinding beams. On the sides of the road, stumpy trees and giant water lilies sprang up at the bus, then dropped into the dusk. Ahead, white moths danced into the headlights. Nora couldn't tell if they smashed into the fender, or rode some air current to safety.

In just a few days, the tour would be over. When they'd first set off, it had seemed interminable. Now it seemed to be streaking past like the scenery outside her window.

Nora knew, like a flare through the fog in her head, that she didn't want to return to her life as she'd left it. The beautiful brownstone she'd loved at first sight, now an excavated mess. All the spaces that Jesse used to fill with his clay sculptures, his well-worn clothes, his warm golden self—now gaping holes.

She couldn't bear the thought of returning to proving herself, day after day, on the trading floor. She needed a better way to be a trailblazer. She needed a rest from trying to be a trailblazer at all.

That morning when her mother had announced she was quitting her job, Nora had found herself saying, *Me too*—and then flinching when her mother seized on this as a moment of togetherness.

She didn't want to end up like her mother, alone in the house in Queens; like her grandmother, alone in her apartment in LA. Enough of drawing lines between strength and weakness, great and ordinary, themselves and other women. They'd drawn lines until they'd drawn themselves into cages.

The moment she got into her hotel room, she reached for the phone.

"You were just in my dream. We were trying to save this little boy. He was—" She bit her lip. "Enough of my dreams. You shouldn't have cheated, but I shouldn't have tested you till you failed."

"Do you really mean that?" Jesse asked.

"Yes. And I've been thinking—I'm quitting finance, once and for all. It's time to make a fresh start."

"Good for you."

He sounded sincere. She strained to detect proprietary interest.

He said, "I've been researching grad programs in art therapy. I've been working on my application. I've been figuring out my life."

"That's great." She took a deep breath. "What if we tried to make a fresh start together?"

"Nora, I don't think we want the same things anymore. Maybe we never did."

"I just want you back." Her breath came and went in shivers. There was a thrill in placing herself, like never before, in his hands.

"You still can't say you want to marry me, can you?"

"I—I'm working on it."

"I don't want you to have to work on wanting to marry me," he said, very slowly. "You never trusted me enough, and you never will, and of course that's mostly my fault, but that's where we are now."

"But I'm done fighting, too," she said. "I love you. I still love you."

Cautiously, he said, "I'll always love you."

"I'll forgive you. It'll take time, but I will."

"I hope so. I really do. But in terms of us, I think it's like you said before. I think it's too late."

"But—" It hit her: At home that last night, on the phone the other night, in asking for forgiveness, in defining forgiveness, he hadn't asked her to take him back.

She hung up. "But I'm pregnant." She heard the words aloud, and she knew they were true.

20

They crossed a moat, entered an archway—and stepped back in time. Irene reached for her camera.

The village wall and the houses were all the same creamy material, mottled and cracked through the centuries, scorched a gorgeous charcoal in some spots. Doors stood open; windows had no glass. Little rosy kids tottered around unsupervised, playing with dogs, sucking on popsicles. Hens and ducks loitered by stoops, surveying their surroundings with an air of ownership. Shabby underwear and mended clothes swayed on bamboo poles overhead. A few villagers washed vegetables in the rivulets of water purling past every house. Others lounged in battered chairs positioned in patches of sun.

Camera raised, Irene kept tripping on the cobblestones, but she felt a pang for every step she took without taking a picture. Through a series of archways, she could see all the way to the rice paddies, where an old man was—surfing? She zoomed in. He was standing on a wooden plow being pulled by a water buffalo, his face serene, brown and creased as a chestnut.

This was the present. An ordinary weekday morning. People lived like this now.

She tugged Kay's arm. "It's like that village in the peach blossom story. Have you read it?"

The tale of a fisherman who follows a stream into a grove of flowering peach trees, enters a cave, and finds himself in a village where old and young, men and women, parents and children, all work and play together. They throw feasts for the fisherman, press him for news of the outside world, and make him promise to keep their little utopia secret. He can't resist leaving markers on his way back and reporting his adventure once he reaches home, but though many die trying, no one ever finds the village again.

Kay said, "Those villagers never had to convert their houses into souvenir shops, or let tourists take pictures of their kids and their underwear."

"But if it wasn't touristed, we couldn't see it. And isn't it beautiful?"

Kay gave herself a little shake. "Yes, and these people are better off financially, and change comes anyway. Don't mind me, I'm just being contrary."

Irene laughed and linked her arm through Kay's, letting her camera dangle. Together, they allowed a growing distance between themselves and the group. Some villagers touted beverages and trinkets as they passed, but with a leisurely air. Most simply sat and gazed back—curious, bemused, unimpressed—as if Irene and her daughter were the ones on display.

One man grinned and winked at Irene. He looked about her age, handsome, with wide cheekbones, taut tanned skin, and crooked teeth.

She smiled back. "*Ni hao.*"

His grin widened. "So you speak Chinese."

"I am Chinese."

"But there's a foreignness about you."

"We're from America."

"But you're Chinese?"

"*Meiguo huaren.*" Kay spoke as if she were incessantly obliged to supply this answer.

"Ah," the man said.

Irene understood the words, of course—*Meiguo*, beautiful country, America; *huaren,* a person of Chinese descent, Chinese essence—but the coinage was unfamiliar, and she sensed it connoted something different to the man, to Kay, to herself. She didn't know what it meant for herself.

Kay nudged her—the group was waiting at the end of the lane, Tommy impatiently waving.

Irene turned to the man's table of wares. A miniature well, with a pail you could draw up, carved from green bamboo. A stone squirrel peeking around a teapot handle. An ink tablet in the shape of a lotus pond.

"You made all these?" she asked.

He gave a proud nod. "With these two hands."

Irene tried to imagine his brown, calloused hands creating such whimsy. Her fingertips caressed the natural surfaces and unfinished edges, then touched on a rock—just a rock, a rough oval, gray streaked with amber.

"That I didn't make," the man said. "That I found. Last year, by the river. Look. What do you see?"

Irene turned and rubbed the rock, stared until a shape emerged from the streaks—a monkey in profile. It was all there, the fuzzed outline, the heavy brow, a swirl of an ear, a fleck of a nose. Her eyes met his.

The man nodded. "You see it."

"That's my year," she said giddily. "I'm the year of the monkey."

"So am I," the man said. "Now that's *yuanfen*."

It occurred to Irene that if her parents hadn't fled, she might be married to a man like him.

Inside the house behind him, a television blasted—his mother and her soap operas, the man said with another wink. Irene blushed and set to choosing her purchases. Kay helped, without protest. The well, the teapot, the ink tablet—all one of a kind, from his hands to hers—and the rock, of course.

Meanwhile, the man related how everyone in the village used to subsist on the rice and lotus crops; how, once they officially opened to tourism, he rediscovered his boyhood talent for carving; how his wife was working the fields that morning, along with his father—could he be the chestnut-faced old man on the plow?—and how they were all counting on his son, who was studying English in the provincial capital in the hopes of becoming a tour guide, to lift them out of the peasantry for good.

"Just the one son?" she asked. All their fates resting on one middling prospect?

Kay elbowed her. "The one-child policy."

"You have more than one daughter?" the man asked.

"Three."

"So you'll never worry about being looked after in old age."

Hastily, Irene said, "I'm sure your son will make you proud. It's a noble undertaking, to give foreigners a deeper understanding of China."

The man grinned again. "He'll earn more in a month than I make all year."

Kay whispered, "Speaking of which—"

Tommy had doubled back to fetch them. In a strained voice, he explained that their local guide was waiting to give them a proper tour, after which they'd visit an official souvenir shop.

Those gargantuan shiny emporiums with troops of perky salespeople. The sense that they were degrading her along with themselves had been eclipsed by Irene's sense of beneficence. This time, her money would go straight into the pocket of this dignified, deserving man. She waved Tommy off, in a way that, she hoped, conveyed no disrespect for his profession.

The man named his price. Very reasonable—cheap, really—but he looked expectant, as if he'd opened a conversation, so Irene named a lower price. They went a couple rounds. Then he sighed, grinned, and pulled out a plastic bag printed with red roses.

"For you, my best bag," he said.

He wrapped each piece in old newspaper and nestled them inside, and she smoothed each bill before handing them over. Kay was right about bargaining. There was a ritual of conflict, then resolution, and now a bond.

The man gave her a business card with both hands holding the edges and a courtly little bow. Irene blushed again, and quickly tucked the card in her purse. He had an English-studying son, a soap-watching mother, a field-working father and wife. A house as old as this village. In the dim doorway, she could see a mop, a ceramic basin, a plastic chair. A whole life, a permanent place.

When Irene and Kay rejoined the group, they were given an aggressively schoolmarmish smile by their local guide, a girl named Xiao Hong who looked Sophie's age, with bluntly chopped bangs and large laminated credentials.

Xiao Hong led them over the threshold of the grandest house in the village, uninhabited but preserved as though the family had just stepped out. In fact they'd scattered in the last decade, Xiao Hong said, as if this were a point of village pride, to Hong Kong, Singapore, even Canada.

Irene had never lived in a house like this, yet everything seemed as it should be. The ancestral shrine, dour black-and-white portraits over bowls of fruit and burned incense. On the mantel, the vase and the mirror, the *ping* and the *jing*, homonyms for balance and harmony. Couplets on faded red paper pasted to twin pillars, Confucian scriptures in calligraphy on the walls. Every room facing the communal courtyard, which was open to the sky. The entire structure like a Chinese character, a system based on symmetry and a center, not linear sequences, closed off and spaced out.

Xiao Hong pointed out a window in the wooden latticework circling the second floor: Back when a marriage was everyone's business but the bride's, the family would gather potential suitors for appraisal, and the daughter could only peek through that window to survey the possibilities for her future. *Jia ji sui ji, jia gou sui gou*—marry a chicken, follow a chicken; marry a dog, follow a dog. The group shook their heads over how backward it was. Yet Irene imagined the thrill of peeking—spotting dandruff, a sweaty back, strong shoulders, polished shoes; a suitor catching her eye and sneaking a grin, even a wink.

Next was the study hall, off-limits to women, where men studied day and night for the imperial exams that would determine their permanent status. Xiao Hong pointed out the scroll painted when society was so *zhong nan qing nü*, weighing male over female, that the character for good, 好, composed of the female radical 女 with a son, 子, was written with a barely legible 女 cowering under the 子. A female had always to obey—first her parents, then her husband and his mother, then her own son, Xiao Hong explained. Looking directly at Irene's daughters, she added, "You know, we are not so lucky as you in America."

Back outside, Kay appeared to be struggling to keep silent.

Irene said, "Her take is a little simplistic."

"She's comparing feudal China to modern America. And even in modern America, there's plenty of backwardness—to take an obvious example, that *he* is still supposed to be universal, when in Chinese, *ta* is truly gender neutral."

Quietly, so as not to embarrass her daughter, Irene explained, "In the written form, there's 他"—she traced the radicals on her palm—"which is male and universal, just like in English, and there's 她, the female pronoun."

"Actually, the female *ta* wasn't invented until the colonial era, when the translation of European texts was mandated." Kay stopped, her attention diverted. She said, "Come on, Mom. We're lagging again."

Irene craned around her daughter. Another handicrafts stall. She walked closer. The same well, the same teapot, the same ink tablet. And a row of rocks—gray rocks with amber blotches. She picked one up: the fuzzy outline of a pig. A dragon, a horse, a rat—all twelve animals of the zodiac, arrayed by a lesser salesman.

"He said he found it by the river," she heard herself say plaintively.

The group gathered, scenting intrigue. "Who did?" "What did you buy?" "How much did she pay?" "She got swindled?" Pitying clucks, smug headshakes.

Tommy said, "Well, when you buy from an unlicensed vendor—"

Kay offered to accompany Irene to return the goods. The man sat a ten-minute walk away, but Irene simply couldn't double back.

She tried to laugh. "Even if they're copies, they are hand-carved. And I guess the rock is hand-painted."

Obligingly, Kay said, "And if you like the stuff, don't worry about authenticity."

They headed to the parking lot, trailing the group again.

Irene couldn't help asking, "So the monkey was just a coincidence?"

"I guess."

"Why did he have to lie? I might've bought it all anyway."

"Just to maximize his profit."

Irene said she blamed the one-child policy—the pressure of the future livelihood of that entire household resting on one son. Kay said that her Beijing friends considered the policy a collective good; that when people's main goal was raising their standard of living, it helped to have just one child to feed and educate. Irene sighed over how mercenary people were forced to be in this new economy. Almost mechanically, Kay said that America was no better.

"You're being contrary again," Irene teased. "Don't you miss home?"

In the pause that followed, she felt her middle—what used to be her gut and, with motherhood, had become her womb—contract.

"Home?" Kay said. "Well, where's home?"

This was a question Irene might contemplate. Not her daughter, whom she'd raised in one country, one city, one house, a very definite home.

"Our house. When we get back, you can have a whole floor to yourself."

Involuntarily, Kay recoiled.

Irene said, "You didn't mind that awful dorm, but you can't stand the thought of home?"

"I just—"

"You think you know China, but you don't know the first thing about being Chinese. It's about family. *Jia*"—Irene slashed the air with it, 家—"family, house, home. In Chinese, it's all one word."

The others were boarding the bus. Byron, hanging back from his father, paused. Nora and Sophie did, too, with glances of commiseration at Kay.

Irene knew she should shut up, for her own good. "And you have it easy. You're not like that poor son who has to"—what was the English word? The man had said *yang,* to look after, to keep, as in children or cattle—"support his parents and grandparents."

"That son isn't living at home."

"Because he's in school! But he'll come back."

"He probably dreams of buying a high-rise condo in the city."

"You don't know that." Perhaps it was true.

"What are we arguing about? If it means that much to you, I'll stay at the house. If I—the summer, at least—" Kay sounded strangled. She turned and boarded the bus.

Irene forced herself to follow Kay up the steps and down the aisle. Tommy and the driver and the rest of the group stared, while her daughters, her sister, and her mother looked away.

It seemed to her that here in China, with all the oppressive dictates of the old ways, with all the teeming scrabble of the new, there was no danger of dying alone. Not the moment of death, that wasn't her concern, but the long way down. Not for a fifty-five-year-old woman who'd raised three daughters in a stationary, solid home, steeped in more love than they could absorb.

But Kay was right that China was chasing American privileges, and American afflictions. As a society prospers, its psychological ills proliferate. Once one set of needs is satisfied, the next starts to clamor. This pursuit of modernization and globalization shot people into solitary orbit, their convergence incidental, at best provisional. Freedom, independence, individuality—eventually, euphemisms for alone. Must there be such a trade-off?

Irene herself was suspended between eras. She could not decree that any of her daughters remain under her roof. She could not conceive of seeking a second love.

Tommy announced they had to pack overnight bags for Huangshan and leave everything else on the bus. They'd ride the cable car up, but they'd still hike to their hotel, and any baggage would be hand-carried on foot—maybe not by them, but hand-carried nonetheless. Who was he to be sanctimonious? He was Hong Kongese, worldly, mobile, not really Chinese either.

Irene tried to turn her mind to the scenic highlight of the tour. Huangshan—literally, Golden Mountains. Peaks that could impale. Ancient evergreens clinging to the cliffs. Piles of whipped cloud.

The bus stopped. Another souvenir shop. There was a collective lack of motion as the driver shut off the engine, and the air-conditioning, and then the realization: shop or suffocate. A litter of salespeople was already scurrying out, greeting Tommy, turning keen faces to their bus. This ravenous developing country, trying to suck her dry.

Irene marched off the bus and up to Tommy. "Enough souvenir shops. Let's go to Huangshan."

He explained, with extreme evenness, that they weren't yet scheduled to arrive in Huangshan, that this was their last chance to buy souvenirs in this province, in an officially licensed store.

Everyone had disembarked now, and Irene felt a rallying around her. She said, "From the first day, you've had us shopping more than sightseeing. At every stop, you hand us off."

"You're never forced to buy anything," Tommy said. "I am only doing my job."

"Are you a guide, or just a broker? This tour is called the Must-Sees, not the Must-Haves. You need some kickbacks—I understand that. But haven't we spent enough? We're not just dumb tourists. We're not just spoiled foreigners. All we wanted was—we're only here to—"

Tommy was staring as if at a madwoman. Irene felt the rallying disperse. Perhaps it hadn't been rallying, only a kind of rubbernecking. And even if the others agreed, no one wanted to side with her, least of all her daughters.

Everyone was moving on, following a cue only she had missed. The salespeople performed a rehearsed greeting and glommed on to their targeted customers, the group straggled toward the air-conditioned entrance, Tommy sauntered ahead.

Everything was slipping away. Irene felt herself teeter. She closed her eyes. It was infinitely worse—a hungry swirling darkness. She reached out and grabbed—Kay's arm.

"Ow."

"Please." Her fingers let go, her arm stayed outstretched. Her daughters stood in a tense arc around her. "Of course I want the three of you to live your lives, but is it too much to ask—just now I had that feeling again, like I'm going to fall. I don't think I should live by myself right now. I'll get better soon, but day after day alone in the house—"

"That's not our fault," Kay said.

"What? Who said—whose fault—"

All three of her daughters had frozen, as if they'd blurted it in unison: Their father's death was her fault. How illogical, and involuntary, and irrevocable, this conviction.

She wished she hadn't said what she said when Bill left—but if she'd sobbed, fallen at his feet, declared her undying love, her daughters would've recoiled, too. She hadn't meant it, and her daughters knew that, but those words rang in their ears, and nearly a year later, they still blamed her.

"He was leaving us!" she shouted. "Have you all forgotten? *He* was leaving *us*."

"No." Sophie's voice was small and shaky. "He was leaving you."

The drop was short, after all. Was that it? Under her soles was the ground, hot asphalt. She stood alone in a vast parking lot. The drop was inside. It was only her heart.

Soon another bus pulled in, a glum face positioned in each window, and another group of salespeople started to scurry outside. Just ahead of them, Susan emerged. She handed Irene a paper cup and tactfully looked away.

Irene took a few sips of water, bracingly cold. Her sister's kindness was real; also distant and limited, like a gift certificate.

Feebly, Irene thanked her.

"You're a better mother than I thought possible," Susan said. "Just try not to take everything so personally."

Irene supposed she had to learn that, after nearly thirty years of doing the opposite.

She'd feared and wanted only daughters. Each birth was another test: Could she quash all worries about an heir, about perpetuating her husband's name? Could she raise them to be *nenggan*—not to be revolutionaries, she'd never inflict that word on them—without sentencing them, the world being what it was, men being who they were, to chafe at their biology? And would they resent her then? Would she resent them? Would they recoil at what they recognized about themselves in one another? Was each generation destined to see the previous as the model to reject? She'd tried to prevent that, but maybe it wasn't possible, wasn't personal.

Even in the womb, daughters resisted their mothers. Those violent bouts of illness, those spells of intense weakness—all a small price to pay, infinitesimal, compared to the gift of her daughters. Everything seemed a small price to pay, ever since that first year with Nora, when she thought she'd never be lonely again.

They ascended into the white sky, slightly swaying. Quiet inside, quieter outside. Solitary raindrops traversing the windows of the cable car vanished into wetness. Irene had never seen anything so inhospitable as these jagged cliffs. Nothing golden about them. If the mist over West Lake was the lull of a peaceful dream, this fog was the grip of a nightmare.

"This is something we can't help," Tommy said tightly, even though Irene hadn't said a word. "No one can predict the weather on Huangshan."

The mountain air was cold, wet, and thin. The path to the hotel went up, down, up—never level for more than a few paces. Watching her own step, Irene bumped into a man toting enormous sacks of rice on a pole across his bare welted shoulders. He lifted weary eyes and gave a disgusted shake of his head. She apologized, twice. He didn't answer. There were dozens of these men crisscrossing the steep, narrow paths, loaded like mules with produce and linens, bottled soda and beer, other people's luggage. They hadn't ridden the cable car, they'd hiked all the way up. Some looked her age, some looked older, most weren't built much bigger. Irene blinked back tears, and saw Kay do the same.

Neither she nor her daughter had anything in common with these laborers, except a claim to being Chinese. A claim that meant everything, or nothing. Back in the hotel in Beijing, Kay had said that they could be anywhere, and perhaps it wasn't far from the truth. Perhaps Irene could have gathered her daughters and sister and mother to tour anywhere, seeking new scenery as a false promise that her own outlook would change, too.

21

"They say Huangshan is best seen in mist."

"Too bad we can't see it."

"We will when we're actually up there, I guess."

"Aren't we already up here?"

Kay felt as disoriented as the others. They all kept their eyes on the rocky steps as they hiked, and when they paused to glance up, they saw only whiteness and pines and one another. She studied the map printed on her cable car ticket, but the peaks and paths drawn in bold black bore no relation to where they stood now, in a vast cold cloud that draped their skin, dewed their hair, seeped into their shoes.

Only Tommy and the local guide were equipped for the weather. She and her family wore disposable slickers Mom had just bought in the hotel lobby. Filmy plastic, polka-dotted red, and one-size-fits-all, the slickers clung to their foreheads and bunched between their legs. Still the damp penetrated.

While the fog crept back, lurked, and crept up again, the local guide rushed them from one signposted spot to the next, urging, "Look there, look now." Deep in the moving mass of white were great hulking presences sensed more than seen.

The local guide told them not to lose hope, that the weather on Huangshan shifted by the minute, his tone entreating them not to blame him. He tried to fill the voids with tourism factoids: the seventy-two named peaks, the ten most famous trees. He pointed into the white and dictated what certain formations resembled: the lion's-head peak, the monkey-gazing-at-the-sea rock, the crags that were, in procession, the goddess Guanyin, a monk picking herbs, two men playing chess, and the emperor in long robes.

More visible were the lovers' locks choking the links of the chain railing. The custom was for couples to pledge their love, click a lock onto the chain, and toss the key.

She felt Byron's nearness in the warmth suffusing her chest, a newly familiar sensation.

He flicked a lock, setting the whole chain clinking. "Those herb-picking monks must get clobbered by keys."

There was a new intimacy in his gaze, a presumptuous tone in his wisecrack. She tried to laugh, but it wouldn't come out.

He gave her a searching glance. "Seems like your mom wants you back home."

Kay nodded. The group was trudging toward the next viewing platform. She looked down at the ridiculous slicker encasing her backpack, her baggy sweatshirt, her ratty jeans.

He tried again. "So that fighting spirit runs in the family, huh?"

She burst out, "That's not funny. I didn't mean that it was my mother's fault. It was—" She stopped, remembering Byron had been out of earshot for that last exchange in the parking lot.

She turned away from his stare and joined the others at the final lookout for the day, the official best site to view the sunset, where they watched the white shade to gray.

Dinner was served in the drafty, dank hotel dining room. Sourness emanated from Byron across the table; from her mother, a helpless melancholy. Everyone munched distractedly and left the table with dishes and rice bowls and opened bottles nearly full—all the supplies shouldered up by those bony, wheezing men. Kay kept silent.

She knew her father's death wasn't her mother's fault. It was an accident. It didn't mean anything. That fact was nearly as hard to accept as the fact that he was gone.

She went to her hotel room and sat alone, huddled in her slicker. It now felt like a protective casing. She couldn't remember sitting alone since the wake of her father's death. After the funeral, all she did was sit in her bedroom alone, not even knowing if Mom and Sophie were downstairs. Then she flew to China and, every day of the year, plunged herself into crowds on the street, in food stalls and teahouses, at tourist attractions; into a dorm room where she and Tomoko slept and studied three feet apart; into seedy parking lots outside karaoke clubs, hair salons, and massage parlors; into the arms of Rick and Du Yi and Mr. Wan.

She picked up the phone and dialed Rick's number. A stranger answered—Rick had already moved out of his dorm. Next she tried Mr. Wan. The moment he answered, she hung up. She called Du Yi. When he answered, she hung up again.

She wandered through the corridors, the stairs, the lobby, telling herself she wasn't looking for Byron. Then she saw, outside, a few sparks, and his silhouette. She wrestled off her slicker and stuffed it in the trash.

"Now you want to talk to me?" He took a drag from his cigarette.

She shivered. "Yes."

He exhaled smoke. It blended into the fog. "I'm actually not a smoker."

"Then why are you smoking?"

"My dad makes me tense."

"Why didn't your mom come along?"

"She has inoperable breast cancer."

"I'm sorry. I didn't—" She gulped. "My dad died last year, in a car accident."

He studied her face, then stubbed out the cigarette. "Let's take a walk."

The fog had opened here and there to show starry patches of sky. The air entering her lungs felt so sheer that it seemed the stars should hang nearly within reach, but they looked farther than ever, minute and brilliant. He started up steps that spiraled to the top of a peak. She followed. If she slipped, her whole body could tumble under the railing. Halfway up, her teeth were chattering. The fog had insinuated itself through every layer of clothing, skin, and muscle to her bones.

"I'm freezing." She sounded like a child.

He took her hand in both of his and briskly rubbed it until the blood coursed. He worked her other hand, her arms, her ears. Wherever he touched her, the other parts were jealous. When he stopped, she nearly cried out in protest. She thought she saw him smirk and she wanted to punch him. What was this feeling, this force befalling her, that seemed to threaten—more than she imagined sex ever could—to make an object, a victim out of her?

She turned away and leaned over the railing. An evergreen thrust itself out of a nook, its top wind-flattened, its gnarled branches all reaching straight out from the face of the cliff. A pine indigenous only to Huangshan, the plaque by its roots said, with its own species name: *Pinus huangshanensis.*

She gave a tinny laugh. "Look. *Pinus huangshanensis*. That doesn't sound very Latin."

He tucked two fingers under her chin and turned her face back to his. She caught her breath, a loud stupid sound. The scent of smoke on him was acrid and lovely. Her hair was full of mountain wind. Against her back, icy locks and chains. Her arms hung slack as he kissed her, as they kissed. Her heart fluttered, fluttered and strained against her rib cage.

The morning revealed where they stood: an exalted space, another stratum between earth and sky. Overhead, clouds like fish scales dappled the blinding blue. Around them, the fog had become wispy, playful mist. And before them was a scene so unprecedented she didn't know how to take it in.

A skyline—not of buildings, but countless mountains—not earthy or rolling, but somehow flat, the color of shadow, jagged and stark, rippling and cresting into a sea of clouds. Flat—not really flat, of course, but governed by different laws of perspective, like the scroll mountainscapes sold in every Chinatown and every souvenir shop in China. They'd always looked hokey to her, but they were true: those serrated arcs to these peaks, those curlicues to this mist, those eyelash-fine brushstrokes to these slender dark pines with upticking needles, those reproductions to this splendor.

And now she remembered a vocabulary lesson from the middle of the year: *yunhai*, sea of clouds. In Chinese, it wasn't a cliché; it was a word.

Her mother stood beside her, clicking away on her camera.

Humbly, contritely, Kay asked, "How would you describe this?"

Mom murmured, "Your aunt is the poet."

"But what words come to mind? Are they all Chinese?"

"Kay, just enjoy the view."

The view was shifting even in that moment, mist rising, peaks vanishing, a spray of pink azalea unveiled, dew on pine needles catching the light.

Byron was there, on the other side of the group, and they hadn't spoken since they kissed good night, but when she closed her eyes, a single slow blink, she could feel a hum in the air between them.

Tommy began to make noises about the time, but even he seemed loath to leave, and they all dragged their feet, turning again and again for one last look.

The consolation for leaving those mountains: their arrival, at last, in the province of her ancestors, the closest she'd get to her *laojia*.

On the bus from the Guangzhou airport, seated across the aisle from her grandmother, Kay was stuffing her sweatshirt into her backpack when she found her grandfather's card crushed at the bottom. It was wet from yesterday's fog, the paper discolored and wavy, the handwritten characters bleeding. Frantically, she tried to press it straight, blow it dry.

"From who?" Grandma asked. "You have a boyfriend in Beijing?"

Kay hesitated, then handed her the card. Grandma squinted at it and thrust it back, her mouth tight.

Seated behind Kay, Nora snapped to attention. "Grandma, there isn't much time left."

Kay ventured, "Did you see his writing? How his hand shakes?"

"What do I care?" Grandma snapped.

"Grandma, he still carries your picture in his wallet," Nora said.

Kay nodded. "He showed me. He's still so proud of your revolutionary work."

"Proud? He doesn't deserve to be proud." Creakily, Grandma's voice scaled.

Nora stammered, "You carry a picture of him, too. I shouldn't have looked, but I found it in your suitcase."

"What picture?" Grandma's chest was heaving.

"The picture of that little boy, in a silver case," Nora said. "Don't make a mistake you'll always regret. Don't wait until it's too late."

Grandma stood up, a haunted look on her face. "Where is he?"

Seated behind her, Mom said, "Ma, sit down. Nora, that's enough."

Nora said, "He's on his way to see you. After all these years—"

"Who do you mean?" Grandma rasped. "How do you know? Where is he?"

Nora looked bewildered. "Grandpa. He's flying to Hong Kong."

"I won't see him," Grandma shouted. "I'll get off this bus right now. I'd rather die in the streets than see him again."

Mom gripped Grandma's shoulders. "Sit down."

Grandma shook her off and tottered toward the front of the bus. Mom lunged after her. So did Nora and Aunt Susan, Sophie and Kay herself. Ahead, she saw the driver gaping in the rearview mirror, Tommy's orange-topped head popping out from the front seat, the startled faces of everyone else in their tour group, and Byron's eyes, widened, showing the pink corners and copper irises. The driver braked.

Grandma pitched forward. They tried to catch her, but their outstretched hands seemed to inflict further injury rather than cushion her fall.

Mom and Aunt Susan had taken hold of Grandma's arms. Leading her back to her seat, Mom repeated over and over, as if to a child, "Sit down. Never mind. *Suan le. Suan le.*"

22

In this city. On these streets. A little boy's legs—the nibs of bone, the tender flesh—how far could they carry him, how fast?

Through the filmy glass, Lin Yulan tried to search the faces outside, but they all blurred by. Wedged between her own body and the side of the bus, her right arm throbbed, the numbness shading to pain. Numbness was a kind of pain, the nerves crying out how they could.

Fifty-one years ago now. This city, their last stronghold, soon to fall. Their passages to Taiwan narrowly secured, with the last of their savings. Already they were the last of their kind—prominent Nationalists, newly declared enemies of the people—to flee.

Her husband on the stoop, a look on his face like it was being eaten from inside.

Why was he sitting there? Where had she been? Why was he sitting there? The house behind him hushed and dim. Where were the children? Inside—their daughters—inside. Their son? He fell before her on knees and hands, forehead to the ground. Their son had wandered off. He'd gone missing. He was gone. A rally, an alarm, pandemonium, gone. The boy, her boy, her son. He'd searched all night, all day. Where had she been?

What was he saying? Where was her son?

He'd taken the boy on an outing. The boy was inconsolable—crying for her—so he took him along while he tended business—bank accounts, the title to his father's house. And then—then—a crowded street, a last desperate rally, shouts about Communist agents, a frenzied crush, their hands forced apart. When the commotion subsided, he was gone.

What street? What rally? What *gone*? A three-year-old couldn't be gone. Her little boy was somewhere. He—this wretched beast before her—would bring her there. He said he'd already searched all night, all day. She slapped him. She could have stomped on his neck. Kneeling before her, he wept. He'd already searched the neighborhood, every lane, every yard. Now they could only wait, and hope— She slapped him again. He would bring her there.

Before they reached the street, she knew. That day she followed him. The girl who lived there. Wei-wei, who begged to volunteer for her organization, was so inspired by her speeches, so admiring of her husband. Doe-eyed with a fine high nose and, when Lin Yulan last saw her, a defiantly swelling belly. There were many *kangzhan furen* in those days, wartime wives; spouses having been left behind or sent out, people sought comfort where they could. Unremarkable that Wei-wei was one. The question was whose.

He broke down. He'd brought their son to the house of a friend. Inconsolable—crying for his mother—that was true. He didn't know where she was. He waited and waited. Finally, thinking a little boy could be pacified by a woman, he brought their son to the house of a friend. A friend, nothing more. Did she remember Wei-wei? She faced him and he went silent, his lips trembling, the color of a corpse.

From their rattling rickshaw, she shouted her little boy's name into the oblivious gray streets.

She could never reconstruct even the circumstances into which he'd vanished. He'd wandered out of the house—out of the yard. He'd been left alone in the yard. He'd wanted to play outside, to look at the flowers.

He wouldn't stop crying. He'd been left out there how long? Not long. Ten minutes. Fifteen. Maybe half an hour.

Only he, the one who'd lost her little boy, could help her find him. His word, the word of a shameless liar, was the closest she could ever get to the truth.

Was there a rally? Yes, a small, ineffectual one—they'd passed it. The shouts about Communist agents? The tending to business? No—yes. Why hadn't he left the boy at home? He'd left the other two, why not her son? He'd already said, the boy wouldn't stop crying, crying for her. Had he wanted the boy to meet his mistress? Had he wanted a cover for a last tryst? Why bother? Why this time? Why her son?

Why any of her children, why any child, but why the one who would go missing? Why her son?

And what was her husband doing while her son vanished? That was the only answerable question, one she did not need to ask.

Wei-wei's eyes were cowlike with terror; the defiant swell was now a toddler. She bleated about the two boys playing together, the older getting bored of the younger, and wandering off. Lin Yulan commanded her to stand on the street with the toddler—the girl held it close, shrouded in a fringed shawl—while she frantically searched the house. Under the beds and tables. Every closet, cabinet, trunk, imagining him leaping out, or lying crushed inside. In the yard were mops, laundry, litter; an overgrown hedge of hibiscus, obscenely pink. Finally, thinking madly, a thief is a thief, Lin Yulan lifted the fringe of the shawl and saw a calm little creature with shining hair, the blackest black, and ears like her husband's.

In the falling dusk, in the half-deserted city, no one knew anything. No one had seen or heard. No one in this neighborhood would have recognized her son as hers.

She had one picture of him, taken on his third birthday, framed in a silver case. She tucked it inside a pair of his shorts, blue with a green button, a button she'd sewn to replace the one he'd plucked off, and carried it against her chest, in both arms. At last one old man said yes, he'd seen a little boy like that. Where? She seized his wrist, the aged skin slipping loose from the bone. Where? In Wei-wei's yard, crying.

That night, the next day and night, the next and the next and the next, she banged on strange doors, searched abandoned lots, screamed down alleys. That street, the streets around it, the streets around those streets, an ever-widening black hole.

The hospital, the orphanage, the monastery. Every police station, against all warnings—no telling who was in charge these days. If she got arrested, she'd put her whole family at risk. She still had two children at home. Two daughters, five and four, capable only of staring with dumb, scared eyes.

Every child was her son in cruel disguise. Every patch of earth could hide a grave, every well could swallow a tiny soul like his with hardly a ripple.

Their ship sailed without them. The borders were closing. Communist troops storming the city any day. They were nearly out of provisions. The price of rice had risen from a satchel, then a sack, and now a wheelbarrow of cash, which would soon be worth more as kindling. Her husband secured berths on another boat out, docking not in Taiwan, but Macau—not even an island, a splinter. Before long, there'd be no escape at all.

She said she didn't care. He grabbed her and shook her. That day—had she heard?—Communist agents had raided the district chief's house, found only a cousin and a housekeeper, made them kneel on broken glass, wrapped them in burlap and tried to beat information out of them, then beat them to death. He shook her until her brain rattled inside her skull. Didn't she know they were next on the list?

He'd left word with every trusted contact. Someone would find their son and keep him safe. Until they returned. A few months, a year at most. Until the Nationalist forces turned back this freak tide. Until their country came back to its senses. That very day, they'd return.

That night, he brought home the calm black-haired creature. Wei-wei would stay, he said, banking on the protection of relatives who'd defected early, willing to take the chance with her own life but not her son's. He said the son's father had agreed.

The last part she knew to be true. The rest, she'd never know. He could have snatched the child, snuck him away, pried him out of Wei-wei's skinny arms. She did not ask. She kept him, this child, conceived when she was nearly due with her missing son. She raised him as her missing son. Upon returning, reclaiming—upon somehow finding him bigger, stronger, safe—it would be a small matter to sort. Many families had chosen to leave children behind—to leave them home—until they could return.

Her daughters gaped. Who's that? Where's our little brother? Who's that?

This is your little brother. Don't dare ask again. She said it, she screamed it. She threatened them, locked them away from him. She might have thrashed them, or ordered her husband to do it. She'd been capable of anything then.

All she remembered packing was that picture.

By the time they boarded the ship, the city's distress signals were wailing nonstop. Each wail held her little boy's cry within.

Her little boy, who loved salt and pronounced his own skin tasty, whose eyes turned down at the corners, who'd crawl beside her and burrow under her arm like a kitten, delicately demanding to be scratched. His restless fingers, tugging at buttons and seams. His pinky toes, always straying off the soles of his sandals. His cool silky earlobes. Cheeks heavy in her cupped hands. His baby hair, like the finest seaweed in bathwater. His tiny bridgeless nose. His low round belly. The rosy bulbs of his toes. His large head, so large that not long before, he'd topple over when she sat him down. His tender little legs.

He could have been picked up by a kind woman, could have saved the life of a barren wife. He could have been apprenticed to monks. Taken as a servant. Crippled and made to beg. He could have been hit by a bus. Trampled by a mob. He could have starved to death. Fallen off a footbridge. Drowned in the Pearl River. He could have been recognized as the son of reactionaries and tortured, carelessly killed. He could have been recognized by someone they knew, someone they could never reach. He could have followed an instinct and found his way home only after they'd fled.

In Macau, with nothing to do, nowhere else to go, she'd wander through the casinos. Fellow refugees would nod and smile—brief eerie smiles. Everyone was haunted, every family maimed in some way.

Hoodlums ruled the streets. Tore off women's earrings, leaving them shrieking, with bloody bisected earlobes. Snatched at bracelets, ready with a cleaver if the metal or the hand resisted. Grabbed unaccompanied children and held them for ransom: this she heard, the rest she saw. Once, she was buying bread, bread like puffed cardboard, when a man ripped the watch off her wrist. On her way home, a different man trailed her, asking if she wanted to buy her watch back. Knees shaking, she laughed in his face.

As soon as they could, they left for Taiwan. With each move, the chance of ever finding her son—of ever being found—got shredded, then shredded again.

In Taiwan, they braced for an attack from the mainland—an attack that wouldn't happen only because the Party had more urgent threats, starting with the Americans in Korea, but they had no way of knowing. They waited for annihilation, and waited for reclamation, until waiting was like breathing.

They were among nearly two million displaced and shell-shocked—servicemen, journalists, teachers, doctors, merchants, artists, engineers, ordinary citizens—all scrambling for food, shelter, position on this tiny island. Not to mention the thousands of elected officials who'd stop at nothing to regain a semblance of power—and, to start, tossed native Taiwanese out of the government, suspended all elections, and established a lifelong dictatorship, with the worst cronyism, corruption, and censorship she'd yet known.

The saying among the Taiwanese was that the dogs, the Japanese, had finally left after fifty years, only to be replaced by the pigs—the Nationalists. Well, people who feel they've lost everything will be ruthless.

Guangzhou was one of the world's largest ports, a major industrial center. Now they lived in shacks with no water, no electricity, no windows, no chairs.

There was no cause for her to fight, not when there was no nation, only this regime reincarnated on an island where suspected subversives simply vanished in the night. Lin Yulan unrolled bedding, boiled water, procured food, watched her children. This was survival, not homemaking.

Her husband was a rotted man, infested with guilt like termites, gnawing his sinews and bones. The one who'd rescued her, the one who'd destroyed her, the only one who knew what she'd lost. They came together, nights, seeking consolation, seeking vengeance; clinging to each other, to nothing but tatters. She conceived and aborted, conceived and miscarried—and then never again.

The little creature had become her precious, carefree Lou. He never made a fuss. He hardly cried. Almost immediately, he accepted her as his mother. So she was.

And almost immediately, her daughters had stopped asking about their little brother. What they had witnessed was incomprehensible; they could only conclude that it hadn't happened. They were five and four when their world disappeared—their house, school, street, language, country—and was never made whole again. She thought at most they remembered a breach, the feeling of a replacement but not the fact.

Now and then, she could not help wondering how they could have lost all remembrance of their brother, the little boy they'd known since his birth, known every day of those three years—at that time, the majority of their own brief lives. Of course, she'd given them no choice. She'd forced them to distrust their senses. She'd trained them to forget.

She shunned family photographs, even when she could afford them, even when they were no longer considered a luxury. It seemed to her that the true purpose of a photograph was to memorialize unspeakable loss.

After a decade of moving at least a dozen times, moving every time her husband spotted an opening in some backwater bureaucracy, he procured a comfortable position as a land official. Eventually, she battled her way to becoming a local magistrate in his district. He resumed his old ways. She fought, until she realized there was little left to fight him for. A women's journal was now expected to translate articles from *Good Housekeeping*. Thanks to American aid and arms, Taiwan was becoming a very rich island, even as its right to exist was soon to be stripped away.

She raised her daughters to be revolutionaries, but in stealth. In their part of the world, in their time, anything else was too dangerous. Poetry and science and fellowships to America—for that era, these would have to substitute for causes. She always knew her daughters would leave to make lives in that richest and most powerful of nations, and they soon did. She hadn't anticipated that Lou would leave, too.

He was a poor student—popular, incorrigible, the class clown. Once grown, he found work in a few commercials and soap operas, decided he liked the sound of California, and asked his sisters to sponsor his immigration.

Before he left, he said to her, *Come along.* As if it were a jaunt. *Forget the old bastard, just come along.*

She thought of her little boy, of placing the diameter of the earth between them. To leave, to stay. One seemed unthinkable, the other unbearable. One allowed a faint ember of hope, the other extinguished it. Which was which? Another unanswerable question.

So her children departed as they'd arrived—one, two, three. For another decade, she stayed. She and her husband never shared a bed, seldom shared a meal, but they were perpetually engaged in a relentless push-and-pull. Each time she spat on his feeble overtures over the years sustained her till the next. She could no longer remember when she hadn't drawn from that dark toxic well for fuel. A measure of her strength: She could live with her enemy and not yield. Or of her weakness: Despite every principle she'd ever blazoned, she didn't know true sovereignty—how to maintain her borders, how to exist, if not in constant resistance against him.

Somewhere in that resistance was her last link to her lost son.

That day, the last morning she'd seen her little boy, she'd gone to her office—the staff long disbanded, the journal essentially defunct—and found it ransacked. The copies she'd saved of each issue, a decade's outpouring of essays and speeches, letters from women all over the province, newspaper profiles, public commendations, a precious handful of photos of her and her sisters-in-arms—all gone.

She spent the day, the night, sifting scraps. At first light, digging through piles of garbage on the street. Then questioning blank and fearful neighbors on when, who, why—until an old colleague yanked her aside and warned her to hush, Communist agents everywhere, lucky enough they hadn't arrested her yet, she'd be luckier still to escape with her family intact.

Instead of watching her son, she'd been trying to salvage evidence of her life's work—by then, mere souvenirs. As if she already knew that no one else would remember.

23

This is it. Susan announced the city to herself. *Here we are.*

Her birthplace, one of many places she'd called home. Guangzhou was a grimy, heaving, sticky city, familiar only the way everything was familiar these days—from a travel show, a newsmagazine, someone else's pictures.

The rest of the group was on their final round of temples and pagodas and souvenir shops—the tour's last gasp. She and Irene and the girls were fending for themselves, despite Tommy's warnings about pickpockets and unsanitary food. They'd left Ma resting at the hotel; she'd hardly spoken since her fit on the bus.

At each juncture, there'd been stirrings, squalls, but not the full storm—until yesterday, when Susan had watched her elderly mother lurch down the bus aisle, and suddenly roused herself. She'd watched her own hands join the others in restraining Ma, heard her own voice murmur as they tried to settle her down. She suspected the storm had turned inward, continuing to devastate Ma as they motored into the city last night, but no one could help that, least of all her.

The people here—their people—were shorter, darker, louder, pushier.

Many manifested the strains of a developing country in jarring physical form. Harelips and clubfoots, hardly one mouthful of good teeth. Gruesome skin protuberances, purple splotches spreading across entire faces, probably treatable with a few pills. Naked jerking stumps for limbs, live exhibits of industrial accidents, none equipped with wheelchairs or prosthetics.

Then the beggars: haggard women wailing, pushing crusty toddlers at their pockets. An old man with an ear swollen to half the size of his head. A boy—she thought it was a boy—burned featureless, his head a shiny knob with raw eyeholes, the wormy brain tissue shrink-wrapped in scar tissue. And, scattered throughout the streets, a legion of cripples with legs bent and crossed behind their heads, as if their feet and necks had been tied into knots, scraping themselves along the pavement on their hands and buttocks. She could not fathom how human bodies had been twisted into these forms.

Kay said she'd often seen them in Beijing, too; she'd heard they'd been abducted as children by gangsters, crippled, and forced to beg—though she'd also heard they were entrepreneurs of a sort, who could untwist themselves at will.

Now Kay asked about taking this chance, their only chance, to find their old street, their old house. Irene told her the house and the street were probably razed. Besides, they had no address, remembered nothing, knew no one.

"But couldn't we explore the neighborhood? Grandma must have some idea."

Dryly, Nora said, "Should we make Grandma our tour guide today?"

"While we're at it," Sophie said, "let's ask her if she wants to see Grandpa."

Irene tsk-tsked, then allowed herself a wry laugh along with the girls. Susan smiled, too, through a haze, the one shrouding her since her call to Ernesto.

The diamond ring glittering from a corner of the phone booth—she'd picked it up and dropped it in her purse, alongside the tattered tissue with those ten digits and the black pearl in its velvet box. Her purse held it all nicely.

The next morning, the group waited by the revolving doors of the hotel while their bus navigated a turnaround. They could have walked across the turnaround in seconds, but they waited, watching the driver wrestle the steering wheel. Cabs idled at the curb, ready to zoom to the airport. She had a suitcase. She had her purse. Her passport—*American, of course*—was in Tommy's fanny pack. When the bus finally swung around, she boarded, telling herself to wait for the next airport. From Shanghai, they'd driven to Hangzhou, then to Nanjing and Huangshan, now Guangzhou. From here, planes flew everywhere in the world, yes—but she couldn't think how to get to Madison, Wisconsin. It was the kind of thing Winston would know.

Winston was meeting Ba at the airport about now. Ba would know soon enough that she'd failed. She didn't have to face the consequences. She didn't have to go to Hong Kong at all. Ernesto was waiting for her. Susan kept this at hand, like a pawn ticket.

The girls seemed to have forgotten about the boy with a Spanish accent at her door in the middle of the night. No one had noticed her bared finger. The shriveled band of skin had filled out, but it retained a pale glow.

They came upon an outdoor market that looked like every knockoff factory in China had spewed onto it. In the next second, they were swarmed.

"CD watch bag!"

"Gucci Prada LV—you like?"

Between the samples and catalogues thrust at their faces by chanting hawkers, Susan glimpsed purses, shoes, wallets, underwear, sunglasses, ski jackets, pendants, perfume, suitcases—all splashed with designer logos.

Delegations of Russians, Arabs, and Africans sifted the goods, flicking stacks of dollars. A cluster of American women who looked older than Susan, each with a Chinese baby in a stroller, marveled at the selection.

"With such quality, why pay for the real thing?"

"With such quality, they *are* the real thing!"

Once they emerged from the main fray, Kay recited some of the more outrageous fakes she'd heard of in this land of counterfeits. Fake landmarks matched with fake tour guides and buses. Fake security slots on bank doors that copied ATM cards. Fake baby formula. Fake chewing gum that crumbled in the mouth. Gony stereos, Odidos sneakers, Sunbucks coffee. Inkless pens, handless clocks, eggless eggshells—she broke off, excited: street food.

Braised duck wings dripping with sauce, sizzling skewers of spicy squid, steaming vats of beef balls in broth. The snacks of Susan's childhood, each bite requiring time and effort, burning tongues and sticky hands—all available in Hong Kong, too, but she'd never craved them as she did now. Irene's face had also lit up. Kay wanted to taste everything in sight. Irene hesitated, then pulled out her wallet. For each of them, a duck wing to gnaw, every bit of skin, meat, and cartilage salty-sweet and tender, even the bone. A cup of beef balls, chewy-soft, with pockets of hot savory soup inside, meant to be slurped. Then a squid skewer, tough and fiery as Susan remembered, each bite releasing more flavor.

Jaws still working on her last piece of squid, Susan flicked through a crate of bootlegged movies. On the packaging, the formatting was scrupulous, with boldfaced blurbs, "Special Features" boxes, the credits in that familiar compressed font, even as the text had been retyped into gibberish or did little to recommend the movie. *Ge treadyf ora drenal ine-ru shexci tem ent! A lackluster effort, too long by half!*

A tap on her knee. Feet—feet framing a face—she recoiled. One of the knotted beggars, a teenage boy, thick-lashed eyes blinking up at her while he wagged his head, rattling the bowl in his jaws. Fake or not, he sat at her feet, and she had visibly recoiled.

She reached into her purse, her fingertips brushing the velvet box. A sudden uneasy throb in her stomach. She dropped a few coins into the bowl. The boy scuttled away with surprising speed.

This is China, Kay had said. *They sell fake water.*

Ahead, Irene and the girls were sniffing and peering at each food stall. Trailing them, her appetite quickly disappearing, Susan spotted a jewelry store with a handwritten poster: "Beware of counterfeits! Trust the old master inside."

Displayed in the window were all sorts of pearls, pink and cream and gray, bumpy and smooth, round and rice-shaped—nothing like hers. She didn't know if that was a good or a bad sign.

Inside, she mumbled something about appraisal, maybe getting it set. Her throat tightened and parched as the jeweler squinted at her pearl, pinched it between thick brown fingers, held it to a light and squinted harder.

"This needs special equipment," he said, and disappeared into a back room with her pearl.

She bit a flake of skin off her lip, scratched at sauce gelled on her wrist. What if he was scraping that perfect sphere with a knife, marring it between decaying teeth? What if he was slipping out a back door, shuffling down an alley with her pearl in his pocket?

She shouldn't have entered this store. She shouldn't have bought the pearl. She shouldn't have come to China at all. She should have just stayed home. In the end, she had to blame herself. She acted in moments. She couldn't think ahead to consequences. She couldn't link cause and effect. *Only connect . . . Dot dot dot.* But she didn't know how. She never had.

At last the jeweler returned frowning. "It's fake."

In the midst of an icy plunge, she managed, "What?"

"Fake. It's fake!"

"It can't be. It's ancient and natural. It came from an oyster. It came from the sea."

He sniggered. "Is that what they told you?"

"Did you rub it against your teeth? Did you scrape it with a knife?"

"Who's the old master here—you or me?"

She stared. He waited. She said, "You."

"That's right." His face softened. "You paid a lot, ah?"

Arms folded over her cold chest, she could only nod.

He took out a cloth and rubbed the counter as if she'd mucked it up. "So you got swindled. It happens. So many cheats out there." When he looked up again, he wore his appraising squint. "Tell you what. It's fake, but a good fake. A very good fake. Only an old master like me can tell. No wonder you were fooled." He leaned close and whispered, "You want to sell? Cut your losses? I'll give you a super price."

She croaked, "Give it back."

He shrugged and held out his hand, the pearl casually cupped like a pebble. She pushed the pearl into its box and dropped it back in her purse.

Outside, she tried to rub the goosebumps from her arms. She'd demand an explanation from Tommy. A full refund. She'd threaten to sue—based on the word of a squinty Cantonese jeweler? She'd call Winston. She had no choice. He knew money, regulations, procedures. He'd tell her what to do.

Irene and the girls were sipping slushy drinks. They wanted her to taste each one. Attempting nonchalance, she said she wanted to head back. They said they were stuffed, and ready for naps, too.

The unease was concentrating in Susan's stomach. In the taxi, her purse on her lap, she sensed the pearl glowing to itself—an oyster's revenge. A sickened laugh rose in her throat.

In her hotel room, she started to dial home, then hung up. Winston would at least expect her to have the receipt ready, the store information, whatever documentation. She upturned her purse. The black velvet box tumbled out, then the diamond ring, lost and loose, then the tissue, scrawled crudely as a ransom note. By now, Ernesto would be hurt, and lusting to hurt her worse.

She needed more light. She turned each dial on the bedside control panel clockwise, then counterclockwise. She flicked each switch up and down. Finally she smacked the panel and it slid off the nightstand. It was a plastic bottomless box. Fake dials, fake switches. No wires, no inner workings, not connected to a thing. She laughed a crazy laugh.

The real lamp switch was on the lamp. The unease in her stomach was tightening to pain.

A knock at the door—Irene, agitated. "It's Ba."

"On the phone?"

"On the plane."

They stared at each other.

A heart attack on the plane, Irene said disjointedly. A message from Tommy. A call from Winston to the tour company.

Susan's stomach twisted tighter. "Is he—?"

"He's in the hospital in Hong Kong." In critical condition, heavily medicated, under evaluation for surgery. Irene's gaze fell on the clutter across the bed, on the velvet box, on the diamond ring near the edge. She muttered, "You should be more careful. There's a safe by the TV."

Susan's head was burning. A surge of jabbering voices. *We try to hold ourselves like so, you and I. What use is a safe?* With her cold, shaky hands, she covered her ears.

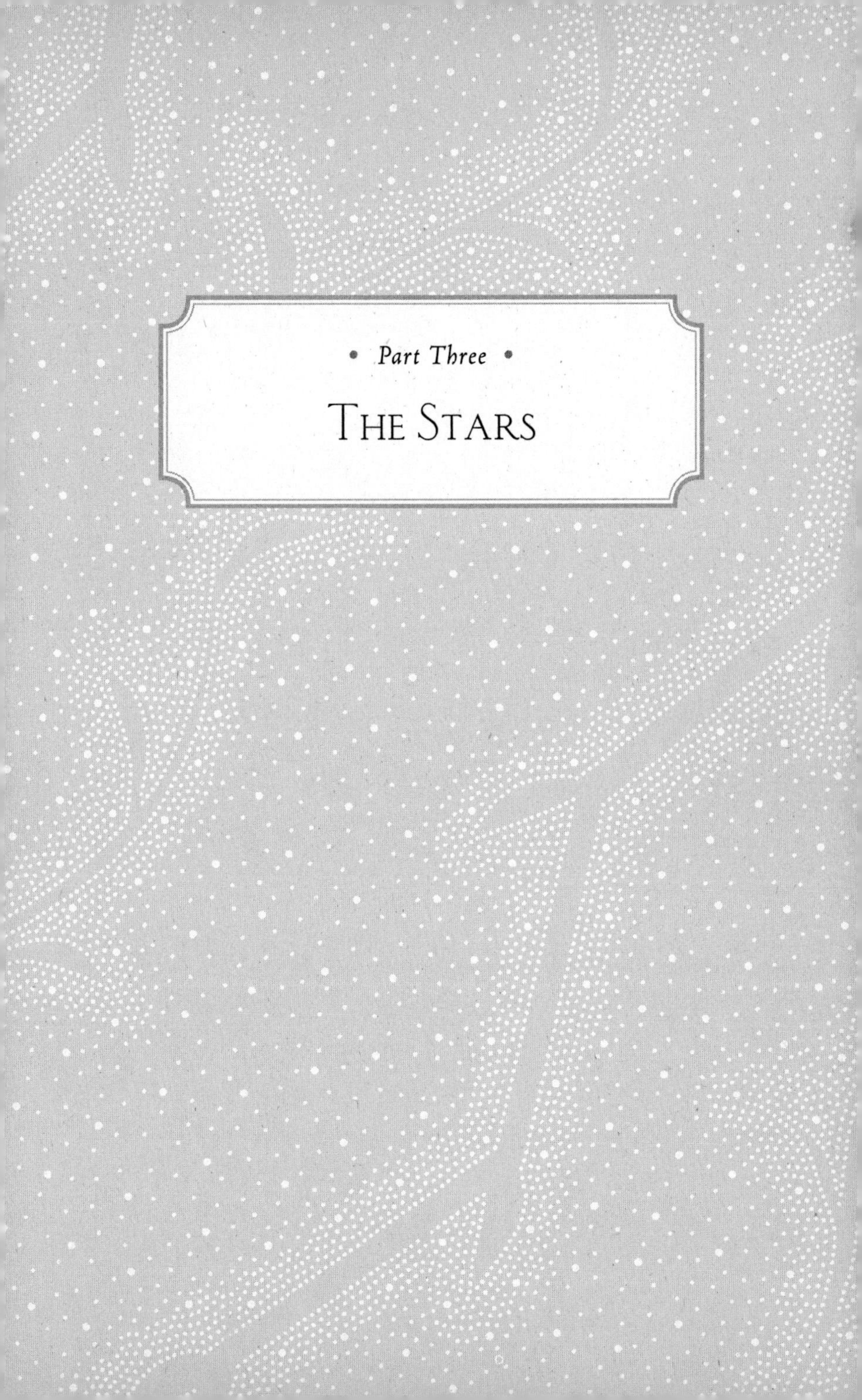

• *Part Three* •

The Stars

24

Sophie felt a swelling in her stomach, a clogging in her chest, all the way up to her throat. As soon as the cab pulled up to their hotel, she rushed ahead of the others and into a waiting elevator.

Those beef balls, the fat floating on the broth. The greasy purple squid. The icy drinks, more dessert than beverage—sesame smoothie, papaya milk, almond bubble tea, lychee milkshake with coconut jelly. *Eat this, try this.* Mom and Kay childlike with excitement, Nora monitoring her intake. So she ate. They ate, too. She was the only one paying for it.

In the mirrored doors, she looked like a little hag, eyes baggy, cheeks sallow. According to mybigfatsecret's blog, one bulimic year equaled ten years of normal wear and tear. Already, the raw spots on her knuckles had festered into red sores. She'd prepared an excuse—a stumble, a scrape—but no one had noticed. She closed her eyes—a mistake. When the elevator stopped, she ran.

She flung herself at the toilet, retching—no time to lock the door. Nothing came out. What was happening? Her whole body hurt, as if a monster were inside, roaring and clawing to get out. She lifted her fingers to her throat. Before she could push, she convulsed. A beastly sound from deep inside, then a torrent of vomit.

Her arm shaking, she flushed. Tears and snot were streaming down her face. This was not her orderly procedure. There was no relief, no control.

Her head wouldn't stay upright. She propped it up on her arm, propped her arm on the toilet. When her arm gave out, her head dropped against it. Bits of unflushed puke floated inches from her face. More tears seeped out, slowly now. From far away, she was aware of chilly tile against her bare legs, the toilet gurgling, the clatter and yammer of the city outside.

She got jolted conscious by more retching, throttling her until she sobbed. *This is what you wanted, isn't it?* a voice inside her snarled. A monster had taken over. She needed to expel it, but it was too big, too terrible; it would kill her. She'd thought she could stay in charge, let it loose whenever she wanted. She didn't want to die.

Mom and Nora and Kay would find her slumped over the toilet. She sobbed harder. They wouldn't be able to bear it. She and Daddy, both dead within a year. She was sorry.

At the very least, she had to flush the toilet again before they found her. Her arms were almost lifeless already. Shaking, sweating, she forced her hand to the lever, then collapsed against the seat again. The whoosh of water washed through her, then over her. She let her eyes close.

Footsteps, voices, louder, at the door. "Sophie?"

She couldn't move, couldn't answer.

"Sophie, what's wrong?"

"Goddammit, I knew it." That was Nora.

Her sisters fell upon her, tugging at her. Limply, she resisted. She would not leave the toilet. She deserved to die here.

A tissue swabbed at her face. She twisted away. From the other direction, a glass was pushed to her lips and tilted. She tried to protest and water slid down her throat. A cool pocket formed deep inside. She accepted another swallow. Then her sisters started to tug at her again.

"Come on, Sophie."

"Get up."

Yes, yes—she should be smarter, better, stronger than this. But she wasn't. So let her die.

"Girls? We need to talk." It was Mom.

Sophie's head throbbed. She wrapped it in both arms.

"Girls? What's going on here?"

Like a homeroom announcement, Nora blared, "Sophie's been throwing up. On purpose—she's bulimic."

"What?" Kay exclaimed.

Sounding bewildered, Mom said, "Sophie wouldn't—what do you mean?"

"No," Sophie croaked. "This isn't on purpose."

"Stop lying," Nora said. "I smelled it on you before. I'm sick of all these secrets. Let's get it out and deal with it."

Suddenly Sophie was alive enough to raise her head. She placed one hand on the toilet seat, one foot flat, the other hand on the toilet tank, the other foot flat, and faced Nora.

"Nobody's as perfect as you," she spat.

Nora flinched.

Knees wobbling, Sophie staggered out of the bathroom and into her bed.

"Girls, please, no arguing now," Mom said. "I have bad news. I need you to listen."

Sophie tried to sit up. Someone else was dead—she was certain. As long as the four of them were here, together, it couldn't be as bad as losing Daddy. To make doubly sure, she counted off—Mom, Nora, Kay, herself, all here. Was it Grandma? Aunt Susan? She braced herself. She could bear it, better than the others. She would be a grown-up this time.

"Your grandfather had a heart attack on the plane. He's in the hospital now."

Sophie felt immense relief—then guilt, but only a little. She tried to listen to the details, but dark choppy waves kept breaking over her.

At some point, Kay rushed out. Mom and Nora sat on the other bed, alternating between tense conversation and even tenser silence.

Then her stomach twisted again. She bolted out of bed and toward the bathroom. Mom and Nora rushed after her. She lurched toward the toilet. A pair of arms latched onto her. She retched. Vomit splattered onto the toilet, the floor, the arm in front of her—Nora's arm.

At last the spasms stopped. Mom was holding Sophie's hair, making soothing sounds, offering tissues and more water.

"I'm not doing it on purpose," Sophie whimpered. "I don't know what's wrong."

Nora was washing the vomit off her arm. Her face looked grayish green. She started to respond—or maybe just opened her mouth—and threw up into the sink.

Mom hurried to Nora's side. Sophie watched, stunned. The phone rang. Nora was still retching.

Holding Nora's head now, Mom said, "Sophie, can you pick up? It might be about Grandpa."

Sophie stumbled toward the ringing.

"Food poisoning." Kay sounded zonked. "I'm next door. I've got the runs. Aunt Susan has a fever. Has it hit Mom and Nora yet? I can send Grandma over."

Sophie wanted to laugh, but she was too weak.

"Food poisoning," she tried to call. Her stomach wrenched.

She curled up in bed, clutching one pillow to her middle, another to her face. The dark choppy waves were breaking over her again. Her head pulsing and burning against the starched sheets, she let herself go under.

Grandma's voice—first beside her, a question Sophie couldn't quite parse, then echoing from the bathroom. "You girls must have weak stomachs. That day in Suzhou, and again today?"

In a strange, high voice, Nora said, "No, Sophie throws up on purpose, and I'm—I think it's—morning sickness."

Sophie pulled the pillow off her face.

Grandma said, "What?"

"Morning sickness?" Mom said. "You mean—"

"I'm pregnant!" It was nearly a shriek.

"Are you sure?"

"Yes. I don't know. I just feel it. Before we left—Jesse—"

Mom's voice was high, too, but steady. "Okay. Calm down. Let's just—"

"Jesse?" Grandma said. "The one who betrayed you? You're pregnant with his child?"

"Ma," Mom barked.

Nora started to retch again.

Sophie finally managed to sit up. "No," she croaked. "It's food poisoning."

"Don't cry," Grandma said. "You made a mistake. You can fix it. Women now, you don't realize how lucky you are. I once drank poison that made me bleed for a month."

"Ma," Mom shouted. "I'm her mother."

"Then you should advise her. He betrayed her. You'd let her tie her life to his?"

"It's her choice. Nobody else's."

"If she makes the wrong choice, she'll regret it for the rest of her life, and so will you."

And then Mom erupted, in a voice shattering and deep, "You still think I made the wrong choice? You think I regret having Sophie?"

"I didn't say that."

"You didn't have to. You and your revolutionary talk. What did you achieve in the end? Your revolution ended more than fifty years ago. China is a new country now. Has anyone here heard of you?"

"No," Grandma said. "But—"

"You had no choice." Mom sounded winded, as if she'd held in the eruption for years—nearly eighteen years, to be exact. "Well, I made my choices, and Nora will make hers, and if you think our lives are worthless, so be it. Nobody's worth anything to you, except for Lou. A car salesman with no wife, no kids. Your precious son."

Grandma's voice was low and ominous. "Don't speak of Lou that way."

"Let him be your legacy. Leave me and my daughters alone."

Now Grandma sounded winded, too. "You'll never understand."

Nora was still retching.

Sophie stumbled out of bed. "Food poisoning! It's food poisoning." She reached the bathroom doorway, panting. "Kay says it's food poisoning. She and Aunt Susan have it, too."

Mom stared as if she'd forgotten Sophie's presence. Finally she said, "I don't feel sick."

"You're pale as a ghost," Grandma snapped. "Just wait."

She was right. By the time Sophie had crawled back to bed and Nora had staggered out, Mom was locking herself in the bathroom.

Through the next groggy hours, Sophie intermittently woke to a rough cool washcloth drawn across her face and neck, a mug of lukewarm water held to her mouth, tingling pungent ointment dabbed on her temples. Grandma's hands sturdy and a little brusque, her face impassive.

At some point Kay returned, muttering that Nora had commandeered the other bathroom, and flopped beside Mom on the other bed. It seemed no one had moved into the empty third room, maybe to keep it for Grandma, but also for some solidarity. They were all helpless victims—all except Grandma.

In a moment of relative lucidity, Mom and Kay tried to pinpoint the source of their illness. That faint sourness in one of the milky drinks. Ice cubes made from tap water. Rancid beef ground into the mix. Dirty chili sauce on the squid.

Sophie kept quiet. She felt like she didn't fully exist.

Suddenly stepping out of the shadows, Grandma said, "Who told you to eat that stuff? What made you think you could handle it?" She shook out a freshly wrung washcloth. They shut their eyes and mouths and submitted to it—Mom with a defiant tilt of her head.

From that tilt, Sophie knew she hadn't imagined anything. So she was unplanned. She'd never guessed it, though she supposed she'd had the sense of an overenthusiastic welcome into an already complete family, two tidy pairs before her arrival. She tried to think of signs that she'd been unwanted. In all the time she'd been alive, she couldn't recall one. Why did Grandma think she was a mistake? Because her father had left? Had Grandma somehow known that he'd eventually want out? Had he wanted only two kids? All this time, she'd tortured herself with all the ways she could've kept him at home, kept him alive, when the reason he'd left was her very existence? But then why would he have waited to leave until she was almost out of the house herself?

Grandma went next door with the washcloth.

Mom said, "We are certainly not telling Tommy about this."

Kay let out a weak laugh, then muttered, "We should be at the hospital."

"You think? That bad?"

"I mean Grandpa. We should be there with him."

Mom sighed. "Tomorrow."

When Kay had locked herself in the bathroom again, Sophie turned toward her mother.

From the other bed, Mom regarded her with a sad smile. "I thought you were asleep."

"So I was unplanned?"

Mom hesitated. "Yes."

"Grandma wanted you to abort me?"

A tear slid from Mom's eye right into the pillow. "She never meant *you*. She didn't know you."

"What about Daddy? Did he want to have me?"

Without hesitating, Mom said, "Yes, very much."

"Don't lie."

Mom was silent.

"Is that why he left?"

"No," Mom said forcefully. "You were right—he was leaving me. Not us, not you—me."

"Then why does Grandma think I was a mistake?"

"I shouldn't have said that. All she knows is that I disappointed her. I valued my daughters over my career. But everyone disappoints her—everyone except Lou."

"She always favored him? Because he was the boy?"

Bitterly, Mom said, "You could say that."

"Maybe it was just that he was the baby—like me."

"You weren't just the baby. You were a gift," Mom said. "You know we never regretted you. Not Daddy or me, not Nora or Kay, not for a second. We adored you from the start. You know that."

Suddenly Mom grimaced, clutching her stomach. Without thinking, Sophie got up, lay beside her, and stroked her head, her shoulders, her back. She could feel Mom's bones so clearly. Her thinness suddenly seemed a fragile quality, not something to envy. Mom was starting to grow old, while Sophie was becoming grown-up. She was stronger than Mom now. Under her touch, she felt Mom gradually relaxing, breathing more evenly, until she fell asleep.

Her own head throbbed, her throat ached, her stomach was in knots. But the monster was out of her, or nearly. Maybe it had meant to warn her, not kill her. Maybe now she'd learn her lesson. She felt the weight of her body as if she might sink right through the mattress. It was a comforting pull; she gave in.

• • •

She woke to Grandma standing at her bedside with a small bottle. "Open your hand," she said, and poured a heap of tiny bronze beads into Sophie's palm.

"What do I do with them?"

"Swallow. What else?"

The beads looked like things to glue or string, not swallow. Sophie tipped them in, along with a mouthful of the water Grandma offered. The beads went down easily, leaving an aftertaste both herbal and metallic.

Mom was still fast asleep, as was Kay on the other bed. Both their brows were furrowed, as if they'd forced themselves into unconsciousness. When Grandma brusquely shook them awake to take the medicine, Sophie winced.

Grandma caught Sophie watching her. "You're the first one up."

That seemed to call for Sophie to get out of bed. She was shaky, but she was up—maybe because her body was conditioned to purge and recover, or simply because it was the youngest. She offered to tend to Nora and Aunt Susan. Grandma handed her the bottle of medicine.

Next door, Aunt Susan lay perfectly still on one bed, Nora curled up on the other. Careful to mimic her mother's touch instead of her grandmother's, Sophie gently woke her aunt and gave her a dose of medicine and water. Then she tiptoed to Nora, her slender limbs folded close, her sculpted face scrunched in sleep. Nora pregnant! And betrayed, then impregnated—or impregnated, then betrayed? She'd abort it—wouldn't she? This wasn't the same as Mom having a third child. Her big sister becoming a mother? Well, Nora was old enough; she had her own house. Sophie supposed Brandon wouldn't be so shocked. Only privileged people could plan the ideal timing and circumstances to have a baby.

Nora groaned. "I can't keep anything down."

"This will help."

Stubbornly, Nora shook her head.

"Hey, I'm the baby," Sophie said. "Say 'ah.'"

Sophie supported Nora's head and watched the faint undulation travel along her fine throat. Nora curled up again. Sophie hesitated, then stood to leave.

"Wait." Nora grabbed her hand. "I know you weren't throwing up on purpose today. I shouldn't have accused you like that. But are you bulimic?"

Nora's pointer was pressing between the two raw knuckles. "I—not the official definition, not yet—but yes," Sophie stammered. "I want to stop. I will stop."

"I'm not perfect," Nora said. "I have my own problems, obviously."

Sophie couldn't help glancing at Nora's middle. It was flat as ever. "Do you really think you're—"

"I don't know. I think so."

"Apparently I was unplanned," Sophie said.

"That was the first I've heard of it. I knew Mom and Grandma fought, but I didn't know why." Nora's expression was full of sisterly concern—not big-sisterly, just sisterly. "Maybe you were an accident, but you were never a mistake."

Sophie nodded. Nora squeezed her hand. Sophie squeezed hers back. Nora's eyes closed. The shadows settled all around them. Sophie stayed on the edge of the bed, holding her sister's hand, until her sister fell asleep again.

In the other room, Grandma was setting out steaming plastic containers, napkins, and spoons. "Can you try to eat? A little bit."

"I'll try."

They sat side by side. Sophie spooned a little congee, but it was too hot. Easily, Grandma slurped hers up.

"I wasn't a mistake," Sophie said.

Grandma laid down her spoon and blotted her mouth. "I was only thinking of your mother's work."

"You think she would've achieved more if she hadn't had me?"

"I don't know anymore." Grandma's face drooped.

Sophie knew her grandmother had suffered in ways she couldn't imagine. "I still want to visit you from Stanford."

Grandma nodded. "We'll hang out."

Sophie grinned.

"Eat while it's hot," Grandma said.

Sophie blew at her congee and took a cautious sip. Her insides welcomed it, a bit of cushioning against the continual grind. She took a bigger sip.

25

Kay woke with a gasp, feeling she'd lost days out of her life. It was nearly midnight, their last night in China. She got up, too suddenly, and her knees gave out. Leaning against the wall, she tried to clear her head. All her indigestion in the last year wasn't as bad as this.

On the other bed, Mom and Sophie slept curved toward each other, like parentheses. On the nightstand were covered containers of plain congee, still warm, the only food in the world she could stomach.

Only after she'd eaten did she think of her grandfather, heart failing, alone in a hospital in Hong Kong. And she'd never written back to him. She'd let his card get ruined in the bottom of her backpack.

Early in the year, when she'd gone to Taiwan to meet him, she'd been gripped by the fear that he'd died. She waited in his lobby as he'd instructed, peering hopefully at every old man who passed by, becoming more convinced by the minute that he'd died. He'd already taken a bad fall. In the days since she'd contacted him, he must have died.

She found his door and knocked, banged, shouted. He finally appeared in a suit reeking of mothballs, stooped over a cane. His watch had stopped; his hearing was poor. Embarrassment seemed to make him gruff. He didn't ask her in. All she could see was that his apartment was cramped, but everything in Taipei looked cramped.

They walked to a neighborhood restaurant, his cane shaking before touching the ground, each of his steps half the length of hers. She had the urge to carry him. Once they sat down, the menu seemed to require his full attention; then chewing did. She chewed, too, and covertly studied his features. His cheekbones resembled Mom's. His hanging earlobes had been passed on to Sophie. His nose reminded her of her own.

After he finished eating, he asked about the weather in Beijing. She tried to craft a thoughtful answer, but while she was still talking, he asked for the check. She was thinking maybe her mother was right, that her visit was an imposition, but then he asked if the rest of her day was free. Eagerly, she said yes. He said he'd take her shopping and, waving off her polite protestations, swung out his cane at a ninety-degree angle to hail a cab, nearly knocking a schoolboy off his bike.

For an interminable hour, they inched their way around a mall, she desperately uninterested in the clothing and jewelry shops, he seeming just as uninterested in her conversation. At last they sat by an Italianesque fountain, where he took out his oily black leather wallet and edged out a yellowed photo of a young woman with a stern forehead and bright eyes.

"You know who that is?" he asked.

"My grandmother?" she hazarded.

"She was one of the most prominent women in our province. A tireless worker for feminism, and for Chinese sovereignty against foreign imperialism."

Kay couldn't hide her astonishment. "This was before the civil war?"

He nodded. "She was about your age, with three children."

"In class we learned that feminism in China started with Communism."

The lines of his face deepened forbiddingly. "Hnh!"

Hastily, Kay asked, "Why didn't Grandma ever tell me? Why didn't Mom?"

"They tell what they want to tell. They are stubborn women. Your grandmother hasn't spoken a word to me in twenty years."

"It's a travesty that we're all so disconnected."

For the first time, he smiled—slightly, wryly. "You have the same fire as your grandmother—the fire of a revolutionary."

She breathed, "How can you tell?" Holding the picture by its edges, she searched for the grandma in her memory, her mother's face, her own reflection. It no longer mattered that her grandfather knew almost nothing about her, that he'd never tried to contact her, that he hadn't asked about her father.

"I know," he said. "I can still see."

When the time came for her to leave, he took her hand. His skin felt like ancient silk. His shaky grip was, for one determined moment, iron-strong. Frantically, she thought to say, *Take care, I'll miss you,* even *I love you.* But she'd said all that to her father before he drove off, and it was no consolation when she learned he'd died. If anything, it seemed crueler. There was nothing to say that wasn't grossly inadequate. There was no good way to say good-bye. Perhaps her grandfather felt the same way, because once he released her hand, he simply swung out his cane to hail another cab.

All year, she hadn't let herself dwell on the fact that her father was gone. She was gone, too—here on the other side of the world. But the truth was, she'd seen him everywhere in China—in all the words she'd collected in her notebook, in all the words she hadn't managed to learn; in the sandstorm, in the *liuxu* or *yangxu* and the confusion between the two; in Rick and Du Yi and Mr. Wan; in everyone in this country who made her heart ache; in all the sights she couldn't simply see; in the concept of history, of memory; in *gone,* the very feeling.

And in her grandfather, the closest thing she had left to her father. Now he, too, was dying.

In the next room, Aunt Susan slept on one bed, Nora on the other, Grandma on the couch. That left the third room, her and Nora's room, empty. She washed up and changed into the jeans she'd bought on Women's Street and a camisole of Nora's, telling herself it was only because everything else needed laundering.

The front desk clerk eyed her suspiciously and refused to tell her Byron's room number until she asked in English. She was walking to the house phone when she realized the clerk had probably taken her for a hooker. She dialed the number, prepared to hang up if Mr. Chu answered. When Byron answered, she nearly dropped the receiver.

The lobby was frenetically lit and air-conditioned. She waited by the elevators, leaning against a cold marble pillar. When Byron stepped out, his matted hair looked like sunbaked hay. She wanted to burrow her fingers in it.

"You okay?"

"We all got food poisoning. And my grandfather had a heart attack." She fought back a sob.

Byron reached under her hair and gripped the back of her neck. His touch was startling, unyielding, but tender. Her sob dried up.

He let go. "My mom used to do that to me. I used to do it to my dog. He was pretty emotional."

How could it be, that a brief squeeze from his hand was more comforting than anything she'd felt before, that miscellany from his childhood was the most endearing thing she'd ever heard?

Now his eyes seemed to be taking in her shoulders, her clavicles, everything bared. "Want to take a walk?"

"Not really."

"Any better ideas?"

She thought of the empty room. She shook her head.

The night outside was thick and close. It made her skimpy clothes cling, cocooned her separately from him. Her hand sought his but made scant progress, her tremendous effort and desire transmitting into a feeble rippling of her fingers. It was all she could do to keep walking. Soon they'd walk the night away.

"I don't want to walk anymore."

"What do you want to do?"

She could not meet his gaze, but her hand finally found his.

In the empty hotel room, they faced each other. He touched her cheek, and she melted, and tripped backward against the dresser.

He smirked. "You're weak in the knees."

She wanted to punch him, but she could hardly breathe.

He kissed her, pressed against her. She held on to him as if a tide were tugging her under. Then his kiss became tentative. His hands strayed gently around her waist. His brow was quizzical. He seemed to be waiting for some instruction. Maybe she wasn't giving the right signals. Maybe she was supposed to take the initiative. But she could only let this happen. She nearly wept with frustration.

Abruptly, he backed away and led her to the bed, and she wasn't sure if he pushed or she simply fell, but she found herself prostrate below him, eyes closed, limbs useless, while he maneuvered her out of her clothes. She succumbed to the dark pull, wallowed in it, drowned in it. When she came up to breathe, there they were, laid bare. His copper skin was smoother than hers, holding muscles that seemed about to shift, like tectonic plates.

Their bodies took over, pushing and pulling, working up to a rhythmic frenzy. Sounds entered the air as though wrung from their guts.

They would have sex. There was no other way. The night unspooled, one dark reel, with one ending. The solid tip of him was probing her, pushing against her, while the core of her caved, her body hollowing like a vase. Was this the line between virgin and not? Between hooking up and having sex? Was she crossing it now?

He pulled back. "I don't have any protection," he panted.

She was panting, too. She whispered, "I've never done this before."

He gaped. "Are you serious? I don't know if—"

She pulled him in. When was it again? One moment he was pushing against her. Another moment, he was inside her. It felt seamless. Had she missed it?

He pushed. She gasped. He'd been holding still. Pain, sustained—the seam? Here, now, this moment? Her mouth burst open, but no sound came out. He touched her face. She bit his hand. They gripped each other and kissed.

They were having sex. Unsafe sex. How terrible. How ravishing.

How providential, the empty hotel room. If not for the food poisoning, she and her family in disarray—then where? With him, anywhere—in a stairway, on a roof, in the backseat of a cab. Suddenly she believed in fate. She believed in soul mates. She believed he was the one. She understood, in a jolt, that this could be a lifetime. And that if he promised her that, and then left her, she might never recover.

He reached down and touched her, pushed deeper and touched her. This pushing was different. Her body strained and flopped. Her mouth stuck fast to his tense sinewy neck. This pushing was different, a pushing up and up, up and up—then over, over an edge but not down, not yet.

She flailed, soundless still, hanging on to this tide, a force like the opposite of gravity, and then she cried out and plunged—through the thinnest air—into a soft pile, and from its depths, she heard herself whimper, "I love you."

When she could bear to, she stole a glance at him. He caught it. He'd been gazing at the ceiling, absently playing with her arm fuzz.

"So." He kissed her ear. "What now?"

She wondered if the kiss was charitable, if the talk was obligatory. She mumbled, "Look, I didn't mean—before, when we—"

"It was your first time."

Her heart collapsed.

He said, "I just meant, where are you headed after this?"

"To the hospital in Hong Kong, to see my grandfather."

"Do you know which hospital?"

She snapped, "Why? You want to meet my dying grandfather? You want to be introduced as the guy who just took my virginity?"

"I spend lots of time in Hong Kong hospitals with my mom."

"Oh. Sorry."

After a minute, he said, "And then what? You still might stay in Beijing?"

She mumbled, "There's a lot happening there." And none of it involved her anymore.

"It'd be hard to visit between Boston and Beijing, but not impossible. Between Boston and New York would be much easier."

Kay replayed this a half-dozen times. Living at home with her mother would be tolerable if she spent weekends in Boston with him. At last she said, very carefully, "The truth is, I'll probably head to law school. I don't know what I'd do if I stayed here."

He nodded. His fingers strayed back to her arm fuzz.

She breathed, "You seeing anyone in Boston?"

"Not seriously. You seeing anyone in Beijing?"

"Not seriously."

He smirked. "Obviously."

She punched him. He laughed and kissed her again, on the lips.

"Let's get some sleep," he said.

He settled an arm around her. She laid her cheek on his chest. She closed her eyes, and recalled his hesitation: *I don't know if—* If he liked her enough? Wanted to break in a virgin? She recalled how she flailed. How she whimpered. How he sped up, jerked out, spurted against her thigh. Uncontrollably, she shuddered.

"I have to get a morning-after pill."

"But I—"

"Still." She tried a wry grin. "At least we're in a country that stresses birth control."

He wanted to know how it worked, where to go. He offered to get it for her, to go with her to get it. Was he just being conscientious? Come morning, they'd separate. What if this first night together turned out to be their last? What if they saw each other again, but what they'd shared was gone? Hong Kong and Boston, New York and Beijing, the world so interconnected, the distances so far. Anything could happen in those gaps between them.

She wrapped the sheets around herself. "I'll take care of it. You should go."

"Can't we get a little sleep together first?"

"No." She gave him a shove. "Just go."

"You're really kicking me out?"

"Let's just say good-bye now. Things will be too hectic tomorrow."

Yanking on his clothes, he looked like an angry boy. "Bye."

"Bye."

Goosebumps were surfacing across her naked body. She turned into the pillow. He let the door slam.

She lay in the starched white sheets, in the empty hotel room. She checked the clock. Six hours until breakfast time, until opening time for shops. Eight hours before the tour's final flight, their departure from the mainland. She supposed she'd known all along that she was leaving China. She just hadn't known how to say good-bye.

Even if they never saw each other again—even if he broke her heart—she wanted the rest of this night with Byron. She wanted to ask him all about his mother, his dog, the girls he wasn't seriously seeing in Boston; what he was like in high school, as a little kid; how he spent previous summers; how his parents met. Maybe his history was exciting, probably it was mundane, but it was his, and now he would figure in hers, and even if he answered every question, offered every memory, she'd crave more, more guideposts to his geography, more clues to that everyday mystery—not *Where are you from?* but *How did you get here, like this?*

She jumped up and ran out, clutching the sheets to her chest. He was down the corridor, jabbing the elevator button.

"Come back," she called desperately. "Stay the night. Please?"

He came back, his eyes shadowed and wary. She started to speak. He put a finger to his lips. He lay down and tucked her in his arms. She nestled against his chest. He slept. She watched him.

In the morning, she stalked resolutely through the cold brilliant lobby, past the same sharp-eyed clerk, out the revolving glass doors, onto a just-swept sidewalk, and wavered.

The early clamor of food stalls and traffic, the industriousness of bicyclists and beggars, the leather gleam and brass glint of businessmen. A procession of rickshaw men labored past her into a neighboring lane, announcing their business in song: fresh vegetables, knife sharpening, secondhand electronics. She was looking for a morning-after pill in her ancestral city, in last night's clingy clothes, slightly raw between her legs.

She walked and walked, past office towers anchored by malls, past alleys reeking of fish. Soon her tour group would be surveying the breakfast buffet, packing for the last time, gathering to board the bus.

At last she spotted the "Adult Health" sign. Behind the glass storefront were hanging strips of condoms, a shelf of pornographic magazines and DVDs, a neat row of dildos, flesh-colored and neon—and a grandmotherly woman with bobbed gray hair reading a newspaper.

Kay's legs sped right past the store to the next intersection. She watched the lights blink from green to red to green. She took a deep breath and turned back.

The old woman looked up, perfectly expressionless.

"Good morning. I'm looking for—" She could not remember the translation, if she'd ever known it. "Next morning medicine?"

The woman only raised her eyebrows.

"I'm sorry," Kay stammered. "I'm not from here. I'm Chinese American. I don't know how to say it. Next-day medicine? Anti-pregnancy medicine?"

Still the old woman stared.

Kay gritted her teeth and said, word by word, "The kind of medicine you take if you had sex the night before and you don't want to get pregnant."

The old woman placed a little box on the counter. "Take it right away. But eat something first."

Kay proffered a hundred-*kuai* bill. The old woman accepted it and offered no change.

Next door, a man in an undershirt and boxers, hair sticking up in all directions, was fastidiously arranging a rainbow of fruit in color-coordinated foam and tissue paper. Kay asked for a banana. He gave her a bunch, pocketed her money, and set to perfecting the arrangement again. Standing on a square of pavement between the two shops, Kay hurriedly ate a banana and swallowed the pill dry.

Turning back toward the hotel, she couldn't help glancing at the "Adult Health" storefront again, and from this angle, perfectly aligned with the elderly woman's placid, bespectacled face, on a shelf just above, sat a rubber head with lemon-yellow hair, blue goggle eyes, an open red hole of a mouth. Kay stared. It was an image she could ponder to no end, or she could just let it be.

She walked in the massive shadows of razor-edged skyscrapers and raised concrete expressways, but all around her were squat walk-ups, their balconies bursting with potted plants and fresh laundry, and lush trees dripping full blooms, and people pedaling, strolling, haggling, chatting. There was, under the industrial rush and toil, not a Third World languor, but a thorough equanimity, a deep-rooted way of going about the primordial business of living, the unshakable sense—here as in America—that they simply were who they were: citizens of a country at the center of the world.

26

Nora's arms were still so weak, she couldn't scrub her hair. She shut off the shower. By the time she wrapped herself in a towel, her vision was dissolving into black dots. She plunked onto the floor, beside her suitcase. For the last time, they had to pack up, board the bus, catch a flight.

Kay entered, hair mussed, face flushed, wearing one of Nora's camisoles.

"Where have you been?" Nora asked.

"Convenience store," Kay stammered. "Got my period."

Nora looked at the bananas in Kay's hand. "Have you renounced tampons for some ancient Chinese method?"

"Huh? Oh—the store was closed."

Nora dug up her box of tampons and tossed it to Kay. A little jerkily, Kay put down the bananas and took the tampons into the bathroom. Nora sifted through her clothes. There was a clink, a curious weight in her cardigan—the tin of candy from her grandmother.

Late last night, she'd woken to find Grandma facing the window. The drawn curtains let in just a sliver of the night outside, so dark that all Nora could see was a bit of her grandmother's reflection. Clasped in front of her, nearly hidden in both hands, was the tarnished silver case. Perhaps Grandma, from her angle, saw Nora's reflection, because she abruptly turned, folding the picture to her chest. Nora had closed her eyes and soon fallen into a heavy, dreamless sleep.

Kay burst out of the bathroom, tampons still in hand. "I had sex with Byron."

"What?"

"Last night. I had sex with Byron. Unsafe sex. I just took a morning-after pill."

"I did the same thing with Jesse. After we broke up, right before this trip. But I didn't take a pill. And now I think I'm pregnant."

Kay gaped.

"There's more. He cheated on me. So I threw him out. Then, a few days ago, I asked if we could make a fresh start. He said it's too late. I didn't tell him about—this." Feeling winded, Nora gestured toward her midsection.

Kay gaped wider. At last she said, "How have you survived this trip?"

Wryly, Nora said, "Aren't we descendants of a revolutionary?"

Kay managed a laugh. "Do you want—I could go out and get—"

"A morning-after pill? It's too late for me."

"A pregnancy test? The sooner you find out—"

Nora sighed. "I guess."

"The shopkeeper will think I'm deranged." Kay hurried off.

Nora turned back to her suitcase. She pried open the little tin and lifted the wax paper. Gingerly—her stomach was still skittish—she placed a candy on her tongue. The pale dusty feel she remembered, then a mouth-puckering tartness, and finally the sweetness, hard and spare. She sucked it, the measured dose of sugar seeping into her starved bloodstream.

She'd never shaken the lifelong fear that if she revealed her weaknesses, especially to her family, she'd somehow cease to exist. Yesterday she'd had no choice; she couldn't hold anything in a moment longer. Now she felt severely depleted, but lighter. Maybe this was the same feeling Sophie, in a warped way, had been after.

Nora finally understood, perhaps with the certainty her mother had had from the start, that her grandmother would not see her grandfather—not even as she held a memory of him at an innocent, blameless moment to her heart. But now that her grandfather lay dying, Nora needed to make one last effort on her grandmother's behalf.

In the next room, the beds were empty, the shower was running, and her grandmother's suitcase stood by the door, ready for transport. Nora unzipped it, dug out the picture frame, and slipped it into her own purse.

At the Hong Kong airport, her mother enlisted a custodian to photograph the entire group, including Tommy. Then Tommy produced a sheaf of hotel bills—room numbers, phone numbers, duration of each call.

Nora reached out, saying, "Let me—"

But her mother, Aunt Susan, Kay, and Sophie had all started forward, with the same exposed look.

"This should cover it," her mother said firmly, handing Tommy a wad of cash.

There was a spate of polite good-byes—Byron and Kay managing an embrace, a few whispers, a quick kiss—and then Tommy, George and Joyce, Mr. and Mrs. Wong, and Mr. Chu and Byron nimbly joined the efficient crowds, while the six of them muddled along, fumbling with their suitcases, their plastic-wrapped and string-tied souvenirs, their just-returned passports, their immigration and customs forms. But they moved together from one line to the next, more docilely than they ever had on the tour. Without discussion, without dissent, they drove to Aunt Susan's, where they dropped off Grandma and their luggage, and continued on to the hospital.

In the waiting area, anxious visitors toted bouquets draped in tinsel, fruit baskets wrapped in red cellophane, fat primped babies. In an adjoining room, bleary-eyed, uncombed relatives hunched on bunk beds sipping jars of tea, sucking up instant noodles, staring blankly at one of two TVs—a soap opera and a legislative gathering in Taiwan, the sounds bleeding together.

Kay cried, "We didn't bring anything."

"He wouldn't want a fuss," Aunt Susan said.

"We don't even have a get-well card."

"Why don't you make one?" her mother said. "Aunt Susan and I will go in first."

The two of them walked down the corridor, their postures tired, purposeful, and nearly symmetrical.

In her newly soothing manner, Sophie offered to make a drawing for the card, but after a few minutes, Kay crumpled her sheet of paper. "I'm blanking on my characters. Isn't there anything we can give him?"

Nora felt for the silver case in her purse, alongside the opened tin of candy and the unopened pregnancy test.

A commotion—the legislative gathering had erupted into a brawl, paunchy politicians lunging at one another, others clasping them from behind, chairs and papers upturned, cameramen crowding in. Nora wondered if she'd mixed up the two programs, but on the other screen, a tearful woman was storming away from a strong-jawed man.

When her mother and aunt returned, their faces were grave.

"He's conscious," Aunt Susan said. "He can talk."

"He's too weak for surgery. His heart is stiff with calcium. He has hypertension and diabetes. And they just found a lung infection." Her mother covered her face and wept.

"Don't worry. We'll take good care of him." Awkwardly, Aunt Susan patted her mother's arm, then slipped off, she said, to call Uncle Winston.

To Nora and her sisters, her mother raised a tear-streaked face. "I didn't mean it. I didn't mean for your father to die. I didn't mean what I said when he left."

"We know you didn't," Kay said. "I didn't mean what I said. His death was an accident, that's all."

"I meant to tell you—I brought a little vial of his ashes to China. I thought maybe we'd find a place to scatter them, like you girls wanted."

"I think you were right," Kay said. "Home is the right place."

"Are you coming home? It's your choice, really."

"I'll come home. Not forever, but for now."

"I'll be okay, as long as you all visit."

Sophie said, "I'm not gone yet. And of course I'll visit. College isn't home."

Nora groped for a reply. She clasped her arms around her mother. Her mother fell against her. Nurses, doctors, visitors simply sidestepped them—another family in distress.

After a minute, her mother stood upright, wiping her eyes, steadying her breath. "Kay, Sophie, let me talk to Nora for a second."

Nora braced herself. She wasn't sure she could handle any more revelations.

"Whatever you decide, I'll support you," her mother said. "I'll just say this. Once you become a mother, that's the rest of your life. It never belongs to you again. And you're tied to him—the father—forever. But you might never feel ready to be a mother, until you become a mother. That's when your child teaches you how. That's what you did for me."

Nora nodded, unable to meet her mother's gaze.

"One more thing. I never thanked you. You did everything, after the accident. I don't know how you did it, I just know you did it all."

Nora hadn't realized, until then, that she'd been waiting to hear this. "You don't need to thank me," she said. She meant it.

Their grandfather's bed was angled so his face was nearly level with their own. His head was large and rectangular, with sparse steely strands webbing the spotted pate. His grayish lips receded from thin dark gums, which receded from stained, jagged teeth. His arms were punctured by tubes, the yellowed skin slackly encasing sharp bones. Inside the hospital gown, beneath a pale green sheet, his body was hard to envision upright or in motion, let alone virile. Hovering over him, underneath the scent of sterilizer, was an unrelenting, musty sourness.

To Nora's relief, Kay took charge, asking how he felt, expressing their regrets, exuding a confident familiarity Nora couldn't begin to attempt.

In raspy grunts, he pronounced them pretty. He said Kay resembled Aunt Susan, Sophie their mother, Nora their grandmother; after some hesitation, they agreed. He said he could tell they were "number one" at school and work. He asked about boyfriends, and when none of them claimed one, he said, "Too independent, ah? I could see it right away."

Nora noted Kay trying to hide her disappointment, his declaration about her revolutionary fire now buried amid these arbitrary and no less authoritative statements.

Kay said, "I'm sorry I never wrote back."

"To what?" he said.

The nurse looked in: Five more minutes, then time for him to rest.

"I'm glad to have seen the three of you." His tone suggested he'd dispensed with a not unpleasant task.

He had not asked about Grandma. Maybe her mother and aunt had made it clear the cause was lost. Maybe his impending death had resigned him to never being forgiven, to never getting one last chance to ask.

Nora reached into her purse. This wasn't the rekindling of a romance, or the catharsis of a reunion. It was all she could do—maybe all anyone could do—to comfort someone who was dying, to say: *You will not be forgotten.*

"I wanted you to see this. Grandma carries it with her." She opened the silver case.

He moved to hold it, but he couldn't raise his arms. She held it before him. He was silent, squinting. She held it higher, lower, closer, farther. Her hands started to shake.

At last, he grunted.

Kay reached out. "That's really him? Can I see?"

"Where did you get that?" her grandfather asked.

Shamefaced, Nora said, "I took it from Grandma's suitcase. I wanted you to see that even though she's not here, even if she can't admit it, she—"

"You should put it back," he said.

Kay was staring intently into the picture. "What year is this? Where was it taken?"

Her grandfather said nothing. Suddenly Nora knew she'd made a terrible mistake.

Peering over Kay's arm, Sophie said shyly, "Grandpa, you were so cute."

He barked, "That's not me."

Her sisters started.

"Then who is it?" Kay asked.

"A son."

"Uncle Lou?" Sophie asked.

"A son we lost. In Guangzhou. During the war, right before we fled." His breathing was labored now. "No one else knows."

Kay started to speak. Nora could feel the flood of questions surging. She shook her head.

At last her grandfather said, "Your grandmother is as stubborn as ever, ah?"

They nodded.

"Try to be like her." His eyes closed. "But not too much like her."

The nurse entered and flicked the IV bag, jiggled the tubes, flipped his arm. Nora averted her eyes from his bruised inner elbow.

"Time to let him rest," the nurse said. "Come back tomorrow."

"Tomorrow they're going home to America," her grandfather said.

"America! They came all the way from America? You must be some grandfather."

He grunted.

Nora summoned her courage and leaned over the bed to hug him.

There was a sudden series of loud beeps, an electronic whine, a gasp from her grandfather, a thud.

He now lay supine, face contorted. The nurse clucked, pointing to red buttons on the side of the bed. Apparently Nora had leaned on the button that popped the bed flat. She babbled frantic apologies. Her grandfather, wheezing, raised one feeble hand for silence.

Her sisters said carefully distanced good-byes, Sophie bending to peck his cheek, Kay clasping his hand with both of hers.

Once they'd eased into the corridor, Nora hissed, "I can't believe I did that."

Unwilling laughter crept up her sisters' throats, and then her own. They erupted, covering their mouths and holding their stomachs, desperately trying to hush themselves.

"Well," Sophie gasped, "at least that was a moment to remember."

Kay hiccupped into a sob. "I guess that's good-bye. That's it. And now we leave him to die."

"There's nothing else we can do," Nora said.

Kay still held the silver case. "What about this? A lost son we've never heard of? That's our uncle. We'll never know what happened?"

It now seemed indecent to subject the little boy in the picture to the glare of the hospital lights, the smudging of their fingertips. Nora took the silver case, closed the clasp, and tucked it back in her purse.

"It's their secret. They want to keep it that way. I misunderstood."

The picture, her grandmother's wishes, her own dreams—she'd misunderstood everything.

The hospital bathroom was white tile and stainless steel, sanitized and quiet. She recognized the brand of the test, but the brand was the only English word on or inside the box. On the instruction booklet, she picked out numbers: 5 and 4. Five seconds for the test to take effect, four minutes to wait for the results? There was an illustration of the two possible results, but which was which? She guessed that the positive result was displayed first. She guessed that two lines instead of one was positive.

She performed the test. She wrapped the stick in tissue and placed it on the dispenser. She would not look until the time was up.

The toilet automatically flushed. She sat. The edges of the booklet dampened in her hands.

The single vertical line—rotated, a minus, a negative. The double vertical lines—eleven, two els, an equal symbol. Signs, all signs. She knew these tests were fallible. She knew a sign was all she could bear. But couldn't she at least have some certainty in the meaning of that sign?

She checked her watch. She picked up the test.

Two lines. Of course. Two lives.

She'd always felt the responsibility of embodying the future, of carrying the hopes of her mother, her grandmother, perhaps ancestors she couldn't name. She'd thought she was meant to fulfill the promise of equal opportunity, of immigration, of progress.

She'd feared marriage and children, feared not being different enough from her parents, not only because their future together had ended tragically, but because everyone's future ended. That was why nobody wanted to be like their parents. It meant accepting your limits, accepting being just one more turn in the cycle of blood-soaked, squalling birth and lonely, foul-smelling death.

This new life inside her, if she chose to bear it, was the next generation. In becoming ready for it, in making way for it, she would become the past. The past, that eternally imperfect, increasingly musty thing, hope steadily leaking, and filling the only place that could hold it—the future, a child.

For now, the present, she discarded the test and found a pay phone.

"It's me. I—I'm—I'm pregnant."

"Nora?" Jesse said.

"Did you hear me?"

"No."

She repeated it.

"Can you talk louder?"

Doctors and nurses clacking by, patients being wheeled past, relatives pacing all around, and her own family somewhere down the corridor. "I'm pregnant!"

There was another pause, taut and breathless, and she knew he'd heard.

"Are you sure?"

"Not a hundred percent."

"Let's go to a doctor. When are you back?"

"Tomorrow."

"You don't want to have it," he said. "Do you?"

"No. I don't know." She asked, "Do you?"

"I don't know. Should I meet you at the airport?"

"No. Meet me at home."

He'd meet her at home. That was one certainty. For now, it was enough.

27

Alone in the apartment, her own footsteps sounded ghostly. For a moment, Lin Yulan held her breath. Shadows loomed. The light hurt her eyes. The glass walls threatened to shriek and break. White walls, white upholstery, white carpeting—the color of truth, the color of death.

She shook herself. There was nothing haunted here—just the opposite. Despite the excess of appliances, the stacks of English books and journals, the glossy decorative plants—even a perfect white orchid that looked so real, she had to touch the fabric petals twice—the apartment reminded her of her own. Contemporary spaces, stark and tidy, thickly quiet. Not a place to accommodate previous generations, or the next. Or the kind of constant friction and collision—the kind provoked by love—she remembered in Irene's house.

On Susan's desk, there was no evidence of new work, no evidence of any work at all. Decades ago, when Lin Yulan read her daughter's first published poems in Taiwan, they made her feel dreamy, lost. Only after she roused herself and her pulse resumed its normal pace did she realize it had slowed. She couldn't say what the poems were about. She'd told

Susan they were well-crafted, with hints of original ideas—but was that enough? What was their purpose? When there was so much wrong in the world, and you had the chance to hold people's attention, imprint words in their minds, ignite flames in their hearts, why settle for providing a moment's pause?

She'd give a great deal to read them now, to feel that lull.

The kettle she'd put on the stove started to wail. She hastened to turn off the heat. Hanging beside the cupboards was a scroll calendar, the kind distributed by Chinese banks and banquet restaurants, each day marked with the solar date in black boldface, the lunar date in fine red print. Squinting, tracing the red with her fingertip, Lin Yulan realized that today was her eightieth birthday.

Most years, she let herself forget. This year, it was the ostensible reason for the tour. A little celebration would have been nice after all.

Such *timing* he had. Right now he was being tended by her daughters and granddaughters. Laying a claim, the final claim, to being the righteous one, the truly wronged one.

Death is final, Nora had said. Perhaps this was a new consideration for her granddaughters, but not for Lin Yulan. When she'd left Taiwan at sixty years of age, finality was the point.

So let him lay his claim. And let her daughters and granddaughters go home with this picture of her—a bitter old woman, bitter over a faithless husband. The same grievance as women everywhere, housewives and career women, feudal women and modern women, women in folktales and soap operas, women through the centuries.

He had not flown his failing body to express everlasting love, or dying regrets. He'd tried to seize this last chance to see the one person in the world who understood, to say: *I remember, too.* Perhaps, when her time came, she would feel the same yearning. If so, it would be futile, even more futile than his yearning now.

A secret passed on was only that. And it was no one's to keep but theirs—hers and his. Soon hers alone. And then it would be nothing. No secret, no burden, nothing.

Somehow Nora had found that picture in her suitcase, and concocted her own explanation. It was just as well. Lin Yulan could not divulge what no one else would understand. She could not relive a tragedy she'd barely survived. She could not betray Lou, a bachelor car salesman in California—and yes, her precious son.

That day in Guangzhou, while her daughters and granddaughters ate themselves sick, she'd sat in the hotel room with the lights on, the TV blaring, the curtains closed. She'd kept the picture in her suitcase. She'd sipped a little soup and tea in the hotel café. A day, even a day in the city she'd fled without her son, could simply be borne that way. Only at night, when everyone was asleep, and the streets were empty and black, did she take out the picture and clasp it before her, facing a sliver of window. Only then, and only for a moment, did she look out and see herself holding her little boy again, in the glass.

She harbored no illusions, except, perhaps, this: that her revolutionary years—which ended when she wasn't yet thirty, more than fifty years ago, as Irene said—were worth something. Even though the achievements of women like her were erased from history. Even though they'd go down as nothing but Nationalists—on the mainland, the arrogant rich who got their comeuppance; in Taiwan, the last and most resented wave of settlers. Even though the gap between rich and poor was greater in China today than before the revolution, and it was hard for anyone now to say what it had all been for.

She was no martyr. As Susan had joked: No one wanted to embalm her body. But her sacrifices, even forgotten, had made a difference. If that was an illusion, she'd take it to her tomb.

She still wanted her daughters and granddaughters to know what it was to leave a legacy. She still wanted that, though she could not say, in their place, what she would fight for; what cause was so crucial it could only consume them, so noble it couldn't be shamed by the flawed individuals propelling it. If they'd ever led a thundering protest, they would know there is not only power in masses, there is beauty, beauty that compels you to take the long view.

But in the long view, the lives of those you love are so small. Small as the plastic beads she'd bought on her way to the airport, small as the drops of sweat she'd wiped from the faces of her daughters and granddaughters, small as the granules of medicine she'd poured into their palms.

Well, if nothing else, this tour had allowed them to hang out—that term she'd learned from Lou. And if they could hang out in China, they could hang out in California, or in New York. They could hang out again, and again. And hanging out together was something. In her old age, it was certainly something.

She stepped out on the balcony, the wind flowing under her blouse, ruffling her thinned hair. The view was similar to—possibly the same as—what she'd seen on the boat to Macau, between the two frenzied ports. Back then, those rocky green islets had looked like utter desolation. Now they looked like potential resorts.

She stood before the darkening sky and sea, waiting for her daughters and granddaughters, waiting for this journey to end—even as waiting for anything, at this stage of life, was waiting for her own passing. Too much wind, too much air, too much view. She turned and went inside to heat the kettle again.

28

There was her husband, back home from a day of lectures and meetings. She was his wife, back home from a two-week tour of China.

"Let's get away," Susan whispered.

"Where?" Winston whispered back.

"Anywhere."

He thought for a moment. "We need groceries."

Away from these women and their luggage. Down the hall, down the elevator. Across an overpass, onto a bus. They sat in a seat for two.

He touched her hand. "You're not wearing your ring."

She dug into her purse, fumbling around the velvet box. She found the ring, the metal and gem cast for a particular part of a particular finger—hers. She slid it on. It rested to cover the same exact band of skin.

"It felt a little loose," she said. "I was afraid it might fall off."

He studied her hand. "You haven't been eating well."

"I've missed your cooking."

A little shyly, he smiled, then turned his steady gaze out the window. She rested her head on his shoulder. There'd be time to try to describe the tour. There'd be time to discuss her father's expiring body, the vestiges of his life in Taiwan. And there would be the credit card bill to explain. She could tell Winston she'd bought gifts for Ma and Irene and the girls. She could tell him she'd bought an extravagant gift for herself. She could show him the pearl. Even then, it would be her secret to keep.

She hadn't really wanted to leave him. She'd needed to test the parameters of her life, to feel how breakable yet how solid, this container that held her.

They climbed off the bus and stepped onto stairs chipped into a hill, onto an escalator laid into the mountainside. As they glided up, she patted his rear, the squared, solid curve. He started. She grinned. Their hands clasped.

Sooner or later, you need structure. You have a life to build. You can build it around another person, children, a career, your art; you can pick a guiding principle—resistance, ease, duty, pleasure, mobility, permanence. There is love, the usual scaffolding. By the time it corrodes, the building is standing. Some use love like that and varnish it, bolster it, prop it up. Some use love like that and let it rot, then start again.

With Winston, she'd found herself, for the first time, in a home. A new life, ready-built. And love—maybe not poetry, maybe not passion, but love, so steady it was more than scaffolding. It was the very walls.

Perhaps the metaphor breaks down, as metaphors, in any language, eventually do.

"I love you," she whispered.

Winston turned. "This?" A fish pulsing on ice, glinting electric blue.

She nodded. The fish was grabbed and scaled, flopped into a clear pouch and spun, sealed with a knot. Now silken tofu, preserved duck eggs, tomatoes ripe to splitting. Slender eggplant, firm and pearlescent. Pears and peaches, fat and fragrant. Beef tendon, ground pork, chicken thighs and wings. A jar of bamboo shoots in chili oil, a can of black bean sauce. Leafy greens, soil clinging to the roots. Cilantro, scallions, garlic, ginger. The weight collected in translucent plastic, the strained handles scoring her palms. This, too, is love. This and this and this.

29

As if the wind had risen: When Irene turned, boarding passes in hand, the five of them were already drifting off—to the duty-free store, the newsstand, the restroom, the nearest chairs, the sanitized and refrigerated spaces in between. Irene wandered through an array of last-minute souvenirs, dazzling as fireworks, and just as fleeting.

There was something she'd forgotten. Something she'd forgotten to pack? The Forbidden City book and prints, the Tiantan knickknacks, the plum flower silk screen. The silk quilt, the Longjing tea. The villager's carvings—though not his business card. In the end, not much mass. Once she emptied her suitcase—except for the innermost pocket, where the vial of ashes had stayed wrapped tight and tucked deep—and started over, everything fit.

Something she'd forgotten to buy, then? She picked up a calendar, half-price, the year being more than half over: *Top Twelve Landmarks of China, Ancient and Wondrous.* The glossy pictures taunted her, like trick windows. So much she hadn't seen: terra-cotta warriors, baby pandas, the Three Gorges, Mongolian grassland, Silk Road desert, snowcapped and prayer-flagged Tibet. All ancient and wondrous, indeed; also endangered, commercialized, preserved like a wax corpse.

How crass, this ranking, a neat dozen. And how unfair, really. What about the nameless section of Great Wall they'd climbed? The mass graves in Nanjing? The cobblestone paths of the village? And that thread of sky in the dark, damp cave?

But what about these landmarks? She'd seen half of them, in just one trip. Not quite like this, front and center, unobstructed, gorgeously lit. But she'd seen them with her daughters and sister and mother, and together they'd paused, looked, taken pictures, traveled on. People needed landmarks, not only to mark the land but, like holidays, to punctuate life.

Irene put down the calendar. She fingered a satin robe, a teapot, a kite.

At Ba's bedside, she'd tried to call up images of him young, quick, arrogant, fatherly, but all she could see was the decaying skin puckered around his IV, the yellowed and blood-clotted whites of his eyes, the vacillations on his electrocardiogram, the outlines of his wasted legs and lifeless pelvis.

Now, a memory: kite-flying. He took her once. Just her and her father, in a park or a lot. Empty ground, empty air. They waited for wind. The kite, a fiendish blue face, glowered and puffed against his leg. It was taller than her. It could wrap her whole father. Other people flew birds, butterflies, goldfish.

He lit a cigarette and inhaled; talk streamed out. How the first kite was invented when a peasant tied a string to his hat to keep it from blowing away. How kites became weapons of war. The invading general who flew one over city walls to measure the distance past the defenses, and sent his troops tunneling under. Then, most ingenious: warrior kites, painted masks with hollow bamboo frames. Spies spread tales of soul-stealing demons, and in the predawn hours before battle, enemy soldiers woke to a sky swarming with swooping, shrieking faces.

That's the way to win, he said. *Steal your enemy's spirit.* Laowai *say we Chinese invented gunpowder but only used it for fireworks, and that's why we lost to them. But we invented kites and used them as weapons. Hnh!*

She tried to nod like a worthy heir to this history. *Hnh!* she repeated, under her breath. A fiery sting to her cheek—cigarette ash. The kite toppled. Ba snapped to attention. She daubed her burned cheek with spit. He switched his cigarette from one spindly hand to the other. Two steps back and a few hard tugs and the kite leaped up. He emitted another grunt, triumphant. She grabbed the only part of him she could, a handful of his trousers at one knee, and she thought she could feel the power of the kite pulsing all the way down the string through her father to her.

He said, *Now you fly it.*

Trembling, she released his knee and took hold of the string. He let go. She was flying the blue demon. He nodded his approval. She thought her face might shatter with joy.

Then the wind lifted, and the kite soared so fast the string singed her hand. She cried out in pain.

Keep it tight, Ba said. *If you don't feel it straining, it'll fall. Pull. Pull.*

With each pull the demon menaced her. Still she pulled, one fist over the other, until a pile of string lay at her feet. The demon dipped, then dived. Ba was lighting another cigarette. Frantically, she pulled. The kite hurtled to the ground, the blue demon's face in the dirt.

Ba said, *Well, Lou was worse.*

Lou was a little kid. He'd probably just stood there. And when had Ba taken Lou? She thought she was special.

Ba told her to gather the string and fold the kite. That was it, the end of their kite-flying. He gave his assessments. Lou was too *suibian*—loose, going with the flow. She was too *jinzhang*—anxious, tightly wound. Susan, he said, was not bad. She operated on feeling, from her hand to her eye to her hand, but she was fickle.

When had he taken Susan? How many times? She figured Lou hadn't told her because he hadn't thought much of it, while Susan hadn't told her because she'd been hoarding it, secretly gloating. And perhaps that was how Ba kept a hold over Susan, with such allotments of praise, meager but marked for her alone: *not bad*.

For a time, perhaps while she hoped for a chance to redeem herself, even Irene held those assessments as profound truths, the kind only the man who'd given you life could bestow. Then she realized the most casual acquaintance could have tossed them off.

Yet something of that day stayed with her. The moment after Ba handed her the kite, before the wind rose again. The kite aloft, the tension coursing through the cord and her own arm, the surprising weight of her body, her feet steadfast—her whole being suspended, amid open space, in perfect equilibrium between the pull from the sky and the pull from the earth.

Irene turned away from the souvenirs. Across the passageway, Ma sat alone. Irene braced herself and went to join her.

Trying to smile, she said, "This trip didn't turn out exactly as I planned."

"I don't know what you planned."

"It had nothing to do with Ba. It was for the six of us." Irene waited. "If you regret coming, I understand."

"I never valued Lou above you," Ma said. "I knew you and Susan were stronger."

"You forced us to be." Irene blinked back sudden, hot tears. "I don't want to argue. I don't blame you anymore. Daughters are hard on their mothers. Mothers want too much from their daughters. Maybe if I'd had a son—"

"It wasn't because he was the son. It was because I lost him once, and I could not bear for anything to happen to him, ever again. That's all I can say. That much you can understand."

Irene tried to take this in. "I guess it was selfish of me to bring you back here. I just thought, somehow, it would do us all good."

"You were right."

The tears reappeared. This was the moment when a mother would hug a daughter. Instead, Ma handed her a tissue. Irene turned away and dabbed her eyes.

After a minute, she said, "You could visit New York. We could visit LA. We don't have to fly across the world."

Ma nodded.

Irene tried to imagine a future reunion. Passing around pictures of this one. Laughing over things that had made them cry. Surely, among the six of them, they could devise a new tradition. Surely once a year wasn't too much to ask. Together, they'd mark the passage of time, even the loss of one more year from each of their lives.

And then she remembered what she'd forgotten.

"I'll be back," she stammered. "You wait here."

She found Nora, who waved over Kay, who grabbed Sophie, who spotted Susan.

"Grandma's birthday. Ma's eightieth. We don't have much time."

Like tentacles of one organism, they spread to the shops and kiosks, to the aisles and counters, swung back heavily laden, and propelled themselves over to Ma as quickly and stealthily as they could. Ma saw them almost immediately, of course, and Irene faltered, but her daughters charged forward—Nora brandishing aromatherapy candles, Kay tossing popcorn in lieu of confetti, Sophie unfurling crepelike pink toilet paper.

"*Wei!*" Ma said. "What is this?"

On the table, instead of longevity noodles, instead of an ice cream cake, they placed a heap of lo mein, a pepperoni pizza, a monstrous cinnamon bun, a red tin of out-of-season moon cakes.

There was much fumbling, increasingly nervous, to light the candles—a search for matches, a borrowed lighter, uncooperative wicks—and then, as the scent of synthetic florals filled the air, they sang a ragged rendition of "Happy Birthday."

After a long pause, Sophie said encouragingly, "Make a wish and blow out the candles."

"I know," Ma said. "I've seen your sisters do this. Your mother's supposed to take a picture first."

Irene rushed to get her camera. Hands shaking, she clicked again and again, to be sure of one decent shot.

Ma blew out the candles. The aromatherapy scent filled the air, thick and cloying over the smell of greasy food. Susan produced paper cups and a bottle of champagne. The cork was plastic, emerging with more of a sigh than a pop.

Nora raised her cup. "To Grandma."

"To all of us," Kay said.

"To the end of our tour," Susan said, with a slight grin.

"To Mom, for planning the tour." And Sophie, her baby daughter who'd soothed Irene to sleep the other night, now caressed her head, a gesture that felt strangely protective, even maternal.

Bubbles were sparkling through Irene's chest. She decided that whatever they devised for their annual tradition, it ought to include champagne. "This isn't enough of a celebration, of course."

"Yes, it is," Ma said.

"No, no. We'll celebrate again. When we—next time we—" Her daughters, her sister, her mother looked alarmed. "Well, if you feel this is enough," Irene said, to their open relief.

They picked at the food. The lo mein and pizza were already congealing, while the cinnamon bun and moon cakes seemed to glint with varnish. Irene studied the fizzing at the bottom of her cup. She'd gulped her champagne with each toast, while the others had taken little sips.

To break the silence, she exclaimed, "What a mess we made."

Her daughters flinched—her daughters, fatherless, one sabotaging her adolescent body, one mourning an entire nation, one pregnant by a cheating ex.

"I meant all this," Irene said hastily, indicating the toilet paper, the popcorn, the candle wax.

"This," Ma said, "is my souvenir."

"You're taking this home?" Susan looked dubious.

Ma emptied the red tin of moon cakes and placed inside one kernel of popcorn, a square of pink toilet paper, the champagne cork, a blackened candlewick. She snapped the lid shut and put the tin in her purse. "You see?"

Irene took one more picture—self-timed, the camera precariously balanced on a stack of takeout containers, all six of them nestled together to fit inside the frame.

Her sister would separate from the five of them at security, her mother would separate from the four of them upon the first landing, and her daughters would separate from her soon after their final arrival, always too soon. But for now they were close, so close Irene didn't need to reach out at all.

And if all she had in the end was a glimmer, she could feel how it connected the six of them to one another, connected them to this part of the world, perhaps even connected them to the heavens.

She was unprepared for the sense of loss that flooded her at takeoff. The wheels suddenly spinning on nothing, the plane pointing its nose to the dusky sky, pulling her up and away with such force, such finality. She closed her eyes. Thrumming in her ears, the vigor of a young arm beside hers, the solid grip of her seat above so much space—the space surging and surging. Now she saw how the skyscrapers were built—out of arrogance, out of hope—to vie with mountains. Higher, how the roads emulated rivers. And, just before they broke through a skin of cloud, how the little lights strung all across the islands below shone in answer to the stars.

• *Acknowledgments* •

In the summer of 2000, I toured China with my mother, my sisters, my aunt, and my grandmother—five extraordinary women. While this book was, in part, inspired by them, it is not about them; it does not depict their histories or their personalities. I offer them my apologies for potential misunderstandings, and my lifelong admiration.

I've received crucial guidance and support from the faculty and administration of Amherst College and the Iowa Writers' Workshop, most notably Barry O'Connell, Rhonda Cobham-Sander, Shen Tong, Elizabeth McCracken, Ethan Canin, and Marilynne Robinson. Grants from the Fulbright Program, the New York Foundation for the Arts, and the Chinese Ministry of Education have also been invaluable.

The following friends and acquaintances helped enlighten me on fields from architecture to poetry, offered lodging and laptops, or otherwise gave sustenance: Sang Yul Bae, Doug Bradley, Berrick Chang, Chris Chen, Chi-Lien Cheng, Juan Du, Anton Harder, Loren Kajikawa, Jen Lin-Liu, Alice Liu, Dima and Kate Lorenz, Judith Riven, Sarah Rogers, Jennifer Schneider, Dorjee Sun, and Virginia Tusher. Special thanks to Diane

Chang and Serah Choi for their scientific insights and all-around brilliance.

The passages on Alzheimer's disease were greatly improved by Diane Chang, who compiled and elucidated key papers that were, to me, nearly impenetrable, and applied her keen eye to numerous drafts. Sherwin B. Nuland's *How We Die: Reflections on Life's Final Chapter* was also a valuable reference.

In my historical research, I'm particularly indebted to the books *Women of the Chinese Enlightenment* by Wang Zheng and *The Chinese in America* by Iris Chang, and to letters from Lisand Hsiao, my grandmother.

I'll always be grateful to Lisa Bankoff for plucking me out of her slush pile, Ann Godoff for bringing me under her auspices, and Janie Fleming for lavishing such care on the manuscript. My thanks also go to Lindsay Whalen, Abigail Cleaves, and Tracy Locke for their tremendous efforts on behalf of this book.

Since the seventh grade, I've relied on Ji Yoon Chung for long talks, sarcastic wit, and loyal support. Since our Iowa years, Frances de Pontes Peebles and Mika Tanner have been beloved friends and ideal readers.

Finally, my eternal love and gratitude go to my precious parents, first and foremost; to Bebe and Jessie, my superstar sisters; and to Peter—my husband, my shelter.